The Baton

The Baton

The story of William Hildebrand (1882 – 1965) who passed the baton from Gustav Mahler to Leonard Bernstein

Mike Maran

© 2023 Mike Maran

All rights reserved

Some of the characters and events portrayed in this book are fictitious. The similarity of other characters to real persons is not coincidental and is intended by the author.

No part of this book may be reproduced, or stored in a retrieval system, or transmitted in any form or by any means, electronic, mechanical, photocopying, recording, or otherwise, without express written permission of the publisher.

ISBN-13: 9798393675400

Cover design by: John Williams

Published by Mike Maran Productions
www.mikemaran.com
mike@mikemaran.com

For the Edinburgh Festival Chorus
who sang both the Scottish Premiere of Mahler's
Eighth Symphony at the opening concert of the Nineteenth
Edinburgh Festival in 1965 conducted by Alexander Gibson
and Mahler's Second Symphony conducted by Leonard
Bernstein in Ely Cathedral in 1974 and for our inspiring
choirmaster, Arthur Oldham.

We were, and we are, all of us, in heaven.

'...all the right notes but not necessarily in the right order.'

Eric Morecambe

Foreword

In 2003 I wrote produced and performed a musical theatre show about the life and music of Gustav Mahler called 'Song & Dance Man' with music by Karen Wimhurst who arranged extracts from Mahler's music performed live on stage by a string quartet clarinet and accordion. The following year 'Song & Dance Man' was presented at the Edinburgh Fringe where it was critically acclaimed with five- star reviews and awarded a Herald Angel (a sort of Oscar with wings). I told the story of 'Song & Dance Man' in the character of William Hildebrand, Mahler's gofer and chauffeur. Mahler never had one. William is entirely my invention. Mahler, however, did have a car. It was a wedding present from the Emperor and in this story William gets to drive it.

    I had long harboured the ambition to write a similar show to celebrate the life and music of Leonard Bernstein and, fortunately, William Hildebrand lived long enough to gofer and chauffeur for Bernstein too. Unfortunately my own days on the road performing one-night stands in theatres are over so, instead, I have arranged the material from the Mahler show and the Bernstein show that never toured, to write a novel about William Hildebrand who goffered and chauffeured both and passed the baton from one to the other.

    This is a work of fiction. Nevertheless the public events described in the novel all really happened – with one exception. Bernstein never conducted Mahler's Sixth so early in his career. But then William Hildebrand never lived in the real world and if he had he would have fixed it exactly as I have described in the book

    Mahler famously claimed the symphony must contain 'everything' and to my ears that includes laughter. I have put into 'The Baton' as much as I can and I hope you have a lot of fun reading it. The soundtrack, of course, is magnificent.

Mike Maran

Contents

1. Mahler's Fourth Symphony 2
2. Hugo Wolf 9
3. Gustav & Alma 11
4. Mahler's Third Symphony 16
5. Richard Strauss 18
6. Maria 21
7. Mahler's Fifth Symphony 23
8. Unhappy Birthdays 26
9. Arnold Schönberg 33
10. Mahler's Sixth Symphony 35
11. Mahler leaves Vienna 39
12. New York 43
13. Christmas 1907 48
14. A Letter to Johnny Stanko 55
15. Mahler's New York Debut 57
16. Mechtilde Müller 59
17. The Met 65
18. A Chinese Restaurant 67
19. Mahler's First Symphony 70
20. The Horse With No Name 74
21. Mahler's Seventh Symphony 79
22. Mahler's Second Symphony 84
23. Mahler Gets Lost 89
24. A Letter for William 97
25. La Semaine Littéraire 99
26. La Semaine Littéraire (2) 103
27. Voyage Home 106
28. A Séance in New York 111
29. La Semaine Littéraire (3) 114
30. Another Chinese Restaurant 117

31. La Semaine Littéraire (4) 119
32. Home Again 123
33. A Nightmare in Rome 128
34. Gropius 132
35. Freud 137
36. Mahler's Eighth Symphony 142
37. Johnny Stanko to New York 146
38. Mahler's Funeral 1911 155
39. The Merry Widow 160
40. Das Lied von der Erde 184
41. Kokoschka 188
42. Christmas 1911 196
43. New Year 1912 199
44. A Grand Tour of Italy 203
45. Mahler's 9th Symphony 234
46. War 248
47. Another Grand Tour of Italy 256
48. Anna Mahler. Franz Werfel 265
49. Meddi and Johnny Stanko 280
50. Flight from Europe 297
51. William Meets Leonard 308
52. Bernstein's Assistant 321
53. On Tour with Bernstein 350
54. Johnny Stanko's Trumpet 361
55. Edinburgh Festival 1950 368
56. Hollywood and HUAC 371
57. 'West Side Story' 376
58. A Gay Bar in Tokyo 388
59. The Chichester Psalms and The Opening Concert
    of the Nineteenth Edinburgh Festival 397
Acknowledgments 409

PART ONE

1900-1911

William and Mahler

CHAPTER 1

Mahler's Fourth Symphony

To be young in Vienna at the beginning of the twentieth century was no fun at all. Young men wanted to get their youth over and done with as quickly as possible. They grew beards, wore spectacles, and aped the manners of their elders. Boys disguised themselves as middle-aged men. Girls rushed into marriages with these elderly young men and got themselves safely pregnant. It was no fun. Syphilis was everywhere.

Before he left Basel to study viola at the conservatoire in Vienna, William Hildebrand's mother advised him to be careful. William understood but wasn't concerned. He'd never had a girlfriend and had no ambitions to find one. However, on his first day in Vienna he met and fell in love with Johnny Stanko who had come from Prague to study the trumpet. William and Johnny often went to art galleries together. They especially enjoyed looking at pictures of naked men and they liked looking at each other. They spent happy hours exploring one another. William and Johnny became a couple. Everyone knew them as Willy and Stinky. They were a handsome pair. They didn't look middle-aged like all the other youngsters at the conservatoire. They were two beautiful young men of similar height and slightly built. They both had dark hair which they wore long. They dressed comfortably in clothes that looked one size too large and as they walked hand in hand from the conservatoire to the Hofoper, their long hair flapping in the breeze, they might be mistaken for sisters in men's clothing.

William played a beautiful viola lent to him by an elderly neighbour. It had belonged to her late husband and she was happy to know that it was being played. When William went home to Basel to visit his mother at Christmas he took the viola with him in case the generous neighbour wanted him to return it, but she was happy for him to keep it. William never felt fully in possession of the instrument and struggled to make progress. His teachers were more interested in the beautiful viola than they were in him. Before the end of his second year William knew that he was not good enough for the viola and that he never would be.

Johnny's trumpet was a present from his father. It was an ordinary instrument suited to a student. Johnny's teachers were impressed by the tone he produced. He sculpted sounds on his trumpet that were unique. Johnny had in mind that one day he would build his own instrument. He sketched drawings of his ideal trumpet which had a raised length of upper tubing so that the horn pointed upwards. Johnny knew the difference between the sound a trumpet makes when the musician is reading the score and when he is playing from memory. The latter holds his trumpet higher whereas the sight-reader's instrument points to the floor. Johnny's design compensates for this and throws the sight-reader's sound into the hall. His drawings showed the horn raised at different angles from 20 degrees to 45 degrees. Meanwhile, on his standard instrument, Johnny created an inimitable sound, and his teachers knew that he was destined to be a leader.

In any performance there will always be deps. When a viola dep or a trumpet dep was required Johnny frequently, and William less frequently, found themselves sitting in the orchestra pit at the opera where the best students gained valuable work experience, allowing old, tired, sick, or bored, members of the orchestra a night off. Mahler was never pleased to see deps in his orchestra. More than six or seven deps and the quality falls away sharply. The viola section might just be able to carry a passenger, but the more exposed trumpet section cannot. Johnny, a good trumpeter, always contributed to a performance whereas on the few occasions William played he was happy to hide his modest talents behind the other violas.

William and Johnny would go most evenings to the opera. The Weiner Hofoper stood on the south side of the Ringstrasse. It was an imposing and controversial building which the Viennese referred to as a turtle because of the shape of its roof which looked like a large shell. The two architects suffered an avalanche of abuse in the Vienna newspapers. The attacks were so poisonous that before the Opera House opened its doors, one of them committed suicide and the other died of a broken heart.

On the other side of the Ringstrasse, set back a few hundred yards from the main road, stands The Secession gallery which houses the work of the artists who had resigned from the Academy of Fine Arts. The Gallery was topped by a golden cupola which the Viennese called a 'golden cabbage.' Flying south a bird might look down first onto The Secession's cabbage and then onto the Hofoper's turtle shell. Vienna may have vied with Paris for pre-eminence in the visual arts but in music there was no contest. Vienna was the capital of the musical world and its Opera House, directed by Gustav Mahler, stood at the very summit of European music-making.

When Mahler first came to the Hofoper the orchestra that performed in the evening was regularly sprinkled with deps and bore little resemblance to the orchestra which had rehearsed in the afternoon. On Wagner nights the problem was acute. Mahler hardly recognized anyone in the orchestra. Wagner operas, which might last five hours or more, were performed largely by deputies because the regular musicians would otherwise miss the last tram and need to hire a cab. For a musician living outside Vienna the cab fare might be more than the performance fee. Mahler went to the Emperor with a demand for a musicians' pay rise and a travel allowance. This did not endear Mahler to his administrators who felt he had gone to the Emperor behind their backs. The administration was also unhappy to see musicians' rates of pay leapfrog their own. These changes, however, went down well with musicians and audiences. Musicians were better paid, and the music was better played.

Although the number of deps went down after Mahler's reforms, they were still required to cover for musicians who were either sick or who claimed to be sick and were working elsewhere. Johnny Stanko quickly made it to the top of the fixer's list while William slipped down the list of viola deps.

Music pours out of many windows in Vienna, filling the air with scales and exercises - a singer here, a piano there, a string quartet, a tuba, 'Tristan' at an upper window, 'Isolde' at a window below and a Bach cello suite rising from the basement. The daylight hours in Vienna are filled with a variety of musical sounds as diverse as birdsong before dawn. It's the same in Prague and in Budapest where youngsters at the beginning of the twentieth century learned the musical language of the Empire.

There is a limit to the number of hours a trumpeter can blow before he spoils his lip and cheeks. Johnny Stanko was blessed with strong chops. He spent the first hour of the day blowing glissandos and arpeggios into the mouthpiece until his lip felt good. Then he would insert the mouthpiece into the trumpet and do the same all over again. Only when these hours were done did he feel ready to start practising. William would go out for the morning bread while Johnny was warming up. Johnny's trumpet followed him down the stairs and around the corner. He heard it as he waited in the baker shop. It accompanied his request for rolls and pastries, and he followed the sound back to their room, climbing the stairs slowly to prolong the pleasure of Johnny's call. William's ears were caressed by Johnny's kiss. When William got home Johnny kissed his eyes, his forehead, the tip of his nose, and explored William with his lips and his tongue.

William searched but never found in the viola what Johnny found in his trumpet. William bowed and scraped efficiently but never made a sound that drew the listener towards him like Johnny did. William believed there was a bright, cheerful world of daylight open to the trumpet that was forever closed to the viola, an instrument full of darkness. William was happy listening to Johnny's cheerfulness and was not inclined to explore his own pain.

William Hildebrand was a passenger among the violas. Mahler had no use for passengers.

William and Johnny went to the opera every night because they got free tickets from Suttner who organized the claque. Suttner took the money from the singers, bought the tickets, and distributed them to the members of the claque who were responsible for leading the applause. To say that the claque led the applause does not do justice to the complex and subtle role William and Johnny and the other *claquers* played at the opera. Strategically placed in locations around the auditorium, the claque carefully exploited the spaces in the performance to stimulate applause. The claque not only had to judge the right moment, it also had to be sensitive to the mood of the auditorium and the quality of the performance. It would never do for *claquers* to promote applause for a singer that wasn't good enough.

Mahler hated the claque. He considered it to be a vulgar intrusion into the art of the opera house. Suttner and Mahler were bitter enemies. Suttner hated Mahler not because he was a Jew but because he considered him to be a megalomaniac. Mahler, conducting in the orchestra pit, was frustrated by *claquers* conducting the audience from somewhere else in the house. When Mahler was forced to wait until the clapping ended, he would gesture with bad grace at the score as if to ask, 'Where does the composer ask for applause?'

Mahler went to war against the claque. At first, anticipating applause, Mahler would rush the production forwards to delete those moments that might be used by the claque to interrupt the performance – a cure that was worse than the disease. Although Mahler cut down the opportunities for applause, he could only achieve this by losing control over the tempo of his production. This infuriated Mahler, gave no satisfaction to Suttner, lowered the quality of the performance, and increased the temperature of the hostility which became more serious when Mahler employed plain clothes policemen to infiltrate the audience, locate, and arrest the *claquers*. There were wrongful arrests of innocent people and the Emperor had to ask Mahler to back down after members of his Imperial household who had been enthusiastically enjoying a performance of *Die Meistersinger von Nürnberg* spent a night in the police cells.

Suttner objected not only to Mahler's megalomania but also to his hypocrisy. He accused Mahler of behaving one way in the opera house and the opposite way in the concert hall. At the opera Mahler strictly observed the composer's intentions and attempted to silence the applause because it interfered with the composition. In the concert hall Mahler took a more flexible attitude towards the composition and would, for example, re-orchestrate Beethoven by adding a part for an E flat clarinet and giving Beethoven's flute parts to the oboe. Audiences might not notice Mahler's re-touchings, but Suttner was aware of them because musicians coming out of rehearsals told him about it. Altering the composer's work in the concert hall and forbidding the claque to interrupt the composer's work in the opera house was not only hypocritical, it also showed a lack of respect for the Viennese audience – bad manners, which in Suttner's opinion was typically Jewish.

The opera singers took Suttner's side. Even those singers who approved of Mahler took Suttner's side because every singer wants applause, and the claque could get it for them. Singers were happy to pay for the applause and audiences liked applauding, so everybody was happy, except Mahler.

Everyone in the claque loved opera. No one in the claque liked Mahler.

The claque got their chance to let Mahler know what they thought of him at the Grosser Musikvereinsaal at the Viennese Premier of his Fourth Symphony on January 12th 1902. It had already been performed in Berlin and Munich. The *claquers* in Vienna had read the bad reviews. They already knew that the symphony wasn't any good. The opinions of the German critics were affirmed by the Viennese musicians who grumbled about the difficult rehearsals. The atmosphere was further enhanced by rumours about Mahler and Alma Schindler who was 19 years younger than him. The claque went to jeer at him and feast their eyes on her.

Many in the audience enjoyed the music. The *claquers* enjoyed themselves because they hated it. When the symphony opened with jingling sleigh bells the claque burst out laughing. 'Is it a horse? Is it a mule?' The opening subject sounded like Haydn – not the classical

Haydn but a twentieth century Haydn riding around Vienna in an automobile that stank of oil and gasoline. Then four flutes played a tune you might hear a delivery boy whistling in the street. The claque joined in and whistled too. Then they heard a diabolical scherzo which was followed by a beautiful adagio that irritated the claque because beauty had no place in such a grotesque farrago. It was like being asked to watch a circus in a cathedral. The final movement was a song, and when it was all over, they called out 'shame!' They were not as successful at stimulating disapproval in the Musikvereinsaal as they were at stimulating applause in the Hofoper. Many in the audience enjoyed driving around Vienna with Haydn in an automobile and thrilled at the violent contrasts in the scherzo. They were moved by the heartfelt adagio and wept at the innocence of the song. They disapproved of the claque's bad manners. Suttner thought these people must be Jewish. Bruno Walter, who *was* Jewish and who was Mahler's deputy at the Hofoper, called out in response to the *claquers'* jeers, 'Mahler and his immortal work will still be alive after you are dead and buried.' Bruno Walter's real name was Bruno Schlesinger. Mahler suggested he change it because one Jew at the head of the Opera was enough. Suttner couldn't see how Bruno Schlesinger's new name made any difference. Nor was Suttner impressed with Mahler's new coat – the one Mahler put on when he came out of the church after he was baptized a Catholic in order to get the job at the Opera House.

> *'Gustav Mahler's so-called Symphony No.4 is nothing but a silly joke in poor taste, a really silly joke. He has put together a little Vienneseishness, some Hungarianishness, a lot of boredom and written four movements. Rightly surmising that the boredom would send his audience to sleep Mahler asks the orchestra to occasionally shriek fortissimo in order to terrify them.'*
> Neue Frei Presse

In the café after the concert the *claquers* shared their low opinion of Mahler's music and their high opinion of Alma Schindler's beauty. William's abiding memory of the concert had nothing to do with the claque's jeering nor Alma's ample bosom. It was the tune that sounded like a delivery boy whistling in the street. William couldn't get it out of his head. He liked it. It made him feel happy. The *claquers* looked at him awkwardly when he started whistling it in the café. Johnny squeezed William's hand and he stopped.

As the drink flowed so did the racism. The worst anti-Semites in Austrian society, according to Suttner, were wealthy Jews, who looked down on the more recent Jewish immigrants – poor orientals of the trading and lower classes. According to Suttner, rich Jews who looked down on poor Jews while pretending to be German were poisoning Austria. It was a familiar theme of Suttner's. What bothered Suttner was not so much that the Jews who appeared to have successfully integrated into Teutonic culture looked down on the Jews who had not yet integrated. What really bothered him was that the Jews who had successfully integrated looked down on him. Suttner was one of many Austrians who not only do not like Jews, they also don't much care for Germans either, although this latter prejudice was more a matter of taste than of race. Austrians prefer Mozart to Wagner. They prefer Haydn to Brahms. They find Wagner and Brahms too Germanic for their more refined Austrian tastes. And these Austrians had a problem with Jews, like Mahler, who appeared to be more German than Austrian.

Suttner hated Mahler but denied that he himself was anti-Semitic. 'Each to his own' was Suttner's view. Germans are Germans and Jews are Jews. Germans don't pretend to be Jews. Why do Jews pretend to be German? And Jews should not be permitted to make changes in Beethoven's scores. If they want to tamper with a composer's work let them meddle with one of their own – like Mendelssohn.

There were many in the Empire who would not have been able to understand the Viennese arrogance of the *claquers* in the bar that night because they did not speak German – subjects of Emperor Franz Joseph like Hungarians, or Bohemians or Slavs. William Hildebrand was Swiss. His first language was the French his mother spoke. Johnny was Bohemian and spoke Czech. Nevertheless, they both understood the language of racism well enough, finished their drinks and left the *claquers* to crow their racial superiority. William and Johnny walked home hand in hand whistling the flautists' tune from the first movement of Mahler's Fourth.

The baton Mahler used to conduct his Fourth Symphony was stolen from the conductor' podium after the performance that night by a member of the audience. The thief was the composer, Alban Berg. He loved the symphony and stole the baton which he kept in a pot on his desk where he wrote his orchestral works, songs, and operas.

CHAPTER 2

Hugo Wolf

William, Johnny, and the *claquers* went with Suttner to a house concert of Lieder at Hugo Wolf's. Suttner admired Wolf's songs and did what he could to support the composer who relied on the charity of his friends. Wolf was also a fierce enemy of Mahler's.

The director of the Hofoper inevitably attracts the hostility of hopeful composers whose work he rejects. Mahler had a secret bell button on his desk to summon help if he felt threatened by the thwarted ambition of a rejected composer and had occasion to use the bell during his last interview with Hugo Wolf.

The house concert offered the *claquers* an evening of Lieder and, for Suttner, the opportunity to support a friend with whom he shared an enemy. There must have been thirty or so in the room when Hugo Wolf stood up and took from his pocket the programme for the following season at the Hofoper and read out the dates for a new opera by Richard Strauss called *Feursnot*. He then read from the programme for the next Krefeld Festival, whose director was Richard Strauss, the date for the premier of Mahler's Third Symphony. The two directors had booked each other's work. 'To have one's work performed,' Wolf announced, 'it is necessary not only to be a composer but also to be a director!'

William and Johnny were surprised when Suttner clapped. The *claquers* in Wolf's audience who were used to applauding music rather than speeches, missed the moment, and didn't join in. Suttner filled the embarrassed silence which followed his solitary applause by calling out, 'Well said!' The rest of the room waited for the music, but Wolf was in no mood to sing. He recited a litany of Mahler's disasters beginning with his first production at the Hofoper – Leoncavallo's *La Bohème*. Mahler had gone to Milan to hear the opera and while he was there also heard Puccini's *La Bohème*, which, in Wolf's opinion, was nearly as bad. Mahler nevertheless returned to Vienna with a contract to perform Leoncavallo's version.

With Italy and Italians in his sights Wolf then took aim at Mahler's contract with Enrico Caruso. Whatever the Italian tenor's merits, and Wolf thought they were few, Caruso's morals disqualified the singer from the platform at the Hofoper. Mahler had paid Caruso a fortune and arranged for him to be awarded Imperial medals while covering up the singer's disgraceful conduct towards the women of the chorus.

A couple got up and left the room. The rest of Wolf's audience sat in silence. The door of an automobile slammed. The engine started. Those who had depended on this couple for a lift home looked around them anxiously.

Wolf referred to Zemlinsky's opera, *Es War Einmal*, which had received its premiere at the Hofoper after the composer had sent his lover, Alma Schindler, to Mahler. 'The director,' said Wolf, 'agreed to mount both her and the opera.'

Those who had just missed their lift home got up and left the room followed by several more. William and Johnny turned to Suttner. The *claquers* wanted out. Suttner pleaded with Wolf for some music.

Wolf addressed his remaining audience as 'dear brothers and sisters' and announced that he had been appointed by the Emperor to be the new director of the Hofoper and that his first task after dismissing Gustav Mahler would be to ban sex in the dressing rooms.

Suttner told Wolf he was mad and left the room followed by William, Johnny, the *claquers* and everyone else except for a woman who called out after them, 'Clear out, all of you! You haven't the least understanding. There's need of understanding here.'

Hugo Wolf sat on the stool, spread his arms to grasp the sides of the piano, then thrust his head onto the keyboard. The piano yielded a loud, painful, dissonant cry.

CHAPTER 3

Gustav & Alma

In the weeks after the Vienna premier of Mahler's Fourth William Hildebrand loitered around the opera house during the day hoping to catch a glimpse of Mahler. It didn't take Hildebrand long to discover Mahler's regular hours. Mahler walked home from the opera to his apartment in Auenbruggergasse every day for lunch, always leaving the Hofoper punctually at twelve noon. Hildebrand followed him. At first he followed Mahler from a discreet distance but after a few days he followed Mahler more closely. Mahler was a small man who walked briskly with quick steps but would then abruptly stop for no apparent reason and touch the back of his left leg with the toe of his right foot before going on his way. Between the Hofoper and his apartment Mahler would stop and perform this strange ritual again and again. Hildebrand was convinced there must be some meaning to these pauses – some music underlying the rhythm of Mahler's strange gait. As he followed Mahler he counted and tried to predict when he would stop but these moments were unpredictable. Mahler might walk a hundred metres without stopping and then stop twice within the next twenty metres. In his effort to understand, Hildebrand found himself walking more closely behind Mahler so when Mahler stopped Hildebrand had to stop too. One day Hildebrand was following Mahler so closely that when Mahler stopped Hildebrand walked straight into him. Mahler's hat fell off and he dropped the scores he was carrying. Hildebrand got down on his knees to retrieve Mahler's hat and the music from the pavement. He handed them back, apologising profusely. Mahler said nothing and the two of them went their separate ways, Mahler to his apartment and Hildebrand in the opposite direction back to the Hofoper and away from the scene of his shame.

    The following day Hildebrand's guilt brought him back to the same spot at the same time and when he saw Mahler coming he walked in front of him where there was no danger of accidentally walking into him. He started to whistle the melody played by the four flutes from the first movement of the Fourth Symphony – the tune that sounds like a delivery boy whistling in the street. Mahler's ears pricked up. He walked more quickly to catch up with the whistler. Hildebrand heard Mahler behind him calling out, 'Excuse me!' Hildebrand stopped and Mahler walked straight into him. Mahler's hat flew off and he dropped his music. Hildebrand got down on his knees to retrieve Mahler's hat and music and he apologized to Mahler again. Mahler, recognizing him from the day before, smiled the most beautiful smile. William's flesh tingled and thrilled to the light in Mahler's eyes. He handed Mahler his hat and carried his music until they arrived at Mahler's apartment. They walked together in silence. Mahler never once stopped to touch his left leg with his right. When they arrived at Mahler's door the maestro lifted his hat to the student and bade him good day. Hildebrand returned to the Hofoper walking on air.

Hildebrand waited for Mahler at the same time in the same place every day and Mahler looked out for him. They walked along the street together. Mahler often stopped to buy apples and Hildebrand would wait outside the shop holding Mahler's hat and music. If Mahler was caught short and went into a café to relieve himself Hildebrand would wait outside holding Mahler's hat, his music, and his apples. And when they arrived at Mahler's apartment Mahler would doff his hat, flash William a beautiful smile, and wish the young student a good day. William wanted to hold Mahler. He wanted to be held by Mahler.

William told Johnny about his daily encounters with Mahler but as every day seemed to be much the same Johnny showed little interest. Every day was not quite the same because with each encounter William Hildebrand fell more deeply in love with Gustav Mahler.

Eventually, William found his way into Mahler's household and occasionally ran errands for Mahler and his sister, Justi. Johnny wasn't jealous. He loved William and was happy for William to have Mahler's feather in his cap. William wanted to share his feather, but Johnny preferred to let William wear it himself. Johnny knew that William and Gustav would never be lovers. When Johnny and William held each other there was no room between them for Mahler.

Mahler was having trouble in his own bedroom. He had tried making love with Alma Schindler but the first time his strength had ebbed away. It was a disappointment for them both. Alma wrote about it in her diary. When they tried a second time it was so successful that Alma became pregnant. A wedding was hastily arranged, and the 41-year-old Mahler held an engagement party to introduce his 22-year-old fiancée. William went shopping with Mahler's sister to fetch cakes and bottles of beer for the party. William helped Justi to serve the guests. William, Johnny, and Alma were the only young people in the room.

The other guests were Mahler's age or even older. They were surprised that Mahler had chosen such a young bride and examined her closely. She was the daughter of the late Emil Schindler, the Emperor's favourite landscape painter. William went around the guests with the beer and cakes, but no one wanted to eat or drink except for Alma, who, after a few beers, was a bit tipsy.

William had heard the rumours that, despite her youth, Alma was not inexperienced and that when she was sixteen had been intimately involved with Gustav Klimt. She was a competent musician who had studied composition with Zemlinsky. Everyone knew that Alma was walking out on Zemlinsky to marry Mahler. Mahler started biting his nails. Alma slapped Mahler's hand and told him to stop it. He poured himself a bottle of beer and picked at the label, scratching it away from the bottle while his friends asked Alma questions about philosophy. She told them that *Plato's Symposium* had 'tickled her pink.' Mahler's friends asked her about Mahler's music. She told them that she had heard very little of it and the little she had heard she did not like. Mahler burst out laughing, took Alma by the hand and rushed out of the room with her. Mahler's guests sat in silence as Justi went around with a grimace and a tray of cakes. William and Johnny sat holding hands. There was knocking on the other side of the wall which everyone ignored even as it accelerated and got louder. On a table next to the wall a candlestick wobbled. Pictures on the wall hung askew as the banging from the other room vibrated throughout the apartment until Alma shrieked, 'Ja!' then all was quiet. Johnny squeezed William's hand.

William made himself useful to Alma. On the nights when Alma came to the Hofoper she sat in the director's box and William would take her a cup of tea at the interval until she told him she preferred Benedictine.

William made himself useful to Mahler too. Mahler kept his tails and dress shirt in a wardrobe behind the desk in his office and got into these working clothes five minutes before a performance. He then walked briskly from his office to the auditorium and onto the podium without inviting the confidence of a mirror. With the lights dimmed and the conductor sitting in the pit below the level of the audience in the orchestra stalls no one noticed Mahler's poor dress sense. William convinced Mahler that he should have a second set of working clothes so that his one suit could be taken to the tailor for essential repairs which were urgently needed after the last of the buttons on his flies popped off. Mahler had been conducting with three buttons, then two, and then one, and it was only after he lost the last one that Mahler noticed a problem. William wondered why Mahler was late and went to his office where he found the conductor staring in dismay at his open flies. William found some pins on Mahler's desk and was on his knees trying to close Mahler's flies when the stage manager, looking for Mahler, ran into the office, misunderstood what was going on, and ran out again. Mahler's flies would not stay closed with the pins and William suggested that Mahler put his trousers on back to front. Mahler made his way to the auditorium with his open flies behind him concealed beneath his tails. As soon as the overture started Mahler did not give another thought to the way he was dressed. No one in the auditorium would have guessed Mahler was wearing his trousers back to front and it would have gone unnoticed but at the end of the performance Mahler turned to acknowledge the audience's applause, bowed, and presented the orchestra with a sight which was the subject of great mirth in the cafes long after the final curtain.

William measured Mahler and, with blank Hofoper cheques that Mahler had signed, he ordered a second suit of working clothes better fitted to the new century and two pairs of shoes in the modern style without laces so they could be easily slipped on and off. William explained to the shoemaker that they were for a small man and asked for an extra half inch on the heels which would allow Mahler to look a little taller when he stood next to Alma. Mahler did not notice the improvements. Alma, however, did and she asked William's advice regarding her wedding dress.

The Catholic church does not light many candles for mixed marriages. The marriage of Gustav and Alma was mixed not because Mahler was a Jew but because Alma was a Protestant. In order to get married to a Protestant, Mahler, who was baptized a Catholic, had to persuade Alma to agree that they would bring up their children as Catholics. The Catholic Church insisted on that. Mahler also insisted that Alma give up composing. He told her that the idea of two composers in the house was unthinkable and that her role was to look after his happiness.

On their wedding day, after walking down the aisle stopping now and then to touch his left leg with the toe of his right shoe Mahler waited for his bride at the altar. Alma arrived with her stepfather, Carl Moll, and a bridesmaid who paused on the way down the aisle to touch her left leg with the toe of her right shoe. The little girl's witty gesture punctured the solemnity of the occasion. William and Johnny tried not to laugh. It was difficult to restore an air of solemnity after Alma's mother slapped the little girl's legs and marched her out of the church.

After the ceremony William and Johnny skipped home from the church laughing in the sunshine, hand in hand, all the way down the street and, like two delivery boys, whistling the tune from the opening movement of Mahler's Fourth and sometimes stopping to touch their left legs with the toes of their right shoes.

The following day Gustav and Alma left Vienna to honeymoon in Russia where Mahler was booked to conduct three concerts in St Petersburg.

With Mahler in Russia musical life in Vienna dropped into a lower gear. Many musicians took advantage of Mahler's honeymoon to take a few days off themselves. The orchestra that Mahler's deputy, Bruno Walter, conducted in Mahler's absence was full of deputies. Johnny was in the orchestra every night. William, who had now slipped off the fixer's lists, spent every night in the auditorium with the claque but there was nothing in any of the performances that merited the claque's intervention. Bruno Walter's performances were attended, just as Mahler would have wished, without any interruptions.

William counted the days when Gustav and Alma would return so that he could fulfill the new vocation in his life. The Emperor's wedding present to the Mahlers was a four-seater, straight-ahead, four-cylinder, eight-litre Benz. William knew that neither Gustav nor Alma would ever drive it. The future that beckoned to William Hildebrand was not a seat in the viola section of Mahler's orchestra but a seat behind the wheel of Mahler's car.

CHAPTER 4

Mahler's Third Symphony

Richard Strauss arranged for the world premiere of Mahler's 3rd Symphony to be performed at the festival in Krefeld in June.

William had only ever heard Mahler's Fourth. Nothing in the Fourth could possibly have prepared him for the mountainous music of the Third Symphony. Even before a note was played William was astonished by the size of the orchestra. There must have been more than a hundred instruments, a soloist, a boys' choir, an adult choir, and offstage musicians in the corridors all around the hall. Richard Strauss was a powerful influence on the festival committee and had pushed through Mahler's demand for an extra 30 musicians and four extra rehearsals. At the first rehearsal when the symphony opened with eight horns playing in unison, William was pinned back in his seat. He was in heaven.

Mahler gave Alma little jobs making corrections and copying out parts. William gave Alma a hand. His hand was neat. Alma's was almost illegible.

The symphony's six movements lasted for an hour and a half. The first movement, a mixture of the bizarre, the cheap, and the profound, was filled with fairground music, barrel organs, fanfares, brass bands, and socialist marching songs. At the end of the movement Strauss marched up and down the aisle leading the applause. The second movement wafted through the audience like a breeze through a meadow of flowers. The audience listened to the third like startled animals in a forest. The mysterious fourth dug below a layer of pain to reveal an even deeper layer of joy. As the boys' choir sang in the fifth movement the infectious smiles on the faces of the choristers spread throughout the audience and when the last movement rose to a warm and satisfying conclusion Strauss was no longer leading the applause. Strauss had hoped that it would be good but did not realise it would be quite so good. It was modern. It was original. It took the audience on an adventure they could never have imagined. It was playful. It was fun. Alma looked on proudly and for the first time she felt the baby inside her kick. After the last movement, an adagio of incomparable nobility, the ovation lasted for fifteen minutes. Mahler was called back onto the podium twelve times. When it was all over Mahler would have swapped all the applause for just one word from Strauss. In the restaurant afterwards William sat several places away from Mahler and watched him move the food around on his plate. Mahler ate nothing. William wished that Alma, somebody, anybody, would reach out to the exhausted and sad composer, hold him in their arms and let him fall asleep.

When Mahler was waiting in the conductor's room after the concert for Strauss to come and say something, Strauss was standing on the conductor's podium above the empty auditorium looking at Mahler's score and was lost in his thoughts. When two stagehands came on to the platform to remove the chairs and music stands Strauss, absent-mindedly, picked up Mahler's baton, put it in his inside pocket and left the building.

CHAPTER 5

Richard Strauss

Richard Strauss was engaged to Pauline de Ahna, a soprano with a big voice and a huge temper. Once, in Berlin, she threw the score at the conductor and stormed off the stage. The orchestra informed the conductor that if she returned they would refuse to play. The conductor, Richard Strauss, pleaded with them not to walk out and confessed that Pauline was his fiancée. Not wishing to add to their conductor's difficulties the musicians stayed and finished the rehearsal.

Strauss and Pauline, now husband and wife, arrived in Vienna for the first night of Strauss's *Feuersnot* at the Hofoper. It was performed to a small audience and although it was beautifully played and beautifully sung there was nothing the claque could do to stimulate applause in the half-empty auditorium. The performance, nevertheless, was good. Strauss had never heard a work of his played so well. When it was over, William took a glass of Benedictine to Alma and a cup of tea for Pauline. He stopped outside the director's box wondering how to knock on the door with a drink in each hand when he heard Pauline's raised voice denouncing her husband's opera. William didn't want to interrupt, and he didn't want to eavesdrop, but couldn't help overhearing Pauline accuse her husband of plagiarism, of raking through Wagner's waste-paper bin, throwing away the best of Wagner's rubbish and copying the worst of it. William waited for Pauline to take a breath and then tapped on the door with his foot. Pauline took the tea and Benedictine dismissed him. Before he closed the door, William looked at Alma to let her know that he had heard. She looked at him and let him know she needed help.

William went to Mahler's office where he found Mahler and Strauss smoking cigars. Strauss, who never understood Mahler the composer but had the greatest respect for Mahler the conductor, told Mahler he could not have conducted his own opera better himself. He complimented the orchestra, the singers, and referred to himself as Richard the Second. Mahler, who had heard the influence of Richard Wagner, told Strauss that his homage to 'Richard the First' was intelligently done. Strauss agreed. William interrupted and offered to drive them and their wives to the restaurant in the automobile.

William fetched Alma and Pauline from the director's box and Johnny from the orchestra room and returned with them to Mahler's office where Pauline launched into a furious onslaught on her husband's 'feeble opera.' Mahler ushered the quarrelling pair towards the room that had been reserved for Strauss. Pauline pushed her husband into the room and slammed the door behind them. The sign on the door, *'The Hofoper welcomes Herr R. Strauss'* was knocked sideways. Everyone heard Pauline's solo accompanied by objects thrown and broken until something struck the door with great force, Pauline screamed, 'Nein!' and the sign welcoming Herr Strauss to the Hofoper leapt off the door and onto the floor. William and Johnny, remembering the banging on the bedroom wall when Alma and Mahler left their engagement party to have noisy sex in an adjacent bedroom, wondered if all heterosexual couples were similarly noisy. Mahler opened the door an inch and speaking into the crack said it was time to go to the restaurant. Herr Strauss emerged from the room, face red, hair disheveled, and said that Pauline wasn't feeling hungry. William drove Alma and Mahler, Strauss, and Johnny to dinner. Strauss spent the whole evening in the restaurant talking about royalties.

Johnny sometimes went for after-concert dinners with William and Mahler but more often went for a beer with the other musicians. He enjoyed the company of those who played the music more than those who wrote it.

William drove the Mahlers to visit the Strausses. Alma and Gustav were surprised to find Pauline still in bed. Richard was not at home. He was out shopping. He returned with a diamond ring and went to his wife's bedside, gave it to her and said, 'Now will you get up!'

Over lunch Pauline accused her husband of using too much toilet paper in the lavatory. She asked Mahler how much toilet paper he used.

Mahler and Strauss retired to the study. Strauss wanted to talk to Mahler about his new opera based on Oscar Wilde's *Salome*. Alma was left with Pauline and William. Pauline wanted to know about hairdressers, department stores and fashions in Vienna. Alma turned to William for help.

In Strauss's study the two composers looked at rough drafts of the new opera. When Herod's daughter dances naked for him he promises to grant her whatever she wishes. Strauss believed the soprano's naked dance would be a box office sensation. At the piano Strauss played the music for Salome demanding the head of John the Baptist, then the music which would accompany the head being brought to her on a platter, followed by the music to accompany Salome kissing the severed head. Strauss thought nudity and necrophilia was a winning combination. Mahler thought the Hofoper might cope with the nudity but not necessarily the necrophilia.

William Hildebrand coughed politely. Mahler and Strauss turned to find him at the door where he mimed 'baby in the womb' and 'need to sleep.' Mahler stubbed out his cigar and took his leave.

CHAPTER 6

Maria

William drove Alma and Mahler to Maiernigg on the Worthersee where they had a summer house and where Mahler had a composing hut. He worked there on his fifth symphony and took Alma for long walks in the hills. Occasionally he would stop and make notes. He wrote a song for her.

Liebst du um Schönheit o nicht mich liebe!
Liebe die Sonne, sie tragt ein gold'nes Haar.
Liebst du um Jugend, O nicht mich liebe!
Liebe den Fruhling, der jung ist jedes Jahr.
Liebst du um Schätze, o nicht mich liebe
Liebe die Meerfrau, sie hat viel Perlen klar.
Liebst du um Liebe, o ja, mich liebe!
Liebe mich immer, dich lieb'ich immerdar.

If you love me for beauty– don't love me.
If you love me for youth – don't ...
If you love me for wealth – don't ...
If you love me for love – yes,
Love me forever.

Mahler rarely went out with Alma. However, they did both go to the theatre together and enjoyed a matinée performance of *The Merry Widow*. Back home they danced the widow's waltz but got stuck when they forgot the tune. They went to a music shop and while Mahler engaged the shopkeeper in conversation Alma found a copy of the music, memorised the waltz then hummed the tune to her husband who committed it to memory. They got home, sang for each other, and finished their dance.

When Alma went into labour William ran from the kitchen to the bedroom with boiling water and towels for Alma and from the bedroom back to the kitchen to make tea for Alma's mother.

Mahler tried to help too. As she lay there calling out obscenities and writhing in agony, he read to her from Plato's *Symposium*. The baby was breech born. Mahler held his baby daughter and told her how pleased he was that she had decided to present her backside to the world first. 'That's my girl!' said the proud father kissing his daughter while the midwife with needle and thread tried to repair his torn and bleeding wife. The child was named Maria after Mahler's mother. Mahler loved this child beyond measure from the first day.

CHAPTER 7

Mahler's Fifth Symphony

The relationship between any orchestra and conductor is never moderate. It is either very good or very bad and is frequently both. Mahler's relationship with the Vienna players was normal. They liked him a lot and they disliked him in equal measure. They were supportive, prickly, defiant, and dedicated, ready to walk out at a moment's notice and prepared to stay behind and rehearse overtime if necessary. After work they would discuss the limitations of all conductors, and remind each other over a beer how the sound in the concert hall was only ever made by musicians – never by conductors. The musician who produced a baton from his inside pocket, beat time with it, and asked if anyone could hear anything, always got a laugh. In the concert hall, it was different. The players had one eye on their music and the other on Mahler. Mahler, with one eye on his score and the other on his musicians, played his orchestra with body language the players instinctively understood. Mahler would close the back desks of the second violins with a shake of the head, bring in the flutes and oboes just ahead of the beat with a raised eyebrow, make a diminuendo in the first violins by lowering his left hand, take out one of the trombones with the raised index finger of his left hand while anticipating a rallentando with a slight bend of his knees. Like a sailor trimming his sails into a favourable wind, Mahler would steer his orchestral ship across a symphonic ocean. The Vienna Philharmonic musicians, who were bemused when asked to play slower so that the music would sound faster, or quieter so that it would sound louder, laughed about their conductor in the café but in the concert hall it was no joke. They could clearly hear that Mahler was right.

Mahler asked the Vienna Philharmonic Orchestra to hire another ten musicians. Mahler's argument was simple. Eighteenth and nineteenth century composers did not write for large twentieth century concert halls. To play in bigger halls you need bigger orchestras. Double the strings and you must double the brass and the woodwinds so that large audiences could hear the music as the composer intended. The Vienna orchestra's argument was also simple. Their ensemble was a co-operative. They shared their profits and were not prepared to cut their income into another ten shares. Mahler needed a larger orchestra to conduct the music the way he wanted. More controversially, he needed a larger orchestra to perform his own work. The players refused.

It was not the best time for Mahler to ask the Vienna players to read through his fifth symphony. He wanted to hear what he had written and offered the orchestra an appropriate remuneration. The orchestra gave Mahler two rehearsals and refused remuneration. They played the symphony for him twice for free. They didn't just hate him. They loved him.

The Grosser Musikvereinsaal smelled of fresh paint for the birth of Mahler's new symphony. This was even more exciting than a premier. The silent scores on the music stands were about to be given life. Rhythms, harmonies, and melodies that had never been heard before were about to make their way into the world at the hands of the Vienna players. Strings, woodwinds, and brass took their seats in front of a percussion section which stretched from one end of the platform to the other. Musicians nervously turned the pages of their scores to see what lay in store for them. Mahler had called for extra musicians and several of the best students from the conservatoire had been invited to play. William arrived with his viola but there was no seat for him. Johnny Stanko, the star student, was given the lead trumpet's seat. He looked at the first page and his jaw dropped. He waved at William to come and see. The symphony opened with his solo trumpet. Johnny had spent the last three hours warming up, his lip was in good shape and he was ready. William was happy for him. William sat on a step beside the organ with his viola on his knees ready to step in if by chance one of the viola section should leave.

Mahler smiled at the first trumpet, nodded, and Johnny opened Mahler's Fifth Symphony.

William was not in a good place to hear the music. On his step behind the orchestra the symphony sounded like a concerto for percussion. As the players grew in confidence Mahler asked for more from the cymbals and more from the timpani. It was deafening. Then the percussion stopped for the fourth movement which was for strings only. Johnny left his seat to come and sit on the step beside William and together they listened to the *adagietto*. It was the most beautiful thing William had ever heard. William took Johnny's hand and together they were captivated by the tender intimacy of a melody that appeared to have no end. It was so full of sweetness and nostalgia. William and Johnny wept.

Johnny returned to the trumpet section for the final movement and William saw a white stripe on the backside of Johnny's concert black trousers. The step where they were sitting had been freshly painted.

After it was all over William, wearing an apron to conceal the paint on his own backside, took a large glass of Benedictine to Alma. She wasn't happy. She hated the percussion, told her husband so, and insisted that he remove it all.

Conducting at the Opera was different from conducting in the concert hall. Mahler kept time with the baton and anticipated time with his eyes. This was necessary because the house was so big that the singers onstage and the musicians in the pit reached different parts of the hall at different times. The distance from the stage to the Imperial Box was greater than the distance from the orchestra pit to the Imperial Box and in such a big house the difference was crucial, and, to an Emperor's ears, painful. There are conductors who think it is all going well but someone sitting in the boxes at the back of the stalls could tell them that it isn't. Mahler understood the Hofoper's acoustics. He conducted the singers with his eyes in anticipation of the beat and conducted the orchestra with his baton on the beat, so that the Emperor in his Imperial Box heard the words and the music at the same time.

Mahler did not confine these skills to the Hofoper. His ability to conduct on the beat with his hands, ahead of the beat with his eyes, and behind the beat with his hips, allowed orchestras to explore tempos flexibly. Mahler, dancing in front of his orchestra, could step in and out of time, making music sound as natural as wind whistling through the grass, animals chasing each other through the undergrowth, or waves lapping on the shore. Mahler always knew the exact position of the first beat of every bar even if he rarely referred to it. He could transform a simple waltzing 1-2-3 into an exhilarating helter-skelter ride by bringing in the 2 early and the 3 late but not necessarily in all the parts, sometimes holding the second violins a little behind the first violins while, at the same time, keeping strict tempo in the percussion. It was hard work and such good fun.

CHAPTER 8

Unhappy Birthdays

Alma's second daughter, Anna, was born in June 1904. After the birth Alma was depressed. She stayed in bed. When William brought her a glass of Benedictine she told him, 'I've lost all my friends and won a friend who doesn't know me.'

The following day she was feeling better and told William of her decision 'to sacrifice my happiness for that of another, and in so doing find happiness myself.'

On the third day she told William, 'One moment I'm dying of love for him – the next moment I feel nothing.'

On August 31st she showed William her husband's greeting: 'I hope that, instead of an expensive gift, you will welcome my most heartfelt greetings for your birthday – what more can one give when he has already given all of himself?'"

William travelled with Alma and Mahler to Cologne for the premier of his fifth Symphony. William sat with Alma in front of the orchestra where it sounded better than it did in Vienna when he sat on a step behind the orchestra. The percussion was still there – all of it. Mahler hadn't deleted a rattle, a switch, a clapper, or a stroke. The triangles, bells and cymbals swished, crashed, and rang. It was as loud as thunder in a storm. The planets swirled around the sun to the beat of the drums, the universe danced, and the critics hated it. So did Alma, who put down her glass of Benedictine and put her hands over her ears. She was still holding her ears at the beginning of the fourth movement – the adagietto for strings. William knew this movement was a love song for her and he wanted her to hear it. He poured her a glass of Benedictine. She took her hands from her ears to accept the glass. At the beginning of the final movement she covered her ears again. The critics covered their ears too.

> *'How could the audience applaud with such enthusiasm a symphony which tortures healthy minds? The public has allowed itself to be seduced by a piece of shameless music that is unable to sustain the same manner or direction for more than four bars without becoming trite... No doctor would prescribe it for his patient for he would not sleep well, it would give him*

bad dreams, and leave him depressed in the daytime...First Mahler scoffs at sadness, then he scoffs at gaiety, and finally he scoffs at himself.'
Kölnische Zeitung

When Alma was ill in bed William would go to her room and refill her glass with another dose of medicinal Benedictine. Alma was always unwell when Anna von Mildenburg, the Hofoper's soprano, came to visit. She never told her husband how much she disliked his former lover. Instead, she shared her feelings with William. Alma also told William all about her mother's affair with Carl Moll who eventually married her mother and became her stepfather. She told him how Moll had banned Klimt from the house after he learned of the artist's intimacy with Alma. She confessed to missing her former lover, Zemlinsky. She told him how badly she missed her music. William showed an interest in her songs and asked if he could hear them. She refused. Her husband had stipulated there must only be one composer in the house. She was determined to keep it that way and to suffer. William wondered if it might be a good idea to invite Zemlinsky for a musical evening. She perked up and thought it was an excellent idea. It was such a good idea she came to believe that she had thought of it herself. If it was all right for Gustav to have a former lover in the house, then it was all right for her too.

The day before Zemlinsky's visit Alma was in great form. She was playing hide and seek with her daughter. Maria was hiding in the automobile while William polished it. Alma, shielding her eyes from the afternoon sun like a sailor scanning the horizon, searched for her daughter. She knew Maria couldn't be far away. She didn't know Maria was in the automobile. The little girl put her finger to her lips and gave William a 'sssh', inviting his complicity. Alma walked all around the automobile. William kept polishing. She stepped away from the automobile and turned towards the house calling out, 'Maria!' Her daughter sprang out of her hiding place. 'I won! I won!' Alma picked Maria up in her arms. Gustav and Anna von Mildenburg came out of the house to see what all the laughter was about. Alma told Gustav that William had kidnapped their daughter but now that Maria was rescued Alma hoped that Anna would be staying to join them for supper.

That night Johnny was surprised by William's request to play hide and seek before they went to bed.

Mahler was not at home when Zemlinsky came to visit. He was conducting at the Hofoper. William brought pastries and his viola. Zemlinsky, bashful and apologetic, stumbled in the doorway and dropped all his music. As William picked up the papers he saw that Zemlinsky had brought Wagner piano arrangements for four hands. There was no room in these piano duets for a viola. William took Zemlinsky's coat, served the coffee and the pastries, a bottle of Benedictine and two glasses, opened the lid of the piano, propped up the music stand above the keyboard and, taking his viola with him, left the room.

Alma and Zemlinsky sat at the piano and played Wagner all evening. When the music stopped William returned to take away the coffee cups. The bottle of Benedictine was unopened. Alma was exhausted. At the front door she asked Zemlinsky to come again. Zemlinsky kissed Alma on the cheek as he bid her good night.

William got home well before Johnny who was having a long evening of Wagner at the Hofoper.

The next day William went to the Mahlers' with a bag of apples. Mahler was at work and Alma was ill in bed with a bottle of Benedictine. She told William that her husband had been unhappy about the previous evening's soirée. Mahler himself had no ill feelings about Alma receiving Zemlinsky into their home. He was concerned only for Zemlinsky's feelings. Mahler thought his wife had been careless about the difficult situation into which she had thrust the young composer. He felt she had not behaved responsibly. Her husband's sympathies were all for Zemlinsky and none for her. She complained to William that Gustav was not her father and that she was not a mischievous child. He could play Wagner all night at the Hofoper with Anna von Mildenburg so why couldn't she play Wagner in her own home with Zemlinsky?

William wondered if it might be an idea to invite Zemlinsky again and this time to invite Zemlinsky's sister, Mathilde, to come with him. Alma perked up. She thought it was an excellent idea. It was such a good idea she believed she had thought of it herself.

For William and Mathilde's visit William prepared a tray with pastries, coffee, Benedictine and three glasses. William took their coats, served coffee, opened the lid of the piano, and propped up the music stand above the keyboard. Mathilde asked him what he was going to play. William told her that he didn't play, not the piano anyway, but he did play the viola, sort of, but not very well. He used to study at the conservatoire. His name was William and of course he would be happy to show her his viola if she would like to see it.

From the auditorium the difference between a viola and a violin is not obvious. Closer and you can easily see that a viola is much bigger. Mathilde held William's viola under her chin. She said it felt all wrong. William agreed. Violins and cellos are 'right' and violas are 'wrong.' That was what he found attractive about the viola. In a quartet the viola is the odd one out – and that's how William felt about himself.

She gave it back to him and asked him if he knew the similarity between a viola player's fingers and lightning. William didn't understand. 'The similarity between a viola player's fingers and lightning?' he repeated looking puzzled. She nodded. William shook his head. She told him that lightning never strikes the same place twice. William didn't know what she was talking about, but it sounded like a compliment. He put the viola back in its case, poured a cup of coffee, gave it to her and left the room. She settled down in an armchair and took a book from her bag. Alma and Zemlinsky pounded out the four-hand piano reduction of Wagner, Mathilde read her book. William waited in the kitchen.

At the end of the evening Zemlinsky kissed Alma on the cheek and bid her good night. Mathilde kissed William. He carried the tray to the kitchen with the pastries, one dirty coffee cup, three clean glasses, and the unopened bottle of Benedictine.

That night William asked Johnny about the similarity between a viola player's fingers and lightning. Johnny told him that lightning never strikes the same place twice.

William went to the Mahlers' the next day with a bag of apples. The Mahlers seemed to get through a lot of apples. Then William discovered that Alma didn't like apples, neither did the children, and that Mahler ate them all himself. William made it his mission to supply Mahler's apple addiction and keep his barrel full. Alma left a glass in the kitchen with petty cash for William to spend on apples, pastries, and other household goods. William always counted out the change carefully and put it back into this magical glass where the cash never diminished. William knew he was trusted. He was helpful, honest, and invisible. They would have given him the keys to the house if he had asked.

William had often listened to Alma complain but had never imagined that she would ever be displeased with him. The day after Zemlinsky's second visit Alma was angry with William. She complained that William had abandoned Mathilde and left her with nothing to do all evening except read her book. Alma thought it unlikely she would want to come back and accused William of ill-manners.

If Alma needed a foursome then William wondered whether Alma might ask Zemlinsky to bring a friend with him the next time. Alma perked up. She thought this was an excellent idea. It was such a good idea that she believed she had thought of it herself.

William, relieved that Alma's temper had improved, asked her if she knew the similarity between lightning and a viola player's fingers. Alma asked William how she was supposed to know that!

There was no performance at the Hofoper on the evening of Zemlinsky's third visit, and Mahler was at home. Gustav and Alma welcomed their guests and William prepared a tray of coffee and pastries. He knew that Alma would not require Benedictine. He opened a bottle of beer for Mahler.

Arnold Schönberg was eight years older than William and looked a great deal older than that. He had lost most of his hair and his eyes were so deeply sunken that his expression resembled a skull. William wondered if Schönberg had ever smiled.

Alma declined to join Zemlinsky at the piano. He played solo. Mozart. Beethoven. Schubert. Schönberg played some of his own work. Sparse, brief, and ghostly. Mathilde looked over to William and smiled as if to ask him what he thought of Schönberg's music. William didn't know what he thought about it. Mathilde went over to the piano, put her hand on Schönberg's shoulder and whispered a 'Thank you' in his ear. Schönberg stopped playing and the atmosphere in the room lifted. Mahler smoked a cigar.

Zemlinsky asked Mahler how the first performance of his Fifth Symphony had been received in Cologne. Mahler told Zemlinsky that he would rather have given the first performance fifty years after his death. Schönberg told Mahler he hoped his Fifth was better than his Fourth which sounded like a symphony of tea and cakes. Mahler smiled and with a small movement of his head, a gesture familiar to any musician in his orchestra, encouraged Schönberg to continue. Schönberg told Mahler that music cannot be a means to escape the human condition. Music is an expression of the human condition and although one may visit ballrooms and cafes on the road to the grave, the human journey nevertheless moved relentlessly towards death. A symphony that directed its audience towards a happy ending and a pretty cadence was a lie. Schönberg said it was the duty of the composer to say 'no' with every note. Mathilde laughed and told Schönberg he was being 'naughty.' William would like to have said something about the mischief in Mahler's Fourth and how the Fifth was full of love and counterpoint, that the adagietto was the most beautiful music he had ever heard, and that the last movement was a glorious life-affirming 'yes.' If William had said anything the others would have been surprised to discover he was in the room.

Zemlinsky asked Mahler what he was working on. Mahler told him, Kindertotenlieder. Alma paled. 'Songs on the deaths of children?' She was shocked. So was William. Schönberg wanted to know who wrote the lyrics.

'Ruckert,' said Mahler.

Schönberg thought Ruckert was a second-rate poet.

Mahler agreed that Ruckert was not of the very first rank but explained that one would not set the very finest poetry to music. The words of great poets were already full of music, but Ruckert's poetry left sufficient room for a musical contribution. Mahler was proposing little journeys from the cradle to the grave so brief there would be no time for visiting ballrooms or cafes on the way.

Alma left the room to check on her children not because she thought they were in danger from their father's settings of Ruckert's poems but because she was having a miserable evening. She had enjoyed Zemlinsky's first two visits but not this third. Nothing could have persuaded her to sit at the piano in front of her husband. She had warmed to Schönberg's criticism of her husband's music and was disappointed when Schönberg had no response to Mahler's enthusiasm for Ruckert's poems.

Mahler said goodnight to his guests by himself. William took the tray back to the kitchen. Mahler had scratched the labels off the beer bottles

Alma asked William why her husband had bound to him a splendid bird so happy in flight when a heavy grey one would have suited him better? William suggested she invite Zemlinsky, Schoenberg and Mathilde for another musical evening. She didn't want to see her friends. She didn't want to see her children. She didn't want to see her husband. She wanted to be on her own. She withdrew to her room. She had never engaged with her elder daughter. Maria was daddy's girl. Maria often went to her father in his composing hut. Mahler, who hated any kind of disturbance when composing, nevertheless welcomed Maria who often emerged from the hut covered in jam. Alma didn't spend much time with the younger daughter, Anna, who had a nurse. Alma didn't like either of her girls. They were Jewish.

On August 31st Alma showed William her husband's birthday greeting.

'Dear Alma, I'm afraid it's too late for a birthday present – and with the best will in the world I can't think of anything suitable to buy you. Almschi! You know how hopeless I am about things like that.'

To cheer her up William took her for a drive. When they got back, as Alma was getting out of the automobile, she looked up at the house and saw Maria at the window. The child who had endlessly beautiful dark curls waved to her mother. Alma hissed, 'That girl has got to go……and so has Gustav!'

CHAPTER 9

Arnold Schönberg

Mahler told William that he would like to invite Schönberg to the house so that they could continue their interesting discussion. Mahler admired Schönberg's description of his Fourth Symphony as 'tea and cakes.' It was mischievous just like the symphony itself and Mahler delighted at the prospect of making further mischief with the young composer.

Schoenberg became a regular visitor and he and Mahler spent hours together talking about music while Mahler scratched the labels off the beer bottles. One day Schönberg brought bottles of beer with the labels already scratched off. Mahler was not amused, called him 'a conceited young puppy,' and threw him out.

Mahler supported Schönberg even though his music maddened and puzzled him. Schönberg concerts sometimes ended in brawls among warring factions in the audience. At one concert William pulled Mahler out of a brawl after he had thrown a punch at one of Schönberg's hecklers and bruised the knuckles on his right hand. On the way home Mahler told William he thought it would be better if Alma didn't know about the fight. Later, in Alma's hearing, William apologized to Mahler for catching his hand in the door of the automobile and Mahler told William not to worry, that it had been his own fault, and that he would be more careful getting in and out of the automobile in future. The next time Schönberg visited he thanked Mahler for knocking out that stupid heckler with 'one stupendous blow.' William told Alma that Schönberg was only joking. Alma assured William that Schönberg did not have a sense of humour.

There are artists who will not let anyone see their work until it is finished, in the belief that you can jinx a work if you talk about it before it's done. Mahler wasn't like that and would return from his composing hut with daily progress reports. He told Alma that he had composed her into the first movement of his Sixth and their two daughters into the second movement. He told Schönberg too. Schönberg did not believe it was possible to translate a wife and daughters into sound patterns and expect them to be translated into images of a wife and daughters in the ears of an audience. However, Schönberg knew that Mahler could create extraordinary patterns in sound, and he looked forward to hearing this new music more than Alma did.

CHAPTER 10

Mahler's Sixth Symphony

On a fine May morning in 1906 William accompanied the family to Essen for the premier of Mahler's Sixth Symphony. The musicians were excellent, and the rehearsal proceeded in great good humour. The rhythmic intensity at the start of the opening movements kept everyone on their toes. The long lines of melody, especially in the third movement, had the players smiling in disbelief. Mahler had magically constructed harmony out of dissonance. The 'wrong notes' which the musicians read in their scores sounded right when all the parts were played together. This transformation of 'wrong notes' into 'right notes' was miraculous – like turning water into wine. The sum of their individual parts added up to a colossal orchestral whole.

Mahler's percussion section got bigger with each symphony and his Sixth required cowbells which transported the Essen players from their North Rhineland river plain to a Tyrolean mountainside. Mahler asked his musicians to listen to the bells as if they were the very last earthly sounds heard on a mountaintop before they ascended to heaven.

What caused most mirth in rehearsal was the hammer. Mahler wanted seven hammer blows in the last movement. He experimented with various drums, but nothing sounded flat enough. Mahler wanted a loud short-pitched sound that ended with no reverberation or echo. A bass drum was constructed for Mahler, three times bigger than a normal bass drum but, no matter how tight or loose the skin or how many towels were used to dampen it, the blow still rang out. In the end he asked for something to be constructed to his own specifications and was given a huge wooden hammer and anvil. It looked more like something you would see on the opera stage than in the concert hall. The hammer was bigger than the percussionist and this musician's problem was to strike the anvil on the beat. He had to lift this huge hammer high above his head, swing its weight through an arc and bring it down onto a wooden block which was at knee height. The first few attempts landed wide of the beat. There was a lot of laughter as they went over it again and again. Mahler wanted the blow to be struck just off the beat. It would sound cleaner and clearer if it was just a tiny bit early creating a small space for itself. The percussionist was being asked to miss the beat but only by a little. If he missed it by a little bit more it would sound like a mistake. Swinging the hammer was like pulling on a bell rope. The gap between pulling the rope and hearing the clapper strike the bell was not dissimilar to the gap between swinging the hammer and striking the anvil. Percussionist and conductor agreed on five clear beats ahead of the blow to get the hammer onto the anvil – four beats to raise the hammer above his head and one beat to bring it down onto the anvil. Mahler would hold the orchestra back just a fraction to let the blow anticipate the beat. When he got it right the orchestra put their instruments down to applaud. The final movement stopped seven times at every hammer blow for applause from the rehearsing musicians.

The herdsman with his cowbells and the blacksmith with his hammer and anvil both watched Mahler carefully during these rehearsals as he frequently cancelled their parts with the blink of an eye. At the rehearsal on the day before the performance the hammer blows were reduced from seven to three.

Richard Strauss arrived to hear the dress rehearsal and premier. He knew that Mahler had something he himself didn't have and he came to Essen hoping to find out what it might be. At the final rehearsal Mahler was overwhelmed by the music and badly shaken by what he had written. In the conductor's room in the last hours before the premiere he wept in Strauss's arms. William watched. He saw Mahler's pain. He saw Strauss's confusion. William wanted to hold the sobbing composer in his arms. Instead, he watched Strauss trying to cheer him up. Strauss went through the four movements one at a time telling Mahler how good they were. Mahler was not comforted. He knew they were good. That wasn't the problem. It was the sum of the four movements that Mahler was struggling with – the enormity of the whole thing! Mahler had not anticipated his own response as the musicians moved from the peaceful beauty of his third movement to the spiralling downhill career of his terrifying last movement. It was a step further than Mahler could manage and he was undone by it.

Strauss suggested swapping the inner movements around. Play the beautiful 'andante' second instead of third. Then, instead of taking a leap from the andante into the abyss of the final movement, Strauss's suggestion would allow for a smaller and more manageable step from the scherzo to the last movement. Everything sorted without changing a note!

And that's what Mahler did.

William was swept away with the rhythms, the melody, the beauty, and the drama of the symphony. He wondered how a listener might translate into words the sublime feelings conveyed by music which has no words? William knew these four movements made a journey from A minor to C minor, but he didn't believe the audience made a tonal voyage. He thought it more likely the audience were struggling to stay afloat as white-water rapids hurled them towards a great waterfall. He listened to the comments as the audience left the hall. Some heard soldiers marching, others heard children playing, some heard beautiful melodies, others heard no melody at all. A bald man said it made his hair stand on end, there were people in tears, someone was singing Alma's theme and someone else said he felt the great hammer blows vibrating through the floor and up his back. Some people said nothing. The critics attacked Mahler with his own hammer.

> *'The audience heard a symphony full of bells and percussion and were beguiled by a successful charlatan. The music was a failure. If Mahler were capable of expressing tragic feelings he would gladly do without the hammer and its fateful blows. But he does not possess the true inner creative power. Thus he resorts to hammer blows. That is entirely natural. Speakers, who at the decisive moment cannot find the right words, beat the table with their fists. Mahler's example may one day revolutionise symphonic creation. In order to arouse feelings of anguish, hitherto evoked by a sorrowful melody, the score will simply ask the orchestral musician to break something.'*
> Arbeiter Zeitung

As the story of the changed order of the movements emerged the critics realized that Mahler's approach to symphonic creation was even more revolutionary than they had feared. Here was now proof, if proof was ever needed, that Mahler really had no understanding of symphonic form at all. Can you switch the movements around in a Mozart symphony? The architecture of a Mozart or Beethoven symphony did not allow a change in the order of movements and the critics argued that Mahler switched the movements around in his Sixth because his symphony wasn't really a symphony at all.

Two professors, Karl Matthias at the conservatoire in Berlin and Dieter Matthias at the conservatoire in Leipzig, Mahler supporters who frequently defended the composer from critical hostility, both waded into the controversy but on opposite sides. Mahler's enemies followed the disagreement between Berlin and Leipzig with delight because the professors were brothers!

For William, the answer was obvious – scherzo, then andante – just as Mahler had written and rehearsed it. For William, a Mahler experience is huge and intensely emotional. If it is too emotional for Mahler to conduct, then William thought he should let someone else do it. The only way William would ever want to hear the symphony is the way he heard it at the final rehearsal before the movements were switched around.

CHAPTER 11

Mahler leaves Vienna

William drove the family to Maiernigg where they had a summer house on the Worthersee. The children fell ill. Anna recovered but Maria's health deteriorated.

The symptoms were alarming. Scarlet fever and diphtheria. The night the tracheotomy was performed Mahler ran along the shore of the Worthersee screaming. The beautiful child lay with her eyes wide open – gasping for breath for another day – until it was all over.

Maria was lowered into her grave in a little white coffin on a fine sunny day.

'Oft denk' ich sie sund nur ausgegangen!
Bald werden sie wieder nach Hause gelangen!
Der Tag ist schon. O, sei nich bang!
Sie machen nur einen weiten Gang.
(from Ruckert's *Kindertotenlieder*)

I often think they've merely gone for a walk.
Soon, they will be coming home again.
The day is bright. Oh, never fear.
They have only gone for a long walk.

Gustav and Alma left Maiernigg never to return. Mahler was diagnosed with an irregular heartbeat and the doctor told him he must slow down and take it easy. Mahler left the Hofoper never to return. He turned his back on the old world where his daughter had died and took his wife away with him to the New World. He signed a contract to conduct at the Metropolitan Opera in New York, earning more in four months than his annual salary in Vienna. William organized the luggage, the taxis, and booked a hotel in Paris. Gustav and Alma were to travel by train from Vienna to Cherbourg via Paris and then to New York aboard the *Kaiserin Auguste Viktoria*. Their daughter, Anna, stayed in Vienna with Anna's mother and stepfather. William sold his viola.

The train left Vienna's Westbahnhof station at 8.30am. The platform was crowded with friends who came to see them off. Arnold Schönberg was there, Alban Berg, Arnold Rose, Gustav Klimt and many more, some of them including William Hildebrand and Johnny Stanko, in tears. Johnny Stanko said, 'Vorbei – 'it's over,' and it was. Before the train pulled away from the platform William Hildebrand hugged his lover for the last time, boarded the train, and left Vienna to go to New York with the Mahlers.

When Johnny got home he found on their bed a large sum of money which William had raised by selling the viola, and a bunch of flowers. Johnny used the cash to settle with the landlord, put the flowers in the bin, resigned his new job as first trumpet in Hofoper orchestra, and left Vienna.

The sale of the viola had raised a small fortune. William left half the cash in the flat for Johnny and, after paying for his own train fare, the Paris hotel, and his passage to New York, he still had a substantial sum in his pocket.

Neither Gustav nor Alma were surprised to see him in Paris when he attended to their luggage, nor were they surprised to see him on the train to Cherbourg where he supervised their embarkation on the *Kaiserin Auguste Viktoria*.

On board William travelled steerage in the mens' bunkhouse which smelled of urine, sickness, and bleach. Some of the men never left their beds but, like animals in hibernation, closed themselves down and only stirred when they sensed their destination. The first three days were rough. Everyone in steerage was sick. The ship lurched and rolled, William retched, and although there was nothing left to throw up, he contracted violently as if trying to bring up his stomach itself.

William had left Johnny without a word, sold the viola which was not his to sell, and now found himself in hell. On the fourth day when the weather calmed William ventured out to look at the horizon. He held the rail and let the pale winter sunshine soothe him. On the fifth day William ate some bread, kept it down, and stayed away from the stench in the bunkhouse. He was standing at the rail when a steward called his name and beckoned him to follow. Mahler was waiting for him in first class. He took William's arm and said, 'My wife.' Mahler knocked on the door of their suite and stepped back to let William enter alone. Alma, lying in bed, gestured William towards the armchair.

The Mahler suite was opulently furnished and carefully attended. First class passengers enjoying top deck luxury in the middle of the ship could have no idea what it was like in steerage. Likewise, steerage passengers, with no thought beyond surviving the crossing, had little idea of the care and attention lavished on those voyaging in luxury above them.

Alma was unhappy. Between sobs she told William how her husband was responsible for the death of their daughter. How could he possibly have written *Kindertotenlieder* without contemplating the death of his own children? She said the same thing again and again with long silences between the repetitions. When she had exhausted herself, she thanked William and asked him to come back the next day. The steward escorted William back to the door that sealed the first-class passengers from the rest of the ship. He told William he was sorry that Mr Mahler's daughter was unwell.

The following day William waited in the same place for the steward and returned with him to the first class. Mahler took his arm, and said, 'Thank you.'

Nothing in the room had moved since the previous day. William sat by the bed and she told him about the three hammer blows in the last movement of the Sixth. The first was the death of their daughter, the second was the diagnosis of her husband's irregular heartbeat, and the third was his resignation from the Hofoper. Alma accused her husband of writing those hammer blows and then making it all happen. She said the same thing again and again. In the long silences between the repetitions William thought of telling her there had originally been seven hammer blows, but he said nothing. She asked him to come back the following day.

William told the steward that she seemed a little better. The steward was happy to hear about her improvement and acknowledged that her illness must be a terrible worry for her father.

When William visited Alma on the third day, she told him she was bored. She knew what her husband was going to say before he said it and he always said what she knew he was going to say. She told William she found more companionship in his silence than in her husband's predictability. She was, nevertheless, grateful to her husband for asking William to accompany them to New York. She did not know how she would have managed without him.

William realized that Mahler might similarly think it was Alma who had invited him and that neither of them understood that he was travelling with them uninvited.

William didn't go back to the bunkhouse. He stood at the rail scanning the horizon. Perhaps it would first appear as a light or maybe a low-lying cloud. William didn't know what to look out for, but he knew that sometime in the next few hours someone would see it and call out, 'America!'

CHAPTER 12

New York

In the early morning of Sunday December 22$^{nd.}$ 1907 the call of 'America!' echoed around the ship. William gathered up his things and left the bunkhouse for the first class where he supervised the Mahlers' disembarkation. The ship docked at 10.30am. The welcoming party from the Opera House smoothed their way through immigration and no one questioned William's presence. His arrival did not appear to be unexpected. There was a seat for him in the car to the hotel where the bellboys took the luggage to the Mahlers' suite on the eleventh floor and William was given a room on the same floor. It was furnished with the biggest bed he had ever seen. There was a desk with a telephone and writing paper headed with the address of the 'Hotel Majestic, 72 Central Park West, New York, New York. There were two armchairs and a sofa surrounding a large low circular table, a standard lamp and two bedside lamps, as well as ceiling lights and three large windows that looked onto the Park.

William wrote to Johnny on the hotel's notepaper. He wrote about the train journey from Vienna to Cherbourg and the crossing to New York but said nothing about his seasickness. He described the hotel room and the view from the window but said nothing about how he was feeling. He hoped Johnny was well and said he would write again.

William counted out a roll of Austrian banknotes and went downstairs to the desk to ask where could change his money and where he could find a post office. On the desk was a bell and a name tag, 'Mr. Alvin Chandor.' William touched the plunger gently and was surprised when the bell announced his presence so loudly. It was still echoing around the lobby when Mr. Chandor appeared. He spoke German, gave William a roll of dollar bills for his *Kronen,* and took his letter. William left the hotel with the cash and without the letter, and, with no need to find a bank or post office, he wandered aimlessly. He found a music shop. The shop assistant was German. William played a few notes on a viola which was a poor instrument. He had a drink in a Bierkeller where everyone spoke German. He sat in a café and was served a 'hamburger sandwich' by a German waiter. It was made with ground beef, salad and pickles served between two slices of bread. All the white people spoke

German. William assumed that black people would not speak German and that it might be bad manners to stare at them, so he avoided looking at them at all. He bought a bag of apples and went back to the hotel. He rang the bell at the desk, asked Mr. Chandor for more headed notepaper, and retired to his room.

The apples were large. He ate one of them and it tasted the same as a Viennese apple. He was about to take the apples to Mahler when there was a knock at the door. Alma and Mahler were on their way to Carnegie Hall to hear the New York Symphony perform Berlioz's *Symphonie Fantastique* and they wanted William to go with them.

After the concert they walked back to the Hotel Majestic and stopped at a café where Alma and Mahler ate their first hamburger and William had his second. Back at the hotel Mahler told William to be in the foyer in the morning at 9.45 and they would go by car to the Met for his first rehearsal.

That night William wrote to Johnny about hamburgers, black people, Carnegie Hall, and big apples.

In the morning William spent half an hour working out how to use the shower. It was difficult to adjust the temperature which was either freezing or scalding but when he got it right it was a great pleasure. Standing under a cascade of hot water his flesh tingled with delight. Once he had dried himself William made a little drawing of the taps with a note of the temperature settings, and then he went out into the dark New York Monday morning to find a cup of coffee. At the newspaper stall he bought a copy of the New Yorker Staats-Zeitung and went into a café. He opened the newspaper and saw a picture of himself underneath the headline 'Willkommen.' He was standing at the rail of the *Kaiserin Auguste Viktoria* with Alma and Gustav just before they disembarked. The first three pages of the newspaper were all about Mahler's arrival. As he read the paper the waitress refilled his cup. He nodded a thank you and she said, 'You're welcome.'

It was nearly ten o'clock before Mahler appeared in the hotel foyer. He hadn't been able to find the lift, had run down eleven flights of stairs and was out of breath. The car sent by The Met was waiting for them. Mahler and William were driven south to the opera house in mid-town Manhattan where Mahler would rehearse *Tristan und Isolde* for his New York debut on January 1st.

When Mahler stepped onto the podium the orchestra greeted him with a fanfare. Then they began to rehearse the Prelude. After a few bars Mahler stopped. He could hear singers rehearsing elsewhere in the building and demanded that all other rehearsals in the theatre stop immediately. He conducted the Prelude to the end then spoke to the trumpets asking them for more. The orchestra played it again from the beginning. With the bigger brass sound the whole Prelude was transformed. Mahler told them they were a fine orchestra and said he would now work with the singers.

Mahler took the vocal rehearsal and played the piano accompaniment himself. The nervous singers were taken aback by Mahler's meekness and courtesy. It was less than an hour since Mahler had ordered them to be quiet.

After the rehearsal Mahler and William went to have lunch with the Met's Austrian director. Heinrich Conried was unlike any Austrian William had ever seen. He wore high heeled suede boots, a top hat, and red gloves. His apartment was lit with multi-coloured light bulbs. He had a suit of armour illuminated from within by a red light and a four-poster sofa with carved pillars and a canopy of silks on which Conried reclined to receive his guests.

In the car on their way back to the hotel William wanted to ask Mahler about the suit of armour and the sofa but Mahler, trying not to laugh, shook his head and held a finger to his lips. Only once they were out of the car and earshot of the Met's driver did they burst out laughing. Mahler asked William to come to his suite.

Alma was in the bedroom. There was a grand piano in the sitting room. Mahler took William to the bathroom, showed him the shower and asked William if he knew how to work it. William fetched the drawing he had made for himself that morning, stepped into the Mahlers' shower, turned it on and adjusted the temperature. He emerged from the bathroom in soaking wet clothes and returned to his room leaving puddles on the hallway carpet. He took off his wet clothes, had another shower, dried himself and, dressed in new clothes, returned to Mahler's room with the bag of apples. Mahler, pink and showered, answered the door in a bathrobe, picked one from the bag and said to William, 'What a big apple!'

It was 4pm, dark, and cold when William left the hotel to go for a walk. He stopped at the desk, rang the bell, and asked Mr. Chandor where he might take a stroll before dinner. Mr. Chandor thought William might like to see the Grand Central Station terminus before it was demolished. He gave William directions and told him it would take an hour to walk there. William did not give Mr. Chandor the letter he had written to Johnny. He wanted to find a post office and post it himself.

As William was crossing 57th Street he saw a line of black men shackled together with chains being led into a police station. He found a post office on 7th Avenue and waited in the queue to be served by a black man. He had never heard a black man's voice before. The black man said the postage would cost a quarter. William didn't understand. The black man held up his hand to William – his palm was not as black as his face – and opened and closed his fist five times. 'Fünfundzwanzig'. William counted out twenty-five cents in coins and the black man told him he was 'great to show and good to go!' William hadn't a clue what he meant but loved the sound of the black man's laughter. The street was cheerful with Christmas lights. The stores were decorated with reindeer and Santa's little helpers. William gazed in wonder through the frosted store windows at mechanical displays of scenes from Wunderhorn and Grimm. New York kitsch was the same as Viennese kitsch. William looked for Times Square but couldn't see anything that resembled a square. However, he did find 42nd Street where he turned left and walked three blocks to the station. Inside, on the concourse, there was a Christmas tree where a brass quintet played *Stille Nacht*. The players were excellent. The trumpet player was especially good. William was transfixed. It wasn't just the quality of the quintet that held him. It was the special quality of the trumpet. The tempo was slow. The harmonies were unusual, luxurious, and rich, and the melody, carried by the trumpet, was soft and sweet and although it emerged quietly from the lower end of the trumpet's range it floated over the quintet and took possession of the station building. The trumpet player was black.

On his way back to the hotel William was cold. He bought a hot dog from a street vendor. In Basel William knew it as a 'Wienerli.' In Vienna they called it a 'Frankfurter'. He thought he would tell Mahler about the 'hot dog' because he knew Mahler would be amused, but he wouldn't tell him about the excellent black trumpeter because he thought it unlikely that Mahler would believe him.

Back at the hotel he asked at reception for more headed notepaper. Mr Chandor congratulated William on having so many friends and wanted to know if William had met any new friends at the station. William thought of telling him about the black trumpeter but couldn't think of how to say it. He did, however, tell him about the fairy lights on the station's Christmas tree.

William wrote to Johnny and told him how cold it was and all about the picture on the front of the New Yorker Staats-Zeitung, about how Mahler transformed the Prelude by asking the trumpets to play louder, about Heinrich Conried's apartment, Mahler's shower, the black man at the post office, the kitsch in the stores, the Christmas tree at the station, and the hotdog stall. He told Johnny that he missed him, that he wished he was here. He didn't mention the black trumpet player.

CHAPTER 13

Christmas 1907

9.45am. William waited for Mahler in the foyer. Mahler arrived just before 10am out of breath having run down the stairs from the 11th floor.

Mahler stepped onto the podium and greeted his orchestra. Rehearsals in German were not a problem for this New York orchestra. Most of the players were German. Those who were not German understood German very well. Mahler had been up all night cutting over ninety minutes from Wagner's score. *Tristan und Isolde* lasts five and a half hours. Performances in Vienna started at 6pm. Mahler's New York *Tristan* was scheduled to start at 7.45pm and so there had to be cuts, otherwise the performance would go on well past midnight and finish in front of an empty house. The Met's elderly orchestral players, given their advanced years and the length of the opera may not have managed to finish it at all, and the audience, far from feeling cheated, would be relieved to hear Isolde sing of Love's Death before midnight rather than in the wee small hours.

On the way home from the rehearsal Mahler gave William 1000 dollars. 'You know her tastes. Buy some things for me to give her tonight. And something for the children.'

'Something for Anna?' asked William.

'Yes, and something for Maria. Don't forget Maria.'

William asked Mr. Chandor where he should go Christmas shopping. He suggested Macy's at 34th Street. It was the same route as yesterday but instead of turning left at 42nd street he should keep going until he arrived at Herald Square. On foot it would take a bit more than an hour. Having failed to find Times Square the previous day William didn't want to look for Herald Square. It was freezing cold, it was too far to walk, and William went on the tram. The driver was black. When he called out 'Macy's' William got off.

One floor of the department store was dedicated to ladies' hats. Feathers were in fashion and it seemed to William that tens of thousands of birds had been slaughtered and plucked to create the exotic plumage that decorated the hats on display. William didn't want to buy Alma a hat but he was nevertheless taken with the idea of feathers. Not real feathers but the idea of feathers, the lightness of feathers and their association with flight and display. He found a German saleswoman who showed him shawls that were embroidered in autumn colours with feathers of silk. One was edged in cerise and it shone. William draped it over his own shoulders and he felt as if he could fly. It cost six hundred dollars. The lady wrapped it for William and tied the parcel in russet and purple ribbons to match the gift. William was delighted and now had a picture in his mind of what he wanted to buy with the other four hundred dollars. He found it in the jewellery department – a pair of earrings made with identical moonstones the size of large pearls suspended from two small fluffy down feathers, their tiny quills worked into the precious metal on the earrings' fastenings. One of the feathers reflected every shade from a light pink at the quill to a deep red wine at the extremity. The other was blue with hues that ranged from azure at the quill to indigo at the extremity. Each white opal moonstone reflected the colours of the feather above it. They cost five hundred dollars. The lady wrapped them with ribbons that matched William's other parcel.

William found the toy department. There was a display of Teddy's Bears. He bought one for Mahler's surviving daughter, Anna, and one for his deceased daughter, Maria. He returned to Central Park in the tram with his gifts feeling triumphant. Mr. Chandor gave William a cheery wave and applauded his four parcels. William went directly to Mahlers' suite. Alma was alone at her desk writing a letter. The hotel had given the Mahlers a small Christmas tree and although there were lights it looked naked without any gifts. William put the two parcels for Alma and the two Teddy's Bears under the tree. Alma asked him to wait. She gave him twenty-five dollars and asked him to get something for her to give to Gustav. 'You know his tastes.'

It was three o'clock on Christmas Eve and already dark when William left the Hotel Majestic to find a gift for Mahler. The air was full of swirling white icy dust. He shivered as he walked to Columbus Circle where he bought a box of cigars for thirty dollars. Then he went to a gentleman's outfitters and bought himself a scarf and a pair of gloves. He asked for the scarf and gloves to be wrapped separately. The parcels were finished with three gift cards and three sprigs of holly. William ran back to the hotel and wrote one gift card to himself, 'For William from Alma,' and attached it to the scarf. On the other he wrote, 'To William from Gustav' and attached it to the gloves. He left the third one blank for Alma's to sign, attached it to the cigars, and went to the Mahlers' suite. He gave Alma the gift for Gustav with the blank card, put the two gifts for himself under the tree, went back to his room, and waited. He imagined there might be a little ceremony when gifts were exchanged. Perhaps later. Possibly not until midnight.

Just before midnight there was a knock on the door. It was the man from the desk in the lobby. The man wished William a Merry Christmas and gave him a small beautifully wrapped gift. William's visitor said his name was Alvin Chandor, that he was American, born in New York and that he had worked in the Hotel Majestic for five years and had a room in the hotel on the floor above. The room was number 1217. Alvin hoped that William would enjoy his stay in New York and repeated that his room number was 1217 and that William would always be welcome to come to his room and visit him. William put Alvin's gift on his desk, lay down and waited. Perhaps the Mahlers were not coming. Maybe they would exchange gifts in the morning.

Before he went to sleep William opened Mr. Chandor's gift – a fountain pen. There was a note on Hotel Majestic notepaper.

Dear William, Happy Christmas from Alvin. Room 1217.

The room number was underlined.

At 9.40am William knocked on Mahler's door and wished Mahler 'A Merry Christmas.' Mahler, dressed in his overcoat and hat, was ready to go. He was wearing the gloves and scarf that William had bought for himself. They left for their Christmas Day rehearsal. It was very cold.

William listened to the rehearsal for half an hour then walked back towards the hotel. He sat in Central Park and watched happy families pass him by. Laughing children wearing scarves and gloves played with their hoops and bicycles or cuddled their dolls and Teddy's Bears. William enjoyed their pleasure and returned their smiles.

A black man strolled towards William and sat on the same bench. William flinched and inched himself away. The black man smiled and, mocking William, did the same, inching away, so that they both sat at opposite ends of the bench. The black man turned to William and said, 'Frohes Fest'. William also wished the stranger a Merry Christmas before he realized their greetings had been exchanged in German.

'You speak German?' asked William.

'Yes.'

'But you're not German.'

'No. My father is German.'

William, already astonished to be speaking to a black man in German, was even more astonished to discover that the stranger's father was German. William told the stranger that he didn't come from round here. He came from Basel.

The stranger looked surprised. 'Basel? You dress more Austrian than Swiss. I would have said you came from Vienna.'

William felt naked in front of the stranger who knew where he came from.

And when the black man introduced himself as Tristan Kruezer, William couldn't think of a false name with which to introduce himself.

'Happy Christmas, William. It's a pleasure to meet you.'

Tristan thought that William spoke German with a French accent.

William said his mother was French.

'Ma mère, aussi,' said Tristan.

Tristan's foster parents were both dentists and they ran a flourishing business in Harlem. They had adopted Tristan when he was a baby. They maintained a normal looking household by employing a black housekeeper, so Tristan had grown up in a family foursome with a black mother, a white mother, and a white father. His German papa loved music, had named his son Tristan, bought him a trumpet, sent him to music lessons, and now had got him a place at the Institute of Musical Art.

'Trumpet!' exclaimed William, realizing where he had seen Tristan before. I heard you playing at the station yesterday.'

'That must have been somebody else. It wasn't me. It's an easy mistake. We all look the same.'

When William described the beautiful sound of the trumpet under the Christmas tree at Grand Central Station Tristan said, 'I'm not that good. I do my best. I do it for my father. He got the Institute going. He's a benefactor. He's on the Board. My presence in class helps the Institute appear less European. With me around they get to believe they are American. Have you ever seen a black man in an orchestra?'

William had never seen a black man in an orchestra.

'I should go to medical school and become a dentist like dad. Black people need black dentists. White dentists won't put their hands into black mouths.'

William, out of his depth, tried to regain the shallows where he could put his feet down. He told Tristan about his own family and told him things he had never revealed to anyone, not even Johnny. His mother was Madeleine Hildebrand. Hildebrand was her own name and her father's name and now it was William's name. William had never known his own father who had vanished not long after William was born. William had grown up in a household with his mother, who was a pianist, and her friend, Félicité who played the cello. His mother had given him piano lessons and Félicité had given him cello lessons, but his main instrument was…

'Viola!' interrupted Tristan.

'How did you know that?' William felt himself slipping out of his depth again.

'All you viola players look the same. You all have the same callous under your chins! I'm cold. Let's go and sit somewhere warm.'

Tristan took William's hand and led him out of Central Park. They walked together in the gathering gloom and Tristan didn't let go of William's hand until they sat down in a café.

Tristan spoke Yiddish to the waitress and ordered two hot corned beef sandwiches with cheese and sauerkraut, and coffee for them both.

'Yiddish?'

'Restaurant Yiddish.'

'German, French, and restaurant Yiddish?'

'And English,' added Tristan. 'If you're going to live here you must learn English.'

William told Tristan he had come with Gustav Mahler who was working at the Met and that he was going back to Vienna with Mahler in April.

'You play viola for Mahler?'

'No, I drive the car.'

'In New York?'

'No. The Met send a car.'

'So, what do you do?'

'I fix the shower, do the Christmas shopping, help him find the lift and look after his wife.'

Tristan told him that when he saw him sitting on the bench with his long hair, he thought William was a pretty girl.

'But it turns out you're a pretty boy.' Tristan touched William's hand. 'I'm going to the washroom. Come and join me if you like.'

Tristan left the table. William felt sick, panicked, left a dollar on the table and ran away.

He ran all the way back to the hotel, shut the door of his room behind him, climbed into bed, pulled the blankets around him, and shivering, hugged himself.

'He's awake,' said the doctor who was standing on one side of William's bed.

The man wasn't speaking to William, but to the big bird on the other side of his bed. The doctor shook a thermometer and put it in William's mouth. The doctor and the bird waited in silence. The doctor removed his spectacles, squinted at the thermometer, declared that his patient was fine, packed his bag, wrote out a prescription and a bill, gave the papers to Alma who was wearing her feather shawl, wished her a Happy New Year, and left the room.

'Have I been asleep?' asked William?'

'For a few hours. Before that, you were crazy. You've had a fever. Tristan drove you mad. No more Wagner until you are strong enough.'

'I'm good.'

'No, you're not. You are weak. You haven't eaten since Wednesday.'

'Wednesday? What day is it?'

'Saturday.'

'I've slept for three days?'

'You've been crazy for three days. Tristan drove you mad. The doctor took blood from you to calm you down. You had a fever. 102, 103, 104, and you kept shouting - calling out that you wanted nothing to do with Tristan. We thought we'd lost you. Once the doctor took away your bad blood, you stopped raving and fell asleep like a child. Now you're weak and hungry and I am going to look after you. You need to eat and drink.'

'Can I have a beer and a hot dog?'

'Dog!!! You're mad. Three days raving about Tristan and now you want to eat a dog! The doctor said you were better and gave me a bill but you're still crazy.'

'A frankfurter, Frau Mahler. They call it a hotdog. Can I have two?'

Alma picked up the telephone and looked at William.

'Hotdog? You sure?'

William nodded and Alma ordered three hotdogs, a beer, and a bottle of mineral water.

The drinks and frankfurters arrived. Alma gave William his hotdogs and the bottle of water. She took the beer, barked at her hotdog, and giggled.

William wondered what he had said in his sleep. He knew it had nothing to do with Wagner. It was the nightmare about the black man who played the trumpet, spoke four languages including restaurant Yiddish, held his hand, took him to a café and proposed they go to the washroom together.

Alma asked William if he was homesick? Did he not miss his boyfriend? Alma told him he would get better if he allowed himself to be sad.

William protested. He wasn't homesick. He wasn't lonely. He didn't miss anyone.

'That's not what you said yesterday. Better to be sad, and angry, and jealous, than to be sick. Now go to sleep.'

CHAPTER 14

A Letter to Johnny Stanko

December 29th 1907

Dear Johnny,

Winter in New York is colder than Vienna and I got a chill. I have been in bed for the last three days with a fever but I am much better now. Tomorrow I will buy myself gloves and a scarf.

I have missed three rehearsals, but Alma tells me it is going well. Gustav says he likes the American orchestra although I cannot see how it's American. The musicians are all German grandfathers. Mahler puts up with it because we are only staying here for a few months. If we were staying longer he would bring in younger musicians.

Mahler has cut Tristan to three hours! It should be called Tristan or Isolde. I don't see how it can be both. Three hours is probably long enough for these ancient musicians who might not survive if Mahler insisted on playing it all.

In New York a frankfurter is called a hot dog. Alma got one and barked before she ate it. It made me laugh. I feel sad and homesick and I miss you, but she cheered me up.

What do you think of this pen? It was a Christmas present from the hotel.

I have decided to cut my hair short and to grow a moustache.

I would like to wish you a Happy Christmas, but it will be the middle of January before you receive this. How you are? Your reply will take two weeks to cross the ocean. With love. Willy.

December 29th 1907

Dear Mr. Chandor,

I am writing this thank you note with the pen which you presented to me from the Hotel. Please convey my gratitude to the management. When I return to Vienna in March the hotel's Christmas gift will remind me of the happy days I spent in New York and of the Hotel's *generous hospitality. I am happy to call myself a Majestic guest. Yours sincerely, William Hildebrand.*

CHAPTER 15

Mahler's New York Debut

William knocked on Mahler's door at 7pm. Alma and Mahler were ready to go. Mahler was wrapped in his hat, scarf, and gloves. He wore his conductor's tails underneath his overcoat. She was wearing a hat with an enormous brim and underneath her coat a full-length gown that trailed on the floor behind her. On their way to the lift William was careful not to stand on the gown. There was just enough room in the lift for the three of them and Alma's hat. In the lobby Mahler stepped on the gown. The rip was loud. Mahler said he would wait in the car while Alma went back to their suite with William. She took the pins out of her hair, threw her hat onto the piano, dropped her coat onto the floor and as William picked it up and put it on a chair Alma unhooked and removed her torn gown. William had never given any thought to what Alma might be wearing underneath her gown. He had no interest in ladies' underwear. Alma wasn't wearing any. She appeared to be quite comfortable standing naked with her back to him as she looked through the gowns in her wardrobe. He was surprised by her nakedness but neither drawn nor repelled by it. From her ankles to her knees Alma's legs looked not dissimilar to his own or to Johnny's but above the knee her thighs became wide and soft and pink beneath the great curves of her bottom. She chose a gown and asked William to hook her up. Her expansive pink flesh was now covered in silk of shining sea and sky blues and rich reds of roses and wine flowing to the floor in graceful pleats and folds. He helped her on with her coat. She adjusted her hat in the mirror and pinned it into place and they went back down in the lift. The car had gone and so had Mahler. Alma snapped her fingers at Mr. Chandor. Another car appeared. Mr. Chandor opened the door for Alma. William ran to the other side and opened the door for himself.

The Met buzzed with an expectant hum. The diamond horseshoe was filling up with New York aristocrcy who had come to be seen at Mahler's debut. The cuts in the opera would not bother them. Many of them would leave before the third act.

Once he had seated Alma in the director's box and ordered a glass of Benedictine, a second glass for the first interval and a third glass for the second interval, William went backstage where he found Mahler relaxing with the singers. He pictured Mahler naked. He imagined Mahler had the beautiful muscles of an athlete beneath his taut skin. Mahler told his 'Tristan' and his 'Isolde' what wonderful singers they were and that they needn't worry about anything because he would be there with them, that he would watch over them, and they would triumph. William told Mahler that his wife wished him good luck. Mahler told William that they did not need luck – they needed only to do their duty.

Alma paid no attention to the diamond horseshoe although the diamond horseshoe paid a great deal of attention to her. She had no interest in being seen and this only stimulated further the interest of those who watched her. William suspected he was the only person in the auditorium who knew that Alma was wearing only her gown and nothing else.

Compared with previous accounts of Wagner in New York Mahler's debut was restrained. This was surprising given Mahler's reputation for blood and thunder. He reined in the orchestra and gave the evening to the singers. Anyone who cared to listen could hear every word.

CHAPTER 16

Mechtilde Müller

Mahler the conductor in New York did not have to work as hard as Mahler the director in Vienna. On most days Mahler never left the hotel. He stayed in bed reading or working with his books or manuscript paper on a board in front of him. In Austria Mahler had required complete silence when he was composing. It was Alma's responsibility to chase away visitors and to purchase and slaughter the neighbour's noisy chickens. In America things were different. Mahler was not bothered by the noise that drifted up from Central Park eleven floors below. Alma took some time to adjust to her husband's changed working practices and when a hurdy gurdy man started busking in the street below she knocked on William's door, gave him twenty dollars and asked him to go downstairs and tell the busker to move away. William gave the busker ten dollars. The delighted busker took the cash and left. When William went back to Alma with the dollars he'd saved, Mahler was looking out of the window wondering where the hurdy gurdy player had gone.

On another occasion Mahler watched a funeral procession of firemen marching up Central Park West. The uniformed mourners stopped in front of the hotel and Mahler heard their captain speak about the bravery of their fallen colleague. At the end of his speech there was a single muffled beat on a bass drum and the procession moved on. Mahler stepped back from the window in a flood of tears, went back to bed, and resumed his work.

Mahler liked to be left alone. He avoided making social engagements. He was not comfortable in the company of strangers and strangers were uncomfortable with him. William wanted to be left alone too. He did not want to explore New York any further in case it brought him more bad dreams. He preferred to stay in his hotel room and read cowboy stories.

Alma, bored and lonely, craved company. Every day she would visit William and order beer and hotdogs for them both. She gave William the dinner invitations she had received that day. They were generally from wealthy women who collected art and were married to rich men who did nothing interesting, and who saw Gustav and Alma as the

Emperor and Empress of music. Alma had an anthropological interest in how these female natives compared with Viennese society. She expected their conversation would be unrefined and their culture understandably shallow given how far they lived from centres of civilization. Alma was, nevertheless, curious to discover what effect modern ideas and new wealth had on their manners, fashions, and relationships. The price of satisfying this curiosity was high. The first invitation Alma accepted ended in disaster when Mahler, bored with the conversation about railroad stocks, ignored the host and hostess and read a book. The host, politely trying to draw Mahler back into conversation, said something about Wagner. Mahler remarked on the stupidity of the comment. The hostess asked Alma if her husband was always this rude. Alma said 'No,' changed her mind, said, 'Yes,' and they both left. After that, Alma was wary about accepting any further invitations and gave William the job of declining them because 'regretfully Gustav was unwell' or 'busy' or 'had to remain in Philadelphia longer than he had anticipated'. William signed the refusal 'With heartfelt thanks and greetings, Alma Mahler'. William did this with his new fountain pen in his best handwriting. He made no attempt to forge Alma's hand which would have rendered the reply illegible.

William always checked the invitations to see if there might be an acceptable one, possibly from a lady married to a medical practitioner, or an academic with an interest in the natural sciences, or Chinese poetry. William would then discuss the suitability of this invitation with the front-of-house manager at the Met who knew everything about everybody. William learned a lot about the Met's more eccentric customers. Alma was delighted with William's grotesque and wonderful tales about New York's aristocracy. On the few occasions when William found something suitable, she grasped the opportunity to reach out and find a friend.

Alma invited Mechtilde Müller, a young seamstress who worked in the wardrobe at the Met, to join her for coffee in the hotel. Meddi had come to New York after leaving Oberkochen, a small village near Ulm, to get away from her family and from the expectation that she would marry one of the village boys. She didn't want to marry anyone. She was horrified at the idea of making a lifetime commitment to a man and to bear his children in return for gifts and poems presented to her in a passing romantic fancy. When men gave her flowers, she threw them in the bucket. They said she was mad – that there must be something the matter with her. She had seen her mother and her aunts cope with the violence, resignation, and defeat in their own lives as their dreams of princes turned into nightmares. She did not believe that one day her prince would come but, just in case he did, she decided to get out before it was too late. She left the village to seek her fortune in America.

She enjoyed her work at the Met where she had been working for six months before the Mahlers arrived. On the day Alma was shown around the wardrobe Meddi was pushed forward to say something welcoming in German to the conductor's wife. She told Alma how much she enjoyed her work at the Met, that she liked working in a female environment, that she enjoyed the opera, and admired the strength of the women who sang but did not understand why all the female characters in the operas committed suicide or were murdered or suffered debilitating and terminal illnesses. Alma thought it was because operas were written by men. Meddi thought a woman should write an opera. That was when Alma asked Meddi if she would come to the Hotel Majestic on her day off to take coffee and cakes with her.

When Alma returned to the hotel she told William she was going to write an opera. It would be based on *Macbeth* but it would be different from Verdi's version. In her opera Lady Macbeth would not ask Macbeth to murder Duncan. Lady Macbeth would do it herself. When Macbeth discovers what his wife has done, he commits suicide and Lady Macbeth becomes Queen. Alma's opera was to be called, 'Lady Macbeth.'

'Oh, by the way,' she said, 'I've found a girlfriend for you.' William was horrified. Alma told him to calm down.

'You are just right for each other,' she said. 'Her name is Meddi. She's coming for coffee and cakes on Sunday. First, we must choose material. Take me to the store where my husband found that beautiful shawl. We will buy the material and Meddi will make clothes for me. We are going to live in New York for five months every year so you will have to learn English, and so will she. You and Mechtilde will go to English lessons and learn how to be good Americans.'

William went in a car with Alma to Macy's where they collected samples of cloth to show Meddi. William bought himself a scarf and a pair of gloves.

When Meddi came to the hotel they looked though the samples and chose silk that matched the shawl and earrings which Alma was wearing. Meddi measured Alma twice, first from head to toe then from toe to head. Meddi told Alma that her measurements would be different when she was wearing her corset. Alma told Meddi that she never wore a corset. Meddi showed Alma the undergarment she herself was wearing. It was not a corset but something she had fashioned for herself from two pieces of silk which supported her breasts. The silks were fastened to a strip of elastic which passed under her arms and clipped together behind her back, and two ribbons which passed over her shoulders and were buttoned to the elastic. Three buttonholes on the shoulder ribbons offered three degrees of support. The first pair of buttonholes held her breasts loosely. The middle pair offered firmer support. The third offered considerable lift. William, thinking about the car, wondered if this design might be adapted to adjust the headlights so that they lit up the road immediately in front, or further ahead, or all the way to the horizon. Alma dismissed William and said she would come for him in an hour. William happily retired to his room and read cowboy stories while Alma and Meddi got on with their fitting session. William was lost in the Wild West when Alma knocked on his door and told him to accompany Meddi downstairs and ask Mr. Chandor for a car to take her home.

'When you come out of the lift take Meddi's arm like this. When you speak to Mr. Chandor put your arm around Meddi's waist like this. Open the car door for Meddi, then kiss her like this.' Alma kissed William on his lips.

William and Meddi took the lift in silence. When they got out of the lift William forgot to put his arm around her. Meddi took his arm and pulled it around her waist. He remembered to open the car door for her but didn't want to kiss her. She kissed him.

William and Meddi attended Professor Schiller's English classes on Sunday afternoons in the hall of Our Lady of the Rosary just behind the South Ferry terminal in Lower Manhattan. Meddi and William rode the Broadway line from 72nd Street. The express took them to South Ferry Terminal in 20 minutes.

Ten German speakers with little or no English assembled for the professor's first class. The students were bemused at the professor's refusal to speak German and his insistence on communicating with them only in English. He registered their names, teaching them how to introduce themselves in English. William learned to say, 'My name is William. What is your name?' and so William discovered the names of his fellow students. The next exercise involved the class describing what they did. Gerhardt was a carpenter, Matthias a priest, Sebastian a teacher, Annike a piano teacher, and when it was William's turn, he did not know what to say. He could only think of what he didn't do. He wasn't a student. He wasn't a musician. He wasn't a secretary, servant, or chauffeur. Meddi whispered in his ear and William announced, 'My name is William, and I am a friend.' Then he asked Meddi, 'What is your name and what do you do? Meddi replied, 'My name is Mechtilde, I am a dressmaker, and you are my friend.'

When the class was over the exhausted students relaxed into German. Everyone seemed especially friendly towards William. Meddi suggested a ride on the Staten Island ferry. It took twenty-five minutes. They stayed on the boat and came straight back again, enjoying the sea air, the Statue of Liberty, and each other. None of them spoke a word of English on the boat except William who told everyone that his name was William and that he was a friend.

When they got back to the hotel Meddi took William's arm and slipped it around her waist. As they waited for the lift Meddi kissed him. In Alma's suite Meddi took two sleeves from her handbag for Alma to try, and as Meddi pinned them, William told Alma about their English lesson. He taught Alma how to say, 'Hallo, my name is Alma.' He said his name was William and that he was a friend. Meddi, with her mouth full of pins mumbled, 'My name is Mechtilde and I am a dressmaker.' Alma could not describe herself in English or German. She couldn't say she was a composer. Her husband had forbidden that. She could have described herself as a mother, but her daughter, Anna, was Jewish and in Austria with her mother and stepfather. She could describe herself as Mahler's wife but the thought irritated her. Alma dismissed William and said she would come for him in an hour.

Hotel Majestic

Dear Johnny,

I go to English lessons every Sunday. The teacher, Professor Schiller, will not allow German to be spoken in the classroom. In the first lesson we learned how to introduce ourselves. At the beginning of the next lesson Professor Schiller put an empty jar on the desk and told us there would be a fine of two cents for anyone who spoke in German. We must mime or speak with our hands otherwise the lessons become costly. Afterwards, I go for a ride on the ferry to Staten Island. I stay on the boat and come back again. New Yorkers are quite different from Viennese. It is acceptable to introduce yourself to strangers. I ride back to the hotel on the subway. I don't talk to people on the train because it is very noisy. I have learned the names of the stations which is good for counting in English. Between 14th Street and 72nd Street where I get off the train stops at 18th, 23rd, 28th, 33rd, 42nd, 50th, 59th, and 66th. Sometimes, if it's not too cold, I get off at 59th or 66th and walk the rest of the way.

Alma has made friends with a dressmaker who works in the wardrobe at the Met. She is making dresses for Alma. Alma will come back to Vienna looking like an American.

The Met's director is ill and Mahler has been asked to take the job. He doesn't want it. He likes New York but he is also homesick for Vienna. I'm sure you would like it here too. I miss you. Willy

CHAPTER 17

The Met

Mahler's debut of *Tristan und Isolde* was sold out. The subsequent performances did not do so well. The Met was suffering from the competition of the other opera house in New York. Oscar Hammerstein had opened his Manhattan Opera House on 34th Street. The Manhattan's big salaries attracted star singers, and its low ticket prices attracted big audiences. Disgruntled minor aristocrats frustrated at their exclusion from the diamond horseshoe at the Met were attracted to the more egalitarian ethos at the Manhattan Opera. New York opera buffs who didn't want to miss anything would run from the Manhattan in 34th Street to the Met in 37th Street, catching the start of one opera and the end of the other and sometimes bumping into opera buffs who were doing the same thing the other way around.

Mahler's second production at the Met was *Don Giovanni*. Mozart was not popular in New York and was rarely performed. Americans were not as comfortable with eighteenth century European culture as they were with the moderns like Wagner, Debussy or Strauss. Music which might be older than America itself was not received well in the New World. Europeans working in America did well to beware of bruising the New World's sense of cultural inferiority. Americans would not have taken to Mahler if he had brought with him any suggestion of Viennese superiority. His restrained 'Tristan' had surprised his potential critics and his *Don Giovanni* was performed by a small orchestra with Mahler himself accompanying the recitatives at a piano whose strings were covered in brown paper to make it sound like a harpsichord. New York critics were favourably disposed to Mahler's sensitivity.

William went with Mahler and Alma when they took *Don Giovanni* to Philadelphia. The performance space in Philadelphia was narrower than the space in New York. The stagehands had put up as much of the set as they could. This did not include the door through which Donna Elvira enters to sing her aria *Mi tradi*. Her entrance was delayed when she could not find the door. Mahler signalled for the orchestra to wait. Lost and desperate Elvira pushed and prodded at the doorless wall which wobbled like scenery put up by a third-rate travelling amateur theatre company. Mahler waited smiling. He would not have smiled in Vienna but things in America were more relaxed. With the set reeling and rocking it took the cast several minutes to slide the wall sufficiently sideways for the singer to squeeze through a gap. Singer and orchestra then performed the aria beautifully. It was greeted with a standing ovation and cries of *brava!* and *encore* which may have been for a repeat of the entrance rather than the song.

For his third production Mahler gave New York his favourite opera, *Fidelio*.

Mahler's Viennese production of *Fidelio* was designed by Alfred Roller who was no longer in favour at the Hofoper after Mahler had left. Alma wrote to Roller asking for drawings of the Vienna costumes. Roller, who felt no obligation to his former employers, was happy to oblige and sent Alma everything she needed. She took the drawings to Mechtilde and the ladies at the Met set about dressing Mahler's New York *Fidelio* exactly as it had been dressed in Vienna. Alma went to the wardrobe every day to meet Mechtilde and supervise the work.

Meddi worked on the *Fidelio* costumes during the week and after the English class on Sundays she came to the Hotel Majestic and worked on costumes for Alma. Everybody was happy with this arrangement. Mahler was delighted to have something of Vienna in his New York *Fidelio* and Alma was pleased both with her new friend and to hear the rumour going around the hotel about Meddi's secret affair with William. William had bought a dictionary and was trying to read Karl May's German cowboy stories in English.

CHAPTER 18

A Chinese Restaurant

At the beginning of March, after William and Meddi's Sunday morning English lesson and after Alma and Meddi had finished their fitting session, Meddi took William out for a walk in the park. The days were getting longer, spring was in the air, and Central Park, covered in crocuses, seemed an inviting place for her to stroll with William and rehearse their English lesson. William didn't want to go into the park but Meddi took his hand and dragged him through the gate. They sat on a bench. William tried to leave a polite gap between them. She moved towards him, closing the gap, and spoke to him in English.

'How old are you?'
'I am 25.'
'Where do you come from?'
'I come from Basel.'
'Are you married?'
'Yes, I am married.'
'How many children do you have?'
'I have three children.'
Then it was William's turn.
'How old are you?'
'I am 21'
Where do you come from?'
'I come from Oberkochen.'
'Are you married?'
'No, I am not married?'
'How many children do you have?'

Meddi laughed and told William, in German, that it was not very polite to ask an unmarried woman how many children she had. William protested that he was only repeating the questions and answers they had learned in class and that he himself was neither married nor had children. He reframed his question in the negative and asked her how many children she didn't have? She pushed him off the bench and the two of them skipped back to the hotel.

The following Sunday, after Alma and Meddi had finished their fitting session, Gustav and Alma took William and Meddi out for dinner. As they walked out of the hotel lobby Alma took her husband's arm and Meddi took William's arm. Mahler was keen to try Chinese food and had been recommended a restaurant in Chinatown owned by a German pianist who played Beethoven sonatas while his German customers ate chop suey. Mahler was reading a small volume of translations of Chinese poetry, *Die Chinesische Flöte* and it was enthusiasm for Chinese literature that had tempted him to visit a Chinese restaurant. It was just as well Mahler was more interested in Chinese poetry than Chinese food because the restaurant wasn't very good. Mahler was nevertheless amused by the adventure and enjoyed being an avuncular host to Meddi and William. Alma was satisfied that her foursome was working out well and they didn't stop talking, not even when the restaurant owner, a man with limited musical abilities, sat at the piano and started playing. Mahler would not normally allow conversation during Beethoven sonatas but made an exception for this pianist.

Meddi spoke to William in English.
'What time did you rise this morning.'
'I rose at eight o'clock, washed my face and cleaned my teeth.'
'What did you have for breakfast.'
'For breakfast I drank orange juice and coffee.'
William asked Meddi, 'What did you do after your English lesson?'
'After my lesson I went to visit Alma.'
'What did you and Alma do?'
Meddi couldn't answer in English and wouldn't answer in German.
Meddi asked William what he had for dinner.
'For my dinner I ate…'
William looked at the Chinese dinner in front of him and couldn't answer in English or German either.

Gustav and Alma congratulated the young students on their progress.

On their way home they passed other Chinese restaurants in the street which were busier than the one they had just left. Mahler suggested they come back another day and eat spareribs without the *Moonlight Sonata*.

March 21st 1908

Dear Mother,

I am sorry I didn't come to visit you at Christmas. I hope you and Félicité had a good time. I am in New York working with Herr Mahler at the Metropolitan Opera House. Last night he conducted his first American performance of Fidelio and it was good. I have been going to English classes. I think I may have forgotten how to speak French. Perhaps I will write to you in English after Mahler and I return to Vienna in April.

With love from your son, Guillaume.

CHAPTER 19

Mahler's First Symphony

Mahler accepted a conducting contract at the Met for the following year. The director of La Scala in Milan accepted the directorship of the Met on condition that he could bring his senior conductor, Arturo Toscanini. Mahler was not unhappy with this new arrangement. Sharing the conducting would mean less work for himself. He imagined that Toscanini would take the Italian repertoire, leaving him the German work.

Walter Damrosch, who managed and conducted the New York Symphony Orchestra which had performed the American premier of Mahler's Fourth asked Mahler to conduct the orchestra in one of his own symphonies. Mahler was delighted and suggested his Second Symphony which required a large orchestra, off-stage musicians, solo singers, and a choir.

Mahler was also approached by a committee of very wealthy ladies who offered him his own orchestra for a series of concerts during the following season.

On April 23rd 1908 Mahler, Alma and William sailed back to Europe on the *Kaiserin Auguste Viktoria*. William sailed with them first class. They docked in Hamburg on May 2nd. Mahler and Alma went to Wiesbaden where he was due to conduct his First Symphony. William went to Vienna. He ran from the station to find Johnny. The people now living in the apartment knew nothing about Johnny Stanko except for the letters that arrived for him from New York which lay by the door unopened. There was also a letter from Basel for M. Guillaume Hildebrand. It was from a lawyer acting on behalf of the estate of Mme Jasmine Gerard. He was sorry to inform M. Guillaume Hildebrand of the death of Mme Gerard and advised him that she had left him a viola which he believed was already in M. Hildebrand's possession. The lawyer would be grateful if M. Hildebrand would inform the estate that he agreed to accept possession as Mme Gerard willed.

William left his former home with the letters, dropped them into a waste-paper bin and returned to the station to take a train from Vienna to join the Mahlers in Wiesbaden.

William had to wait more than three hours for a train. He hadn't eaten all day and although he wasn't hungry he went to the restaurant and ate some sausage and bread and drank a beer. He found a seat by himself in a first-class compartment. The compartment filled up with another five passengers who were impeccably dressed. Sitting opposite William an elderly lady carefully peeled an apple and cut it into segments with a small sharp knife. She wore a tiny feather in her hat. Next to her a young lady with carefully braided blonde hair. Next to her was an officer of the Austrian army wearing a sharply pressed uniform and highly polished straps. Two more passengers sat on William's right. William deliberately kept his eyes to the left and looked out of the window. No one spoke. They avoided each other but William could clearly see in the carriage window the reflections of his fellow passengers.

He wished he hadn't eaten. He was sweating. He wiped his brow and it felt cold. William shivered and felt nauseous. He closed his eyes and tried to imagine Mahler's First Symphony. He had heard the Third, Fourth, Fifth and Sixth and tried to imagine the music that had come before. He knew the first symphony had been poorly reviewed, but William now understood that if the critics hadn't liked it then it must be good. He felt sick. He thought if he could concentrate on the music then his nausea might pass. He guessed that some of the First Symphony would sound like a song, and some of it would sound like a dance. He knew the orchestra would make sounds that had never been heard before and he tried to imagine what they might be. He couldn't hold on to any of his thoughts for very long. His stomach rejected the sausages and beer. He stood up to get out of the compartment. He heaved and his mouth filled with vomit. He couldn't get out of the compartment in time when he heaved again, turned away from his fellow passengers and was sick on the seat where he had been sitting. The compartment filled with the acrid stench of sickness. He turned to find the others on their feet with bits of barely digested sausage and bread sticking to their clothes and hands and faces. They looked at William with disgust. He fled the compartment and bolted himself in the toilet, sat behind the locked door and wept. His nausea had passed but he continued heaving with giant sobs. He ignored the banging on the toilet door. When the train stopped, he let himself out of the toilet, leapt off the train, and fled. Once the train pulled away William discovered he was at Sankt Polten and there were no more trains that day. He found the lavatory, rinsed out his mouth and tried to remove the sickness from his clothes. He wondered how he had lost everything so easily – Johnny, his studies, and the viola. They had come easily and now they were gone. He had nothing left to bring up. His stomach was empty. He was empty.

He took the first train in the morning from Sankt Polten towards Stuttgart. It was a slow train that stopped at every station. Shortly after leaving Ulm the train stopped at Oberkochen and he thought about Meddi, the Met, and New York now so far away.

Late in the afternoon William arrived in Wiesbaden. He asked for a room at the Station Hotel but it was fully booked. He asked at another hotel which was also full. William didn't ask for a room anywhere else. He knew there was no room in Wiesbaden for an unshaven, filthy traveller whose clothes were stained with sickness. He came to a church. He walked around the church to a side door and knocked. A cleric answered the door, told him to wait and closed it again. The cleric returned, gave him a few coins, and shut the door. William spoke to the closed door. 'I have money,' he whispered. I was looking for somewhere to wash and shave.' He left the church and walked to a gentlemen's outfitters. He put a large roll of American dollars on the counter and asked for new clothes. He threw his old clothes away and, dressed in a new suit, found a hotel, washed and shaved, and then looked for the concert hall.

The opening of Mahler's First is the beginning of all Mahler's symphonies. William immediately recognized the sound palette. All the bricks that Mahler would use in his later works were already in place here. The first sound in the symphony was eerie. The strings played the same note in unison octaves apart from bowed basses to a high harmonic in the violins. It was a call to attention but not a fanfare. It sounded more like an impenetrable morning mist. The basses moved out of the depths repeating a figure over and over as they climbed towards the daylight. Then the sun broke through the clouds and the whole orchestra broke into song. In the second movement the orchestra began to dance a primitive waltz. This was not a waltz for sophisticated urban Viennese nor a waltz for Austrian peasantry. It was a waltz for elephants. The third movement opened with a tune that William knew as *Frère Jacques* and which the audience in Wiesbaden would have recognized as *Bruder Jakob*. It was played by a solo bass in the tempo of a funeral march before being interrupted by a klezmer band. The musicians were carrying the coffins of dead children out the back door while at the same time having a party in the front room. It was dark, exhilarating, and diabolical. This was the sort of mischief that got Mahler into trouble with critics who accused the clever little Jew of disrespect towards the German classical tradition. The Wiesbaden audience felt uneasy. When the grotesqueries of the third movement were over, the last movement opened with a fortissimo shriek. An elderly lady near the front dropped her knitting. The tone was triumphant. The percussionist beat his timpani as the symphony beat its chest before the movement leaped into a new key without any preparation, no modulation, just one mighty leap that left the audience high and dry. The applause was muted. William clapped enthusiastically but despite all his experience at the claque in Vienna there was nothing he could do to prolong the applause in Wiesbaden which ground to a halt before Mahler left the platform. After the concert William went to the conductor's room. Mahler was exhausted. Alma looked embarrassed. She asked William to walk her back to her hotel.

CHAPTER 20

The Horse With No Name

Mahler wanted to go immediately to visit their old summer house in Maiernigg. Alma would not return to the place where their daughter had died. She went with her mother and stepfather into the mountains to find another house where Mahler could spend his composing summers. William and Mahler made the twelve-hour journey from Vienna to Maiernigg in the car. They spent the night in a hotel in Klagenfurt before setting off along the Worthersee to Maiernigg. William waited in the car while Mahler carried the Teddy's Bear which William had bought in Macy's in New York to place on Maria's grave.

Vienna was preparing the jubilee for the sixtieth anniversary of the Emperor's accession. A spectacular celebration was planned for June 12th and the Viennese went ahead with their big party even though Italians, Hungarians, Czechs, Bohemians, Serbians, Croats and all the Emperor's other subjects turned their backs on Vienna. So did the Mahlers. On June 10th, two days before the jubilee, they left Vienna for the summer house which Alma had found in the mountains.

Alma dictated the following letter which William transcribed faithfully.

June 11th 1908

Dear Meddi,

I am writing to you from Toblach where I am staying with Alma and Mahler. Three weeks ago Mahler performed his First Symphony in Wiesbaden. The ticket prices were high and it was a beautiful spring evening so the audience was small. Alma does not like funeral music or Jewish music and there is a lot of both. The last movement is loud and heroic. She says the music which travels from self-pity to bravado was composed by her husband for an audience of men.

I miss you very much. Are you going to continue with your English lessons while I am away? I expect you will be an expert by the time we return. Mahler is going to conduct his Second Symphony in New York with Damrosch's orchestra and then he will conduct his own orchestra in a season of symphonic works as well as conducting at the Met. He will be so busy that Alma expects she will hardly see her husband at all.

At the concert in Wiesbaden Alma wore one of the outfits that you made for her – the cerise costume with pink lace. She looked a million dollars.

When you reply I would be happy to receive a photograph of you. Please send me a different photograph from the one Alma has. She has the photograph of you feeding pigeons in the park. I would like a photograph which shows more of your face, preferably smiling. You can write to me c/o Mahler, Trenkerhof, Altschluderbach, Austria.

Your friend,

William.

PS When I was on the train from Ulm to Stuttgart it stopped at Oberkochen.

William asked if he might add the sentence of his own about the train stopping at Oberkochen. Alma thought the postscript was entirely appropriate.

    William asked the landlord, Herr Trenker, to show him how to drive the horse and cart so that he could take the wagon to the station whenever any of Herr Mahler's friends came to visit. Herr Trenker agreed but told him the horse would go to the station and return by himself. William should pick up the reins as a sign that they were ready to set off. The horse would not acknowledge any further commands. If William did attempt a verbal instruction like 'gee up' or if he accidentally pulled on the reins then the horse would stop and stubbornly refuse to go any further. His role as wagon driver would only be to comfort Herr Mahler's guests who might be alarmed to ride in a driverless carriage. Herr Trenker's own friends were well used to being driven by the horse from the station to the house and would be every bit as puzzled to find a driver on board as Herr Mahler's guests would be to find none.

    Trenker took William on the wagon for a driving lesson. Trenker sat beside him and told him to pick up the reins and the horse pulled the wagon to the station. William was careful to do nothing. The horse stopped at the station. William and Herr Trenker stepped down from the wagon. Herr Trenker whispered something to the horse. William suspected these might be words of explanation as to why they had come to the station at a time when there was no train. Trenker gave William a sugar lump and showed him how to hold his hand flat. William flinched as the horse accepted the sugar with his wet and bristly lips. William wiped his hand on his trousers. They stepped back on to the wagon. William picked up the reins and the horse turned and headed back to Trenkerhof. William found that holding the reins slackly was tiring and when they arrived back at Trenkerhof he was exhausted. Trenker congratulated him and told him he had passed.

'What's the horse's name?'

'The horse doesn't have a name,' said Herr Trenker.

The Mahlers lived on the top two floors and the landlord's family lived on the bottom floor. Mahler arranged for the construction of a composing hut where he could escape from the overwhelming odour of the cheese Herr Trenker made and stored in his cellar. Alma kept the cockerels and dogs quiet while Mahler worked undisturbed on his settings of Chinese poems. She turned away journalists, travelling salesmen, and admirers, but encouraged friends to visit and entertain her.

Among the visitors that William collected from the station that summer was the young conductor, Ossip Gabrilowitsch. While Mahler was composing William took Alma and Ossip out for picnics. William carried the picnic basket, laid out the cloth and the food then retreated a discreet distance.

Another visitor that summer was the biologist Paul Kammerer. William did not like him. This was not so much because William disapproved of Alma's flirting. She flirted with all her visitors. What really bothered William was Paul Kammerer's desire to drive the cart, wash the dishes, sweep the floors, clean the windows, babysit for Anna, weed the garden, chop wood, and perform any other task which might be of service to the Mahlers. The biologist not only fell in love with Alma; he was also infatuated with her husband. William felt his own position under threat. But where William was silent Kammerer was noisy and where William was invisible Kammerer was all too visible. Kammerer got on Mahler's nerves and much to William's relief Alma had to let him go. William was happy to take the biologist back to the station. It seemed to William that the horse went a bit faster than usual.

July 1st Toblach
Dear Mother,

I am sorry I missed your birthday. I hope you and Félicité had a good day. I am living with Herr Mahler and his wife in the mountains where he is composing a new symphonic work based on Chinese poems. We do not use the car up here and I have learned to drive a horse and cart. I am now an experienced cavalier. I often take the wagon to the station to collect Herr Mahler's distinguished visitors. I will be going to Prague with Herr Mahler in September to help him prepare the premiere of his Seventh Symphony. My address is c/o Mahler, Trenkerhof, Altschluderbach, Austria.

With love from your son,
Guillaume

July 1st
New York

Dear William,

I was delighted to hear news of you and Herr Mahler and his wife. I have looked up Altschluderbach in the atlas and I see that it is in the mountains. It must be a beautiful place to live. I imagine that Herr Mahler works hard and spends long hours composing music. I am pleased to hear that Frau Mahler looks good in the cerise costume. It is her favourite colour. She moves very gracefully between the sharpness of paprika and the depth of purple. I will make her a coat in similar colours. I hope you look after her when her husband is busy.

I am happy with my work here although it is not so interesting without Herr Mahler. The musicians have fond memories of him and I know they are all looking forward to his return. I have heard that there is some anxiety about the new Italian conductor. He has a reputation for being ill-tempered.

I have enclosed a portrait as you requested. When the photographer came to take publicity photographs of the singers, I asked him if he would make this portrait of me. I am smiling as you requested. Please show the picture to Herr Mahler and his wife.

I am your friend.
Meddi.

Mechtilde had written the last four words in English. William gave the letter and photograph to Alma.

One day, in tears, Alma told William about the guilt she felt over Maria's death. She didn't blame her husband. She blamed herself. She told William that she had been punished by God for conceiving the child before she and Gustav were married.

CHAPTER 21

Mahler's Seventh Symphony

William and Mahler left Toblach and took an overnight train to Vienna where they ate lunch with his father-in-law, Carl Moll, and his former Hofoper colleague, the set designer Alfred Roller. Mahler never met any of his other Viennese friends and hastened to get out of town on an overnight train to Prague where an exhibition orchestra had been assembled for him to conduct the premiere of his Seventh Symphony. The orchestra was composed of members of the Neues Deutsches Theater and the Czech Philharmonic. National feelings were running high in Prague. The Emperor's Jubilee Year was winding down and so was the Empire. The Czech musicians did not look upon Mahler as a returning Bohemian hero but as a German speaking former director of the Vienna Opera – a senior, if now retired, Imperial civil servant. Mahler had asked for a large orchestra and two weeks of rehearsals. The musicians were happy with two weeks' pay but the Czech musicians were uncomfortable about sharing the platform with Germans. A few of the Czech Philharmonic players had declined to take part. The most notable absentee was their new young first trumpet player. It was a difficult orchestra to conduct and the rehearsal facilities didn't make it any easier. The Exhibition Concert Hall was also a restaurant. As Mahler rehearsed on the platform waiters on the floor moved back and forward between tables in a manner which suggested that the rehearsal was interfering with their work. He rehearsed each section separately and when they questioned his composition Mahler had to patiently explain how their parts would eventually fit into the whole. Mahler had to work with this orchestra because there had been no other offers. It was Prague or nowhere. Vienna was closed to him. His Fifth in Cologne and his Sixth in Essen were regarded as failures. Mahler kept calm during the rehearsals and didn't show his feelings until he got back to the hotel. William had never seen Mahler so angry. He threw cushions around the room – nothing that would break or make a noise – just cushions. He threw them at trumpeters who didn't like the long high notes, at cellists who thought their low notes should be scored for basses and their high notes should be scored for violas, and at viola players who thought their low notes should be scored for cellos and he threw a cushion at the orchestra manager who questioned Mahler's need for two mandolins and a guitar. William lit a small cigar and gave it to Mahler who paced up and down the room smoking while William put the cushions back on the chairs. William filled the fruit bowl with apples, opened a bottle of beer for Mahler, laid his writing materials on his desk, and left him to pour out his frustrations in the long nightly letters he wrote to his wife.

William had listened to the musicians grumbling for the first five days. But on the sixth day when Mahler assembled the whole orchestra the grumbling stopped. Parts that no one believed could possibly fit together slotted into a counterpoint that was surprising, breath-taking, and magical. It had one foot in the German classical tradition and another foot on a different planet. Mahler was bringing to life a musical landscape that had never been heard before. William sat and listened with goosebumps. Cellists, basses, harps, and percussion played open-mouthed and violins, violas, brass, and woodwind wide-eyed in wonder at what they were hearing. Waiters stood and forgot all about their customers. Diners forgot all about their dinners. In the first of the 'night music' movements musical candles flickering in the darkness made ghostly shadows. In the second 'night music' movement by some miracle of orchestration two mandolins and a guitar sang out above the strings all around them. The final movement opened with a fanfare on timpani. Mahler asked for more and again for more and again for still more until the timpani player said he was afraid to break the skins. Mahler dared the player to go for it. The rest of the orchestra roared him on. This final movement was an even bigger 'yes' than the final movement of his Fifth. Friends, supporters, waiters, diners all rose to their feet to applaud. Mahler thanked his orchestra and hoped they would enjoy their day off but the musicians refused to leave the platform and begged to be allowed to play the whole symphony again from the beginning. They didn't wait for their conductor's permission and started without him. Mahler shrugged his shoulders, turned back the pages of his score and joined in.

The following rehearsals were all about tempi, dynamics, and re-writing. Orchestral parts normally follow similar dynamic instructions. They all play loudly, or they all play quietly. Mahler asked for something altogether more subtle and required each section to carefully observe their own dynamic instructions which sometimes asked them to play forte while others were playing piano and vice versa. Mahler would diminish the volume in one section with his left hand while at the same time asking more from another section with his right. He would sometimes leave the podium with the baton in his teeth, pencil in his hand, and go around the desks altering scores as the musicians played, taking out sounds he no longer wanted and writing in new phrases that he required.

Alma arrived for the final rehearsal as the orchestra was tuning up. The musicians welcomed her with a fanfare and a round of applause. Mahler seated her at a table by herself, bade his musicians good morning, and then conducted his Seventh Symphony for her.

William, who had listened as the symphony took shape throughout the rehearsals, watched Alma as she heard it for the first time and his heart sank. During the first movement William fancied that Alma revisited the summer house in Maiernigg by the Worthersee where their daughter, Maria, had died, where she had vowed never to return and where her husband had written this music. During the night music scenes on either side of the scherzo Alma appeared to be troubled by the darkness and to be unaffected by the gaiety which overcame the shadows. During the scherzo William thought he saw her shake her head in disapproval. When the final movement began with the huge fanfare on the timpani and strident fortissimo brass Alma held her head in her hands and covered her ears. William was no longer having a Mahler experience. He was having an Alma experience and the final movement disintegrated in his own ears. It went two up and then one down and then one up and then two down and finished where it started. The inventiveness, the novelty, the joy, the gaiety – everything that was good about the movement – evaporated. Alma frowned. Mahler, on the other hand, appeared to be enjoying himself. With his elbows at his sides he swayed from side to side like a dancer. His gestures were so small he might have been conducting with a toothpick rather than a baton. Although he turned the pages of the score he never once looked at it. He only had eyes for his orchestra and they only had eyes for him. They knew by heart every note and how it should be played. They gave their all to their conductor and brought his symphony to a triumphant conclusion. As the last sound faded Mahler did not lower his baton but listened carefully to the silence. Then with his baton still in his right hand he stepped down from the podium and approached the table where Alma was sitting. He sat opposite her, baton in hand, gazed at his wife and waited. The orchestra waited. William waited. Did she not know what to say? Anything would do. Anything other than this silence which became terrible. Alma and her husband looked at one another.

William looked at Alma. He tried to send her three words to say to her husband. 'I love you.' She didn't hear them. Then William tried to send her just two words. 'Thank you.' She didn't hear that either. Then William sent her no words at all – just a small gesture. He begged her to take her husband's hand. Perhaps she heard. Perhaps she misheard. She reached out to her husband, took the baton from his hand, and laid it down on the table. The orchestra shifted in their seats and put down their instruments. Mahler stood up, turned away from his wife, thanked his musicians, then Alma and her husband left the rehearsal together.

Dear Meddi,

I am writing to you from Prague where Mahler conducted the premiere of his Seventh. The symphony was appreciated without controversy by the Czech audience which was a relief after all the difficulties with his Fifth and Sixth symphonies in Germany. Alma has not been feeling very well and is quite impatient to return to America. There are two more performances of the symphony in Munich and Hamburg, Alma will join us in Hamburg and we will depart from there on board the Amerika on November 12$^{th.}$ Arriving NY November 22nd. Staying at the Savoy.

The new Italian conductor at the Met is giving Mahler a headache. He has insisted on opening with 'Tristan.' Mahler has flatly refused. Mahler had assumed that the Italian would conduct the Italian repertoire and he would take responsibility for the German repertoire. Mahler considers the Met's production of 'Tristan' to be his intellectual property and is in no mind to give it to the Italian. Mahler has prevailed and he will open the season with 'Tristan'. Alma feels anxious about all these troubles but knows at the Met she has in you a good friend.

Mahler has agreed to conduct three symphony concerts in Carnegie Hall for the New York Symphony Society. The first is a Schumann symphony and some overtures. The third is a Beethoven and some overtures. The middle one is Mahler's Second. The orchestra might be good enough for the Schumann and the Beethoven but it is difficult to imagine how they will be able to play the Mahler. I believe their performance of Mahler's Fourth wasn't very good. I can't imagine why anyone believes that these same musicians could manage his Second, which is bigger, longer, and more complex.

There is a committee of very wealthy ladies who want to establish a permanent orchestra for Mahler and he is interested in working with them as it would allow him to step away from the Met and its new Italian conductor. Alma, who was pleased to get away from the musical warfare in Vienna, has no appetite for more musical warfare in New York.

Alma's daughter, Anna, will be travelling with us. She is four and will be looked after by her Scottish nanny.

Have you been going to your English lessons?

I am your friend.
William

CHAPTER 22

Mahler's Second Symphony

The Mahlers voyaged to New York with their daughter, Anna, and the Scottish nanny, Lizzie Turner. William played hide and seek with Anna and Lizzie in the electric lift and in the ship's gardens. William thought Lizzie was great fun. Anna ate her meals with William and Lizzie and in the evening was taken to her parents to say goodnight before being tucked into her first-class bed in Lizzie's cabin.

Alma wasn't much fun. She made William sit at her bedside while her husband was working in the adjacent suite and told him Schönberg and Zemlinsky's sister, Mathilde, had married and had two children. She told him that Schönberg had written *Pélleas and Mélisande*, a tone poem on the theme of marital infidelity, but the music had not prepared Schönberg to deal with his wife's infidelity. Alma told William that the painter, Richard Gerstl, who had painted Schönberg's portrait, had inspired the composer to try his own hand at painting. Schönberg asked Gerstl for lessons. Gerstl taught Schönberg during the day and slept with Schönberg's wife during the night. When the affair was discovered Mathilde ran off with the painter leaving her husband with their two young children. Zemlinsky ran after his sister and persuaded her to return to the marriage for her children's sake. Gerstl, ostracised by Zemlinsky's and Schönberg s circles, burned all his work and then hanged himself in front of the full-length mirror which he used for his portraiture. William asked Alma if it was all his fault.

Anna snapped at him, 'How could it be your fault?'

'Because I suggested Zemlinsky bring a friend to join you and Mathilde for a musical soireé. That's where Mathilde met Schönberg, confessed William. It's all my fault!'

'Who do you think you are, God?' cried Alma in disbelief. It's his fault!' She shook her fist at the ceiling and cried out, 'You created us in your own image and likeness so why do our clumsy attempts to love one another lead to so much unhappiness and death? What am I supposed to do?'

Alma was not expecting an answer and was shocked when William said, 'Love Meddi'. William was shocked too. He had meant to say, 'Love Mahler.'

The Mahlers installed themselves on the ninth floor of the Savoy Hotel on the corner of 59th and 5th. Gustav and Alma had a suite of rooms that overlooked Central Park. Anna and Lizzie were next door, and William next to them. When Alma walked into her room she found a mannequin dressed in a beautiful cerise gown with a note, 'To Alma for the American premiere of Mahler's Second Symphony.'

William went with Mahler every day to Carnegie Hall for his Symphony Orchestra rehearsals and was frequently required to come and go from the hall to the hotel fetching and carrying whatever it was Mahler had forgotten. William was given a weekly allowance to pay for Mahler's lunches, his apples, his cigars, and Alma's liquor. The Mahlers never asked for anything to be sent up to their room and so avoided contact with hotel staff. They sent William to fetch whatever they needed. William was also the chaperone for Lizzie and Anna and accompanied them to the park and to the shops. On the street they looked like a young family.

William had to go down to the foyer to meet and greet Meddi whenever she arrived for one of her sessions with Alma. He would welcome Meddi with a kiss on both cheeks, take her hand and lead her to the lift as Alma had instructed. William would then leave the two women alone and when their session was over Meddi would knock on William's door and he would accompany her to the foyer where she would talk to him for a few minutes before they kissed and waved each other goodbye. William was responsible for going through all the Mahlers' dinner invitations and discussing anything that might be potentially suitable with the Met's front-of-house manager, before replying to them all in Alma's name. He had to go to the liquor store twice a week, once to collect six bottles of Benedictine for Alma and once again to collect six bottles of beer for her husband. He carried the bottles wrapped in napkins in two shopping bags, as Alma had instructed, so that he could bring them through the hotel foyer unaccompanied by the sound of clinking glass. William took Alma's correspondence to the post office apart from the few letters Alma wrote to her mother and stepfather which he left at the hotel reception. Occasionally an envelope would arrive addressed to William which contained a sealed envelope addressed to Alma. The first time this happened William opened the first envelope and handed the sealed envelope to Alma. After that William realized that anything addressed to him was really for her.

William accompanied Alma and Meddi to Carnegie Hall for the first of Mahler's New York Symphony concerts on November 29th. The rehearsals had been difficult. Not all the musicians had turned up. Some of the absentees sent deputies and others did not. Some of those who did turn up arrived late in the hope of being sent home. One of the double bass players tried to get himself fired so that he could take a more lucrative job in Minneapolis. Mahler would not fire him because he was the only bass player in the section who was any good. On the night of the concert the half-empty hall nevertheless heard music that resembled the overtures to *Coriolan*, *The Bartered Bride*, and *The Meistersingers* and they heard the Schumann symphony. There was nothing William could contribute to this lacklustre evening. The claque in Vienna would not have attempted to stimulate applause for this performance. It was difficult to imagine this orchestra playing Mahler's Second Symphony. Mahler had successfully negotiated extra rehearsals and extra musicians, but the real difficulty would be with the orchestra's professionalism and musicianship.

William did not attend many of the rehearsals because he was required by Alma to meet and greet Meddi for the daily fitting sessions in the days before the concert.

On December 8th 1908 William accompanied Alma and Meddi to the premiere. The gown Meddi had made for Alma was beautiful. Meddi wore a plain outfit that allowed Alma to shine alone. William knew what he expected from a Mahler experience in the concert hall and knew he wouldn't get it if he had to sit next to Alma so excused himself and found a seat on the other side of the half-empty hall. She had already heard it and William knew she didn't like it. He was going to hear it for the first time. He knew there would be a funeral march, a song, a dance, a wicked scherzo and that the symphony would finish with the resurrection of the dead – a final movement when the orchestra would be joined by a chorus. If the orchestra didn't manage to play it as well as Mahler deserved William hoped he would be able to use his inner ear and imagination to make up the shortfall for himself.

And so William heard a different performance from the rest of the audience and complemented the orchestra's shortcomings with his own imagination. His inner ear cleaned the fluff off the double bassists' bows and oiled the cellists' strings. In the second movement he listened to the graceful waltz without hearing the floorboards creak beneath the dancers' heavy shoes. In the third movement, when heavenly music went to war with hellish music, which is what often happens in a Mahler scherzo, William tried to ignore the orchestra's inferno in order to hear the diabolical score that Mahler had actually written. William was only able to relax when the mezzo soprano joined the orchestra. She sang beautifully,

> 'O Röschen rot!
> Der Mensch liegt in gröster Not!
> Der Mensch liegt in gröster Pein!
> Je lieber möcht'ichim Himmel sein.'

The singer was first class and William walked beside her on the road to heaven as she pushed the angel aside declaring that she had come from God and to God she would return. In the final movement the *Dies Irae* moved from minor to major, music from offstage bands poured into the hall as if they were playing in the streets outside, the last two living creatures on earth, two birds, a flute and a piccolo, fluttered and fell, and as the choir whispered *Aufersteh'n* Mahler's vision was recreated in Carnegie Hall and the souls of the dead rose again. The singers were wonderful and saved the night. William could not hold back his tears as the solo soprano peeled away from the choir and soared.

Applause for the resurrection seemed to be an inappropriately flimsy gesture. William would rather the symphony had been greeted with silence.

He walked back to the hotel with Alma and Meddi. Alma said nothing about the music. She had a toothache.

Mahler arrived back at the hotel and complained about his painful orchestra. Alma complained about her painful tooth. He told her that he had changed the advertised programme for his third and final concert. He would not ask the orchestra to tackle Beethoven's Seventh because he didn't think they would be able to play it and that he would let them have a go at Beethoven's Fifth instead.

The following morning Mahler knocked on William's door and asked him to find a dentist. William took a car to the Met to see the front-of-house manager, who recommended a German dentist who had a box at the opera. He wrote down the address of Dr Winfried Kreuzer's surgery and William put the slip of paper in his pocket, fetched Meddi from the costume department, and they both returned to the Savoy where Meddi called the dentist. She explained who the patient was and arranged for Alma to visit the surgery within the hour. Alma had already taken a large dose of Benedictine to help dull the pain.

When they arrived at the surgery they were surprised to be welcomed by a black receptionist who told them her name was Martha. She showed them into the waiting room, gave William and Meddi coffee and Alma a glass of water. Alma had never spoken to a black person before and was not sure if it was safe to drink the water. She asked Meddi if she was sure this was the dentist the Met had recommended. Meddi looked at William. William held out the slip of paper with the dentist's address written in the hand of the front-of-house manager.

A lady wearing a white coat entered, introduced herself as Madame Kreuzer, and made a little curtsey towards Alma who was pressing her sore cheek with one hand and holding the glass of water in the other. Madame Kreuzer explained that her husband was busy with another patient but rather than asking Frau Mahler to wait she proposed to examine Alma herself. Her husband normally treated their male patients while female patients sometimes preferred to be treated by a woman. She hoped that she would be able to relieve Alma's pain and help her to feel comfortable. She told Meddi she was very welcome to accompany Alma into the treatment room if that was agreeable to Frau Mahler. She told Alma that her name was Jasmine. Alma followed Jasmine to the treatment room taking Meddi with her. William was left alone in the waiting room. Madame Kreuzer spoke good German, but William could hear that she was French. William, losing his balance as he stood on the brink of a nightmare, left the waiting room to find the toilet. He asked the receptionist for the 'wash-room'. On the wall behind the receptionist there was a family photograph. Madame Kreuzer, Herr Kreuzer, the black receptionist, and a smiling black youngster holding a trumpet. William fainted.

When he came round William found himself sitting in the waiting room. Dr Winfried Kreuzer gently encouraged him to lower his head between his knees. Martha, the receptionist, brought William a glass of water and brought Dr Kreuzer his tool bag. He took William's temperature and blood pressure. 'Have you eaten this morning?' William shook his head. Dr Kreuzer tutted and Martha fetched William a glass of milk and a Nabisco. Dr Kreuzer talked with William until he was satisfied that William was fully recovered. Half an hour later, Alma and Meddi emerged from Madame Kreuzer's treatment room.

CHAPTER 3

Mahler Gets Lost

William visited the department stores looking at possible gifts in case Mahler asked him once again to buy something for his wife. He knew that the gifts he got last year were a success and he wanted to succeed again. William went to Macy's and looked at the fashions and the jewellery, and in the toy department he found, instead of last year's display of Teddy's Bears, a new display of Billy's Possums. He bought one of them for Anna and a tartan scarf for Lizzie.

Meddi now attended Professor Schiller's Saturday class for intermediate students. On the Saturday before Christmas William went with her to the lesson. Although he could just about follow what the other students were saying he was not able to join in the conversation. He had none of the grammar that would allow him to build a sentence and sat dumbly throughout the class. Professor Schiller invited him to return to the beginners' class.

Mahler had given Meddi money to buy something for him to give Alma at Christmas and she asked William if he would like to go shopping with her. William was disappointed that Mahler had passed the responsibility of his Christmas shopping to Meddi but was happy to accompany her to a fur shop where she had her eye on a hat and stole made from a piece of white wolf fur. Meddi put it on. The wolf's ears stood alert on top of Meddi's head and the forelegs draped over her breasts. William would never have bought such a thing. The fur that once kept a hungry wolf warm now clothed Meddi's smiling face. Meddi's little nose protruded from where there had once been the wolf's snout and Meddi's mouth where there had once been the wolf's fangs. She stuck her tongue out at him. She paid two thousand dollars for it.

As they walked back towards the Met Meddi told William about the Czech national costumes the ladies were making for Mahler's production of *The Bartered Bride*. Mahler had hired traditional Czech dancers who were coming from Europe for the American performances. The dancers were bringing their own costumes. The ladies at the Met were busy making costumes for the singers and were under pressure to get it right. Czech national feeling was running high and there was no room for any error. Meddi thought it fortunate for *The Bartered Bride* that Mahler was Czech and not Austrian. William told Meddi that Mahler would conduct the opera just as Smetana intended. He did not tell Meddi that in Czech eyes Mahler was a retired Imperial Civil Servant.

Outside the Met William looked up, saw the full moon, and sang from *La Bohème, 'Ma per fortuna è una notte di luna'*. Meddi joined in howling at the moon, then opened the bag where she was carrying the fur and told the wolf to be quiet.

Dec 22nd. The orchestra insisted that Mahler join them for a Christmas celebration. William would like to have gone with them but wasn't asked. He walked back to the hotel through a blizzard.

Alma came to William's room and asked him where her husband was. He told Alma he had gone out with the musicians. He didn't know if Alma was shaking her head because she was cross with him or with her husband. He didn't think it was his fault that Mahler had gone out drinking with the orchestra. William went down to the foyer and looked out onto the street which lay under a blanket of snow and waited for Mahler. It was a silent night.

Mahler had gone with the musicians to a bar and then to a restaurant and then to another bar, then tried to walk back to the hotel, and got lost. There were very few cars out in the snow. A cab did stop for Mahler and agreed to take him to the hotel but the drunken driver hit a tree and fell asleep. Mahler dropped his pince-nez in the snow. A tipsy passer-by helped Mahler to find his spectacles and then walked with Mahler to the Savoy. They kept turning left and left again. After walking in a circle for an hour Mahler left the drunk man and struck out at a tangent on his own. The grid of streets and avenues which makes New York easy to navigate got the better of Mahler. He had walked around the Savoy Hotel in ever decreasing circles until he stumbled into William's arms in the foyer at 1am. Mahler was cold and anxious about Alma. William took Mahler to his room where he could have a hot shower to warm himself up before returning to his own suite.

Dec 23rd William accompanied Alma and Mahler to the Met for Mahler's opening night – a repeat of last year's *Tristan und Isolde*. When they got into the lift William bent over and picked up the trail of Alma's gown and handed it to her. She took it without looking at him but William caught her expression in the mirror and saw she remembered last year's ripped gown.

Alma told her husband that as they were going to be staying in New York it was important to cultivate the friendship of excellent dentists and doctors and on Christmas Eve Alma and Mahler went to dinner with their new dentist friends, the Kreutzers and their friends, Dr and Frau Fraenkel. Dr Fraenkel was a general practitioner and an eminent neuroscientist who was interested in spiritualism. Frau Frankel was silent and almost invisible. Herr Kreuzer not only had a beautiful wife, he was also on the Board of the Institute of Musical Art. Mahler looked forward to an evening of sausage, sachertorte, and a bottle of good German beer.

William went out with Anna and Lizzie for a Christmas dinner of soda pops and hot dogs. When they got back to the Savoy William went to Lizzie and Anna's room and gave Anna the gift-wrapped Billy's Possum. Anna tore open the wrapping and hugged the Possum declaring eternal love for the soft toy, hugging and squeezing it. She caught Lizzie frowning at her, calmed herself, and in formal German thanked 'Uncle William.'

Anna had made four little papier-mâché sculptures. Anna introduced them to William. The man with a raised right arm holding a baton was Papa. Then a seated female figure, her arms and hands held in front of her with fingers extended. 'That's Mama playing the piano.' Then a seated male figure holding a steering wheel which she gave to William. 'That's Uncle William driving a car! Happy Christmas, Uncle William.'

William was undone. Taken completely by surprise he was overwhelmed with Anna's gift. 'Dear Anna, It's beautiful. You are so clever. It looks just like me. I will look after him and he will always remind me of you. Thank you.' William leaned over and kissed her on her forehead. Anna ran off to her bed to cuddle Billy's Possum.

William asked Lizzie about the fourth sculpture – a female figure kneeling. Lizzie said, 'It's me saying my prayers.' He gave her the tartan scarf and she gave him an English-German dictionary. They looked at one another both wondering whether they might share a kiss, and the moment passed. When he got back to his room he put the little sculpture on his bedside table and when he opened the dictionary he saw that Lizzie had written on the fly-leaf, 'From your friend, Lizzie'.

The Savoy Hotel
59th Street
New York

December 25th

Dear Mother,

I am writing to you on Christmas Day because I am lonely and I want to talk to you. I know that we have not spoken to each other for a long time. I am now twenty-six. I should have graduated from the Vienna Conservatoire, married, and presented you with grandchildren. I have done none of that.

I was not able to graduate because I was not good enough. Please believe me when I tell you that I did my best. I wanted to do it for you as much as for myself and I worked at it for three years but I did not have what the other students had. At first I thought I lacked the ear, or perhaps the intelligence, or the skill, but I have come to believe that I lack the soul. When I hear music, I know that I am listening to another person's soul. The music that others play floods the empty space inside me where my own soul should be. My playing was never more than an expression of that emptiness. My teachers gave me exercises to help me develop a fuller sound but whenever the professor played my instrument the difference was clear and inescapable. I required spiritual exercises rather than musical ones. There was no decisive moment when I left the conservatoire. I just drifted out. It was several months before I realized that I had left. I didn't tell you because I didn't know what I was doing, and when I realised what I had done I didn't tell you because I did not want to disappoint you. It is another one of many mistakes I have made. I am sorry.

Shortly after arriving in Vienna I moved in with a friend who was studying trumpet. I was very fond of him and we lived together for five years. At first, I did not know what was happening to us both. Then I was taken by surprise to discover that we might be a couple just like you and Félicité. He was gentle and I found in his soul what was lacking in myself. He was very fond of me. He enjoyed my cheerfulness and generosity. I am not boasting. I know I have these qualities and that they sound admirable but my cheerfulness and generosity are expressions of a need to be liked. My friend loved me but I cannot say that I loved him. I know that we were never a couple like you and Félicité. We lived together comfortably and easily. Then one day I left him and went with Mahler to America. If hell is a place for those who have failed to love, then I must go there. I have not sold my soul to the devil. If the devil wanted my soul he would not be able to find it. I do not have a soul.

I do not blame anyone for my loneliness, least of all you. I know that you cared for me, looked after me, loved me, and believed in me and that my words today will only bring you sadness and disappointment.

I want to tell you about Madame Gerard's viola. I sold it. I walked away from the dealer with cash in my pocket, leaving him the viola. There may have been a possibility that I might have been able to atone for this sin but when the lawyer wrote to tell me that Madame Gerard's lifetime was over and that she had left the viola to me in her will, a viola that I had already sold, my wickedness was sealed. I look in the mirror and I see a thief. The viola had been in my possession for ten years. I played it less and less and then not at all. I had failed at the conservatoire. I desired to serve Mahler. I needed funds. I took it to the dealer only to have it valued and I left the dealer with a huge sum of money.

Is there not a voice somewhere that will say, 'He did not take the cash for himself. He gave half of it to the man he was leaving and now uses the other half to support himself while serving Mahler?' The only voice I hear tells me there are no mitigating circumstances. Dear Mother, I am sorry.

Mahler needs me. His wife does not look after him and he is unable to look after himself. When he went out with the orchestra for a Christmas drink, I did not go with him. It snowed. He got lost and spent several hours wandering the streets of New York in a blizzard before finding his way back to the hotel. That is what happens if I don't keep a careful watch.

Last night I went out with Anna Mahler, who is four, and her nanny, Miss Lizzie Turner, who is Scottish, and we ate frankfurters for Christmas dinner. We had a splendid evening and exchanged gifts. I gave Miss Turner a scarf and Miss Anna a cuddly toy. Miss Turner gave me a dictionary which she signed 'From your friend,' and Miss Anna made a small sculpture of me driving her father's car. She is a special little girl.

I know my letter will disappoint you. I am writing because I want to reach out to you and to try and make things right between us. I will be staying in New York until April 10th.

Your son, Guillaume.

The Savoy Hotel
59th Street
New York

December 25th

Dear Johnny,

I am writing to share Christmas day with you. I will not trouble you because I do not know where you are and so I will not be sending you this letter.

I wonder if you are in Prague and playing lead trumpet with the Czech Philharmonic. I was there in September with Mahler for the premier of his Seventh. I believe there were a few Czech musicians who preferred not to perform and that one of them was the lead trumpeter. It was you, wasn't it? And your absence had more to do with my presence rather than any nationalist sentiments. I think I am responsible for all the bad things that happen around me.

I hope the cash I left was useful. I was astonished to discover how much the viola was worth. We shared everything and I kept it that way right up to the end and left you half. I am not a good person, but I don't think I am irredeemably bad.

I have let you down, and my mother, and the lady who gave me the viola. On the other hand, I serve Mahler. That doesn't balance the scales but perhaps it lifts me just a little off the bottom. I was a poor musician. You knew that. Mahler would never have had me in his orchestra, but he did need me. As long as Mahler remained in Vienna I did not have to make any difficult decisions. I could share my life with you and share my life with Mahler. When he decided to go to America I was thrown into confusion. I was still confused when I returned to Vienna in April last year, went back to our apartment and found that you were gone. How could I possibly have expected to find you there? It was a horrible thing to see other people in our rooms. I felt sick.

I needed to look after Mahler. Before his marriage Mahler's sister, Justi, looked after him. She took care of his meals, looked after his diary, and saw to his small comforts – apples, cigars, and beers. Alma doesn't look after him. She needs him to look after her. She gets depressed and feels sorry for herself. I listen to her, sometimes for hours on end. These are hours that Mahler is able to spend free from worry. Mahler's journey is a solitary one. Alma craves company. She especially enjoys the company of men and does not discourage anyone she fancies from falling in love with her. I am her chaperone. One day it may all end badly and, if it does, Mahler will need me even more.

I never imagined what it would be like to have an intimate relationship until I met you. I miss you. I miss the joy, the touch, the calm, and the gentle peace that we shared. I cannot imagine what it would be like to have a relationship like that with anyone else.

I have made friends with a German dressmaker. Her name is Mechtilde and we hold hands in the street in New York just like you and I used to do in Vienna. We sometimes hug and kiss each other. She likes me and I like her. We make each other laugh. She makes gowns for Alma and they have long fitting sessions together. I am not required to be a chaperone during these sessions. Alma does not think her relationship with Meddi is dangerous. Mahler certainly doesn't worry about it. You might be amused to know that the gossip around the hotel and the opera is not about Meddi and Alma – it's about Meddi and me!

Once there was a man in Central Park who took me to a café, told me that I was a pretty boy and asked me to go to the washroom with him. Another time the receptionist at the Majestic Hotel gave me his room number and asked me to meet him there. How do strangers imagine they can be intimate with one another?

I have two other friends, Anna, and Lizzie. Anna is Mahler's daughter. She's four. Lizzie is her nurse. The three of us went out for Christmas dinner yesterday. We had hotdogs and soda pops and gave each other presents.

I am bad but I am not all bad. My place in this family is important. I am liked and I am needed. I am sorry I let you down. I am writing to you today because it's Christmas Day and I am lonely.

I hope you are not lonely.
Willy.

After Christmas Mahler embarked on a sequence of twenty-five rehearsals for 'Figaro' before performing the opera on January 13th. Mahler considered *The Marriage of Figaro* to be the summit of Mozart's operatic art. He rehearsed with a small orchestra and staged the opera using only the very front of the proscenium. In this way Mahler produced an eighteenth-century opera in a twentieth-century opera house. Mozart is often seen as a concert in costumes. Mahler rehearsed something quite different. He prepared a dramatic theatre work to be performed up front and right under the noses of the Met's audience.

Before Mahler left the hotel for the opening night he knocked on William's door and said, 'My wife.'

Alma was in bed and in distress. She whispered loudly to William, 'Go with Mahler to the opera. Find Mechtilde. Bring her to me! Now!'

William and Mahler went to the Met. William found Meddi and as the curtain went up on *Figaro* the two of them rushed back to the Savoy. Alma wanted only Meddi and told William to go back to the opera.

Mahler was enjoying a huge triumph. The Met's audience fell in love with both Mozart and Mahler. After fifteen curtain calls and a standing ovation Mahler and William returned to the Savoy. Dr Fraenkel was in the room sitting beside Alma who was in bed asleep. All the linen on the bed had been changed. Dr Fraenkel told Mahler that his wife had lost her little burden but that she was fine – very tired, but otherwise well. He had given her something to help her sleep and that she must stay in bed and rest for two or three days.

Meddi was waiting for William in his room. 'She's had a miscarriage. I want you to walk me home.'

The next day William knocked on Mahler's door with a bunch of grapes, a glass of milk, and a hotdog for Alma. Mahler looked at the tray and smiled his thanks. William said he had a message for Alma, pointed to the hotdog, and barked.

CHAPTER 24

A Letter for William

On January 18th William Hildebrand went to collect the Mahlers' post from reception. There was a parcel of books for Gustav, a letter for Alma and a letter for William. William gave everything to Alma. Half an hour later she knocked on his door and gave him back the letter which had been addressed to William and said, 'I don't read French! This must be for you.'

January 6th 1909
Basel

Dear Guillaume,

The letter which you wrote in New York on Christmas Day arrived in Basel today, the Feast of the Epiphany. If my reply takes twelve days to reach you, I want you to know that on January 18th I will be thinking of you as you read and I will be holding your hand.

There have been many times when I have felt sad and disappointed. Reading your Christmas letter was not one of them. The birthday cards and Christmas cards you have sent me over the years reminded me of notes I received from your father when he left us just after you were born. He hoped we were both well and told me things I didn't want to know. Your greetings sounded just like his and I could not reply to you. I felt that I had lost you just as I had lost him. But your father could never have written a letter like the one I received from you today.

Failure at the conservatoire and failure with your relationship cannot be offered as evidence for the absence of a soul. As an animal hibernates to survive the winter so your soul may have gone to sleep to recover from its injuries. I can see that you are anxious to blame yourself for all that goes on around you and it may be that your injuries are self-inflicted. I don't know. I do know that you have a cheerful and generous soul. You want to be liked? So do I. Accept the love you are given and allow it to awaken the love in your own soul. The gift of love from others will heal your unhappiness. But you already know that. You wrote about it in the last lines of your letter when you described the gifts from the little girl and her nurse. They have not befriended a man with no soul. Don't get in a panic looking for your soul. Let the love of others awaken it gently. This is a love letter from your mama and I am holding your hand as you read.

Thank you for telling me about the viola. Here is another story about that viola. The last time you came to visit us, I think it was Christmas seven years ago, Madame Gerard was pleased to see you and touched that you should bring the viola with you. She was impressed with your good manners. She never wanted you to return it. She always wanted you to have it. It was shortly after your last visit when I first saw signs of Madame Gerard's illness. She had difficulty remembering things. I told Madame Gerard that she should make a will and I helped her to write it. She left everything to her family except for the viola which she left to you. If you had come back to see her again she would not have recognised you. Her family rarely visited. It was Félicité and I who looked after her. We fed and cleaned her when she was no longer Madame Gerard. We loved her and cared for her because of who she once was, and we were relieved when she died. Her sons have complained to the lawyer about the viola. The lawyer has told them there is nothing he can do about it. When they complained to me, I told them there is nothing I can do about it. Her sons have called me a thief. Do not be as harsh on yourself as Madame Gerard's sons are with me.

I hold you in my arms, Guillaume. Here's a suggestion. Earn your own living and don't depend on the funds you raised with the viola which will inevitably run out. There are magazines that would be interested in articles about musical life in America. You are well placed to write about this and if you feel inclined to send me something Félicité will bring it to the attention of an editor.

Trust your little sculptress, trust her nurse, and trust your mother,

Madeleine Hildebrand

CHAPTER 25

La Semaine Littéraire

'War has been declared between the two opera houses and two symphony orchestras in New York. There are not enough musicians or audiences to sustain the four institutions who are now fighting over scarce resources. There will be winners and there will be losers. If Mahler thought that he might enjoy a quiet life in New York after his difficulties in Vienna he was mistaken.'

'Let us begin with the opera house. Last year Mahler conducted a successful season at the Met but this year he finds that his honeymoon is over. A new manager hired Arturo Toscanini to share the conductor's responsibilities. Mahler assumed the Italian would conduct the Italian repertoire, but Toscanini proposed to open with *Tristan und Isolde*. Mahler refused and prevailed. Fortunately, these issues are no longer settled with pistols at dawn, but Toscanini seeks revenge. Mahler may have had his *Tristan* but Toscanini has taken almost everything else. During this season Mahler will conduct only *The Marriage of Figaro* and *The Bartered Bride* while Toscanini conducts his way through the French, Italian and German repertoire, fulfilling far more than his contract requires. Mahler is content to let Toscanini work twice as hard for his salary while he works less. Toscanini conducts the quantity. Mahler conducts the quality. His Mozart and Smetana are meticulously rehearsed.'

'So, the Met's a winner? No!'

'The winner is the Manhattan Opera which Oscar Hammerstein has opened to compete with the Met. The Met has star conductors, the Manhattan has star singers, and it is the singers Americans want to hear. The Met is rarely full when Toscanini and Mahler are conducting while audiences fill the Manhattan to hear Luisa Tetrazzini, Nellie Melba and Mary Garden. Mary Garden is a sensation. Her dance of the seven veils in Strauss's *Salome* ends in complete nudity – something which has never been seen before in an American opera house. Her performance has been called 'degenerate' and the production runs and runs. Every night there are queues of eager young men with a new-found interest in opera hoping to hear her sing. Strauss receives five hundred dollars in royalties for every performance. The Met cannot compete with this. The two opera houses programme aggressively against one another and the nadir was reached when the two houses performed *Aida* on the same night. When news filtered through to the mischievous Manhattan that the Met's *Aida* was almost empty the cast of the Manhattan production performed a jig on the stage that was not in Verdi's score. When the Met performs in Philadelphia so does the Manhattan. When the Met performs in Brooklyn so does the Manhattan. They are trying to kill each other. Their rivalry is truly operatic.'

'Mahler may not return to the opera battleground if he accepts an offer to conduct the New York Philharmonic Orchestra in a season of concerts next year but may discover that he has leapt from the frying pan to the fire. Conducting the Philharmonic will be a hazardous enterprise because there already exists the New York Symphony Orchestra, funded by wealthy and important New Yorkers and managed by the popular Damrosch brothers. This orchestra is not very good. Mahler has conducted them in three concerts, Schumann's First, his own Second and Beethoven's Fifth. The third of these concerts was supposed to be Beethoven's Seventh but Mahler changed the programme because he did not think the orchestra was good enough to play it. Given their limitations, the New York Symphony performed reasonably well under Mahler's instruction. None of the three concerts was more than half full, not even Mahler's Second, which had the potential to be as big an occasion as the night Tchaikovsky conducted his own Sixth at the opening of Carnegie Hall. Why were the concerts undersold? The Damrosch brothers are masters at papering Carnegie Hall when tickets are selling slowly so why did they leave Mahler's concerts so poorly attended? Had word reached the Damrosch brothers that Mahler was being offered the Philharmonic? Was the New York Symphony sending a message to the Philharmonic to let them know they had made a mistake hiring Mahler?'

'If Mahler takes the Philharmonic, how will he manage to recruit musicians of sufficient calibre to perform his programmes with three other orchestras in town? If Mahler thinks he can import musicians from Europe, he must think again. To join the New York Union a musician must be resident in the city for six months. This not only forbids European musicians from taking jobs in New York, it also prohibits Americans from elsewhere in the United States. European orchestras do not operate such restrictive practices. But let me stir a deeper dye. The Philharmonic Society is a co-operative which chooses

its own conductor and its own programmes. The committee of wealthy ladies who administer the orchestra is attempting to rewrite the Philharmonic's constitution, imposing a conductor on the orchestra who will tell them what to play. We await the result of these negotiations and so does Mahler.
Avi Bacharach
New York'

A week after this article appeared in Switzerland the Austrian *Neue Freie Press* paid the magazine twenty-five crowns for permission to reprint it in Vienna. The Viennese newspaper commissioned a translation and did not credit Avi Bacharach. They guessed, correctly, it was a pen name. They did not want to spoil the impact of the piece by associating it with a Jew and so credited the story instead to 'Our special correspondent in New York.' Two weeks later the article was reprinted in English 'By kind permission' in the *New York Tribune* which had neither asked for, nor been given, permission.

Toscanini was furious to find himself described as a conductor of 'quantity' rather than 'quality.' Oscar Hammerstein was delighted to read that the Manhattan was a clear winner. The New York Union was dismayed to read that their musicians were so unfavourably compared to their Viennese cousins and the committee of ladies involved in talks with both the Philharmonic Society and the Union were frustrated to see their delicate negotiations treated so indelicately. The musicians at the New York Symphony were displeased to read such low opinions of their musicianship and Damrosch urged Mahler to write a letter to the New York Tribune offering a different and higher opinion of the Symphony Orchestra. Mahler told Damrosch that he did not think it was a good idea to reply to bad publicity because it only ever led to more bad publicity. Mahler himself did not read the article.

Basel
February 19th 1909

Dear Guillaume,

The editor of La Semaine Littéraire liked the piece. The magazine paid fifty crowns and published it in the last issue. I have just heard that the Neue Freie Press in Vienna has paid a further twenty-five crowns to reprint. Will you write another piece? Readers like celebrities so you should only write about famous people. That way you will hold their attention. For your own safety I have given you a pen name, Avi Bacharach.

With love,
Mama

Professor Schiller, Meddi's English teacher, had been asked by the *New York Tribune* for a translation of the German article in the Vienna *Neue Freie Press* from 'Our special correspondent in New York' and the professor used the article in his lesson as a translation exercise for the amusement of his students. Meddi showed the article to William who did his best to read it as if he had never seen it before. Meddi wondered who in New York could possibly have written it, rubbed her nose against William's, and kissed his eyelashes with hers. It tickled.

CHAPTER 26

La Semaine Littéraire (2)

'Mahler introduced *The Bartered Bride* to New York in a new production at the Met. It was wonderful to hear and beautiful to see thanks to the Czech dancers brought in from Europe. One notable absentee from the premiere was Mrs. Astor who died a few weeks before the opening night. The question on everybody's lips was, 'Who would replace her as Queen of the Met?' It soon emerged that Mrs. Cornelius Vanderbilt the Third had all the qualities that were required to take possession of the vacant throne and at the opening of *The Bartered Bride* all eyes in the auditorium turned to see her enter her box at the centre of the diamond horseshoe, resplendent in one of her celebrated turbans. Below her, Mahler took his place among the musicians and Alma took her seat in the director's box. Mrs. Vanderbilt and Mahler were both surprised when a loud wolf whistle echoed around the auditorium. Alma, wearing a hat and stole of fur made from the front part of a white wolf, its forelegs hanging over her breasts and its ears standing alert on the top of her head, ignored the whistle and sat down. All eyes in the auditorium followed Mrs. Vanderbilt's furious stare towards the conductor's wife and a chorus of wolf whistles broke out. Mahler knew of Mrs. Vanderbilt's presence and had been advised that it would do no harm if he turned to her box to acknowledge her. When Mahler, who may not have understood the meaning of the whistling, turned to Mrs. Vanderbilt and bowed deferentially he associated himself in the eyes of many with his wife's unusual headdress. Mahler may not be associated with the Met for very much longer.'

'Mahler has signed a contract with the Philharmonic Society in New York to conduct a series of forty-six concerts in the 1910 season for which he will be paid a fee of $25,000. Before he finishes this season Mahler will conduct two try-out concerts with his new orchestra and so bring to an end their 67-year history as a co-operative society of professional musicians, democratically deciding who their conductor will be, what music they will play, where they will play it and how much they will charge the audience for the privilege of hearing it. On March 31st when Mahler mounts the podium to conduct Beethoven's Seventh the orchestra will be transformed into a band of musicians hired by committee of wealthy ladies. The choice of Beethoven's Seventh may strike readers as controversial when they remember this is a work Mahler felt the New York Symphony Orchestra was not fit to perform.'

'Marcella Sembrech made her official farewell to the Met at a Gala performance on February 6th which was also the twenty-fifth anniversary of her Met debut. Admirers fought in the streets for tickets which changed hands at enormous prices. The programme comprised three acts from three operas with which she had been closely identified – *Don Pasquale* with Scotti, *Il Barbiere di Siviglia* with Bonci and Campanari, and *La Traviata* with Caruso. The evening concluded with Mahler conducting her in the third act of *Figaro*. The entire auditorium thundered with applause and groups of children emptied baskets of roses at her feet. Later that week Mahler and Alma attended the ball hosted by Sembrech and her husband in The Savoy Hotel's ballroom. New York's high society was represented by J.P. Morgan and his daughter, and there was a sprinkling of Vanderbilts, Alexanders, Harrimans, Drexels and Twomblys. The Metropolitan Opera was there in force, and a long-standing friend of Sembrech, the Polish pianist, Jan Paderewski, came from Europe especially for the occasion. Caruso spent the evening pursuing his favourite pastime – drawing caricatures which he showed to everyone except the victim. Caruso told me, 'People often say beforehand that they won't mind but when they see my drawings, they are usually angry.'

'Enrico Caruso has made a brief appearance in a New York court charged with making an obscene gesture towards a chimpanzee in the monkey house of New York Zoo. The lady who complained to the police refused to describe Caruso's lewd behaviour and did not attend the hearing. Caruso told the judge that after observing the chimpanzee for a few minutes he had decided to join his fellow primate in an act of solidarity that was compassionate and no business of the lady who complained. The judge, who adored Caruso's singing, told the accused that he would be able to close the case if Caruso agreed to pay a fine of $10. Caruso offered to pay half if the chimpanzee agreed to pay the other half. A far higher sum of money was bound over by the Met to keep the story out of the newspapers. Nobody thought to give anything to your incorruptible correspondent in New York.' Avi Bacharach

The article 'from our special correspondent in New York,' was reprinted by the *Neue Freie Press* in Vienna on March 13th. When it was reprinted 'By kind permission' in the *New York Tribune* on March 31st

Bruno Zirato, a burly Neapolitan who was Caruso's manager, marched into the newspaper offices with a loaded gun looking for Avi Bacharach but as the newspaper had pirated the copy from the *Neue Freie Press* there was nothing they could do to satisfy the angry Neapolitan or endanger Mr Bacharach, whoever he was. The newspaper was happy to report an increase in its circulation. There was also a rise in the numbers visiting New York Zoo. An enterprising keeper left a collecting tin with a note from the chimpanzee asking for '$5 to help me pay my fine' and raised over $1000. Caruso's entire run of performances quickly sold out. His first stage entrance at the Met was greeted with monkey noises from one section of the auditorium. At the end of the performance Caruso took several curtain calls and was presented with a hand of bananas.'

CHAPTER 27

Voyage Home

After conducting his two try-out concerts with the New York Philharmonic Orchestra Mahler knew which musicians could be retained and which had to be let go. He left the committee of wealthy ladies to get on with the job of hiring and firing. The committee gave Mahler a budget to purchase a set of modern timpani that could be tuned with a pedal, and to have them shipped from Vienna to New York. The New York Union gave Mahler special dispensation to bring in four musicians from Europe – a concertmaster, a timpanist, principal flute, and principal trombone. Mahler left for Europe satisfied with his second American season and looking forward to his third.

Mahler arrived in Paris on April 19th. He sat for the sculptor, Rodin. The bust of Mahler's head had been commissioned by Alma's mother, but Mahler was told that it was Rodin himself who had asked to make the sculpture and so Mahler believed he was sitting at the sculptor's invitation. Mahler spoke no French and Rodin spoke no German. William, who spoke both, knew about the subterfuge and was sworn to secrecy. Miss Turner came with Miss Anna to the first session. She was keen to let the child show Rodin her papier-maché models. The four-year-old sculptress was excited about meeting the world-famous sculptor. Miss Turner, dismayed to discover the number of young women Rodin kept in his establishment, told Anna they were his 'models' and they left Rodin's studio to go sightseeing without meeting him.

Mahler sat for Rodin over twelve days and William sat with them to interpret. When the sculptor asked the composer to kneel there was a misunderstanding but William was able to assure Mahler that Rodin only needed to examine the top of his head.

Mahler's music had never been performed in France. The poster advertising his First Symphony, which was to be performed in Paris and conducted by a French conductor, misspelled the composer's name as 'Malheur' - an unhappy mistake. Mahler decided to forego an evening of French antipathy towards all things German and left Paris before the concert.

In Vienna he started preparing his next American season. He found and hired the timpanist. Then the percussionist and conductor went together to the factory to get a set of pedal-tuned timpani custom-built to the timpanist's own specifications. Mahler also got the flautist, the trombonist, and the concert master he needed and was delighted to discover his new concert master was born in New York. This musician had not lived in New York for forty years, but Mahler considered that to be a trifling matter. Convinced that his concert master's place of birth more than satisfied the union's six-month registration requirement Mahler considered himself free to find a fifth musician to add to the four he had been given permission to recruit. He wanted the young trumpet player. The one who used to play at the Hofoper. Mahler sent William to the Opera House to find him. 'You know who I mean,' said Mahler.

William walked the streets of Vienna listening to the music that emerged from the windows. He knew what he was listening for and he knew he would never find it in Vienna. No one made a sound that came close to the one that once filled William's heart. He hadn't heard Johnny Stanko play for nearly two years. He suspected if he went to Prague he would find him there.

Alma was depressed. She missed America. She was not happy to be back in Vienna. Her husband visited his old friends, but no one paid any attention to her. Her doctor thought she should take a cure at Levico in the Italian Tyrol on the sunny side of the Alps. William drove Alma and Mahler there. Alma was accompanied by Anna and Miss Turner. Once Mahler had got Alma settled into the hotel William went with Mahler by train to Toblach where they were met at the station by the horse with no name. For Mahler's comfort and safety, William sat up top in the driver's seat holding the reins lightly as the horse made its way back up the hill to Altschluderbach.

While Alma, Anna, and Miss Turner lived under the sun on the south facing alpine slopes, Mahler, William, and the cook, Agnes, lived in the shadows on the Austrian side of the Tyrol where it hardly felt like summer. It was too cold for Mahler to use his composing hut and he tried to work in Trenkerhof where he moved from room to room looking for a warm corner where he could work on his Ninth Symphony. The house was overwhelmed by the pungent smell of the cheese that Herr Trenker made and kept in the cellar. Agnes, the cook, made the mistake bringing one of Trenker's cheeses into the house, increasing Mahler's discomfort, and then compounded her error by presenting

Mahler with a cheese omelette. Mahler loved humanity but was not very good with people. He turned up his nose, left the table and Agnes burst into tears. William comforted her. He knew what Mahler liked to eat and he suggested they go shopping together and offered to drive the horse and cart first thing in the morning to the store in Toblach. He helped her to plan menus for the rest of the week.

Mahler sat in his bedroom sitting next to the stove reading a book. William brought him an opened bottle of beer, a glass, a pack of cigars, an ashtray, and a box of matches. In the morning he took him a pot of coffee and three softly boiled eggs with bread and butter. Then he drove Agnes into Toblach. William knew how to go to the station but he didn't know how to drive the horse and cart to the store. The horse didn't stop at the store but went on to the station. William and Agnes walked back to the store. They bought chickens, eggs, rice, spaghetti, sausages, hams, butter, flour, vegetables, herbs and spices, cases of beer and wine, boxes of cigars, pastries, chocolates, apples, more apples, and no cheese. William put it all on Mahler's account. The shopkeeper helped Agnes and William carry everything down to the station and the horse took them back to Altschluderbach. Agnes showed William how to pluck a chicken and to remove the stubble over a candleflame, tear the carcass into small pieces, cover it with water and to boil it with some chopped celery and salt. She strained the soup, broke the spaghetti into small pieces and put the spaghetti shards into the clear broth. She showed William how to separate the yolks from three eggs and beat them with a fork. Just before the soup was served she tossed the eggs into the broth and stirred it once. Mahler ate his soup in silence with two slices of bread and an apple then left the table with four more apples in his pockets to go back to work.

William went to see Herr Trenker and asked him if the horse only went to the station or was it possible to take the wagon to the store. Herr Trenker said 'Yes.' William asked him if it was difficult. Herr Trenker said, 'No.' William asked Herr Trenker if he would tell him how to do it. Herr Trenker said, 'Yes. Before you set off give him a lump of sugar and say you want to go to the store.'

Agnes spent the afternoon boiling ham and showed William how to make a chicken and ham pie which she served with cabbage for Mahler's supper. She gave William a pan with hot water and cloves to leave overnight on the stove in Mahler's bedroom to drive away the smell of the Trenkers' cheese.

Every evening Mahler wrote to his wife and every morning William went to the post office with the letter. Before setting off he gave the horse a lump of sugar and said he wanted to go to the post office. William was delighted that his driving horizons were broadened and felt confident the horse would take him wherever he wanted to go. Most days William returned from the post office with mail for Mahler but rarely was there anything from his wife. Mahler enjoyed lunches of bohnen eintopf speck and kartoffelstock. He was especially fond of leberlet mit rösti. He drank beer and ate chocolates as he wrote to Alma before going to bed. Mahler made quick progress with his Ninth before Alma arrived. William warmed a room in the house for her and Mahler had a haircut. The barber in Toblach was not a competent hairdresser and Mahler's short hair stuck out in tufts. Alma was appalled by his appearance – not just the haircut but his belly too. Her husband's figure, once trim, now sagged in the middle. She thought he looked like 'a scruffy old Jew'. After he had written about his row with the cook, and how he would never allow another morsel from her kitchen to pass his lips, she had expected that he might have lost weight rather than put it on. She was surprised to find the smell of cheese had been driven out of the house by the smell of cloves. Alma resumed her role in the household as 'Minister of Foreign Affairs' and took responsibility for their social lives. Her mother came to help her.

Richard and Pauline Strauss on a motoring holiday with several friends were Alma's first visitors. The Strauss party had booked rooms in the Grand Hotel in Toblach. William gave the horse a lump of sugar, said he wanted to go to the Grand Hotel, and drove Alma, her mother, and Mahler there to meet Strauss for dinner. Strauss, standing outside the hotel called out across the square as the wagon approached, 'Hallo Mahler. How was America? Did you make a lot of money?' Strauss's friends, who didn't know Mahler's family, assumed Alma's mother to be Mahler's wife. At the dinner table Strauss tried to sit everybody down and as Mahler was about to take his place beside Pauline she said, 'Only if you don't fidget.' Mahler decided not to sit there and found a seat at the other end of the table beside Strauss, leaving Alma and her mother to deal with Pauline. At the other end of the table Strauss talked about his new opera *Der Rosenkavalier*.

Back at the house William chopped wood to feed the stoves and warm the house. Friends came and went but they never managed to warm the atmosphere. Mahler went to his composing hut every morning and worked on his symphony wearing a cap and a scarf. At the end of August they all left Trenkerhof before the weather got any worse. William drove to the station. Alma and Anna went to hospital to have their tonsils scraped. William and Mahler got the train for Vienna. The horse with no name went back to Trenkerhof by itself.

Mahler told William that he did not wish to freeze in the Alps again. He wanted a summer house in the countryside in a warm neighbourhood with no mountains. William added house-hunting to his lengthening list of responsibilities.

Back in Vienna Mahler was delighted to discover that the chicken soup William prepared in the kitchen in Auenbruggerstrasse tasted almost as good as the soup Agnes made in Altschluderbach. Bruno Walter came to visit. The two conductors studied the manuscript of *Das Lied von der Erde*. Mahler told Walter he did not see how anyone could possibly conduct it and entrusted its performance to his friend.

During these September days when her husband was in Vienna Alma was in a hospital with her daughter where they were both undergoing uncomfortable procedures on their tonsils. Mahler wrote to his wife everyday but rarely got a reply. Lizzie spent her daytimes in the hospital with Anna. Alma spent her time in hospital alone. Mahler left for Holland to conduct his Seventh Symphony in Den Haag. He continued his correspondence from the Netherlands writing to Alma every day before eventually meeting up with his wife in Paris where he had three more sessions with Rodin before the couple, with Anna, Miss Turner and William boarded the *Kaiserwilhelm* in Cherbourg to return to New York. Mahler and Alma had spent most of their six months in Europe living apart. He had written to her every day. He had also written his ninth symphony, prepared forty-six concerts for his forthcoming New York Philharmonic season, hired five musicians for his new American orchestra, opened negotiations with an impresario regarding the premier of his Eighth Symphony in Munich, and had discussed with Bruno Walter how to conduct *Das Lied von der Erde*.

William never wondered what Mahler was thinking about because he always knew. He never knew what Alma was thinking about. Neither did Mahler.

CHAPTER 28

A Séance in New York

The Mahlers checked into the Savoy Hotel where Alma found in her bedroom a manikin wearing a beautiful gown and a note, 'To Frau Mahler for the opening concert of the New York Philharmonic season.'

Meddi's English was now so good Alma suggested she come to the hotel to teach William. She came to the Savoy twice a week and after William's lesson she took tea with Alma while Mahler was rehearsing his orchestra. William fetched and carried for Alma, fetched and carried for Mahler, and chaperoned Miss Turner and Anna. In the evening Miss Turner read Anna a bedtime story in English and William provided a rough German translation. When William read Anna a story in German Anna provided Miss Turner with a rough English translation. Anna's English was better than William's.

On Christmas Eve Alma and Mahler went to the Kreuzers for Christmas dinner. William, Anna, and Miss Turner went out for hotdogs and then returned to the hotel to exchange gifts. Miss Turner gave William a copy of Mr. Robert Louis Stevenson's *A Child's Garden of Verses* in which she wrote 'For William and Anna, with love, Elizabeth.' William gave Miss Turner a woollen knitted hat with earflaps to protect her from the New York winter, and for Anna a painting box of water colours, a set of brushes, and a pad of cartridge paper. Anna gave William a big kiss and a small sculpture of his head in plasticene. She had made four of them – Mama, Papa, Miss Turner, and William. William kept it carefully beside the papier-mâché sculpture she had given him the previous year.

December 25th 1909
Savoy Hotel, New York

Dear Johnny,

I am writing to you care of the Prague Philharmonic in the hope that I might find you there. I have a message for you from Herr Mahler. He has an American orchestra and hopes to achieve the high standards he achieved in Vienna. He wants you to lead the trumpet section and hopes that you will consider the position. I am writing to you not with any hope of turning the clock back for you and me but only with hope that you may turn the clock forward for yourself. It's a great orchestra. You'd love it.

William

On New Year's Eve the Mahlers went to the Fraenkels for dinner. Alma wore the necklace of tiny golden tubular bells which Mahler had given her for Christmas. He wore the bowtie she had given him. William and Meddi went too. Mahler particularly enjoyed Dr Fraenkel's conversation. He was an eminent neuroscientist and engaged Mahler's interest with talk of the latest developments in natural science. Dr Fraenkel was also interested in telepathy and the paranormal. He had organised an unusual after-dinner entertainment and booked a séance with Madam Eusapia Palladino, a celebrated Italian medium. Frau Fraenkel had no time for 'such nonsense' and she stayed at home. The other five drove to Madame Palladino's in Dr. Fraenkel's car. They were all sceptical about the paranormal and Dr Fraenkel agreed that there was strong evidence of fraudulence among the spiritualist community and, if they looked carefully, he was sure they would observe something of Madame Palladino's sleight of hand. He also surmised that the medium's box of tricks might be the ordinary means of making the extraordinary possible. 'Whatever happens,' he told them, 'it won't be dull.'

Madame Palladino's assistants showed them into a room dimly lit by flickering candlelight. They were invited to look behind the curtain and inspect the empty alcove, the closed windows, and to look under the table where they were to sit. There were musical instruments and clocks on the wall, a painting of a lakeside view, a grandfather clock in one corner, and a cello in another.

Madame Palladino, a small round woman with long black hair, entered the room wearing a red gown that trailed on the floor and a necklace of pearls that hung to her waist. She sat between Mahler and Alma. She took Mahler's right hand and Alma's left hand and asked the rest of the party to join hands. Madame Palladino stared at Mahler and said, 'You frighten me.' She turned his hand, looked at his palm and shook her head. They all stared at the table, holding hands, and waited. Madame Palladino coughed. She coughed again and then was seized by a fit of coughing. Her cough became harsher and deeper and then stopped suddenly as the table jerked upwards. Holding hands, everyone could feel the unsteadiness of the raised table as if it was repelled from the floor by some magnetic force. The curtains in front of the closed windows and in front of the alcove flapped and the temperature in the room dropped sharply. The instruments on the walls, a mandolin, a trumpet, and a guitar, made a noise as if they were being scraped and crushed. Something William heard in the harmonics that floated above the screech disturbed him and, in the candlelight, the violin's bow flew towards the wall, stabbed the painting of the lake, and dropped to the floor. The clocks chimed and kept on chiming past twelve until the grandfather clock toppled over and crashed to the floor. Time stopped, and all was silent as tiny particles of white dropped from the ceiling onto the floating table and disappeared. Madame Palladino's eyeballs turned backwards, leaving only the whites staring blindly as a deep bass voice issued from her mouth, 'Mama said I had to go and that Papa has to go too!' The table dropped back to the floor and the candles went out. They sat in darkness until the secretaries returned and switched on the lights. Madame Palladino's chair was empty. William had fainted. One of the secretaries went to fetch a glass of water for him. The other went to pick up the grandfather clock. Meddi went to help and was warned sharply not to touch. Mahler gazed at the torn canvas of the lakeside. When William regained consciousness Alma and Meddi took an arm each and helped him down the stairs and into the car.

William wanted to go straight to his room but Dr Fraenkel thought it wiser if they stayed together in the lounge for a few minutes to share their experience. He ordered a glass of milk and a biscuit for William. Alma said that Madame Palladino's performance was like a night at the circus and Dr Fraenkel agreed that she was a very skilful magician. Mahler was fascinated by the wobbly table, the flapping curtains, and the drop in temperature. He thought it was magical but found the sound of the broken instruments disturbing. He wondered if they might all have been hypnotised, and, if so, Madame Palladino was very good at it. Meddi did not speak. Neither did William. If Alma really believed she had spent a night at the circus and if Mahler really did not know why the broken instruments disturbed him then William was not prepared to share his own experience with them. He got up to leave the lounge and go to his room. Dr Fraenkel insisted on accompanying him. William didn't tell Dr Fraenkel that the lakeside painting reminded him of the Worthersee or that the sound of the broken instruments suggested *Kindertotenlieder* because he wasn't sure if it was true. Dr Fraenkel said, 'It was not Madame Palladino who spoke, was it? Do you know who spoke?'

William said, 'Yes. It was Mahler's daughter, Maria.'

CHAPTER 29

La Semaine Littéraire (3)

'War has broken out in New York between Gustav Mahler, conductor of the New York Philharmonic Orchestra, and Henry Krehbiel, chief music critic of the New York Tribune.

'Gustav Mahler opened his Philharmonic season on November 4th with Beethoven's Third Symphony. The conductor included in the performance a part for an E flat clarinet which is not in Beethoven's score. Whereas Mahler's retouching of Beethoven caused outrage in Vienna it has passed unnoticed in New York. This may be attributed to fine performances enjoyed by New York audiences and favourable reviews by critics who admire Mahler's interpretation and are not inclined to go looking into details of instrumentation. Henry Krehbiel's reviews were not enthusiastic, but his disapproval had nothing to do with Mahler's instrumentation because this New York Tribune critic cannot read music. How Mr. Krehbiel has risen to a position of such critical eminence given this significant limitation is one of the minor mysteries of the New York musical scene. Mahler has programmed a complete cycle of Beethoven symphonies and over the first month Mr. Krehbiel has told the Tribune's readers that the performances are too fast, too slow, too loud, or too quiet. It is unlikely that Mahler could ever find a tempo or dynamic to suit Mr. Krehbiel because this critic is a close ally of Mr. Damrosch and his New York Symphony Orchestra. He writes their programme notes, makes programming suggestions, writes promotional articles advertising their concerts and favourably reviews them in his newspaper, so earning for himself an elevated status within the musical scene in New York and the warm gratitude of Damrosch and his Symphony Orchestra. The Philharmonic's arrival is viewed by the Symphony Orchestra as hostile competition. Krehbiel shares that view and his relationship with the Philharmonic is as cool as his relationship with the Symphony is warm. You might take a dim view of a critic who cannot read music and who sits comfortably in the pocket of a rival orchestra, but Mahler doesn't, because Mahler doesn't read the reviews.

'For a month or more the New York Tribune published Krehbiel's faint praise of Mahler's Philharmonic concerts but then relations between Krehbiel and the Philharmonic sharply deteriorated when Mahler performed his own First Symphony. Krehbiel asked Mahler for the Symphony's programme so that he could write notes to aid the audience's appreciation of the music. Mahler refused. Krehbiel felt slighted.

'Mahler had provided programmes for his early symphonies. He even named the first symphony 'Titan'. His second was called the 'Resurrection' Symphony. Each movement of his Third had its own title – what the mountains tell me, what the flowers tell me, what the animals of the forest tell me, and so on. If you had asked the young Mahler to tell you what his music was all about he might have attempted an answer. But from his Fourth Symphony onwards Mahler did away with programmes and provided the audience with no information. He declared that his music was about nothing other than itself. He did not want to give the audience a story to help them to hear it. He took the view that programmes could only get in the way of the music. Mahler now permits nothing to intrude between the performance and the listener and refused Krehbield's request for a programme

'Mr. Krehbiel, in bad humour, produced notes which declared:

"In deference to the wish of Mr. Mahler this programme refrains from even an outline analysis of the symphony which he is performing for the first time in New York. This programme also refrains from any attempt to suggest what might be its possible poetical, dramatical, or emotional contents." Mr. Krehbiel went on refraining until the closing sentence, which correctly attributed to Mahler the view that 'all writing about music is injurious to musical enjoyment.'

'Having been robbed of one of his toys, Mr. Krehbiel sulked. But Mahler took more away from Krehbiel than a toy – he took away Krehbiel's crutch. The New York Tribune's critic, unlike many who write about or listen to music, has never played a musical instrument, never attended a conservatoire and never studied music, so when he enters an auditorium he needs help to listen because he cannot help himself. His study of law and his experience of journalism have not equipped him to listen to music. He needs someone to tell him what it is about, and he aspires to be that very person. The Tribune's critic considers himself to be the high priest of music in New York. According to Krehbiel, Mahler's refusal to defer to his request for programme notes left the critic without a role, and the audience without a clue. Without a programme neither critic nor audience could approach 'the muddle' of his First Symphony.

'Krehbiel wrote a damning review of the symphony which he described as 'disjointed and incoherent' and then he proposed a solution. He suggested that Mahler should permit the critics to attend dress rehearsals so that they could give him better criticism after hearing both the rehearsal and the performance. Mahler replied to Krehbiel and told him he could not criticise his music no matter how many times he heard it.

'Krehbiel, who had never written a word about Mahler's retouching of Beethoven scores, now went in search of information that might damage Mahler. Looking for revenge he ingratiated himself with Philharmonic musicians, some of whom were chafing under Mahler's strict discipline, and Krehbiel encouraged them to gossip. He gathered information about how Mahler doubled bassoons with cellos, how he transposed the piccolo an octave higher, and so on – retouchings of Beethoven that Krehbiel could never have heard for himself because he does not have sufficiently good ears. The committee of ladies whose wealth supports the Philharmonic orchestra might wish that Mahler was more diplomatic in his dealings with the press. One of these wealthy ladies did approach Mahler and asked him if Krehbiel might not be right to complain about changes to a composer's work. Mahler informed the lady that he respected the composer but his first duty was to the composition which he would perform as he believed the composer would perform it if the composer were to conduct it himself. Mahler has told me of his hope that conductors in the future would respect his own compositions in the same manner.

'We look forward to hearing Mahler's first concert of 1910 – Berlioz's 'Symphonie Fantastique' which promises to be a wonderfully graphic, vivid, and powerful reading of the score.'

Avi Bacharach

This article, published in the *La Semaine Littéraire*, and which also appeared in the *Neue Freie Press* in Vienna, was not reprinted by the *New York Tribune*. After consulting their lawyers, the *New York Evening Post* published it.

CHAPTER 30

Another Chinese Restaurant

Alma received a letter from one of her admirers, the young conductor, Ossip Gabrilowitsch, telling her about his forthcoming marriage. This letter put Alma in a bad mood which she dealt with by seeing Meddi on three consecutive days and by organising an outing for herself, her husband, William and Meddi to a Chinese restaurant on Canal Street.

They found a busy restaurant and were given a table before they noticed that all the other customers in the restaurant were women. The menu was in Chinese. No one spoke English. William and Meddi walked around the tables pointing out to their waiter dishes that the women were eating. Twenty minutes later these same dishes were brought to Mahler's table. A huge bowl of broth was placed in the centre of the table on top of a burner on a dumb waiter with smaller dishes all around with morsels to be picked up and cooked in the soup. A helpful waiter replaced their chopsticks with forks and the cheerful foursome cooked and ate. Meddi thought that the men had likely been served their meal earlier in the day and now it was the turn of the ladies. Women at an adjacent table quarrelled over the bill. One woman who wanted to pay was slapped down by another who insisted on paying, only to be bested by a third who was outdone by a fourth as tempers rose. There was some pushing and shoving. A chair went over, tipping an angry lady onto the floor. A manager arrived on the scene and said something to the satisfaction of all and the quarrel ended as abruptly as it had started.

As he ate Mahler talked about his difficulty with the committee of wealthy ladies who financed his orchestra. They had asked for an interval during the concerts. Mahler had declined but the ladies insisted. The matter was not yet resolved. Mahler felt that his concert programmes were carefully chosen to make best use of an audience's capacity to concentrate and that these programmes never included an interval which would only serve to break their concentration. Alma thought an interval would allow the audience the opportunity to discuss the first half and anticipate the second half. Mahler felt he had not been hired to run a social club but to raise the standards of orchestral performance and audience appreciation. Meddi thought most people went to concerts to be seen and that an interval would best serve their purposes. William agreed with everyone.

When the Mahlers finished their meal, they were invited by the restaurant manager to follow him upstairs where they were taken into a large dormitory where customers lay on bunks drowsy with opium. It appeared to the Mahlers that their Chinese hosts might be showing off their facilities or they may possibly have been inviting the Mahlers to join in. The Mahlers backed off, settled their bill and emerged onto Canal Street where Mahler declared that soup with quarrelling ladies beneath an opium den was superior to spareribs with Beethoven's Moonlight Sonata, but not by a lot. They stopped at an Italian café and ate ice cream before taking a taxi back to the Savoy.

CHAPTER 31

La Semaine Littéraire (4)

'There are rumours in New York that Mahler will not return to America at the end of the present season. Although the orchestra plays well, the concerts are poorly attended and the committee of wealthy ladies have presented Mahler with proposals to remedy the situation. They have requested more popular works and the inclusion of an interval. Mahler declined the request, whereupon the ladies of the committee have insisted. They not only require Mahler to include more popular works, they have stipulated that they want Tchaikovsky's Sixth Symphony. Mahler has no recent experience of being told what to do. Moreover, he has strong feelings about Tchaikovsky's last symphony. He doesn't like it. He has a low opinion of Tchaikovsky as a symphonist although he rates the composer's operatic works highly. Indeed, Mahler has just agreed to conduct *The Queen of Spades* for The Met which we look forward to seeing when it opens on March 5th.

'The ladies of the Philharmonic have prevailed. There will now be intervals in the forthcoming Philharmonic concerts and the season includes a performance of Tchaikovsky's Sixth on January 20th.

'On January 16th Mahler conducted Rachmaninov playing his Third Piano Concerto. The pairing of Mahler and Rachmaninov lived up to all expectations but despite being such a very popular work, which Rachmaninov has performed in New York once before with the Symphony orchestra to huge acclaim, there were still empty seats all around Carnegie Hall for this second performance. Rachmaninov declared himself entirely satisfied with Mahler and his Philharmonic Orchestra. Those who heard the concert witnessed a breath-taking performance by two musical giants at the top of their form. This may have given some comfort to the ladies of the committee but perhaps not to the treasurer, who yet again dipped into the committee's reserves to make up for concert losses. During rehearsals Rachmaninov joked with the Russian speakers in the orchestra. Those of us who do not speak Russian are at a loss to know why they laughed so much.

'There was no humour at the Tchaikovsky rehearsal. The rehearsal not only lacked humour, it lacked everything. The orchestra played without interruption until the last movement when Mahler stopped to congratulate them for playing with so much feeling. He thought it unnecessary to continue rehearsing music they were so familiar with. He believed they could play the symphony beautifully without a conductor. Fortunately, Mahler did not go that far and for the concert he stood in front of the Philharmonic beating time for a performance which *The New York Herald* described as 'boring.' *The New York Evening Post* noted that the Philharmonic musicians were now 'so well trained that their conductor could lead them with the most minimal gestures.

'The ladies got their Tchaikovsky and Mahler gave them a lacklustre performance – honour hardly satisfied on either side. We wait to see how the relationship between the committee and Mahler develops, especially as they were both required to handle a much hotter potato when the Philharmonic engaged Joseph Weiss to perform the Schumann piano concerto.

'Weiss, a former pupil of Franz Liszt, had a sporadic career in Europe and eventually turned up in America hoping for better opportunities. He broke into the Mahler circle. Mahler was fascinated by this brilliant but wild pianist and took it upon himself to break in this unbridled colt. Taking pity on the poor boy Mahler offered him the Schumann Piano Concerto and negotiated a huge fee to help him out. At the rehearsal Weiss was on edge and muttered complaints about the orchestra which Mahler chose not to hear. To put the pianist at his ease, and to offer him encouragement, Mahler called out to him. 'Good!' at which point Weiss slammed down the lid of the piano and threw the score at Mahler. He was about to storm the podium when he was overwhelmed by musicians who prevented him from attacking Mahler. A replacement was found to play the concerto. I cannot remember the replacement's name, which is best forgotten anyway. The concert was a mess. Weiss was in the auditorium. He had come with a lawyer to present an invoice for his fee. A few days later Weiss was admitted to a lunatic asylum.

'Mahler put the Weiss scandal behind him and started rehearsing the new Debussy programme Every new concert for Mahler is a fresh start and he does not let past difficulties distract him. The committee of wealthy ladies may not so quickly put difficulties behind them and as their problems mount they may be asking if Mahler is the right man for them.

'The Manhattan will be full to bursting for Strauss's new opera, *Elektra,* which opens on February 1st. Strauss has been paid $28,000 in advance royalties. This new opera has neither nudity nor necrophilia and it will be interesting to see if it enjoys the same success as 'Salome'.'

Avi Bacharach

February 12th 1910

Dear Guillaume, La Semaine Littéraire liked your piece which is published today. I suggest that you do an interview with Mahler. Readers in Europe will be interested to know what America looks like through his eyes.

With love, from your mother, Madeleine Hildebrand

Four days later William took the mail to the Mahlers including a letter addressed to himself in handwriting he did not recognise. Alma opened the letter and returned it to William.

Basel
February 16th 1910

To Guillaume Hildebrand,

I am writing to send you sad news. Your mother has passed and gone to her eternal rest. She died in the early hours of Sunday morning, February 13th. Her funeral was held this morning.

From your mother's friend, Félicité Deschamps

Meddi held William in her arms before going to visit Alma. That evening at Anna's bedtime the child presented William with a card she had made saying how unhappy she was to hear William's sad news. The card was signed by Anna Mahler and Elizabeth Turner.

    William walked the streets between Carnegie Hall and the Savoy fetching and carrying for Mahler. He went shopping for Alma. He took Anna and Lizzie to picnic in Central Park. The world around him felt like a bad dream set in New York. There were moments when he would test the real world by letting his hand linger on a door handle or test the ground beneath his feet as he walked. He would pause and breathe in the air from the bakery and then in the florist's doorway and look at the sun and the moon lighting up a world in which his mother was no longer present. Every morning when he awoke he re-read the short letter from Félicité Deschamps which lay open on his desk. He flipped in and out of fantasies. In his dreams his mother was dead. When he woke up he thought it was all a bad dream and she wasn't dead. The relief lasted a few seconds and his mother was dead again. At one moment he planned to visit his mother to confess his failure, knowing she would soothe him. He wanted to hear her insist it was in the natural order for sons to leave their mothers and find their own place in the world. When Anna asked him to play hide and seek he found himself looking for his mother.

When Meddi turned up for his next English lesson the letter from Félicité was still lying on the desk. Meddi asked William if he had replied. He had not thought the letter required a reply. Meddi suggested that he send Félicité his condolences and ask her for information about his mother's illness, the circumstances of her death, and where she was buried.

New York
March 1st

Dear Madame Deschamps,

I received your terrible news a week ago and I am numb with shock. As you know my mother and I corresponded over the articles which you kindly brought to the attention of the Semaine Littéraire. She never mentioned any problems with her health. In fact, she wrote to me on February 12th with a suggestion that I interview Mahler. I am bewildered to discover that when I received this letter my mother was no longer alive and that she died the day after writing to me. I find this tragic news incomprehensible.

I know that you were my mother's dearest friend and closest companion and I cannot imagine the depth of your own grief at this tragic loss. If you feel able, I would be most grateful if you would write to me and tell me something of the circumstances of my mother's death and where I may visit her grave.

I will return from New York on April 5th and will come directly from Cherbourg to Basel. You and my mother are both constantly in my thoughts.

Guillaume

CHAPTER 32

Home Again

Mahler was struggling to make time to study the scores for the final concerts of his New York season and deal with correspondence relating to his European projects which included the French debut of his Second Symphony in Paris scheduled within days of arriving in Cherbourg, followed by concerts with the Santa Cecilia orchestra in Rome and, the biggest and most difficult project, the premier of his Eighth in Munich. Mahler wrote to the Munich promoter threatening to pull out if his demands for rehearsal time were not met. Mahler was stressed, overworked, and tired.

For his penultimate New York concert Mahler made cuts in Bruckner's Fourth and Schumann's Second and William relieved Mahler of the tedious chore of copying the changes into the orchestral parts before the rehearsal. William also wrote Mahler's changes into the parts for his closing performance of Beethoven's Ninth. As William marked Mahler's changes to Beethoven's scores he imagined he was overhearing a conversation between the two composers. Henry Krehbiel, the New York Tribune's chief critic, did not attend but sent one of his assistants who damned the concert with faint praise to please his boss. The New York Evening Post's critic, Henry Finck, thought the concert was 'astonishing and delightful'. Whenever the Tribune and the Evening Post attended a Mahler concert they invariably heard completely different performances.

Basel
March 24th

Guillaume,

Your mother had difficulty breathing for some years. Her effort to breathe brought on fits of coughing which she calmed by taking morphine. Despite her shallow breathing she was still able to smoke cigarettes. Towards the end she ate very little, she lost weight, and her breathing became more shallow until she lost the strength to breathe and stopped. When you come to Basel in April do not come to the rooms I shared with your mother. I no longer live there. Your mother is buried in the Friedhof Cemetery which you will find on Hegenheimerstrasse. Félicité Deschamps

On April 5th. 1910 William and the Mahlers left New York on board the *Kaiser Wilhelm*.

Anna knocked on the door of William's cabin and asked if he would like to play hide and seek. He told her to go away.

The next morning Miss Turner knocked on William's cabin door. William told her to go away. She spoke to William through the locked door and told him that she would come back again tomorrow. She asked if she might be permitted to bring him something to eat and drink. William didn't answer.

Two days out from New York the *Kaiser Wilhelm* ran into a storm. Passengers were advised to remain inside their cabins as the ship tossed and rolled violently. A steward brought Alma a message from the ship's doctor asking her to come to the medical room where he was looking after William. She arrived to find the doctor wrapping a tight bandage around William's hand, wrist and forearm which was held fast to a splint.

The doctor said. 'He may have broken a finger. It is difficult to tell. This should keep his hand straight and still. Is he a musician?'

William answered, 'No!'

'Ah,' said the doctor, so you *can* speak Well, Mr. Hildebrand. I don't think you will be able to return to your cabin without having another accident, so I propose to keep you here until the storm blows over.

Alma said, 'I don't think he has eaten since we left New York.'

'Well, aren't you the lucky one, Mr. Hildebrand! Nothing to bring up! When the sea becomes calm you will be hungry and I will ask the stewards to provide you with a left-handed breakfast! Can you come back in the morning, Frau Mahler, and help Mr. Hildebrand back to his cabin?'

Alma found the door to William's cabin unlocked. She went in. There was broken glass and blood on the floor. William had smashed the mirror. The desk was covered in sheets of paper. There were letters in French to 'Dear Mother,' and letters in German to 'Dear Johnny.'

Alma went to see the purser and reported the damage. She hoped it would be possible for him to accept a payment from her to cover the damages and inconvenience and asked him to fix William's cabin without bringing it to the attention of her husband who was exhausted after his demanding work in New York.

In the morning William and Alma emerged from the medical room with his right forearm held stiffly in front of him in a sling. She tried to take his left hand, but William preferred to hold on to the rail. He felt vulnerable with his injured hand strapped in front of him and he tried walking sideways. William and Alma eventually made some progress with William walking backwards.

The cabin had been made good and the mirror replaced. Alma told William that no one had intruded on his privacy. The ship stewards had tidied the room with the utmost discretion and she herself had collected his papers and put them all in the desk drawer. Alma went on to say that it was quite normal for things on ships to become broken in storms. William wondered why, if this was normal, it was necessary to tidy his cabin with 'utmost discretion.'

'Because you are being looked after,' she snapped. 'You are so good at looking after others but you're useless at being looked after!'

She made him lie down, ordered scrambled eggs and coffee, and she fed him despite his protest that his left hand was still good. After breakfast William was still hungry.

'Good,' said Alma, 'then I will bring you some dinner this evening.' She stood and sternly told William that it was normal for mothers to die and for their children to grieve. 'It is the natural order of things. It is not in the natural order of things for a child to predecease her mother and the sadness never leaves the parent. I know something of this sadness. Grieve, William! Heal and become whole again and perhaps you will find atonement. When you are at one with yourself then you may be at one with your mother, too. I also know something of your anger which will be better taken out on a pillow than a mirror.'

'I wasn't taking it out on the mirror – it was the man in the mirror!'

'I will leave your door open for Anna. She wants to come and visit you.'

When Anna came William apologised for telling her to go away. She brought the paints and brushes that William had given her for Christmas and once she got William settled comfortably with his right arm up in the air she started work on the bandage and splint on the underside of his forearm. She painted in silence. William found the sound of the brushes on the bandages soothing and the concentration on the child's face banished all other anxiety from the cabin. As the child worked William fell asleep.

Miss Turner came with tea and pastries. William fed himself with his left hand while she admired the painting under his right forearm. She told William that the rest of the voyage was expected to be smooth and that the captain was hoping to make up time as they were a day behind schedule.

Alma brought a dinner tray with a dish of meat and vegetables cut into small pieces and a fork. She asked to see her daughter's painting and then left William to eat alone.

Mahler came to William's cabin with two bottles of beer and two glasses. He opened one for William and one for himself and settled himself down on a chair beside William's bed. He stroked William's bandaged hand and said, 'You must stop attending Schönberg's recitals!' William did not know what Mahler was talking about. Mahler flashed William a big smile and said, 'Or perhaps you should be more careful getting out of the car!' Mahler's eyes flashed again and his laughter lit up the cabin. William laughed too, remembering the brawl at Schönberg's recital when Mahler threw a punch, hurt his hand, and tried to keep it a secret from Alma. Mahler drank his beer. 'You told the ship's doctor you were not a musician. What kind of mischief is that? You are my right hand and today I see it is injured. I have only two rehearsals before I conduct for the first time in France and there are changes I need to make to the score. You are not ambidextrous by any chance? No? Pity! Nobody can read anything my wife writes. Now your right hand is in bandages. What am I to do? Will you be healed by the time we get to Rome? Should I open in Italy with Beethoven's Seventh followed by my own Seventh? I think it may not be a very good orchestra. Perhaps it would be wiser to play Beethoven's Fifth followed by my own Fifth? What do you think? Either way there are changes to be made to the Beethoven parts and to my parts whether we do the Fifths or the Sevenths. Then we must prepare the parts for the first performance of my Eighth in Munich. There will be two choirs, a boys' choir, quadruple woodwind, extra brass – one mistake could go a long way. You don't make mistakes. Get well quickly. I need you.'

Mahler finished his beer, put his arms on William's shoulders, kissed him on his forehead, and left. William levered himself out of bed, went over to the mirror, raised his right arm, and saw that Anna had painted two symmetrical 'f' holes on either side of four strings. The child had painted the shadows under the strings giving the strings tension and the soundboard depth. The black ebony of the fingerboard and the metallic tailpiece reflected the cabin's light. Below the tailpiece of the viola she had written in tiny letters, 'For my friend.'

The *Kaiser Wilhelm* never made up any time and arrived in Cherbourg a day late. Mahler lost a day's rehearsal with the French orchestra which had been so badly prepared that it would have been better if they had not been prepared at all. The choir and the soloists, however, were excellent, and at the rehearsal William realized he was about to hear yet another performance of Mahler's Second Symphony that would be rescued by the singers. When the French singers whispered 'Aufersteh'n' they had an intense focus which spread through all the players.

At the concert that evening Alma and William sat in the director's box. The seat she had reserved for Rodin remained empty. The next box was occupied by Debussy and his friends. Halfway through the gentle second movement, as the under-rehearsed cellos sang the melody beneath the pizzicato of the higher strings, Debussy and his friends got up and left noisily. William tried to keep still. He took a few deep breaths in an attempt to repress his feelings but failed. He quietly got up and left his seat. He caught up with Debussy's party in the foyer where he heard the French composer scornfully dismissing Mahler's symphony as one interminable episode after another. 'German composers drink so much beer,' he said, 'and when they write music they fart. This composer is well named – 'mal air.'

William addressed Debussy in formal French. 'Excuse me, sir!'

William had not meant to interrupt Debussy's rant politely. If his right forearm had not been bandaged and held in a splint he would not have spoken to Debussy at all. He would have hit him as hard as he could.

'I heard your *L'Après Midi d'un Faun* recently in New York. It was performed by musicians led by a conductor who took great care to present your music with honour and respect.' Debussy appeared to think he was being addressed by an admirer. William continued, 'I refer to Gustav Mahler. Your conduct by comparison is uncivilised. You are a barbarian. Compared to Mahler, who is a saint, you are a moral pygmy. Your behaviour is not fit to grace a French sewer, never mind a French concert hall. Fart? That's what your opinion of Mahler's music amounts to – a worthless fart. Why don't you and your stupid friends piss on your shoes and float away?'

Someone approached William from behind and touched him. William turned and Alma slapped his face. Debussy and his friends laughed and left the concert hall. Alma took William's hand and led him back to their box in time for the start of the third movement.

CHAPTER 33

A Nightmare in Rome

Whenever the Mahlers travelled William always supervised the luggage but with his arm in a sling the hotel staff helped him to pack and William engaged porters to move the luggage to the Gare de Lyons for the train to Rome. Alma and Mahler slept in a first-class compartment. Miss Turner and Anna slept in another. William sat up all night looking out into the darkness. He must have fallen asleep to the gentle rocking of the railway carriage because he woke up with a start when the train stopped. He looked out of the window, rubbed his eyes, and looked again. Basel! Half asleep, William knew the train had stopped so that he could get off and visit his mother. Half awake, his shame overwhelmed him. Awake or asleep he felt trapped in a nightmare. He wanted the train to pull out of the station and take him away but the train waited at the platform and stubbornly refused to move on to Rome. William closed the curtains over the window to make himself invisible to the station. But the curtain offered no comfort. He needed to be able to check the empty platform to see if anyone was coming – someone who would knock on the window and say, 'Mr. Hildebrand, at last. Your mother is waiting to see you. Follow me.' The twenty-minute wait in the Basel Bahnhof seemed to take several hours and when the engine finally pulled the train out of the station William was exhausted.

    The train spiralled slowly through the Alps on a line that followed tight circles up and down the mountain. William remembered journeys with his mother when he would look out of the window from a coach near the front of a train to watch the coaches at the back of the train below them apparently going in the opposite direction. At Turin William joined the others for breakfast in the restaurant car. After the train left Genoa William sat beside Anna at the window and they marvelled at the tall palm trees, deep purple bougainvillea, and the Mediterranean. Alma looked at the hilltop villas with steps carved into the rock leading down to the beach. She wanted a holiday. She'd had enough of concerts. William wanted a holiday too. So did Anna. So did Miss Turner. So did Mahler.

    They checked into the hotel in Rome and it all started to go wrong before Alma had finished unpacking. Two precious dresses were missing. She spent several hours and a small fortune speaking on the telephone to the Hotel Majestic in Paris who could not find the dresses nor could they find the maid who had helped to pack them. She finally managed to contact a firm of private detectives to recover the dresses. She told them that she was not interested in prosecuting anyone, she just wanted the dresses, and that she was prepared to offer a reward. Mahler, exhausted after twenty hours on the train, and anxious about the following day's rehearsal, slept through Alma's telephone calls. William, Anna, and Miss Turner went out for ice cream.

At 10am, when the rehearsal with the orchestra of Santa Cecilia was due to start, the only musicians sitting at their desks were two bassoonists who were identical twins. By 10.30 half the orchestra had assembled. Mahler asked to speak to the concert master but he was on holiday. Mahler spoke Italian sufficiently well to understand that some musicians were at a christening, some were at a wedding, and some did not normally attend rehearsals. Mahler was nevertheless assured that all the missing musicians were excellent readers and would turn up for the performance. Those who had kindly come for the rehearsal offered to make a note of any special requests Mahler wanted to make and bring them to the attention of their colleagues.

Mahler bit his tongue. He did not wish to express anger with musicians who had turned up when he was furious with those who were absent. He invited them to read through the overture to 'Tänhauser'. Within a few bars he was also furious with those who had turned up. Could it be that those who turned up could hardly read a note and that the better sight readers only turned up for the performance? The small ensemble struggling to read Wagner's score were exposed and there was nowhere for the incompetent to hide. The one bass player who had turned up sawed away at his instrument on either side of the notes – sometimes flat, sometimes sharp, but never in tune. Mahler asked him to repeat a passage three times and as there was no improvement Mahler questioned his competence. The musician left the platform carrying his bass over his head, stood in the doorway, passed some wind, and then let the door slam behind him.

Mahler spent nearly an hour trying to coax some music from the players until 11.30am when the players announced they would take a break. Mahler sat at the back of the hall with his head in his hands. The twin bassoon players remained on the platform with identical smiles. At midday Mahler asked them when their colleagues might return.

They told him they might return around 4.30pm. Mahler stormed out of the building and returned to the hotel.

Alma, concerned about her missing dresses, could not deal with her husband's anger. He wanted to leave Rome immediately. She insisted he honour his contract. A full-scale row erupted between them. In the years William had been with Alma and Mahler he had never heard anything like it.

William, Anna, and Miss Turner left the hotel to go for lunch. They sat outside a trattoria and were served plates of spaghetti. William discovered that eating spaghetti left-handed with a fork was a challenge. Miss Turner found it a challenge with two hands. She moved her fork and spoon from left to right and back again. Anna had no problem feeding herself and took great delight in helping the two adults. They visited the Pantheon. They strolled into Piazza Navona and admired the fountains. Anna watched an artist who invited tourists to sit for him. She asked if she could have a turn. William, Anna, Miss Turner, and the artist spent a long time negotiating in French, German, English, and Italian before Anna could get the artist to understand that she wanted to make a portrait of the artist. The artist agreed and relinquished his seat to Anna. William counted out the cash to cover the artist's normal fee and then proposed to double the fee if the artist then made a portrait of the child. A crowd gathered and admired Anna's work as a likeness of the artist came alive on the paper in front of the child. It was more than just a likeness because Anna had also managed to capture the artist's discomfort. When she finished there were shouts of 'Brava!' and applause. The artist looked at Anna's picture, took William's money but declined the second part of the bargain. He did not wish to paint Anna's portrait in front of an audience that so admired the child's work. Anna made a gift of the picture to the artist and wished him a good day.

They threw coins into the Fontana di Trevi and ate ice creams on the Spanish Steps before returning to the hotel. Mahler, burdened by the contract with the Roman orchestra, was resting with a sore throat and a headache. Alma, fretting about her missing dresses, was on the phone to Paris.

Mahler fled from Italy before the third concert. As the Mahlers were about to leave the hotel Alma's dresses arrived from Paris. Mahler, travelling with a scarf around his sore throat and a storm raging in his head, was impatient to get the Alps between himself and the Santa Cecilia orchestra. Alma, relieved to have her dresses back, sat quietly thinking of how she could extricate herself from a life she had come to despise. Anna had fallen in love with Italy and knew that she would one day return to live there.

CHAPTER 34

Gropius

In Vienna, while staying with her mother, Alma collapsed with nervous exhaustion. The doctor suggested a rest cure and recommended the waters at Tobelbad, near Graz. William drove Alma, Mahler, Anna, and Miss Turner to Tobelbad and once they were settled William drove Mahler to his summer house in the mountains at Altschluderbach.

William and the horse with no name went into Toblach every day to collect Mahler's post. One day there was a letter addressed to himself. It was written in English.

Dear William,

This letter is private. Do not show it to anyone. Do not let Herr Mahler see it. Alma is with a man and they are together all the time. I don't know what to do. I am looking after Anna. Can you help me?

Elizabeth Turner

William was confounded. His dealings with Alma had compromised him. She had confided in him. He had been present as she flirted with male friends on picnics that she had asked him to organise. William had received letters for her that had been addressed to him in New York from Grabilowisch, Pfizner and Kammerer and, perhaps, others. He had gone along with the happy foursomes Alma put together with her husband, Meddi and himself as if he and Meddi were a couple when in fact, unknown to Mahler, the intimacy was between Meddi and his wife. And now, with Alma behaving recklessly in front of her daughter, Miss Turner needed his help.

William told Mahler that he wanted to take Alma's summer clothes to her in Tobelbad. Mahler thought that was an excellent plan and said he would come too. William told Mahler that he was sure Alma would prefer him to use his time alone to work on his Tenth Symphony. 'Choose some light summer clothes and make a package for me to take to her,' said William. 'I could leave for Tobelbad today and get back tomorrow.' Mahler said he would rather William chose and packed whatever he thought Alma might need. William took the wagon to the station where the car was parked, sent the horse and wagon back to Trenkerhof, then drove to Tobelbad.

William found Alma enjoying a picnic with her mother, her daughter, Miss Turner, and a friend. Alma was surprised that William had come with more summer clothes as she had more than enough that were fashionable and suitable for the climate. William was invited to join them and was introduced to Alma's new friend, Walter Gropius. The weather was fine, the picnic was splendid, and everybody seemed happy. Alma and her mother both looked after Walter Gropius, competing to offer him the best cuts of meat and to refill his glass. Gropius accepted their attention as if he was part of the family. Anna was pleased to see William and dragged him and Miss Turner away from the picnic for a game of hide and seek. Then Anna took them both to her room to see her paintings. She had painted a skeleton rowing a boat. A little girl sitting beside the skeleton waved to the viewer. Anna told William it was a picture of her sister, Maria, waving goodbye. In another picture a man and a woman sat in a boat waving to the viewer. 'That's Mama and her new friend waving goodbye.' In the last picture the oarsman, a woman, and a little girl waved towards the viewer. Anna said, 'That's you and Miss Turner and me waving goodbye to Mama.' William was about to tell Anna that she was very good at painting boats when Anna asked him if he was going to marry Miss Turner. Lizzie blushed.

When Anna was asleep Miss Turner sat with William in the car and told him that Alma was in love with Walter Gropius and that Alma's mother was very happy with this new development. William told Anna that she should not bother about the adults who were old enough to look after themselves and just to look after Anna.

'But Anna can see what's going on as clearly as you or I.'
'Has she said anything about it?'
'Yes.'
'What did she say?'
'She said that if Mama marries her new friend, she would like you and I to adopt her.'

Next morning after breakfast William asked Alma if there was any message for her husband. 'Yes,' she said, 'tell him I will come to Toblach on July 18th. You can come and collect me from the station. I would rather he didn't come with you. Leave him in peace to get on with his symphony.'

William asked if she would like to write anything for her husband. She said, 'No. He cannot read my handwriting. Tell him whatever you think he'd like to hear.'

When he got back to Toblach William did what he could to relieve Mahler's anxiety. Mahler was pleased to hear that Alma looked much better, that she was eating and sleeping well, that she was enjoying her family, and that his mother-in law and his daughter both looked very well too. William thought about warning Mahler against putting any trust in his mother-in-law but could find neither the words nor the opportunity and he meekly followed the conversation where Mahler led, agreeing with Mahler's judgment that he was very lucky to have such a supportive mother-in-law. 'We couldn't possibly manage without her,' said Mahler.

When Alma returned to Toblach life resumed its normal summertime pattern with Mahler in his composing hut and William collecting the post and looking after the needs of Mahler, Alma, Anna, Miss Turner, and Agnes, the cook.

The routine was shattered when William returned from the post office with a letter addressed to Mahler. Mahler opened it and discovered that, although it was addressed to him, it was in fact a love letter to his wife from Gropius. Mahler only read the first few lines before calling out to Alma and asking for an explanation. Miss Turner took Anna out for a walk. William and Agnes waited in the kitchen.

William and Agnes overheard only Alma's strident voice. She told her husband that he had driven her into the arms of another man. She told him that she needed to be loved and that he had turned away and withdrawn from her. She told him that she needed her music and that he had forbidden it to her. She told him that her life with him was meaningless and she could see no point in continuing with it. She told him that the few days of love she had shared in Tobelbad had reminded her what it was like to feel happy. She told him that it was such a long time since she last felt happy – so long, she had forgotten what it felt like. She retired to her room. He retired to his composing hut. That night he knocked on her bedroom door and asked if she would let him have a look at her songs.

When William took the wagon into town to fetch the mail he saw Walter Gropius sitting at the station café drinking a beer and reading the newspaper. He told Mahler. Mahler said, 'Then let us go to him and bring him here.'

William and Mahler went into town on the wagon where they found Gropius who had not moved from the station café. Gropius sat with Mahler on the way back to Altschluderbach. They never spoke to each other. When they arrived at Trenkerhof Mahler left Alma and Gropius alone and asked them to decide whatever it was they wanted to decide and to let him know about their decision. He went to his room and read the bible. Later that day Mahler asked William to take Gropius back to the station.

Alma spent the next three days in her room writing long letters to her mother in Vienna and to Mechtilde Müller and Dr Fraenkel in New York. Mahler spent the next three days in his composing hut searching for the music that would express his pain. Agnes, the cook, showed William how to make bread. It was a recipe for dealing with unhappiness. The first ingredient is the rhythm of kneading. Once you have found a satisfactory rhythm then you fold, push, and turn the dough. As the dough changes texture you cover it and leave it aside in a warm place to rise. Then you allow the rising dough to lift your spirits. William shared his dough between two bread tins and Agnes did the same. As their four loaves were baking in the oven Agnes opened the kitchen door to let the smell of baking bread move through the rooms of the house to soften the edges of the pain that had settled into the Trenkerhof. Agnes turned the four loaves onto a cooling tray. Mahler came into the kitchen and sat with them. He held one of the loaves and warmed his hands. He asked William to take bread to Alma. Agnes put the loaf on a tray beside a pot of honey.

Alma was lying on her bed staring at the ceiling. William left the tray on her desk. She asked him to sit and wait with her.

'He left us alone together to decide. There wasn't the slightest chance that we could decide anything. There was nothing we could do. Gropius is young, he is nothing, he is not at a place in his life where he can decide. I am a wife and I am nothing without my husband. I can only decide to stay with Mahler. If I leave him I would be worthless. Should I embrace madness or step back from it? I am not a fool. Gropius has gone and Mahler repossesses me. Could I leave Mahler and be held up to ridicule, an outcast, scorned by society, penniless, and deemed unfit to be a mother to my child? Could I leave him for a young architect who is no more than a student, who has yet to prove himself, who has no wealth, no reputation, who has yet to achieve anything, who may never achieve anything and has no standing in the community? Everyone would laugh at my foolishness. My lover and I would have each other, but for how long could we withstand the poverty of such a life together? Gropius and I can love each other only if I remain with Mahler. Only when I become his widow will I be free to love. Mahler does not possess my soul. I do not love him. I love another.'

William sat and waited and when it was clear that Alma had finished and had nothing further to say he asked, 'What about your daughter?'

Alma said that the child was Jewish and one day she would give birth to a proper child. She asked William to come back to her before he next went into town as she had some letters for him to take to the post office.

Mahler composed in the morning, took his wife for long walks in the afternoon and spent evenings with her at the piano with suggestions for orchestrating her songs. William, Anna, Miss Turner, and Agnes spent the morning together making bread. Anna rolled her dough into several long thin strands which she carefully braided before setting it to rise. Agnes, William, and Lizzie baked their bread. Anna sculpted hers. She took the braided loaf out of the oven and up to her room to do further work on it.

CHAPTER 35

Freud

On Monday, August 22nd. William took the train to Vienna and knocked on the door at Bergasse 19 and asked to speak with Dr Freud. The woman who answered told him Dr Freud was on holiday.

'Where? 'asked William.

She told William it was none of his business.

'When is he coming back?' asked William.

She told him that was none of his business either.

William explained that he needed to see Dr Freud urgently.

She told him that Dr Freud was not taking any new patients and asked him to leave. As she was closing the door William told her that Herr Mahler needed to see Dr Freud. The door opened a little. She wanted to know if he was referring to Herr Mahler, the Director of the Opera.

She told William that Sigmund Freud was on holiday in the Netherlands, and that if Dr Freud agreed to see him, Herr Mahler would have to go to Holland. She sent a telegram to Leiden. William sent a telegram to Toblach. Mahler and Freud arranged to meet in Leiden. William met Mahler at the Vienna Hautbanhof and they boarded a train for Holland. They sat together in a first-class compartment. Mahler sat opposite William, reading the score of his Eighth Symphony. William watched Mahler's eyes move from side to side and up and down as he read the score horizontally and vertically. Mahler occasionally made a mark on the score. William anxiously watched the door of the compartment guarding the silence that the composer needed. Mahler looked up from his manuscript and said, 'You would be amazed at the sound these notes make!' Mahler put his papers away and fell asleep.

In Frankfurt they ate a breakfast of apples and arrived in Leiden in the early afternoon. Freud met them at the station. William went off by himself to explore the canals. At a market stall he was offered a taste of a hard cheese spiced with caraway seeds. He wanted to buy some but only had Austrian kronen. Neither William not the stall holder knew what his Austrian currency was worth but the cheesemonger thought it was a pretty note and swapped William's ten kronen for ten guilders and gave him a wedge of cheese. He took the ten guilders to a café where he bought a coffee and two large pastries. After his breakfast he paid the bill, left cheese on the table, and went to the washroom. When he returned a cat had torn open the packet and was eating the cheese which was now scored with needle-fine teeth marks. The cat licked its feet and yawned. The café owner laughed. William left the café without his cheese.

He passed the cheese stall where he had bought the cheese. The cheesemonger greeted him with a cheery wave. William was too embarrassed to ask for another piece of cheese. At another stall William pointed to the cheese spiced with caraway seeds. The cheesemonger held his knife over the cheese and William nodded his agreement. The cheesemonger cut it, wrapped it, and asked for twelve guilders. William only had seven. William returned to the station without any cheese, bought a French newspaper and waited for Mahler.

Mahler was delighted with the time he had spent with Freud and talked about it all the way back to Vienna, sometimes to William, sometimes to the landscape rolling past the carriage window, and sometimes to himself. At first it appeared to William that the sane composer he had accompanied to Leiden had been transformed during his meeting with Freud into a madman.

Mahler asked William, 'Do you know my wife's name?'
William was nonplussed.
'My wife's name! Do you know it?' Mahler asked again.
William shrugged and answered tentatively, 'Alma?'
'It's Alma Maria!' roared Mahler.
'Alma Maria,' repeated William, trying to humour Mahler.
'Maria!' repeated Mahler. 'My mother's name was Maria.'
 'And Alma's father – what did he do?
William didn't understand.
'Mahler patiently explained, 'What was his profession?'
'He was a painter, 'ein Kunstler.'
'Another expression for 'Kunstler?' urged Mahler.
'Maler,' answered William.
 'Yes!' roared Mahler. The man's a genius!'
'Emil Schindler?'
'No,' said Mahler. 'Freud.'
Mahler started to giggle, 'I married my mother and she married her father!'
He laughed until he wept.

William stared out of the window.

'Do you know why my music is not of the very first rank?'

William thought it *was* of the very first rank and looked back at Mahler dumbly.

'It is because when I write something noble it is invariably followed by something vulgar. The route of my funeral processions invariably leads the orchestra to a fairground. When my composition climbs a mountain and takes you to summit where you might expect to find yourself closer to heaven, what do you hear? A brass band!'

Mahler started laughing again.

'If I were to compose music that took you all the way to heaven, you would hear my choirs of angels singing socialist anthems!'

Mahler started singing the opening bars of his Third Symphony. Mahler was not a very good singer.

William told Mahler that the juxtaposition of the noble and the vulgar was precisely what he loved about Mahler's music.

Mahler complimented William on understanding music better than Freud. 'Composers, musicians, audiences, all of us, pray, hope, love, and empty our bladders and bowels. A symphony must contain everything. My music leaves nothing out. That's why Freud believes it is not of the very first rank. Freud could never imagine the working class in heaven. But then Freud cannot imagine the working class on earth either. My music is not for today and it is not for Dr Freud. I wouldn't listen to music that carefully leaves out what contemporary refined ears find distasteful, I haven't written any, and I never will. If my music cannot join the very first rank today, then it must wait until tomorrow.'

William listened open-mouthed. Mahler had already said more to William in the last ten minutes that he had said in the previous ten years.

William said, 'I thought you visited Dr Freud to talk about your marriage.'

Mahler was taken aback. William blushed.

Mahler said, 'Dr Freud has assured me that she will never leave. He thinks I need to choose between my wife and my music, but I need both, so here's what I propose. From November until May I conduct. From June until October I compose. But after this next season in New York I will give up conducting and give those months to Alma. Have you heard any of Alma's songs?'

William said he hadn't.

Mahler said, 'They are really quite good. If I wrote orchestral parts, her songs would make a fine opening to a symphony concert. I would insist that any performance of my work was preceded by a selection of her songs. She would like that.'

William reminded Mahler that it was Alma's birthday on Wednesday. Mahler was surprised and asked William to suggest a birthday present. William knew that Alma would like a night of love with Walter Gropius.

William knew there was nothing Mahler could give Alma that would please her – nothing in the way of clothes or jewellery. However, Meddi in New York could give Alma some of the love she craved.

William said, 'Why don't you get in touch with my friend, Meddi, at the Met and arrange for her to give Alma a nice surprise when we return to New York? She knows Alma's colours. She knows Alma's measurements. She knows Alma's tastes. Ask Meddi to wire Alma on her birthday saying that your present is waiting for her in New York.'

Mahler reached out and clasped William's knee. His eyes shone and he was speechless with gratitude. William knew he had betrayed Mahler and looked away.

Mahler talked all the way to Vienna with his hand on William's knee. He told William all about his abusive father. How his mother and father quarrelled. How his father brewed beer and ran a drinking house. That four of his younger brothers died. That on the four occasions little coffins were carried out of the back of the building as riotous drinking parties were going on at the front. That another brother, a better musician than himself, had committed suicide leaving a note saying that he had decided to 'hand back his ticket.' That after their mother died Mahler looked after his surviving siblings and kept the family together. Mahler told William he was no longer aroused by his wife and he asked William to tell him what it was like to be aroused by men. William thought that perhaps some men understood each other's needs better than they understood the needs of women.

'I don't understand your needs, William, and I don't understand Alma's needs, either. Dr Freud thinks he understands my needs, but he doesn't, and neither do I.'

One stop before Vienna the door of the compartment opened. Mahler took his hand from William's knee and sat back. The new arrival, Franz Lehar, recognizing Mahler, put his hand to his lapel to conceal the badge that identified him as a military bandsman. The train approached Vienna Hauptbahnhof and the stranger got up to leave. Mahler stood up and addressed him.

'I think you and I are known to each other, sir. I am an admirer of your work and my wife is also very fond of your music. I enjoyed reading the score you sent me. It was so good I declined to take it for the Hofoper where it would have been performed at most six or seven times a year. Your work deserved more and has achieved its just reward in the theatre. May I congratulate you, sir on... is it five hundred performances? Or is it more?'

'Four hundred and sixty-three performances in Vienna, sir, and now on tour.' The two composers shook hands warmly.

CHAPTER 36

Mahler's Eighth Symphony

William prepared for the journey to Munich where Mahler would rehearse and conduct the premier of his Eighth Symphony. Mahler followed Alma around the house. She escaped his attention for a few hours every morning when she went with William to the post office. William posted Mahler's letters. She posted her own. On August 31st she received Meddi's telegram from New York. She purred with pleasure. William had to remind Mahler again that it was his wife's birthday. Mahler asked cook to make Alma a birthday cake with thirty-one candles. After the evening meal Agnes brought the cake to the table without any candles. William started to sing 'Happy Birthday'. Mahler, irritated, did not join in, but, instead, asked cook, 'Where are the candles? I asked you for thirty-one candles!' Agnes winced. Alma smiled and thanked Agnes for the beautiful cake.

William ordered a new set of working clothes for Mahler and insisted on dressing Mahler to check that it was all in order. Mahler hated dressing up but agreed to let William fuss around him in front of a large mirror. Tails and trousers were a perfect fit and William had ordered a silver cummerbund. Mahler fastened all the buttons of the tailcoat, but William suggested that he unfasten them to free his arms for conducting and allow the flash of silver around his waist to smile at the orchestra. The flies on the trousers were opened and closed by a new-fangled zip fastener. Mahler was intrigued and stood in front of the mirror pulling the zip up and down. He was amused and started to laugh. He walked around the room opening and closing his flies. William told him not to do this in front of the audience or the orchestra. Mahler went to Alma to show her the new zip fastener which was so easy to open and close.

Mahler left for Munich on September 3rd. Alma was due to follow him there on September 6th. On the morning of Mahler's departure William was dismayed to discover that Mahler did not want William to travel with him but to remain with Alma and accompany her to Munich three days later. William took Mahler to the station. Alma came to see her husband off. It was a windy day and Alma's hat blew away. Alma asked William to stop. William knew the horse would stop if he pulled on the reins but he had no idea how to get the horse started again. Alma was furious. At the station she tore her stockings getting down from the wagon and her mood worsened. Mahler tried to make light of it all, which made her even more angry.

After the train departed Alma turned on William. 'Why didn't you stop?' William told her the horse goes to the station and comes back without stopping. Then he ordered her into the cart. William had never ever spoken to her like that and she did what she was told. When they got back to the house he stayed out of Alma's way. He went to the kitchen and offered to help Agnes. They sat together drinking cups of sweet hot milk and discussing menus. William asked Agnes why she never prepared fish. She told William to go and look for a fish in the mountains and if he found one, she would prepare it. There were two rabbits hanging in the larder and she offered to show William how to skin them. Although William liked eating rabbit, he had no wish to skin them. Alma appeared in the kitchen asking to be taken back to the station to meet her mother. Alma spoke to Agnes. 'Please ask Herr Trenker to supply us with one of his excellent cheeses. My mother and I will have cheese and fruit for supper.'

Alma climbed up into the wagon. William said, 'I didn't know your mother was coming.' Alma said, 'There is much that you do not know. Please go directly to the station and do not stop on the way.'

Alma and her mother dined together. Agnes put the cheese, freshly baked bread, and the fruit on the table where Alma and her mother dined alone. Agnes and William ate in the kitchen and looked to the future with foreboding.

William didn't sleep. If Mahler had known that Alma's mother was coming, he would not have asked William to stay and look after his wife. His mother-in-law's attendance would have allowed William to travel to Munich with Mahler. If only he could have gone with Mahler and escaped from the wife and mother-in-law. William's attendance on Alma and her mother implicated him in their betrayal of Mahler.

Alma asked William to go to the post office with a letter. William's heart sank. Alma's letter was addressed to Gropius. When he got to the post office William showed Alma's letter to the horse and asked what he should do with it. 'Should I keep it and show it to Mahler? Should I destroy it? Should I post it?' The horse stared at him. William told the horse he was stupid and went into the post office. When he came out the horse was gone. It took William more than an hour to walk home.

He apologised to the horse and went for a long walk. He had been rambling for two hours or so when he came upon a lake. He approached a fisherman who had landed several large trout and offered to buy two of them. When he got back to Trenkerhof he slammed the fish onto the kitchen table with two loud angry slaps. Agnes got a fright and burst into tears. So did William.

In Munich Alma checked into the Hotel Continental and found her room covered in red roses, a tiara which her husband had commissioned from a jeweller, and a copy of the piano reduction of his Eighth Symphony with its dedication,

To My Dear Wife, Alma Maria.

Mahler also left a piano reduction in his mother-in-law's room which he inscribed,

To our dear mother, who has been everything to us and who gave me Alma – from Gustav, in undying gratitude.

The following morning William went with Mahler to his rehearsal and Alma went to the Regina Palest Hotel to meet Gropius.

There were two choirs, a children's choir, and a large orchestra with double woodwinds and extra brass. Never had so many performers assembled on a concert platform to present a symphonic work. Mahler had a chronic problem with a sore throat and his friends were shocked to see how old and tired he appeared. William knew Mahler was not so much sick as betrayed. While Mahler was pushing himself through the rehearsals for the symphony dedicated to his wife, she was lying in the arms of her lover.

The symphony was the biggest music the audience had ever heard and they greeted it with an ovation that lasted over half an hour. William stood beside Alma and her mother applauding the symphony. Mahler shook hands with every one of the children in the choir. One little boy said, 'Herr Mahler, that was a beautiful song!' Alma was not looking at the platform but gazing at Gropius who stood and enthusiastically applauded her husband's work.

Nothing in the concert hall that night prepared William for the abuse which appeared in the Munich newspapers the following day. William was familiar with the tone and vocabulary of the anti-Semitism commonly employed by Mahler's Viennese critics, but the hostile criticism in the Munich press was violent. Mahler, who never read reviews, was unaware of the hatred his music had unleashed. William, who did read the reviews, wondered what could have aroused so much anger. The Symphony was in two parts – the first, a setting of the Christian Hymn, 'Veni Creator Spiritus', the second, a setting of the final scene of Goethe's 'Faust.' What was it about Mahler's setting of these Latin and German texts that aroused the anti-Semitic critics in Munich to such a fury? Mahler, born a Jew, now baptized, had dared to compose within a Christian and German culture where he had no birthright and which the Teutonic race were anxious to police. It wasn't the composition they hated – it was the composer, and not just the composer – they hated all Jews.

Why had the audience loved it so much? The critics had no doubt that the audience was entirely Jewish.

What kind of adult world was waiting for the youngsters in the children's chorus? Many of these young singers were Jewish – and all of them were German.

CHAPTER 37

Johnny Stanko to New York

Mahler put aside his Tenth Symphony to work on Alma's songs. He came into her room at night and hovered over her as she pretended to sleep. Alma, who used to feel lonely when her husband spent all day in his composing hut now wished he would go away.

William organised the return journey to America. The Mahlers would travel by train to Paris where they would rest for a few days before joining the *Kaiser Wilhelm* in Boulogne for the voyage to New York. Mahler himself preferred to board the *Kaiser Wilhelm* in Bremen. William wanted to go to Bremen with Mahler.

'No,' replied Mahler. 'You will go to Paris with Alma.'

William's heart sank.

'Someone needs to keep an eye on her. Better you that me.'

'I'm useless at this,' pleaded William. 'I don't think I can help you.'

'I am not asking you to help me. I am asking you to help her.'

William shifted uncomfortably in his seat.

'I am not asking you to spy on my wife and report to me. There is nothing you can tell me. In Paris she will meet her young friend. They will spend time together and she will be happy. Then we will all go to New York for the last time. When we return we will find somewhere else to live, somewhere a bit warmer and that doesn't smell of Mr. Trenker's cheese. But for the moment she needs to see her young friend in Paris and it is better that I am not with her when this happens.'

'But her mother is with her. Her mother can look after her.'

'Dear William, you know they have jumped ship together and are both at sea. It would be a comfort for me to know that you were there with them. Your presence will also be reassuring for Anna and Miss Turner, who are both very fond of you. And you speak French. I don't know what I would do without you.'

Alma wanted to know about the travel arrangements in detail and William wrote out the itinerary for her. She wanted to know in which carriage she would be travelling and in which berth, and, armed with this information, she went to the post office and sent a telegram to Gropius.

William spent three days in Paris with Lizzie and Miss Turner. They saw very little of Alma's mother and nothing of Alma. They went on a boat trip on the Seine, climbed the Eiffel Tower, saw the African masks at the Musèe d'Ethnographie du Trocadéro, and went to the Louvre to see the Mona Lisa but it wasn't there. Someone had stolen it.

SS Kaiser Wilhelm
A special concert in the first-class lounge
October 21st at 7pm
John McCormack – tenor
Mary Garden – soprano
Gustav Mahler – piano
Retiring collection in aid of the German Sailors' Pension Fund.

New York. October 25th. Alma was delighted to find a manikin in her suite wearing a purple gown that shone. The deep colour also concealed a rich darkness in the folds of material that tumbled to the floor. It was trimmed at the sleeves and bodice with lace in different shades of cerise. The manikin said, 'Welcome to New York.' Alma reached out to touch the material. The manikin raised its arm and stroked Alma's cheek. Alma gasped and stepped back. Meddi stepped out from behind the manikin.

Dr Fraenkel came to welcome his friends back to New York. William waited for an opportunity to speak with Dr Fraenkel alone He asked if the doctor might be able to help him to get in touch with his mother. Dr Fraenkel asked if she lived in New York.

'No,' replied William, 'she is in Basel.'

'I don't think I understand, William.'

'She died in April and I would like to get in touch with her.'

Dr Fraenkel frowned.

'I want to see Madame Palladino. Don't you remember? You took us to visit her last year. She can help me to get in touch with my mother.'

'I'll see what I can do, William.'

William spent his first day in New York helping Mahler prepare for his opening concert. He took Mahler's new suit of working clothes to be dry cleaned. He polished Mahler's shoes and bought apples and cigars for the conductor's room and a box of pencils and a pencil sharpener to leave on the podium during rehearsals. He collected Mahler's white shirt and tails from the dry cleaner and hung them by an open window to blow away the odour of gasoline. He gathered all the cards welcoming the Mahlers back to New York and asked Alma if she would like him to reply to them. Alma was no longer interested in her social life and told William he could do what he liked with them.

The programme for Mahler's first concert on Tuesday, November 1st was the Bach Orchestral Suite Number 3 in D major, Schubert's C Minor Symphony, Mozart's ballet music from 'Idomeneo' and Strauss's 'Thus Spake Zarathustra.' Alma wasn't feeling well and stayed in the hotel with her mother. In the conductor's room at Carnegie Hall William helped Mahler to get dressed. Mahler paced the room, nervously pulling the new-fangled zipper on his trousers up and down until it stuck. The concert was due to begin and William was kneeling in front of Mahler trying to close the gaping flies with pins when the orchestral manager arrived to tell Mahler the audience was waiting, saw what was going on, apologised, and left. Mahler took his trousers off and quickly pulled them on again back to front. William's told Mahler not to bow to the audience at the end of the concert and the American musicians were deprived of the sight that had once caused so much mirth in Vienna. The audience found Mahler's rigid response to their generous applause a bit stiff and put this down to his genius rather than his pants being back to front.

In the car on the short journey back to the hotel Mahler beamed his satisfaction with his orchestra and his audience. His musicians had performed well, and his audience was eager to listen and to learn. William was struck by Mahler's description of 'my' orchestra and 'my' audience. Mahler and William went up to their rooms on the seventh floor. Mahler waited by William's door and asked if he might come in. He sat down and lit a cigar. He asked William what he thought about the tempo of the Schubert. He asked for William's opinion about the balance of the orchestra, which had fewer strings and more woodwinds than the previous year. He wanted to know if the brass was too loud in the Strauss. Then in an abrupt change of key he confessed he had never thought that William might need a holiday.

'Alma and I need a holiday too. I will take Alma to Egypt where we can visit the pyramids and you must have time for yourself to do whatever you need to do, William. Perhaps you would like to go to Prague and find your friend?'

'Johnny Stanko?'

'An excellent trumpet player. The very best. Perhaps you need to visit Basel? You haven't been there since your mother died. If you want to get in touch with your mother, why not write to her? You could write something and when you go to Basel take the letter with you and leave it at her grave? Do you think she might like that? There's no need to visit the circus lady. She's a fraud. Good night, William. Sleep well.'

Christmas Day 1910
New York

Dear Mother,

I will bring this letter to the cemetery in Basel although I know that you are somewhere in heaven. Last night Gustav and Alma went to the Fraenkels for Christmas dinner. Alma flirts with Dr Fraenkel. I suspect Fraenkel knows she doesn't love Mahler.

Gustav's mood has changed. When he found out about Alma and the young architect, he was distraught. But you should see him now! He not only survives – he thrives.

Alma doesn't know how to deal with this new situation. Mahler didn't ask anyone to help him with Christmas presents. He went to Macy's and got vouchers for everybody. My voucher was for $1,000. Perhaps he meant to give me $100 and made a mistake.

I went out with Anna and Lizzie for a Christmas dinner of hot dogs and soda pops. It has become a regular thing for us in New York. I am amazed at how much Anna can eat! She is only six. When I was six I don't believe I had such a big appetite. After dinner we went back to the hotel and exchanged gifts. I gave Anna a little artist's manikin because she is a little artist. I gave Lizzie a print of a self-portrait by the English painter, Turner, and I gave her a white silk scarf just like the one her namesake is wearing in the picture. Anna gave me a carved wooden sculpture of my head. She had made four of them – Mahler, Alma, Lizzie, and me. They looked just like the African masks that we saw in the Musée d'Ethnographie du Trocadéro. They have a sharp likeness even though they are not realistic. She has made our faces long and narrow so none of us looks happy. The heads Anna made of her mother and father are a bit scary. Alma with her eyes wide open looked like she has just had a big fright and Gustav with his eyes closed looks like he is dead. You would not believe they were made by a child. Lizzie gave me a copy of 'Les Fiancés.' It's a French edition of Manzoni's novel 'The Betrothed.'

Mahler has few friends, but his friendships are all special. I wouldn't say this to anyone else but I can tell you. Mahler counts me among his friends. You know it's true and you know that it makes me feel like a million dollars.

Good night, Mama. I will write again soon.
Guillaume

    Mahler wrote to Johnny Stanko. He asked William to look over the letter before posting it.

January 15th 1911
The Savoy Hotel
New York

Dear Herr Stanko,

I am writing to offer you the position of principal trumpet in the New York Philharmonic for the next season which will run from November 1911 until the following April.

Your salary in New York will be considerably higher than your present salary in Prague and you will find that costs are generally lower in America than in Europe. The orchestra is of a lower standard than the Prague orchestra but the younger musicians are ambitious. The audience is less sophisticated than the Czech audience but they are enthusiastic and anxious to learn.

Please give your present employers the shortest possible notice and come immediately because I would like you to join my orchestra for the last few weeks of this season. I am proposing that you return with me to Europe at the end of March. I would like you to join the orchestras that will perform my Eighth in Amsterdam and Frankfurt, my Fifth in Munich, where I will also conduct a performance of 'Das Klagende Leid', and then three concerts in Paris. It is a busy schedule, but it does leave you some time off before we return to New York for the new season.

I will arrange your contracts with the European orchestras. You will receive a contract from the Philharmonic manager for the American concerts at the end of this season and all of the following season. He will send you the tickets for a second-class passage from Bremen to New York on the Kaiser Wilhelm.

I beg you to accept this offer and I look forward to seeing you in New York.

I have enclosed a note for you to present to the captain of the Kaiser Wilhelm. I know him well and he will look after you during the crossing.

With my very best wishes,
Gustav Mahler

Dear Captain Morgenstern,

The bearer of this note, Herr Jonathan Stanko, is travelling to New York to join my orchestra. I would be most grateful if you would furnish him with the best accommodation you have available during the crossing. I will be indebted to you. I look forward to seeing you again in April during my return voyage to Europe, and to performing for the German Sailors' Pension Fund. Thank you, Gustav Mahler.

February 22nd
Savoy Hotel
New York

Dear Mama,

The last few days have been very difficult.

Last week Mahler attended a meeting of the Board of the orchestra and accepted the Board's offer to conduct the orchestra for the next season. Mahler has agreed to conduct one hundred concerts.

Mahler then presented the Board with a list of musicians which he required to be replaced. The Board have taken exception to Mahler's presumption and informed him that the responsibility to hire and fire musicians is theirs alone. This difficult situation has arisen because Mahler has offered a post in the orchestra to a European musician without consulting the Board. This musician is now on his way to New York. When they pointed out that the Union would not agree to another European musician joining the orchestra Mahler informed the Board that the leader of the orchestra, Theodore Spierling, who was thought to be European, had in fact been born in New York. Mahler assumed this freed up a place for another European musician. The Board agreed that was indeed the case but reminded Mahler that he had already done it once and that he had now overstepped the mark.

This difficulty was made worse by Mahler's unfortunate relationship with the leader of the second violins, Herr Johner. The list of musicians Mahler wishes to fire was drawn up with the help of Mr. Johner who compiled reports on the inadequacies of twenty of the older players. The Board and the orchestra were very unhappy with this behaviour. However, Mr. Johner has foolishly allowed the disputing parties a way out of their difficulty. He reported sick and did not travel with the orchestra on its recent tour. It has now come to the attention of the Board that during the days he was 'sick' he was employed by New York Symphony Orchestra.

The Board have decided to resolve the conflict by firing Mr. Johner and hiring Mahler's new European musician. In this way they have reserved their right to hire and fire and have demonstrated their insistence upon exercising this right. They have rid themselves of Mahler's 'spy' and Mahler gets the young musician he wants. Alma is furious. She says that in Vienna not even the Emperor would dare to treat her husband like that.

The following day Mahler was laid low with a severe throat infection and could not leave his bed. In his absence the rehearsal was taken by Theodore Spierling. Over the week Mahler's health deteriorated and Alma asked Dr Fraenkel to come and see him. The doctor insisted that Mahler stay in bed but yesterday Mahler took the dress rehearsal and conducted the evening concert of Italian music which included Busoni's Berceuse Elégiaque. At the end of the performance he was exhausted. He was too tired to get changed. I brought him back to the hotel still wearing his tails. I carried his baton. His working clothes were soaked with sweat. I got him undressed and into bed. Alma asked Dr Fraenkel to come. The doctor is with him now.

Dear Mama, Mahler has not been very well since the New Year. First it was a toothache and now a throat infection. I hope he gets better soon. If you are in heaven could you have a word with someone who might be able to help.

I love you.
Guillaume

Press Release. March 21st 1911

The Guarantors' Committee
The New York Philharmonic Society.

'In view of the widespread disappointment at the absence of Mr. Gustav Mahler from the recent Philharmonic concerts the Guarantors' Committee of the Philharmonic Society wishes to say to the musical public that only serious illness has kept Mr. Mahler from his post. Mr. Mahler has been confined to his room since the end of February.

The committee shares with the public the deep regret that our season proceeds without Mr. Mahler's reappearance and that the public has thus been deprived of the opportunity of expressing its appreciation of everything Mr. Mahler has done during the past two seasons for the Philharmonic Society and for music in this country.

The achievements of this great master cannot fail to leave their impression on the development of music in America, and it is the sincere hope of the committee that Mr. Mahler's health may soon be restored and that he may resume these activities which mean so much to the world of art.'

Savoy Hotel
March 30th 1911

Dear Mama,

We are leaving New York in the morning and returning to Europe. Mahler has not conducted since February 21st. Theodore Spierling has conducted all the concerts. I have not attended any but I have read the newspaper reviews which are very favourable. The new member of the orchestra arrived from Europe in time to perform with the orchestra on February 26th. I have heard that he is very good.

Dear Mama, I know he is very good. He is Johnny Stanko. I cannot go to the rehearsals or concerts. I cannot look at him again nor can I bear to let him see me.

Dr Fraenkel says that Mahler should be seen by specialists in Paris. Alma and I have spent the last week preparing for the voyage and we have packed forty suitcases.

Mahler is afraid he might die on the ship. Neither his daughter nor Miss Turner know about the gravity of his illness. Dr Fraenkel came *to see me last night after he bid Mahler farewell and told me that in his experience nobody has ever survived the infection which Mahler has contracted. He told me that Mahler wishes to die in Vienna and that I should get him there as quickly as possible. I can't believe what I have just written, Mama. Can you help?*

I love you.
Guillaume

CHAPTER 38

Mahler's Funeral 1911

William sat beside the deathbed and listened to Mahler's shallow breathing. William didn't speak. He just wanted Mahler to know that he was there. Mahler tried to speak. William leaned over and held his ear close to Mahler's lips, took Mahler's hand and said, 'I will bring her to you.' William felt Mahler squeeze his hand.

The day before Mahler's funeral William drove to Maernigg to fulfil Mahler's dying wish and bring Maria to Vienna to be buried beside her father in the cemetery at Grinzing.

William arrived at Maria's grave before dawn. The Teddy's Bear tied to Maria's headstone was bedraggled and weather-beaten. William started to dig. After two hours he had made little progress. Each shovelful was harder than the one before. He was sitting hopelessly on the edge of the grave, weeping, when two policemen approached and led him away.

William spent several hours in a police cell pacing up and down, measuring his determination to fulfil Mahler's last wish against his inability to deal with it.

He was interviewed by an officer who asked him what he thought he was doing. William explained that he was taking Mahler's daughter back to Vienna so that father and daughter could be buried together. It was Mahler's last wish and William's promise to the dying man.

The officer and William looked into each other's eyes. Then the officer spoke.

'Mr Hildebrand, I do not have the authority to open Maria Mahler's grave.'

'I do not want your authority, sir. I want your help. Mahler wants to rest in peace with his daughter. I told him I would see to it. I gave him my word. Help me! Please.'

The officer came out from behind his desk, drew up a chair beside William, and said, 'My name is Jacob Strassman. On the lakeside we are a small community. We know each other and we help one another. We have followed the deterioration of Mahler's health in the newspapers. Whenever the Mahlers were in residence we did what we could to keep our animals and our children from disturbing him. We knew he was there when we saw the car. I recognize the car but I do not recognise you. Who are you, Mr. Hildebrand?'

William told the policeman that he drove Mahler's car, that he did whatever Mahler needed and that he looked after Alma, that he looked after their daughter, Anna, and that he helped Mahler organise his professional life. He knew what Mahler needed better than anyone else and right now he needed to have his daughter beside him. Mahler had trusted him to do it. 'I will not let him down. Please help me.'

'I believe you. I would like to help you, Mr. Hildebrand. It would be helpful if I could speak to someone who would be able to confirm what you have told me about yourself. Is there someone, perhaps a friend of the family, that I could speak to on the telephone?'

William suggested the composer, Zemlinsky. Strassman lifted his telephone and asked someone to find Zemlinsky's number and to get him on the line.

Strassman asked William about the Teddy's Bear on Maria's grave.

William told him that Mahler had put it there himself. Strassman asked William where Mahler had got the bear. William told Strassman that it wasn't Mahler who bought it. 'I bought it,' said William. 'Where?' asked Strassman. 'Macy's in New York.' 'That's correct,' said Strassman. 'You left the price tag pinned to its ear. I found the bear in the forest with the note around its neck 'For Maria, Happy Christmas, from your loving father, Gustav.' I took it back to the grave and tied it to the headstone.'

The phone rang.

'Herr Zemlinsky. Good morning. This is the police station in Klagenfurt. I am sorry to hear about the death of your friend, Herr Mahler, and regret that I am troubling you at such a sad time. I am looking for information that would help me to confirm the identity of Mahler's personal assistant. I see. What about his chauffeur? I see. You're sure? Thank you very much. No, not at all. You've been very helpful.'

'He didn't know Mahler had a personal assistant or a chauffeur. Is there someone else I could speak too?'

'Mathilde. Zemlinsky's sister. Frau Mathilde Schönberg. She'll remember me.'

Strassman lifted his telephone receiver and asked someone to find Arnold Schönberg's number and to put Schoenberg's wife on the line.

Strassman wondered if William was familiar with Mahler's music. William said he knew it very well. Strassman confessed he had not heard any of it and asked William to tell him about the opening of Mahler's Seventh Symphony. William told Strassman that Mahler had spent days looking for a way to open the symphony and how it had come to him one day when someone rowed him across the Worthersee. He had used the atmosphere and the rhythm of these few minutes on the lake to begin his symphony. 'That's correct.,' said Strassman. 'It was my boat. I was the oarsman. Mahler told me that very same story himself.'

The phone rang. 'Frau Schönberg. Good Morning. This is the police station in Klagenfurt. I am sorry to hear about the death of your friend, Herr Mahler, and regret that I am troubling you at such a sad time. Frau Schönberg... Frau Schönberg... I'm terribly sorry. I was only looking for some information...'

Strassman suggested he call Frau Mahler.

'She doesn't know I'm here.'

Strassman lifted his telephone receiver and asked someone to find Alma Mahler's number and to put her on the line.

'What makes you think she does not know that you are here?'

'Because I never told her.'

'Does she only know what you tell her? I think she knows more, Mr Hildebrand.' Strassman opened his wallet, pulled out a twenty Kronen note, and laid it on the table. 'I say that she knows what you are doing here.'

The phone rang. 'Frau Mahler, this is the police station in Klagenfurt. I am sorry to hear about the death of your husband and regret that I am troubling you at such a sad time. I would like to confirm the identity of your personal assistant and chauffeur. That's correct. I have Mr. Hildebrand here with me now. Can you tell me why he has come here? That's correct. I am sorry to have troubled you, Frau Mahler. Thank you for your help. Goodbye.'

Strassman tapped the twenty kronen note on the table and told William he owed twenty kronen. William, who had not thought the police officer was serious fished in his pockets and found a twenty kronen note. 'How did she know what I was doing here?'

'She is Mahler's wife. You have never been married, have you, Mr. Hildebrand?'

Strassman picked up the telephone, 'Put Father Kurtz on the line and get me three policemen and three shovels.'

'The priest will watch over us at this end. You'll need a priest at the other end.

The phone rang. 'Father Kurtz? Strassman here. I am going to exhume Maria Mahler's coffin and send it back to Vienna to be buried beside her father. I need you at the graveside. Full dress. Pail, holy water, brush, everything. Now. Right away. Thank you.'

With shovels, ropes, a ladder, and a priest looking on in prayer, the Klagenfurt policemen brought the coffin to the surface, wrapped it in a blanket and placed it on the back seat of Mahler's car while the priest walked around the vehicle sprinkling it with holy water. Strassman thanked the priest, gave him forty kronen, wished William a safe journey and said he would arrange for him be met by a priest first thing in the morning at the gates of the Grinzing cemetery.

William drove back to Vienna through the night and arrived at Grinzing cemetery where a priest in full vestments, with the pail and the brush, stood waiting for him at the cemetery gate. The priest walked around the car splashing it with holy water and then walked in front as William drove behind him at a slow walking pace to Mahler's grave. The grave was covered in flowers. The grave diggers moved a large raft of timber that covered Mahler's open grave and lowered Maria's coffin to rest on top of her father's. The priest said a few more prayers, splashed more holy water around, and then waited for William to settle with him. William gave the priest forty kronen.

Later that day Alma asked William what he had been doing in the police station in Klagenfurt on the day of the funeral. William told her he had not been able to do it by himself and that he had asked the police to help him.

'To help you to do what?'

'You know what.'

'How should I know what you're up to? I thought you were going to my husband's funeral! Why are you smiling?'

'Because the policeman told me you knew what I was doing, robbed me of twenty kronen and then gave it to a priest.'

'You are one riddle after another.'

William asked, 'How was the funeral?'

Alma answered, 'I didn't go.'

End of Part One

PART TWO

1911-1943

Anna Mahler

Portrait of the Artist as a Young Girl

CHAPTER 39

The Merry Widow

Alma said she would not spend another minute in Mahler's flat and told William to drive her and Anna to her mother's house in Wallergasse.

The silence in the car was awkward and became even more unpleasant when William asked after Miss Turner.

'She's gone back to England!' snapped Alma.

'Scotland,' said Anna.

Alma told her daughter to 'Shut up!'

William tried to concentrate on the road as he wondered what had happened to Lizzie, what was going to happen to him, and what was going to happen in Wallergasse where Alma was proposing to live with her daughter and mother, neither of whom she liked. William hit a kerb, scraped the car against a lamp post and knocked over a dustbin.

William parked outside the Moll's home and opened the car doors for Alma and Anna, as he would normally do, but now feeling more like a chauffeur than one of the family. Alma walked into the Moll household without looking back. Anna turned and waved sadly to William. She had lost her father. She had lost Miss Turner. William wondered if she was about to lose him.

As he drove back to Auenbruggergasse to fetch Alma's luggage, Mahler told William that he was waiting for him in the apartment and that there were things he needed William to do. William knew that Mahler was dead but the prospect of seeing him again lightened his mood and he stopped to buy a bag of apples. He would do whatever Mahler wanted, and, if the opportunity arose, he would ask Mahler if he could live in the apartment until he found a place of his own. William found Mahler sitting at the kitchen table. Mahler's smile warmed William's heart. Although Mahler was dead, William was neither afraid nor surprised to see him. William knew there was much that needed doing and that Mahler trusted him to do it. William put the bag of apples down on the table. Mahler looked at them and then shook his head. 'That's very kind of you, but I don't eat apples anymore. Thank you for going to Mairenigg to fetch Maria. I knew I could rely on you' he said. 'There are other things I need you to do.'

'Of course,' said William. 'I have all the time in the world.'

'I have,' said Mahler. 'You don't. I've been thinking about *Das Lied von der Erde*. Bruno Walter will conduct the premier in Munich. It's difficult to imagine how he might do it. If I had an orchestra every day for a month I might manage. Bruno will be lucky if he gets a week. He needs all the help he can get so he should begin with a clean score. I want you to make a copy. I need you to earn Bruno's trust. Make friends with him. You're good at making friends.'

'And I need you to copy the first movement of my Tenth and then destroy the original which I was composing while my wife was involved with Gropius. I don't want anyone to see what I scribbled in the margins. It may never be performed but I would like Schoenberg to read it. He may be onto something with his twelve-tone row. The symphony opens with a row of eleven tones played by violas. It works well. The missing tone will infuriate Schönberg. I like infuriating him. The eleven tones make a beautiful melody that will drive him mad. The manuscript will be among my papers in one of the suitcases.'

William asked if there was anything else.

'Look after Alma and Anna. Alma's appetites will lead her into one scrape after another. She'll need someone to talk to. You know that Alma has some little difficulties with our daughter and now that Miss Turner has gone back to Scotland, I would be grateful if you would keep an eye on Anna. Perhaps you might think of taking her on holiday to Italy. I know she would like that. You shared a happy time together in Rome, didn't you? Is there anything I can do for you?'

William hesitated, then said, 'No.'

'You can, of course, stay here. You will find the peace and quiet you need to do all your copying and I will know where to find you. Go next door and find my Tenth. It's in one of the suitcases. I don't want Alma to see it. Vai! Vai! Arrivederci!'

There should have been forty suitcases but William counted only thirty-eight. He knew there were forty because he had counted them on and off the boat, into and out of the Paris hotel, on and off the train, and he had carried all forty up the stairs to the apartment. It would be just his luck if the Tenth Symphony was in one of the missing cases. He counted them again. Two were his. Two were Anna's. Two were Miss Turner's. Some were Mahler's and the rest were Alma's. William started to examine Gustav's luggage but the manuscript wasn't there. He had packed Alma's cases himself and did not expect to find the manuscripts among her things. They were unlikely to be in Anna's luggage and they certainly weren't in his. Four hours later he had turned out every one of the thirty-eight suitcases and had not found the manuscript. By the time he had repacked the luggage it was dark, he was exhausted, and it was too late to deliver the bags to Alma. It would have to wait until the morning. He took his own luggage to the smallest bedroom, unpacked his nightclothes, laid out clean clothes for the morning and ran himself a bath. The water was cold. The next time he saw Mahler he must remember to ask him how to get hot water. He lay in bed counting suitcases and as he fell asleep he realised the missing suitcases must be Miss Turner's and she was on her way to Scotland. Why had she left?

William got up early. When he opened the front door to carry the first two bags down to the car, he found Anna sitting on the step. Alma and her mother had quarrelled. Alma had run away. Anna didn't know where.

'But your grandparents don't know where you are!'

Anna didn't think it mattered.

'But what if they report you missing and the police find you here ... with me?'

Anna burst into tears. William knelt down and held her. Through her sobs she told William that she didn't want him. She wanted Miss Turner.

William took her down to the car and drove her back to Wallergasse where her grandparents had not noticed her absence. Frau Moll wished them both a good morning and asked if they had eaten any breakfast. They all sat down and ate together like a happy family. No-one asked where Alma was. After breakfast William asked Anna if she would help him move all the luggage and they drove back to Auenbruggergasse.

They returned with the first twelve of Alma's cases. William took them up to Alma's room and closed the door behind him. He didn't have to look far. Alma had lined up her precious manuscripts on the dresser. All her husband's symphonies were there, including the Tenth and *Das Lied von der Erde*.

William appealed to Mahler for help.

Mahler told him to leave the Tenth where it was. It was too late. 'Alma will have to live with the tears and pain I left in the margins. I will not. Take the *Das Lied von der Erde* and put it back when you've copied it.'

'She'll notice the folder is empty,' said William.

'Then put something else there in the meantime.'

'What?'

'There are some scores in my baggage that I enjoyed reading. Choose one of them.'

'Which one?'

'How about *The Merry Widow*?'

By the end of the morning William and Anna had moved everything from Auenbruggergasse to Wallergasse. Then Anna told her grandmother that she wanted to move all her materials to Auenbruggergasse and live there with William. She planned to set up a studio where she could paint and sculpt without creating a mess in the Moll house. William was surprised how readily the Molls agreed. When they got back to Auenbruggergasse William asked Anna if she knew how to get hot water. She didn't. William went out to buy the groceries leaving Anna to organise her studio. When William returned he could hear the water pipes clanking merrily throughout the building. The tap in the kitchen shuddered and expelled bursts of steaming hot water. William wondered how the little girl had managed to fix the plumbing and get hot water. She told him that she had gone downstairs to the boiler room and asked the caretaker to turn it on.

William and Anna lived happily together for a week, Anna painting in her studio, William copying *Das Lied von der Erde*. Then Alma turned up. She told William she had found an apartment in Pokornygasse and told William to move everything from Wallergasse to the new address. Anna told her mother that it would have to wait until the morning because she and William were both busy.

The following morning William and Anna began moving everything to Pokornygasse. 'This will be mother's room,' Anna said, identifying the largest room with the best view. Anna claimed the room with the best light. There were two other rooms. 'One for a guest,' said Anna, 'and the other one's for you.' William hoped the child was right to include him. Anna told William that he would have to decorate the house and that she would help him.

William returned for the last of Alma's luggage and took the manuscript of *Das Lied von der Erde* to swap for *The Merry Widow*. He found Alma waiting by the door of her mother's house. 'Oh, it's only you,' she cried. 'I thought it was the police.' William went to her room, found the folder with *The Merry Widow* lying on the floor. He took it out and replaced it with *Das Lied von der Erde,* leaving the folder on the floor exactly where he had found it. He went back downstairs to find Alma telling two policemen that she had been robbed. Someone had broken into her room and stolen a precious manuscript. She had only just discovered the theft. She hadn't touched a thing. As the police went upstairs to examine Alma's room William left.

Mahler was waiting for him in the car.

'Well done, William. That was close!'

'Alma's in a terrible state.'

'She's in mourning,' explained Mahler.

'What will she say when the police find *Das Lied von der Erde* in the folder?'

'That's her problem, William. Give her a shoulder to lean on. Nothing is going well for her. Especially Gropius. It was better for the two of them when she was married to me. During the year before my death they exchanged letters of longing for each other but when I died the longing died and now they've reached a crisis. It's just as difficult for young Gropius. He was in love with my wife. Now she is no longer my wife, Gropius is not sure if he still loves her. I believe that Gropius was also in love with me and is unable to be unfaithful to my memory by continuing the affair with my wife. Let the two of them sort it out. I need you to be there to pick up the pieces. Gropius has gone back to Berlin and it may be a while before they see each other again. Presently, she has Franz Schrecker attending on her. Have you heard any of his music? A minor Austrian composer. That's how some people refer to me, but he's the real thing. Alma imagines her role in life is to inspire artists to greatness. She believes my music, even though she doesn't like it, serves as a fine example of her success.'

'And then there's the biologist. Do you remember that silly boy? He came to stay with us in Toblach. He wanted to clean my shoes, light my cigars, and ensure that the chair was clean before I sat on it. He would have accompanied me to the toilet and wiped my arse if I had asked him. You didn't like him, did you? He wanted to learn how to drive the horse and cart to the station.'

'Paul Kammerer?'

'Kammerer. That's right. He was in love with me too. Can you imagine that? And now he is sniffing around my widow.'

'The new director of the opera, Weingarter, is negotiating with Alma a fitting memorial while at the same time trying to forget I ever existed. He'll do anything she asks. She told him that the head of costumes at the Met in New York was looking for a place in Vienna and a senior position in the Hofoper wardrobe immediately became available. So Meddi is coming to Vienna to be with Alma. You've got to admire Alma. I take my hat off to her.'

'The Hofoper are going to purchase the Rodin sculpture and display it in a room named after me, and once a year they will perform one of my symphonies on the anniversary of my death. I don't care for any of it. What I do care about is the premier of my Ninth. Alma hasn't given it any thought, but I have. I want it to be heard first in Vienna. Bruno Walter will need sufficient rehearsal time to make a success of it. Speak to Bruno. He'll need to get started today because the mood in Vienna could change tomorrow.'

'Regarding *Das Lied* tell Bruno that the final *Ewig* is to be sung as a footprint – two syllables, heel and then toe. If he gets it right it will sound like a step in the air and will last forever.'

There were two letters waiting for William in Auenbruggergasse.

New York
August 1911

Dear William

Please forgive me for not writing sooner. I knew that Herr Mahler was unwell, but I did not realise that he was so ill. It must have been a terrible journey for you.

I have missed you all. Herr Mahler made a huge impression here and his legacy in New York is endlessly debated in the newspapers. Some of it would fill you with pride. Some of it would make you angry. It is difficult to believe that he will never return. I don't want to live in this city without Mahler, so when a position became available at the Vienna Opera House, I applied for it and I got the job. I will come to Vienna before the beginning of the new season in October.

I thought I might make something for Alma to wear. I would like to do the same for her daughter. Would you ask Miss Turner to take Anna's measurements and send them to me?

I will arrive in Hamburg on September 14th and I should get to Vienna sometime the following day. I can't wait to see you all again.

With all my love,
Meddi

Kingsburgh Rd,
Murrayfield
Edinburgh

Dear William,

The last few months have been difficult for me and I am writing to tell you how I feel.

I was surprised that neither you nor Alma were at Mr. Mahler's funeral. I went because Anna pleaded with me to take her. I knew that Alma had forbidden her daughter to attend but when the child begged to go I could not refuse. When we got back from the cemetery Alma's mother took Anna away from me and I was dismissed. Mr Moll took me to the station where I was given a ticket to Paris, a month's wages, and put on a train. I sat up all night on the train outraged at my dismissal. The next day on the journey to London I felt sad, then the day after that on the train to Edinburgh I felt angry. I checked into a hotel near the station and stayed in my room for two days feeling outrage at the way I had been treated. It is now four months since the funeral and some of the pain has gone. I wonder how it has affected Anna.

Why were you not at the funeral, William? They would not have treated me so badly if you had been there. Forgive me if my words sound harsh. Perhaps you are in pain too.

I managed to find a position in Edinburgh. The man of the house has remarried and the two boys from his first marriage are difficult. The new wife has a baby and is struggling to cope with this awkward family situation.

I have a little room with its own staircase off the kitchen. The warmth from the kitchen follows me upstairs and my room is private and cosy. I get up early to give the boys their breakfast and send them off to school. I spend all day helping Madam with the baby and then I prepare a meal for the evening. The boys eat a lot and if I feed them well it keeps them quiet. When they are hungry they fight each other. They are unpleasant boys.

I have a day off on Sundays and I usually go for a walk if it's not raining. There is an Italian community living in Edinburgh and there's a shop which sells Italian groceries. I sometimes go there and buy a piece of cheese. Near the Catholic Cathedral there is an Italian ice cream café. I sit there and I think of you and Anna and the time we were in Rome. I know it was a bad time for Mr Mahler and his wife. She lost her dresses and he hated the orchestra. But I will never forget how much Anna loved Italy. I can see her now with her big smile covered in ice cream.

Do you remember that Anna wanted you and me to adopt her? I sometimes dream of the three of us together in Italy. Oh, how I would love to do that, William! I know she would love it, too.

With all my love,
Elizabeth Turner

Anna and William decorated Alma's new house in Pokornygasse. Anna's eye was true. Although the picture rail and the skirting board appeared to be straight, they were not. Anna observed carefully, calculated the angles, and cut the wallpaper to fit. William climbed the ladder and hung the paper on the wall while she squinted at the picture rail, rolled out the next sheet of paper, cut it, and brushed on the paste.

William asked Anna if she would like a new dress.
'No,' she answered.
'What about something special – something that artists wear?'
'Artists don't wear anything special.'
'Don't painters wear a kind of smock?'
'If you have to dress up to be a painter you probably aren't any good.'
'What do good painters wear?'
'Nothing!' said the child and giggled.
'Do you remember Meddi?'
'Mama's girlfriend?'
'She's coming to live in Vienna.'
'Good.'
'Do you like her?'
'Yes. When she's around Mama's a lot easier to manage. Do you like her?'
'Yes.'
'Is she your girlfriend too?'
'She's making your mother a dress and she would like to make a dress for you.'
'I don't want a dress.'
'She wants to bring you something.'
'I'd like plasticene. You can't get it here. In New York you can get it in different colours. Tell her to bring me lots of plasticene.'
'Would you like to go for a holiday in Italy?'
'Yes. This one's ready to hang up.'
'After we've finished this room we should decorate the guest room for Meddi.'

'Meddi won't stay here,' said Anna. 'She'll find her own place to live. Are you her friend or her boyfriend?'
'What do you think?'
'How should I know? I'm only seven.'
William flicked some wallpaper paste onto her nose. She threw a handful back. It slithered down the inside of his shirt. They both went laughing to the bathroom where Anna wiped the paste off her face and William cleaned the paste off his stomach.
'When are we going to Italy?'
'How should I know? I'm only twenty-nine,' said William.
 'Miss Turner said that one day she'd take me back to Italy. She promised.'
'You liked Miss Turner, didn't you?'
'I used to like her.'
'When you're upset, it's her that you want, isn't it?'
'Yes.'
William buttoned up his shirt and took Anna's hand. 'Come on.'
'Where are we going?'
'Back to work.'
'But I want to go to Italy!'
'So do I,' said William.
'Do you think Miss Turner will come back?'
'Maybe.'
'We'll have to ask Mama, but she might still be cross with Miss Turner for walking out on us.'
'Your mother was cross?'
'Very cross. Were you cross with Miss Turner?' asked Anna.
 'No,' said William.
'She left and never even said goodbye, but if she comes back and says sorry Mama will forgive her. When Meddi comes Mama will be in a good mood and then we can ask her to tell Miss Turner to come back.'
'That's a good idea, Anna.'
'Is Miss Turner your girlfriend too?'
'Do you want me to put more wallpaper paste on your face?'
'No. I want Miss Turner to come back and I want Meddi to bring me plasticene from New York. Lots of it. All different colours. But most of all I want to go to Italy.'

Pokornygasse
Vienna

Dear Lizzie,

What a joy it was to hear from you. I'm sorry about the awful circumstances surrounding your departure and your nightmare journey to Scotland but I'm glad to hear you have found a position in Edinburgh. The two difficult boys are lucky to have you.

Anna misses you and so do I. Neither of us knew anything about the circumstances of your departure. Anna would be angry with her mother if she found out. Things are not good between them and it would be a shame if they got any worse.

Alma doesn't have much time for her daughter and would be relieved if you come back. Do you think you might be able to write to Alma and express some regret about taking Anna to the funeral, even if you don't mean it? Anna and I will work on it too and then we'll all go to Italy. How about springtime? La primavera?

Andiamo.
William

Pokornygasse
Vienna

Dear Meddi,

I look forward to welcoming you to Vienna. Anna is looking forward to you coming as well. We are going to prepare the guest room where we hope you will be comfortable.

I understand that New York without Mahler must seem empty. It's the same here. Life goes on but Herr Mahler leaves behind a huge empty space that nobody can fill. You will feel this most sharply in the Opera House. Bruno Walter no longer conducts there. He was closely associated with Mahler and the new director seeks to distance himself from the past and does not employ him. This may have nothing to do with the Jewish Question. But Jews, like Herr Walter, are being made to feel unwelcome in Austria. There is a nasty feeling in our city against Jews and it's led by the mayor. Whenever there's a problem *someone blames the Jews. This wouldn't make any sense in New York, but it is the normal thing here.*

There is still much to enjoy in Vienna. The orchestra sounds wonderful. How does the New York orchestra sound without Mahler? I am particularly interested in the brass section. The trumpets? Are they playing well?

Alma will be very pleased with the dress you are making for her. Anna's wardrobe is full and she doesn't need anything new. She would, however, be grateful if you would bring her the modelling clay that she likes. It's called plasticene. I believe you can get it in a variety of colours. It is not available in Vienna. I know that Anna could use a substantial amount of it.

Miss Turner is not with us at the moment so when I get the chance to show you around Vienna Anna will accompany us instead.

Auf Wiedersehen
William

Anna and William finished decorating Alma's room. When Alma came to inspect, William noticed the beginning of a smile at the corner of Alma's mouth. She looked out of the large window and admired the view that extended from the garden below to the forest beyond and told William she needed curtains. Anna told her mother that Meddi would make the curtains when she arrived. Alma patted her daughter on the head and told them they were going to have a proper Christmas this year, not a Jewish Christmas. She asked William to deal with Anna's education, gave him the address of a language school and told him to take Anna there and enrol in the English class which met twice a week. After Alma left, Anna asked William, 'What is a Jewish Christmas?' William didn't know.

When they got to the language school Anna saw a poster advertising 'Italian for Beginners' and told William she didn't want to learn English. William's heart sank. 'But you have to do what you're told. She's your mother!'

'*You* have to do what you're told because she's my mother, but I don't have to. I am going to the Italian class, and I am going to live in Italy.'

'But your mother said we have to enrol in the English class.'

'You go to the English class and I'll go to the Italian class. When Miss Turner comes back she can teach me English.'

'If you enrol in the Italian class after your mother has told me to take you to the English class she will dismiss me and none of us will go to Italy.'

Anna turned to William. 'That's why Miss Turner left, isn't it? Mama dismissed her. Mama said I wasn't to go to Papa's funeral. Miss Turner took me and so Mama sent her away.'

William said nothing. She wiped away her tears and then said to William, 'Would it work if we went to the English class once a week and to the Italian class once a week?'

William thought it would. They went to the language school twice a week – once for English and once for Italian. When Alma was in the house they spoke in English. When she wasn't, they spoke Italian.

Kingsburgh Rd
Edinburgh

Dear Anna,

Greetings from Edinburgh, the capital of Scotland. I have enclosed some postcards so that you can see how beautiful it is. There's a picture of the Castle which sits high on a rock in the centre of the city. There's a picture of the Scott Monument which stands at the edge of the gardens in memory of the writer, Sir Walter Scott, and there's a picture of the Forth Bridge which is one of the engineering wonders of the world. Sometimes I take a train across the bridge. It is so high the boats far below look like little toys.

I miss you and I hope that one day we can be together again. I am sorry I left Vienna without saying goodbye. The day of your Papa's funeral was a terrible day for all of us and it must have been especially terrible for you. I am so sorry that I was not able to stay and support you. It was a terrible day for me too. I hope you will forgive me.

I have also written to William who thinks we will meet again, but we must be patient. Your mother will be in mourning until next April and you must be kind and helpful to her.

I would love to hear from you.

With love,
Elizabeth

Pokornygasse
Vienna

Carissima Elizabetta,

Grazie per i cartolini. Mi piace molto il castello. In scozia ci sono cavalli? Ci sono mucca? Ci sono giraffe? Ci sono elefanti? Ci sono principe? C'e un mostro nel Lago di Ness? Imparo Italiano perche voglio andare in Italia con te.

Ti voglio bene.
Anna

William went with Alma and Anna to the Hofoper for the unveiling of the Rodin sculpture. William took his copy of *Das Lied von der Erde* for Bruno Walter. Mahler's bust surveyed the space now called *The Mahler Room* where many of the Viennese great and good had gathered. There were representatives from the Imperial household but none from the city council. The mayor, Herr Lüger did not attend. Those who packed the room to listen to Bruno Walter's speech were predominantly Jewish. Alma was veiled and wearing black. Herr Walter invited Alma to speak but she was too overcome to be able to say anything. Walter spoke and said that Mahler had found both immortality and eternal rest. Mahler's music lived on and his spirit would always be with us. He announced the forthcoming performance of *Das Lied von der Erde* in Munich.

Alma left the room with the others who were going to the bar. William approached Bruno Walter and showed him the score of *Das Lied* that he had carefully copied. Bruno Walter looked at the score, astonished and delighted, and asked William where he got it. William told him that Herr Mahler had asked him to make a clean copy for Herr Walter. He told Walter that the last *Ewig* should sound like a footprint, the two syllables stepping toe and heel but not on the ground. Herr Mahler wanted to hear the footprint in the air. Bruno Walter stared at William in amazement. 'Did Herr Mahler tell you anything else?' 'Yes,' said William. 'He told me to that this piece could only be performed after thirty rehearsals. He expressly forbids it to be performed with anything less than thirty rehearsals and he has asked me to place myself at your disposal.'

William went over to the table in the corner where Mahler was sitting.

'Very good, William. Well done. He ought to be able to get a few of those rehearsals. Wasn't that a boring speech? He's got such a dull voice. Do you still have my baton? Good. When it comes to the performance, put it on the podium beside the score. I'd like him to use it. You and Anna are making a good job of the house. I'm glad that Mechtilde's coming. That'll cheer up Alma and it'll be good for the Hofoper costume department too. And Miss Turner's coming too. Well done. That wasn't Alma's finest hour. Her return will be good for you and Anna and it would also let Alma, who feels guilty, off the hook. Grazie mille.'

William asked Mahler why he sometimes spoke in Italian. Mahler told him that everyone in Heaven speaks Italian. 'I'm delighted you and Anna are going to Italian lessons. Now go downstairs to the bar and rescue Alma before she gets drunk. Vai! Vai! Alla prossima volta|! Ciao!'

William collected Meddi from the station and brought her to Pokornygasse. Alma tried on the new gown that Meddi had made for her. Anna went to her studio with a large box of plasticene. Meddi admired the newly decorated house and offered to make curtains. Alma asked Meddi to choose the material. Meddi asked if the stores were far away. Alma said, 'Yes. They're in Paris.' And so the day after Meddi arrived in Vienna, Alma took Meddi with her to Paris.

On the way to the station William asked Meddi about the New York Philharmonic. 'Does it sound as good as it did when Mahler was conducting?'

'It is an even better orchestra now they have taken on some younger players,' she said. 'The new brass section is wonderful. Especially the new lead trumpet.'

William asked Alma if she would tell him where they would be staying in Paris. Alma hesitated.

William pressed her, 'Just in case....'

'Just in case what?'

'In case Anna....'

'I think that's wise,' interrupted Meddi. Anna might want to get in touch with her mother.'

Alma rummaged in her handbag for the reservation, scribbled the name of the hotel for William, and said, 'Only if it's very urgent.'

William helped Alma and Meddi onto the train. Meddi leaned out of the window and said to William, 'There's nothing there for either you or Johnny. You live in different worlds. There's no going back. Move on, William. Vorbei. It's over.' The train pulled out of the station.

It was a glorious late September week in Vienna. William and Anna collected wild fruits as the forest turned gold in the late summer sun. William picked berries, eagerly searching out the biggest and ripest fruit with a hunter's eye and an urgent enthusiasm. Anna sauntered idly among the bushes apparently lost in a daydream. William could not understand how Anna managed to pick so much more than he did. When they got home Anna went to her studio leaving William to pick out the insects, clean the fruit and make the jam.

William was baking bread when Anna came in with a sunflower in a bottle on a plate. She had wrapped a twig in green plasticene and attached the plasticene covered stalk to a circle of card. She had made leaves in yellow and green plasticene and had filled the centre of the flower with hundreds of tiny balls of plasticene – each one no bigger than a pinhead – arranged in a spiral moving from the centre of the flower to the circumference. The flower was sitting in a wine bottle and in place of a label she had arranged, in very finely rolled yellow plasticene, the word 'girasole' in old-fashioned handwriting. The bottle sat at one end of an elliptical white platter which she had painted with black rays extending from the bottle to the circumference.

'Girasole'? It means 'sun wheel.' Let's put it in the garden.'

It was a sunny afternoon. She laid the plate on the ground, turned the flower to the sun, looked at the shadow on the plate and said to William, 'It's four o'clock.' William looked at his watch and said, 'It's three o'clock.' 'No, it's not,' said Anna. 'The sun says four. It's time for bread and jam!'

William was taken aback when he answered a knock at the door and found Mahler's doctor from New York, Dr Joseph Fraenkel, on the doorstep.

Dr Fraenkel said he had come to see Alma.

'She's not here.'

'Do you know where she's gone?'

'She's gone shopping.'

'Do you mind if I wait here until she comes home?'

William explained that she had gone shopping in Paris and wasn't expected home until next week.

Dr Fraenkel asked William if he knew where Alma was staying.

William hesitated, 'Is it urgent?'

'Very urgent.'

William showed Frankel the note that Alma had thrust into his hand before she got onto the train. Fraenkel could not read Alma's handwriting. William, who was more familiar with Alma's hand, managed to decipher 'Hotel Lutetia'. He lifted the telephone, asked the operator to connect him, got through, and, addressing the hotel receptionist in French, asked if he could speak with guest Frau Alma Mahler.

The receptionist said they did not have a guest of that name. William tried again – 'Alma Schindler?' No guest of that name either. William had one last try – 'Mechtilde Mûller?' 'Ah yes. Perhaps you mean her sister, Alma Müller? Hold on and I will put you through to their room.' William waited but there was no answer. The receptionist came back to William to say the sisters had gone out and that he should try later.

William rewrote the name and address of the hotel neatly and gave it to Dr Fraenkel.

Dr Fraenkel asked William if Mahler had died peacefully. He told Dr Fraenkel that right up to the end Mahler had been reading poetry and as he read, instead of turning the pages, he tore them out of the book. Mahler's deathbed was covered in poems. At the very end Mahler was speaking with Mozart. He was urgently trying to tell Mozart something but was running out of breath and when he did finally run out of breath there was a long rattle… William's words were lost in tears. Dr Fraenkel too was weeping. He took William's hand and told him that the swabs he had taken from Mahler in New York indicated that there wasn't the slightest hope that Mahler could survive. No one had ever survived a bacterial infection of the heart. Alma had done well to get her husband back to Vienna before he died.

Dr Fraenkel asked William to tell him about funeral. He was surprised when William said he had not been there. William did not tell Dr Fraenkel why he hadn't gone. Bringing Maria from her grave in Maiernigg to her father's grave at Grinzing was a journey he shared with Mahler and no one else.

'And how is my beautiful Alma?'

William was still trying to digest the information the hotel receptionist had revealed about Alma being Meddi's new sister.

Dr Fraenkel sought William's view on how Alma would react to his feelings. William assured the doctor that his condolences would be a comfort to her. The doctor, who wasn't listening to William, announced, 'I fell in love with Alma the first time I saw her.'

William gazed at Fraenkel in disbelief. The doctor, an elderly respectable Jew, an eminent neuroscientist in America, was, like Mahler, much older than Alma.

Fraenkel, oblivious to William's disbelief, kept going. 'Anyone who has seen us in the same room together knows how I feel. Alma knows how I feel. She is waiting for me to declare my feelings so that the three of us, Mahler, Alma, and me, can be together forever. Our love for each other will overwhelm us all. Our terrible pain will soon be over. I must go to Paris now and tell her.'

Dr Fraenkel picked up his hat and made for the door. William thought to shake hands with the doctor but, in response to William's outstretched hand, the doctor took William in his arms and hugged him.

William wished he had never given Fraenkel the address of the Paris hotel.

When Alma and Meddi came back from Paris Meddi went to work at the Hofoper. Every morning William drove Meddi to work and at the end of the day he went to the Hofoper to bring her home. For two weeks they chatted every morning and every evening on their way to and from the opera. Meddi asked him if he remembered Dr Fraenkel, the New York doctor who took them all to a séance on New Year's Eve. She told William that Dr Fraenkel had turned up at their hotel in Paris. 'Can you believe that? William was unable to say 'yes' or 'no', but he did wonder if Alma had been displeased to have her time in Paris interrupted by the American doctor. Meddi assured William that Alma had been delighted and was very flattered by Dr Fraenkel's attention, until he asked her to marry him. Alma told Fraenkel that she had only ever thought of him as a friend, that he was much too old for her, that she would not be good for him, and anyway, he was already married and she was in mourning. 'Worse than that,' added Meddi, 'nobody in Europe has ever heard of him and he's Jewish. Much better for him to go back to his wife in New York.' William wondered if Meddi thought Dr Fraenkel's behaviour was rather odd. Meddi thought most men behave oddly. 'They want to have a child and, in order to possess the child, they have to possess the mother. There are only a few days in the life of a woman when she is not the property of a father or a husband – the brief period when she is pursued by men and she is able to name her price, which can be as little as a bunch of flowers if she's an ordinary girl or, if she's a princess, she might require a dragon to be slain, or a pearl retrieved from the depths of a magic lake. When the price is met, she yields. Her surrender is blessed by a priest, she becomes the property of her husband and bears his children. What little and very temporary power she enjoyed vanishes forever. At the Met many of the women I worked with spoke to me about their unhappiness. They were unhappy because they were with a man or they were unhappy because they were not with a man. Dr Fraenkel isn't odd. He's unhappy. I imagine his wife is unhappy too.

You're not unhappy, are you, William? You are a good friend. Of all the men I know I think you are the least odd.' As she got out of the car at the Hofoper Meddi told William not to worry about Dr Fraenkel. Alma had never thought about how he had found their hotel in Paris.

Later that day, when he went to collect her, Meddi told William about the two American women they had met in Paris – Gertrude, and Alice. They lived together and their home was open to artists. 'Picasso has the most startling black eyes,' she said. 'They are dark scalpels that cut away your clothes and then they cut away your skin. Gertrude proudly showed us Picasso's portrait of her. There was something of a likeness even though he had transformed Gertrude's face into a mask. I didn't like it and neither did Alma. Picasso offered to paint Alma's portrait. Alma declined. She thought that Picasso didn't like women and would paint something horrible. On the other hand, Matisse was warm and gentle, but he didn't make Alma an offer. Alma is now determined to have a portrait and will get her stepfather to arrange something. She doesn't want Klimt to do it. She wants someone new. She wants the next Viennese genius to paint her and for his reputation to be made by her portrait.'

William had made soup and bread for their evening meal and as they ate William asked Meddi if Gertrude and Alice were a couple? Meddi thought that they were. William told Meddi about his mother and her friend, Félicité, who had lived together in Basel. Meddi thought female couples could live together more comfortably in Basel than in Vienna and that it was probably even easier in Paris.

Meddi invited Anna to spend the day with her at the Hofoper. In the evening Anna brought home a box containing everything she had made. Anna took her box into her studio, did not join Meddi and William for supper.

Meddi told William that Anna wasn't interested in dress making and had spent the day making butterflies. 'Anna's butterflies are rather unusual. They're not symmetrical. The patterns in the cloth are regular and it is easy to cut butterflies shapes which are symmetrical. But Anna cut her cloth at different angles so that the wings are always asymmetrical. At first I thought she had not noticed what she was doing but it soon became clear that she knew exactly what she was doing. I asked her why she was avoiding the symmetry and she told me that if she wanted symmetrical butterflies she would go into the garden and look at real ones. She told me that if God wanted to make butterflies symmetrical that was his business. She thought symmetry was boring.'

Later, when William went to say goodnight to Anna he found a 'do not disturb' sign on the door.

Next morning when William went to Anna's room he found the child was fast asleep in an aviary of fluttering butterflies. She had glued her butterflies onto card and hung them on thread from drinking straws. Each straw was carefully weighted with asymmetrical butterflies and the balance of each assembly hanging from the ceiling was so fragile that William's very presence in the room had set them into motion. William brought Meddi to Anna's room to look at what the child had done. They gazed in wonder, William gently closed the door, and took Meddi to work.

On the way to the Hofoper Meddi asked William if Miss Turner was coming back.

'We haven't spoken to Alma yet. But I'm sure she'll return.'

'What makes you so sure?' asked Meddi.

'Because that's what her father wants,' replied William.

On the way back from the opera Mahler climbed into the car. 'May I join you for the ride home? I have been having second thoughts about Puccini's music. It's better than I thought it was. He is rather clever. His subject is contemporary but his musical palette is not, and so his audiences get today's stories clothed in yesterday's music. A winning combination. His operas will go better at the box office than contemporary works that clothe ancient myths and legends in a dissonant modern idiom. His opera, *Madame Butterfly,* about the American sailor and the geisha girl is especially good. Set in Japan, it's a heart-breaking story, full of good tunes, and I think it would look wonderful if my daughter was involved in the design. The set will float like a butterfly and the story will sting like a hornet. The audience will join in with the humming chorus. The idea for such a project might well come from costumes. It was done once before in Vienna during my time. It was not a success. Weingarter thinks I never rated Puccini and that might be reason enough to encourage the poor chap to have a go at it himself.'

'Meddi won't be staying with you for long. She is looking for a place of her own which will be more convenient for her work at the Hofoper. It will answer Meddi's need for independence and Alma's desire to spend time alone with Meddi without having you and Anna around. That will free up your guest room for Miss Turner. Get in touch with Miss Turner now and ask her to return.'

'It's only a month until the premier of *Das Lied von der Erde*. Bruno Walter has started working with the soloists and there's a problem with the tempo of the fourth song, *Von der Schönheit*. The soloist has complained that the movement cannot be sung at the tempo I marked. Herr Walter agrees and has told her that the copyist, that's you, William, must have made a mistake. You never made a mistake. However, Herr Walter and his soloist are correct when they say it cannot be sung at that tempo. That is exactly the point and I insist that it is sung at the tempo as marked. Do you know the music I am referring to?'

William answered, 'The horse music?'

'Exactly. Did you form an opinion?'

William told Mahler that he couldn't wait to hear it.

'It's music for galloping horses. It may not be obvious to Herr Walter as he sits at the piano that he is dealing with a musical stampede. It will sound far more dangerous with an orchestra. But when the horses stampede the music must fly at the tempo horses gallop, and I want the soloist to sing as if she is clinging onto a stampeding horse! I would rather the audience was afraid the singer was about to be thrown off the horse than to hear the words she is singing. Please tell Herr Walter to rehearse at a tempo that is uncomfortable for the soloist and then when it comes to the performance tell him to take it even faster. I think it is often the case that you can achieve an effect in performance precisely by doing it differently from the way in which it was rehearsed. The performers will be cross with Herr Walter but the audience will be exhilarated. The music is for the excitement of the audience, not the comfort of the musicians.'

At Pokornygasse they both got out of the car. Mahler disappeared and William went upstairs to wake Anna and prepare her breakfast. He sat on the sleeping girl's bed and stroked Anna's hair. He laid his hand on her shoulder. The butterflies above her responded to his movement, but not Anna. She was fast asleep and would not be roused. William looked at the creatures fluttering above his head. He left her to sleep and ate his breakfast alone.

William heard a key in the door. He knew it wasn't Mahler. Mahler didn't need a key and only ever turned up when William was expecting him. He wasn't expecting Alma, who had hardly been to Pokornygasse since she and Meddi had returned from Paris. She was clutching a bouquet of white flowers.

Alma was rather put out to discover that Anna was still fast asleep. 'But it's after mid-day! You are far too soft with her. She needs a firmer hand. When Miss Turner was with us the girl kept regular hours. Miss Turner would never have let her lie in bed all morning.' Alma tried to say something biblical about foolish virgins but couldn't remember how it went so she changed the subject, gave William the flowers and told him to take them to her husband's grave while she got Anna out of bed.

William tried to explain that Anna had been up all night. Alma looked alarmed. 'She started working on something and wouldn't go to sleep until she had finished. Come and see.'

Alma opened her daughter's bedroom door and the butterflies all took flight. Alma looked from the butterflies to her sleeping child and back to the butterflies with a look of incomprehension that reminded William of the way she looked at her husband after she first heard his Seventh Symphony in Prague. Then, as if attempting to blow out all the candles on a birthday cake, Alma blew at the butterflies, which scattered around the room. Alma sat down on the edge of Anna's bed and with an impatient gesture dismissed William.

In the last days of autumn the cemetery looked different from the way it had appeared to William when he had driven there with Maria in the spring. He got lost and had to ask a gardener where Mahler's grave was.

The headstone was a plain monolith engraved with one word, 'Mahler.' Beneath the stone in a huge vase stood a fresh bouquet of flowers with a card, 'Rest in Peace, your loving admirer, Dr Paul Kammerer.' There was no other vase. William arranged Alma's flowers in a vase that he took from a nearby grave, then got the tram home.

Pokornygasse
Vienna

Dear Elizabeth,

Anna and I have prepared a room for you in our new home. Alma misses you and would look very favourably on a request from you to return to your position. Anna is excited about seeing you again and so am I. I shall wire money to a bank in Edinburgh for your train fare.

With love.
William

Alma told William that her daughter needed more discipline. William asked if he could wire sufficient funds to Edinburgh for Miss Turner to purchase a train fare to Vienna? Alma rummaged in her handbag and gave William a handful of notes. William told her the flowers looked splendid on her husband's grave. He said nothing about Kammerer's flowers.

William called through the door to Anna. 'I'm going out to buy something for supper. I'll cook. You wash up!'

He bought spaghetti, tomatoes, carrots, and bacon, a piece of cheese from Parma, two sausages from Bologna, and a bottle of Chianti in a straw flask from Tuscany. He set the table with plates and glasses. He laid out forks and spoons and remembered how clumsily he and Miss Turner had handled the cutlery in Rome and how expertly Anna had eaten her plate of spaghetti.

William and Anna sat down to eat.

'Mama's got a job!'

William wasn't sure if he had heard correctly.

'Mama's got a job in a laboratory where she's doing experiments with spiders.'

William was dumbfounded and did not respond.

Anna continued, 'Are children in Italy allowed to drink wine?'

'Yes, as long as it's well qualified with water.'

Anna poured out two glasses of water and William tipped a thimbleful of wine into hers and two thimblefuls of wine into his.

'I had no idea your mother was looking for a job.'

Anna adopted a pose of grown-up gravitas and explained to William how her mother had wanted to be a composer but as there was room for only one composer in the house she had stepped back from her true vocation and allowed Papa to be the composer. Now that Papa was dead she no longer wanted to compose because her work would always be compared with his, so she had decided to strike out in a new direction. 'Mama doesn't have to work because Papa provided well for us, but Mama says it's now time for her to develop and grow and become an independent woman.'

'But your mother is a talented composer.'

'I know, but she doesn't like the direction modern music is taking and science is more exciting. Can you tell Miss Turner I would like her to bring me a kilt?'

'But kilts are for boys.'

'I can wear a kilt if I want.'

'It will be too warm in Italy for you to wear a kilt.'
'I will wear it when it's cold.'
'But we're going in the springtime.'
'I might stay until winter."
'What does your mother do in the laboratory?'
'She feeds fat juicy worms to spiders.' And with that Anna sucked in a long strand of spaghetti that disappeared into her mouth and splashed her nose with sugo.

William tried to do the same but could not find the end of a piece of spaghetti. He sucked in the dozen juicy strands of spaghetti that hung from his lips until his mouth was full and he had to bite what was left hanging from his mouth and let it drop back onto his plate. Anna thought it would be better if he didn't eat spaghetti while wearing a white shirt. William looked down at the mess and blushed.

'Why does your mother feed worms to the spiders?'
'So that they will learn where to find their food. It's an experiment.'
'And what's the experiment designed to prove?'
'It's to show that when the spiders have babies the baby spiders will also be able to find the food.'
'Because the grown-up spiders teach them?'
'No. Because the babies will already know.'
'How will they know?'
'Because parents can pass on what they have learned to their children in their genes. What are genes?'
'I don't know,' said William. 'Do you feed worms to your butterflies?'
'Don't be silly. They don't eat worms.'
'What do they eat?'
'Colours. Yellow for breakfast, green for lunch, and red for dinner. Can I have some more?'
'You'll get fat!'
'I don't care.

Anna poured herself a glass of water and asked for more wine. William gave her another thimbleful.

'Mama's going to have her portrait painted. It's a Christmas present from Grandpa.'
'Is Grandpa going to do it?'
'No. He asked someone else to do it. Mama told me, but I can't remember his name.'
'If Grandpa has arranged it then it'll be someone really good.'

'When we go to Italy I would like to sit in the Piazza Navona and make portraits. I could make a lot of money doing that. Papa's new music will be played in Munich. It's on November 20th. Mama is going with the scientist who works at her laboratory.'

'What's his name?'

'I can't remember. Will you take me?'

'I'll ask your mother.'

What if she says no?

'Then you won't be able to go.'

'Then neither will you.'

'Why's that?'

'Because you'll have to stay here and look after me. So, you'd better ask Mama very nicely then we can go together.'

CHAPTER 40

Das Lied von der Erde

Bruno Walter asked the orchestra to repeat the last few bars and asked the American mezzo-soprano, Sara Cahier, to deliver the two syllables of the last word *Ewig* as if she was stepping on air – first heel and then toe. Orchestra and soloist repeated the last twenty bars to Bruno Walter's satisfaction. He thanked everyone and looked forward to the dress rehearsal on Sunday.

William approached Herr Walter and congratulated him. He wanted to have a word about the tempo in the fourth movement. Bruno Walter assured William that everything was in hand. He had spotted and corrected the mistake. He told William the score he had copied was otherwise perfect. 'As you can hear, it's going very well.' Bruno Walter picked up his score from the podium and was about to leave but William stood in his way. There was a moment's silence between them before Herr Walter invited William to speak.

'Herr Mahler was concerned about the tempo of the stampede in the fourth movement.'

'I'm not surprised,' said Bruno Walter, laughing. 'Our mezzo-soprano was also concerned, but we have found a tempo with which she is comfortable.'

'Herr Mahler was concerned that the singer should not feel comfortable. When we were working on the final draft, he drew my attention to the tempo, and he told me that the singer would not like it. May I tell you what he said to me?'

Bruno Walter put his score back on the podium and listened.

William told Herr Walter that the stampede should begin at a fair gallop, reins, bridles, stirrups, and spurs moving quickly but initially without danger. When the mezzo-soprano enters it should move more quickly and the accelerando must not slacken. It must keep getting quicker until it is clear the riders are no longer in control. The tempo which is now reckless gets even faster. The soprano, with her arms around the horse's neck and slipping off the saddle, is holding on for dear life and she cannot find a space to breathe. Mahler wishes you to know that's how it is to be heard, that the markings are as he intended, and that he is aware your soprano will not like it.'

'Herr Hidlebrand, Sara will walk out on this!'

'In that case, Herr Walter, you will need to find another singer.'

Bruno Walter waited but William had no more to say. The two men left the platform.

William and Anna collected Alma and Dr Paul Kammerer from Kammerer's Biological Experiment Institute on the Vienna Prater. William opened the door for Alma. Dr Kammerer held her back while he himself leant into the car, removed a scented handkerchief from his top pocket, and carefully wiped the passenger seat. Alma then got in and sat down. Kammerer walked around the car and William let him open the door on the other side for himself. Anna sat in front beside William and they drove to Munich.

Before the performance William found Bruno Walter in the conductor's room, combing his hair in front of the dressing-room mirror.

'Good evening, William. Have you come to wish me good luck?'

'You won't need any luck because you have prepared well.'

William took from his inside pocket Mahler's baton.

'Thank you, William, but I have my own.'

'Mahler insists that you conduct with this.'

Walter looked puzzled and then it dawned on him.

'Is this Mahler's baton?'

'Yes.'

There was great anticipation in the hall where the audience had been thrilled by Mahler's Eighth the previous year. Those in the audience who were expecting to hear similar music were surprised by the change in Mahler's vision. This new work did not look up with awe at the heavens but gazed fondly downwards with love and resignation towards the Earth, a dear green place to which the music finally bade farewell. When the last *Ewig* disappeared into the air the concert ended in silence. There was no applause. No one breathed. Walter stood still holding the baton in front of him. The orchestra and soloists did not move. Bruno Walter waited a very long time before he appeared to reawaken and return to the concert hall. He put the baton down. Some people shifted in their chairs. A few people coughed. The applause which began as a trickle turned into a flood and engulfed the hall. The orchestra stamped their feet and the audience stood and cheered.

At the reception after the concert Alma wept copiously. She was comforted by Dr Kammerer and the two of them left early to return to the hotel. William congratulated Bruno Walter who was reluctant to return Mahler's baton. William assured Walter that he would be able to use it again for the premier of Mahler's Ninth in Vienna. Bruno Walter was unaware of any plans for the premiere of Mahler's last symphony.

Back at the hotel William presented Anna with a gift, 'on the occasion of the premier of *Das Lied von der Erde.*' She unwrapped a willow pattern plate. William told her the Chinese story of the king's beautiful daughter who eloped with the gardener and how they had lived happily on an island until they were discovered by the angry king. He sent his soldiers to put the lovers to death, but they escaped by turning into birds and flying away.

Anna told William that that was what she was going to do.

'Run off with the gardener?'

'No. Turn into a bird and fly away.'

'Where will you fly to?'

'Italy.'

The next day William drove back to Vienna. Alma and Kammerer slept in the back. Anna sat in front with William and as he drove they sang her father's song about the young boys arriving on horseback and showing off to the Chinese girls gathering flowers. When the horses bolted William drove faster. Anna held on to the reins with one hand and slapped her thigh with the other in the thrill of the stampede. William only slowed down when the horses disappeared over the horizon leaving one rider behind. One of the girls looks towards the boy and they fall in love. Anna asked him to sing it again and again and every time the horses stampeded William pushed hard on the accelerator. Alma and Kammerer slept through it all.

Back in Vienna William dropped Alma and Kammerer at the Biological Experiment Institute. Kammerer helped Alma out of the car and then, leaning into the car, he kissed the seat where Alma had been sitting. Anna thought Kammerer was a very silly man.

Back at Pokornygasse Anna went to bed with a cup of hot chocolate and a biscuit on her willow pattern plate.

William asked Mahler what he thought of the performance.

‚Quite good,' said Mahler. Bruno did an excellent job.'

'Was the stampede fast enough?'

'No, but it was good. I don't know if I could have achieved more tension. On the one hand Sara Cahier, clinging on to her horse, was determined not to go any faster while on the other hand Bruno was under a lot of pressure to 'giddy-up'. I thought he did rather well, thanks to you.'

'What did I do?'

'You told him to get another mezzo-soprano. I never told you to say that.'

'I'm sorry. I must have imagined it.'

'You have a wonderful imagination. Bruno Walter is young and tries to please everyone. When you told him to find another soprano you gave him the mettle he lacks. You and Anna achieved the right tempo when you sang in the car. If Herr Walter had driven at that speed what do you think is the worst that could have happened?'

William didn't answer because he knew where Mahler was going with this.

Mahler continued, 'The performance would have veered out of control and crashed. Huge embarrassment all round but no one hurt. When a car veers out of control and crashes there are likely to be fatalities. It's the difference between art and life. There may come a time when the road from Munich to Vienna is good enough for you to drive at forty kilometres an hour. This afternoon was not that time.'

'Forty kilometres an hour?' asked William blushing.

'Forty-two, to be precise. I mention it because there were people in the car whom I love.'

William wondered if Mahler's declaration of love might include Dr Kammerer.

'It includes my daughter, my widow, and you,' said Mahler. 'Paul Kammerer may be tiresome but that is not a capital offence.'

'Who are you talking to?'

William looked around and saw Anna standing in the doorway holding her willow pattern plate. William looked back and Mahler was gone.

Anna asked if she could have another biscuit.

CHAPTER 41

Kokoschka

William and Anna got back from their Italian lesson and found Alma at home. Anna spoke to her mother in English. 'Good evening, Mama. How are you keeping?'

William, replying on Alma's behalf, told Anna, in English, that he thought her mother was keeping very well. Anna was sent to bed with a hot chocolate and a biscuit.

William could see that Alma wanted to talk and he brought the Benedictine to the table. She told William that she was no longer in mourning. Six months was quite enough and now she intended to get on with the rest of her life. She poured out two glasses and drank a toast to the future. Then she poured herself another glass. She intended to host a family dinner on Christmas Eve. She wanted to think about the menu, the gifts, and the guests. William was surprised at Alma's new interest in Christmas. She proposed to invite her mother and stepfather and their daughter Maria, who was fourteen, and her own sister, Gretel, Gretel's husband, Wilhelm, and their son, who was also called Wilhelm. She herself would host the dinner. She wanted Meddi, William and Miss Turner to be her guests and she thought it would be an ideal opportunity to introduce the family to her new friend. Alma poured herself another drink.

'Dr Kammerer?'

'Don't be silly,' said Alma. 'He's Jewish! Jews don't celebrate Christmas. We're Christians, for God's sake! I will invite the young man who is painting my portrait, Oskar Kokoschka. The portrait is a Christmas gift from my stepfather, and the artist will unveil the painting on Christmas Eve.'

William made a note of the guests. He had never heard of Gretel.

'We don't talk about her, said Alma. 'She's not well and is often away on a cure. Gretel inherited something from our father. He once had diphtheria, which left him with a paralysis. There are times when I feel so unhappy, I wonder if I have not inherited the same thing myself. Gretel, her husband, and her son will be with us because it is a family occasion.'

William suspected there was no connection between diphtheria, paralysis and unhappiness but didn't pursue the matter. He counted the guests and said,

'That makes twelve.'

'Yes.'

'Where will they all sit?'

'I will host the dinner at my mother's house. We shall have carp, goose, and a gingerbread house. You and Meddi will buy gifts for everyone. Anna, who is quite the little artist, can make the place settings.'

'What should I get for your sister's family?'

'Whatever you please. I thought you were good at choosing things.'

'But I don't know them.'

'The boy is ten years old, so choose something for a little boy. His father is an artist – cigars or gloves or a scarf – anything will do – and my sister is unhappy so it doesn't matter what you get her. I am giving this apartment to Herr Kokoschka while he works on my portrait. He does not wish to be disturbed. Now that Meddi has her own place you and Anna will stay with her until Christmas. She needs some help getting her new place sorted. Take everything you need because I do not want either of you to return here and disturb Oskar.'

'After Christmas,' continued Alma, 'we will move out of town and live in the country. I am having a house built on a piece of land which my late husband bought in Semmering. I think we will all be healthier and happier living in the fresh air. Vienna has become far too Jewish. We'll be better off living somewhere else.' Alma poured herself another drink. 'We will have a Merry Christmas and then we'll have a Happy New Year,' and she drank a toast to that. Then she drank a toast to 1912 which she hoped would be better than 1911.

Alma got up from the table unsteadily and, taking the bottle with her, bade William good night, and retired to her room.

It didn't take William long to pack everything he needed for the next fortnight at Meddi's, but Anna took all day. She needed to move her entire studio. Alma's patience snapped when Anna insisted on dismantling the butterflies. Her mother told her to leave the butterflies behind. Anna sulked.

When they arrived at Meddi's Anna refused to speak. She took all her bags and materials to her new room. She did not join Meddi and William for the evening meal. William, who had been looking forward to spending two weeks with Meddi, was disappointed at such a poor start. As William was going to bed Anna emerged from her room, told William she couldn't sleep, and insisted on returning to her mother's apartment to collect the butterflies. William sent her back to her room. She burst into tears, went back to her room, slammed the door, and smashed a plate. Meddi came out of her room, sat William down, and gently massaged his head.

In the morning Meddi went to work. Anna didn't appear at breakfast time. William thought it best to leave her alone. He washed up the breakfast dishes, swept the kitchen floor, made his bed, looked at Anna's door, made himself a cup of coffee, looked at Anna's door again and knocked. No answer. He went in. She was fast asleep. He picked up the broken shards of the willow pattern plate and was about to leave the room when his eye was drawn to the sleeping form under the blankets. Anna was far too still. In a panic William pulled back the blankets and saw, instead of Anna, two cushions.

William ran to the car and drove to Alma's where he found Anna with Oskar Kokoschka. On two easels at either end of the room sat two portraits of Alma. One of the canvases showed Alma wearing the cerise gown that Meddi had made for her. The other showed Alma wearing nothing. The table was littered with drawings of female nudes. Some were sketches of the whole female form, others showed only female thighs splayed open with genitalia and pubic hair portrayed in detail. The room smelled of turpentine. Anna was sitting at the table next to Kokoschka with a paintbrush and paper. She looked up from her work and casually introduced William to Kokoschka, then returned to her painting. Kokoschka got up from his seat beside Anna, shook hands with William, then, hearing footsteps on the stairs, went into the hall where he confronted Alma.

'You said you would be half an hour,' complained Kokoschka. 'That was two hours ago. It's now midday. Where have you been?'

Alma told Kokoschka it was none of his 'damn business.'

'Your daughter and her friend are here.'

Alma marched into the room and shouted at them both. 'I told you I was not to be disturbed. 'I told you to stay away from here. What part of that do you not understand? Get the hell out of here, the pair of you!'

William left the room, leaving Anna to deal with her mother's anger. He sat in the car and waited.

A few minutes later Anna appeared, climbed into the passenger seat, and told William that everything was all right now. 'Mama's new friend is going to look after my butterflies and I got a postcard from Miss

Turner.' She showed William a picture of Greyfriars Bobby. They set off back to Meddi's apartment.

That evening William and Meddi dined together while Anna stayed in her room. William confessed to Meddi that he was a weak man. She suggested that after such a difficult day he must be tired. He told her he wasn't weak because he was tired. He was tired because he was weak. He had two mistresses, one of whom was seven years old, and he felt exhausted by his inability to cope. Meddi told William he had done well. 'You are not expected to lock Anna up, and you are not to blame that she ran off. You knew where she had gone, you collected her, and brought her back. Her own father could not have done any better. Don't punish yourself.'

They went to Anna's room with a sandwich and a glass of milk and found the child painting moustaches. She had made portraits of Meddi and William, her mother and grandparents and given them all moustaches. She showed William and Meddi what Kokoschka had taught her. With a thick brush and just the right amount of paint and with gentle pressure on the brush she could use every hair to leave a mark on the paper. 'Look,' she said, and she drew a mouth, picked up a tiny amount of paint on the end of her brush, painted a moustache on the upper lip with two brush strokes – one to the left and one to the right –and in less than two seconds the child had created a thick moustache that looked as if she had meticulously painted every single hair. 'Isn't that clever?'

The following day William and Meddi were surprised to see the direction Anna's expertise had taken. She had moved from moustaches to beards, to heads with long hair, short hair, straight hair and curly hair, then pubic hair.

Meddi brought home from work a book on origami for Anna who disappeared with it into her room and made a paper animal farm.

In the evening Meddi and William ate together – a dish of aubergines, cheese and tomatoes drenched in olive oil, and garnished with basil. Anna was too busy with her animal farm to join them at the table and William took a plate of supper to her room. William took off his apron and sat at the table with Meddi. The aubergines were smooth, the cheese was dense, and the tomatoes were rich.

'Did you make this?'

'Yes'

'I thought you were decorating.'

'I stopped for half an hour, sliced the aubergines, and put them in the oven. It took no time at all. Is it all right?'

'Yes.' Meddi reached out and took William's hand.

William held her hand and told her how much he enjoyed preparing food. 'I like the colours – orange pumpkins, purple aubergines, red tomatoes and all the different shades of green from darkest broccoli to the lightest cabbage – potatoes or radishes so white inside and so different from their richly coloured skins. Apples red and green! Berries black and red! And oranges! I like to see them...'

Meddi looked into his eyes and kept hold of his hand.

'...and to feel them. The hardness that tells you it's not yet ripe – the touch that tells you it is, the kneading that transforms dough from something that feels stodgy and lifeless into something elastic, springy and ready to rise. I love working with my hands.'

Neither of them ate. She kept looking and holding while he talked.

'And the sound! Boiling in one key and frying in another. And the smell!' exclaimed William.

'Tell me about the smell, 'asked Meddi.

William paused. 'I can't. There aren't any words for smells, but every meal smells different. Even the same thing prepared on different days smells different.

'Taste? You forgot taste.'

'Taste?' William took a forkful, savoured it and, waving his knife and fork in the air, said 'Meravigliosa!'

'Well, you're a sensual one, aren't you? Did you cook for Johnny?'

William told Meddi that he and Johnny never ate like this.

'We had coffee and bread in the morning after Johnny had finished warming up, and then we were out all day at the conservatoire and all evening at the opera. We ate in cafes or on the street. Always on the move. We never cooked. It was Agnes in the kitchen at Trenkerhof who showed me how.'

William was about to put another forkful in his mouth when Meddi said, 'You've put on a bit of weight since we first met. It suits you. You look well.'

William lay in bed, masturbating. It was the first time in months. He had often lain awake at night clutching his penis while thinking of Johnny but it never amounted to anything and William was quickly bored. Tonight, it was different. The room he shared in Vienna with Johnny was alive all around him and he felt Johnny's presence. Meddi came into the room and stood beside his bed.

'My room stinks of paint! Can I sleep here?'

She didn't wait for an answer, tossed off her nightgown, and climbed into bed beside him.

'You were thinking of Johnny,' said Meddi.

'How did you know?'

'I could hear you. Can I touch?'

She massaged William's erection. William responded by gently stroking her hair but his erection was collapsing.

'How did Johnny do it?' she asked.

William reached for her hand and adjusted her fingers.

She told him to think of Johnny if he wanted to.

She stroked and then William began to thrust.

She hugged him with her legs. She kissed his ears, his eyes, his cheeks, his lips and kissed his tongue deeply, pushed her breast into his, rubbed herself on his thigh, holding him tight as he shuddered and spilled his seed over her. William buried his head in the hollow between her neck and shoulder and began to weep. She stroked his hair and nibbled his ear.

She asked if he was sad.

'I don't think so.'

'Why are you crying?'

'I feel ashamed.'

She took his hand and placed it between her legs. He was surprised that her pubic hair was as prickly as his own. It wasn't as soft as the hair on her head. She laid her hand on top of his and pressed gently and his middle finger eased into her vagina. He felt the moisture as he followed her directions. When her body became tense he moved more firmly and more quickly. She turned away from him and he felt a harsh thump of excitement explode inside her and then recede in wave after wave that left her exhausted. She turned to him, kissed his forehead, his nose, his mouth and then they fell asleep.

Next day Meddi went to work. Anna stayed in her room and William decorated Meddi's room. He prepared and set a large pot of *bonen ein tumpf* on the stove. At supper time Anna brought a farm of paper pigs and a litter of paper piglets to the table. The soup smelled wonderful. Anna wanted to know what was in it.

'Beans, potatoes, carrots and sausages.'

'What kind of sausages?'

'Pork.'

Anna swept up her pigs, took them to the safety of her room, then returned to her soup.

Meddi asked if it was another recipe from the cook in Toblach.

'I made it up myself. Cooking is like speaking a language. Once you know the grammar and have some vocabulary you can say whatever you like. She taught me the grammar, I chose the ingredients, and the result speaks for itself.'

'Can I have some more?' said Meddi.

Later that night when Meddi came to William's room. He asked her if her room still stank of paint.

'Even worse than last night', she said and climbed in beside him.

She lay her hand on his chest and felt his erection with her elbow.

'Thinking of Johnny again?' she asked.

'Even more than last night,' and he put his arms around her.

She held his erection and licked his eyes, his nose, his mouth, his chin, his breast, his nipples, his stomach, and asked him if Johnny had ever taken it in his mouth.

'Yes.'

'Can I?'

'Yes'

He felt her lips, her tongue, and her teeth. She massaged his erection in her mouth. He told her he was about to come but she kept him in her mouth and swallowed his seed.

They lay beside each other. He buried his head on her shoulder.

'Tears?'

'No.'

'Happy?'

'Yes.'

'Was it all right?'

'Yes.'

William stroked the inside of her thigh and she opened her legs. He leant over her and kissed breasts, licked her nipples, kissed her stomach.

'You don't have to, William.'

'I'd like to try. Does Alma do it?'

'Yes.'

He laid his hand on her pubic hair and heard her gasp with pleasure. She pushed herself up the bed and he knelt between her legs. He moved himself into place first with his nose and then with his tongue. She held his hands tight as he licked her. He felt her guiding him with her hands and her heels on his back moving him towards where she wanted him to go, then she clasped his head. He worked his tongue firmly and vigorously as she dug her fingers into his scalp. She stiffened, moaned, breathed quickly, then she stopped, held her breath, then William felt her climax and release. He pushed himself back up to the bed and they lay in each other's arms.

'Can I stay here with you?'

'Of course.'

'It really doesn't smell good in my room.'

'I know', said William. 'I'm going to put the topcoat of gloss on your window frames tomorrow. Your room will smell even worse.'

'Good,' said Meddi,' and they both fell asleep.

CHAPTER 42

Christmas 1911

At 8am on December 20th at Vienna's Westbanhof station William Hildebrand met Elizabeth Turner. They held each other longer, more tearfully and more joyfully than the other reunions that surrounded them on the platform. Elizabeth was taken aback by the warmth of William's welcome. William carried her luggage to the car. She danced out of the station behind him. He took her to the Hotel Imperial where she would be staying until after Christmas. 'Alma is having her portrait painted and doesn't want to be disturbed. I'm staying with Anna at Meddi's. We'll drop your luggage at the hotel then I'll take you to Anna. We're just around the corner from the hotel.'

When they arrived at Meddi's they found a large sign on the door which said,

'PRINCESS ANNA WELCOMES QUEEN ELIZABETH TO VIENNA'.

On the dining room table Anna displayed a model of the Forth Bridge that she had made with drinking straws and mounted on a blue canvas sheet on which she had painted tiny boats.

Anna was so excited she couldn't keep still. She took Lizzie to her room and showed her the origami farm. Lizzie presented Anna with *The Wind in the Willows* by Mr Kenneth Grahame, a Scottish writer who lived in Rome. Lizzie had inserted a bookmark at the beginning of Chapter Nine. She gave William a little tartan box bearing the name of an Edinburgh jeweller. It contained a circular Celtic brooch. Within a silver band a fine strand of silver traced repeated figures of eight, looping back on itself in a never-ending cycle. Lizzie said it was a 'badge of friendship.' William had never worn a brooch and did not know what to do with it. He thanked her and put it back in its box.

Anna was displeased when William told her that Lizzie would be staying just around the corner in the Hotel Imperial.

'You can sleep in my room,' she told Lizzie.

'But that's your studio and your bed is very small. But thank you anyway, Anna, that's very kind of you.'

'Then you can sleep in William's room.'

William told Anna that Lizzie's hotel couldn't be closer.

'Then I'll stay with you in the hotel,' said Anna and she went away to collect her things.

On December 21st it snowed. Alma was thrilled at the prospect of a perfect Christmas.

On Christmas Eve in the morning Carl Moll fetched the Christmas tree. Alma and Meddi decorated it. Alma's mother placed a large gingerbread house on the table and arranged twelve place settings around it. Anna folded the napkins into elaborate fans and placed a paper animal at each setting – an owl for grandmother, a walrus for grandfather, and for their daughter, Maria, a cow; an elephant for mother, a gorilla for her aunt Gretel, and for Gretel's husband and their son, two monkeys. She gave William an ostrich which stood on its legs and neck to appear as if its head was buried in the plate, for Meddi, a giraffe, and a Loch Ness Monster for Miss Turner in five pieces – a tail, three loops and a head to appear as if it was swimming through the plate. She gave Kokoschka a bear and for herself a lion. Anna Moll had wanted her granddaughter to sit next to her daughter.

'Maria's twelve and she will look after you like a big sister.'

Anna told her grandmother, 'She's not my big sister. She's my aunt. I've already got a big sister called Maria and she's dead.'

Shortly after the staff arrived to cook and serve the dinner Gretel's husband arrived to say that they would not be able to come as Gretel had attempted suicide and had been taken to hospital. Alma and her mother went with Wilhelm to his wife's bedside. Lizzie Turner took Anna and Maria to play in the snow. Meddi went into the kitchen to deal with the staff. Carl Moll sat in an armchair and wept. William sat with him.

Carl Moll told William that he should have refused Alma's insistence on having a family dinner. 'We are not a family. When my wife was married to Schindler she had an affair and became pregnant with Gretel. Alma, Gretel, and Maria are three sisters with different fathers. Maria is my daughter. Alma is Schindler's daughter, and Gretel, who thinks she is Alma's sister, is a bastard and has been unwell for years. When Alma was in America Gretel seemed to recover, but when Alma came back, she relapsed. Gretel doesn't hate Alma. She hates herself. Our world is broken. It can't be fixed. It should be destroyed to let life begin again. Gretel preferred to die than to sit with Alma this evening. Now Alma is sitting with Gretel in hospital. It would help Gretel if you went to the hospital and got Alma out of there.'

Meddi gave the goose, the carp, and the gingerbread house to the staff, paid and dismissed them. William drove to the hospital to fetch Alma. Miss Turner, Maria and Anna went out to build a snowman.

When he arrived at the hospital William found all the family in distress apart from Alma. William drove her back to the Molls and, although she didn't speak, William could sense an air of triumph in Alma's demeanour, as if everything had worked out just as she had planned.

William, Miss Turner and Anna decided to look for a restaurant where they could share a Christmas Eve dinner of hot dogs. On their way they met Oskar Kokoschka carrying a large framed canvas wrapped in a blanket. Anna asked Kokoschka if he had brought the painting of Mama wearing the purple gown or the one with Mama wearing a moustache between her legs? Kokoschka patted the child on the head and wished her a Merry Christmas. William thought about telling Kokoschka what he was walking into but didn't know where to start and so left Kokoschka to knock on the Moll's door and find out for himself.

CHAPTER 43

New Year 1912

Meddi spent New Year's Eve at a party with the ladies from the costumes at the Hofoper. Alma was either with Kokoschka or Kammerer, or perhaps with Gropius in Berlin. William and Anna returned with Lizzie to the apartment in Pornygasse. They spent the morning shopping for San Marzano tomatoes and buffalo mozzarella, pepperoncino, olive oil, and a bottle of Chianti in a straw flask. In the afternoon William set his dough to rise, then he and Anna stretched it. Anna took some of the dough to make pastry flowers. In the evening William made pizzas. He threw a red and white gingham cloth over the table, decanted the wine and stuck a candle into the empty flask and served up the pizzas while singing 'Libiamo' from *La Traviata*. As they ate they made a list of all the places they would visit in the springtime. Lizzie wanted to go to Venice and ride down the Grand Canal on a vaporetto. Anna wanted to go to Ravenna to see the mosaics. William wanted to go to the opera at La Fenice. Lizzie wanted to go to Milan to see the Duomo. Anna wanted to go to Venice to see the Bellini Madonnas in the Academia. William wanted to go to the opera at La Scala. Lizzie wanted to go to Naples to see Mount Vesuvius. Anna wanted to visit Pompeii. William wanted to go to the opera at Teatro San Carlo. Lizzie wanted to go to Rome to see the stray cats at the Torre Argentina. Anna wanted to go to Rome to paint portraits of people with moustaches in Piazza Navona. After Mahler's experience with the St Cecilia Orchestra William decided not to go to the opera in Rome but offered to accompany Lizzie to visit the stray cats. They looked at the map tracing the road from Vienna to Rome and saw that Venice and Ravenna were on the way. At the midnight bells they wished each other a Happy New Year. Lizzie and Anna went to bed. William finished off the wine and went outside to sit in the car.

 Mahler got into the passenger seat, wished William a Happy New Year, and told him that the road from Vienna to Venice passes close to Toblach, where the horse with no name would be pleased to see him again. 'Take a lump of sugar with you. I'm sorry about Christmas. It was a bad idea. I would not have let it happen if I had been alive. I'm not surprised it turned out badly. However, I am very surprised Herr Moll told you what lay behind Gretel's attempted suicide. Gretel and Alma think they are sisters. Neither of them knows the truth, but now you do. Herr Moll was feeling suicidal. He was thinking about setting fire to the house but instead he told you everything, and as you listened his suicidal impulses passed. His idea about destroying the world so that life can start again is nonsense. Breaking eggs to make an omelette is an expression used only by those who want to break eggs and never by those who want to make omelettes. Destruction is always a bad idea. One day Herr Moll will destroy himself.'

'I've been thinking about the silence at the end of *Das Lied von der Erde*. It was one minute and twelve seconds. It is not what Bruno Walter intended but he was unable to put the baton down after the last 'Ewig', and the silence launched the music into eternity. Before you leave for Italy, set Bruno Walter to work on the premier of my Ninth. I have a note for him regarding the conclusion. The music is to slip into eternity before the end so that it never finishes but goes on forever. I would like time to stop before the last sound dies away. On the last page the music must gradually disappear. The conductor may require the back seats of the strings to drop out. In that case I would insist that they continue to bow in unison with the front benches but without touching the strings. They will, of course, object that they are musicians and should not be asked to mime. The conductor will remind them that they are performers and insist they follow his direction. The conductor, in rehearsal, will lead the orchestra over the last six bars as slowly and as quietly as possible so that the sound is barely audible, and he will bring the symphony to its end with a final movement of his baton – but only in rehearsal. In performance the orchestra will perform the last six bars without the conductor. They will look to him for direction and will get none. The remorseless tick-tock in which you live on your side of eternity will cease when Herr Walter ceases to conduct. There will be confusion among the players as they grope their way through those last bars. Barely audible, and without a beat, the fabric of the temporal world will disintegrate, leaving the audience with a glimpse of eternity. Herr Walter must remain absolutely still. When the silence is established, he must continue to remain still.'

Mahler whispered those last words then said nothing. He sat next to William holding a finger in the air and was still. William waited. One minute. Two minutes. Then William broke the silence and asked Mahler, 'How long?'

'Four and a half minutes.'

'Four and a half minutes?' asked William in disbelief.

'Perhaps two or three seconds more,' answered Mahler. 'What do you think?

William didn't speak.

'But you have something in mind?'

'Yes,' said William.

'Have I got a soul?'

'I don't know.'

'I thought…given your situation…that you might be able to see whether I've got a soul or not.'

'How am I supposed to know if you've got one or not?'

'But I thought…you know…that you… being a spirit…'

'I am nothing of the kind. You know very well that I am a figment of your imagination.'

Mahler put his right arm around William and his left hand on William's breast. 'I don't know if you've got a soul, but your heart's in the right place.' Mahler kissed William on the cheek, ruffled William's hair, and got out of the car.

William told Lizzie that he was going to visit Meddi, who had returned from a New Year visit to her sisters.

'Why are you telling me?' asked Lizzie.

'I just thought you'd like to know where I was going.'

He turned to leave and said, 'I'm not in love with her, you know. And she's not in love with me.'

'It's none of my business,' snapped Lizzie.

Meddi could not visit her parents in Oberkochen because her father had refused to see her and so she stayed in a hotel where her sisters came to meet her. She told them all about New York and Vienna and the opera houses and the operas and the singers and the grand hotels and the ocean liners. 'I told them that women don't have to sleep with men if they don't want to and when I told them that I often slept with the widow of a famous composer and that one of my best friends was a homosexual man they giggled and didn't believe me. They loved my clothes, my hair, my perfume, and my jewellery. I gave them the dresses I had made for them. They mustn't say where they came from, but my mother will know. She will notice they are well made and will be impressed. She knew they were meeting me. She'll be pleased to know that I'm well and will keep that pleasure to herself. Nothing, however, will allay her fears about how I will fare in the next life where women go to the eternal rest they deserve after putting up with men in this life.

If there's a heaven, William, it will be a female paradise, because men go to hell.'

'Will I go to hell?'

'No. Homosexuals go to Heaven.'

'Even if they sometimes sleep with women?'

'Especially if they sometimes sleep with women,' said Meddi.

'But you don't believe in Heaven?'

'Of course not.'

'I don't want to believe in Heaven either.'

'Why not?'

'Because I haven't got a soul.'

Meddi put her hand on his breast. 'But your heart's in the right place.' And she kissed him. 'Will you stay here tonight?'

'Yes.'

'I don't want to sleep with you, William. I just don't want to be alone in the house tonight. Is that all right?'

'Do you think that Lizzie might be a bit like you?' asked William.

'She's not a bit like me,' said Meddi. 'Does she know that you are homosexual?'

'I don't think so.'

'Be careful, William.'

CHAPTER 44

A Grand Tour of Italy

William, Lizzie and Anna planned to set off on Friday, February 16th to arrive in Venice in time for the carnival. William asked if there was a carnival in Edinburgh.

'Good heavens, no!' exclaimed Lizzie.

He told her about the carnival in Basel. She asked if he was a Catholic.

'Not really,' said William. We wait until the Catholic cantons have finished their carnivals and then we have ours a week later. Basel erupts into three days of music, drinking and fireworks when the whole of Catholic Europe is wearing sackcloth and ashes. I was in a marching band with my mother but when I was fifteen I had to move to a different group because there are strict rules that do not allow you to be in the same group as your friends or relations. All the marching bands take trains to surrounding Catholic towns and villages where they march all night making a terrific noise. People trying to sleep don't like it. People selling wine love it. After a night of marching and drinking they take the train back to Basel. The station is crowded early in the morning with drummers and piccolo players returning from their night out. They have a breakfast of white wine and cake and then they march all around Basel. It goes on for three days.'

'They don't sound like Protestants to me. Is the carnival in Venice a Catholic one or a Protestant one?' asked Lizzie.

'When you're wearing a mask you can be whatever you want,' said William.

Lizzie wondered if it was true that Mahler was Jewish.

'Yes, but he converted to Catholicism, so he was a Catholic Jew.'

'What about Alma?'

'She's a Protestant so she and Gustav had a mixed marriage. Not because she was a Christian and he was a Jew, but because she was a Protestant and he was a Catholic.'

'Sounds like a mixed-up marriage.'

'It was. And he loved her.'

'And what about Anna?'

'Anna is Jewish. She used to be a Catholic Jew but now she's a Protestant Jew. Alma moved her over so that when Anna gets married she can get divorced if she wants to.'

'Are you trying to make me laugh?'

'Yes, and when we get to Venice I shall wear a cocked hat and a mask with a long nose. You and Anna will have wigs. Meddi will measure us for cloaks. Alma would like nothing better than to have us out of her way. She's busy building her new house and wondering what to do about Kokoschka and Gropius.'

'And when the carnival is over…?'

'Ravenna, Pisa, Florence, Rome, Naples. Let's not come back until June. What do you think?'

She threw her arms around him. He gave her a hug. She didn't let go.

William was concerned about the car. It was eight years old and, unlike newer models, did not have a hood to shelter the passengers. Over the years William had spent many hours fixing problems and had become a good mechanic, but the car was not suitable for a grand tour of Italy. He asked Alma about replacing it. He hoped that Alma would agree to provide them with a Benz touring type – a forty horsepower car with a hood. Alma agreed.

Alma insisted that her daughter should spend some hours of every day in formal education. Anna didn't like the idea. Lizzie suggested that Anna might like to help her to write a syllabus that more or less described what she was already doing but was couched in terms that would get her mother off their backs. Anna agreed to help write a syllabus on condition that it would change nothing. Alma was particularly concerned that Anna had shown little interest in music. Lizzie had no idea what to do about that. William stepped up and assured Alma that he would teach Anna music. William bought two piccolos and packed them in his luggage.

Meddi made cloaks. Lizzie's cloak was a tartan of green and black, William's a herringbone of different greens, and Anna's a check of maroon and deep red. Anna had fashioned three masks in papier-mâché and painted them jet black with painted pearls around the eyes. William's mask had a short beak, Lizzie's was longer, and Anna's the longest. With their masks, tricorn hats, cloaks, and wigs, they could have been anyone, male or female, young or old. In the mirror they saw whoever they wanted to see.

Meddi asked Anna if she would like to help her in the Opera House when she got back from Italy. They would be working on a new production of an opera, set in Japan, called *Madame Butterfly*, to be staged in December. Anna told Miss Turner to put dress-making and costume design on Mama's silly list.

Mahler gave William a list of things to do before the trip to Italy.

'Can you give a clean copy of my Ninth to Bruno Walter. I want him to conduct the premiere in Vienna before the end of June when the days are long. I think the audience will appreciate leaving the hall in daylight. Pay special attention to the marking. Bar 39 is a triple *forte*. Walter may complain that is too early to ask an orchestra for so much when there's still more than an hour to go but at bar 39 they must give everything and then over the next hour find even more. There are places where some instruments are asked to play *forte* while at the same time others are marked *piano*. These are not mistakes. Walter knows this, but he'll need to stand firm with musicians who don't. The orchestration allows everyone to be heard as I intend and when players decide that *mezzo piano* suits them better than *piano*, they must be told that will not suit me. The symphony requires more rehearsals than the budget will allow. You will help Walter to find a way round that. He must rehearse only with the first team. There must be no deps and no passengers. There must be no other concerts programmed for the week of June 26th. This will allow for extra evening rehearsals which can be arranged at short notice. The players will object but Walter will offer them double rates for the extra hours. The administration will object but once all the tickets have been sold, they will have to back down when Bruno Walter threatens to cancel. You will need to help him to stand firm. Make sure you get back from Italy in good time to see that he gets everything the symphony needs. Why don't you send some articles back from Italy for the newspapers? You know what the Viennese enjoy reading. You wrote nonsense for the papers when you were in New York.'

William was surprised. 'I didn't think you knew about that.'

'There is nothing I don't know about you, William.'

'Is Lizzie in love with me?'

'I know everything about you, William, and I don't know any more about Lizzie than you do. However, I think it is very likely and that you should be careful.'

'If you want to talk you know where to find me. Make sure you're back before the beginning of June so that you have at least three weeks to look after my symphony. And no showing off! You're a good driver, William, but the roads in Italy are even worse than the musicians. *Lento* please, not *presto!*'

Mahler ruffled William's hair, kissed him on both cheeks, and disappeared.

Late afternoon on Friday February 16th, 1912, William drove *lentissimo* up the hill to Altschluderbach on a road covered in snow and arrived at Trenkerhof before the light faded. Herr Trenker and the cook came out to welcome them, but not the horse with no name.

'He has gone to the station to meet you. I didn't realise you were coming in your automobile. He'll figure it out and make his way back,' said Mr Trenker.

Cook warmed them up with hot chicken soup and fresh crusty bread straight from the oven. When William went back to the car to fetch the luggage the horse with no name was standing next to the automobile shaking his head in disapproval. William held out his hand with the sugar lumps he had brought. The horse nimbly hoovered them up in his stubbly lips and nodded its thanks.

They were given three freshly made-up rooms, hot baths, warm towels, and then a dinner of shinken mit kartoffelstock followed by one of Herr Trenker's smelly cheeses and a digestivo of schnapps.

After dinner William spread the map on the table and they studied the road south. First to Venice, where they would leave the car on the mainland and take a water taxi to the hotel on Giudecca for a fortnight. Then to Florence and Lucca. Onwards to Perugia from where they would explore Assisi, Todi, Orvieto and Spoleto. Then to Rome for April and then possibly further south to Naples and the Amalfi coast. They hadn't made any plans for the journey home and would return by whichever route took their fancy.

Before they left, William had to rearrange the luggage to find room for a large picnic hamper of sausages, bread, cheese, and wine. William told the horse that if they returned at the beginning of summer they would come in the car and he should not go to the station to meet them. The horse watched the car drive off with people, picnic and luggage, shook his head, and snorted.

They drove south for four hours but the mountains did not appear to recede. It was still daylight when they reached the lagoon. The snow-capped peaks behind them shone pink in the setting sun as the water taxi crossed the lagoon and made for Giudecca.

When darkness fell they put on their cloaks and went into the night to join the masquerade. Disguised and bewigged in the crowded narrow lanes they ate roasted chestnuts and ice cream, drank glühwein and behind their masks imagined themselves to be Venetian, but whenever any of them attempted a word in their halting Italian William was always addressed in French, Lizzie in English and Anna in German. They got hopelessly lost trying to find the stop for the boat back to Giudecca and were fortunate to catch the last vaporetto.

Next day they found a busy fish restaurant near Campo San Barnaba. The waiter found a space for them beside other customers with whom they shared the table. William felt he knew something of the Italian kitchen but the array of fish on offer in this small establishment was far beyond his ken. They sucked the flesh out of all manner of shellfish and ate shrimps on a bed of polenta. Anna had a seafood risotto. William and Lizzie ate spaghetti al mare. They ordered a flatfish and the waiter came to their rescue and removed the bones. They washed it down with a sharp and unpleasant white wine pumped out of a large straw flask which was quite refreshing when well qualified with water. William asked if they could reserve a table and return the following day and the waiter asked for his name.

'Signor Hildebrand.'

'No, your name?'

Anna spoke up, 'Mi chiamo Anna e i mei amici si chiamono Elizabetta e Guiglielmo.'

The waiter beamed. 'Grazia, signorina. A domani alle otto.'

The following day at eight o'clock they arrived to find the restaurant again full but with a reserved ticket on a table where another customer was already seated. The ticket read, 'Capitano Guglielmo, Signorina Elizabetta e la Principessa Anna'. The waiter asked if they would like to see the menu or should she choose for them. They asked the waiter to choose and he brought them sardines in vinegar, then a large tureen of zuppa di pesce followed by pasta con vongole then a platter with a turbot which sat on a bed of thinly-sliced potatoes surrounded by capers and olives and finally a green salad with fennel and anchovies crowned with a lobster surrounded by mussels. These last dishes had the other customers on their feet straining to see and admire what they were eating. The wine was just as bad as the night before.

The customer who shared their table did not offer any conversation and ate his meal in a contented silence until Anna addressed him. 'You look like my Papa.' He was not unhappy to be drawn into conversation with the little girl and speaking German gently asked, 'Who is your Papa?'

'Mahler, and he's dead.'

'Gustav Mahler?... the conductor?'

'...and composer!' added Anna.

'You are Gustav Mahler's daughter?'

'Yes.'

He was dumbfounded and stopped eating. Anna went back to her dinner. He sat in silence watching her eat. Then he stood up and said, 'Your father was the greatest European artist of our times. I was privileged to hear your father conduct his Eighth Symphony in Munich. After the performance I knelt at your father's feet. He was a very great man. What a terrible blow to learn of his illness and death, and what a dreadful bereavement for you, my dear young lady! Please accept my heartfelt condolence. I am honoured to meet you.' He sat down and then asked her name.

'Anna.'

William then inquired his name.

Anna answered, 'It's Gustav! Same as Papa!' And she picked up the stranger's reservation ticket which said, 'Capitano Gustav.'

When the stranger got up to leave William asked if he was Gustav von Aschenbach. The writer bowed deeply and said, 'Yes.'

The next day they took the vaporetto to the Lido to stroll along the sand. Unlike the narrow lanes of San Marco and Dorsoduro the beach on the late February morning was quiet. William took off his socks and shoes to paddle in the Adriatic. It was cold. On a stretch of sand in front of the Hotel des Bains there was a solitary deckchair. It appeared to be abandoned. As they approached, they could see someone sitting in it who was asleep. They recognized von Aschenbach. They intended to pass on and not disturb him, but William held back to look at the sleeping man who bore such a strong resemblance to Mahler. What especially held his eye was von Aschenbach's resemblance to Mahler's corpse. William touched his hand. It was cold.

The hotel staff at the Hotel des Bains did all they could to comfort them. They gave William, Lizzie and Anna a private room and assured them that rumours of an unhealthy influence in the air were grossly exaggerated. Indeed, they were probably false and could be safely discounted. The policemen were similarly anxious to explain that von Aschenbach's death was almost certainly not caused by an infection carried in the air. After they had made and signed their statements the police gave them a thrilling ride back to Giudecca in a police boat which went very much faster than the vaporetto. Lizzie and Anna spent the following days in the hotel. William took himself out and explored Venice on his own. Lizzie and Anna ate breakfast with William and they shared their evening meal but they would not leave the hotel. He found no joy in his solitary visit to the Accademia where the Bellini Madonnas reminded him of Lizzie and the *trompe l'oeil* in the Scuola San Rocca put him in mind of Viennese kitsch. When William returned to the hotel he suggested to Lizzie and Anna that they leave Venice in the morning. When he told the manager they were leaving for Florence William had not anticipated such a helpful response. The manager wired ahead to a hotel in Busetto managed by a distant cousin of her brother-in-law. It was on the road to Florence and an ideal place to break their journey. Then the manager reserved a box at the Teatro Verdi for a performance of *Lucia di Lammermoor*. William did not know the manager was obliged to them after Lizzie and Anna had made him a gift of the masks, cloaks, and wigs. Having decided to leave Venice in the morning the threesome rediscovered their togetherness and went out for a last meal together, 'As long as we do not leave Giudecca,' said Lizzie and Anna. They ate in a small pizzeria next to the hotel. Anna took some plasticene with her. The waiter sat at their table and took their order. He returned with a dish of fried seafood which they had not ordered and sat with them for a few minutes telling them in a mixture of French, German, English and Italian about his brother who was a fisherman. When he brought the pizzas he sat with them again and told Lizzie about a cousin who had travelled to Edinburgh and who had told him it was as beautiful as Venice. He returned with pizza dough blown into a lantern-shaped balloon of fine dough roasted beside the glowing logs and sawdust in his oven. He opened a bottle of wine and proposed a toast to Scotland, to Switzerland and to Austria – great friends of Italy. 'Maybe not the Austrian Empire,' he added, 'but the people of Austria'. He told them that some of his best friends were Austrian and they drank to that. He brought them ice cream and coffee which they hadn't ordered and at the end of the meal he brought three glasses of limoncello and a glass of grappa for himself. William asked for the bill. The waiter said there was no bill. It had been his honour to serve them. He asked Anna for the plasticene and with a few deft strokes he fashioned female breasts. He slid his artwork across the table to Lizzie. They weren't just any breasts. They were her breasts. Anna and William were astonished at the skill and speed with which the waiter had produced these exquisite shapes. Lizzie was silent. When they got out of the pizzeria she burst into tears and ran back to the hotel. That night they quarrelled.

Dear Mama,

We have cut short our visit to Venice. It wasn't a success and Lizzie is furious with me. What kind of man am I to let a waiter insult her? I have tried to apologise but that's not what she needs. She wants me to be different. I wish there was something I could do about that, but there isn't. I do my best and it's not good enough. Perhaps no one would believe this, but I know you will. If anyone tried to hurt Lizzie or Anna I would protect them with my life. William

They drove from Padova to Mantova along the north bank of the Po, crossed the river at Casalmaggiore and fetched up in Busetto just as it was getting dark. They were received at the hotel as if they were long-lost friends. William presented *la padrona* with a gift from the manager of the hotel on Giudecca.

The twin room for Lizzie and Anna and the single room for William were furnished with fresh flowers, fruit, and sweets. The hotel provided them with three bicycles for exploring the riverside. They exchanged embarrassed glances, mumbled their thanks, and then confessed that they did not know how to ride. They were immediately offered bicycle riding lessons and next morning after breakfast they were introduced to three young lads. The six of them walked their bikes to a lawn behind the hotel.

By the end of the morning they could wobble in straight lines on the hotel gardens. It wasn't difficult. The only problem was starting and stopping. They arranged to meet after lunch and learn how to turn corners.

It didn't take them long to describe a wide circle around the lawn, the three young lads leaning slightly, the other three going around the garden bolt upright, tumbling over but suffering nothing worse than muddy hands and knees. Perhaps there was a problem with the bicycles? The young lads had bikes that could be ridden in circles. William, Lizzie, and Anna had bikes with rigid frames that appeared to be insufficiently flexible to go around corners. The boys, who didn't speak German, English, or French, tried to explain in Italian that cornering is more difficult when you ride slowly and upright, and encouraged them to go faster, lean into the corner, and literally follow their feelings. The three students thought this was a recipe for disaster.

They met again the following morning and discovered to their alarm that the plan was to ride along the lanes to Roncole. The hotel manager gave the three young lads the picnic to carry and they set off wobbling north, south and west but, on average, managing to steer a course vaguely westwards for two kilometres towards Roncole, where Verdi was born. Every turn of the pedals took them further away from Venice, away from the corpse on the beach, the plasticene breasts in the restaurant and the quarrel in the hotel.

The ride was slow and the young lads, like sheepdogs, snapped at their heels and got them to press on – 'Vai! Vai!' – and Anna responded, confidently pushing ahead. She didn't make it all the way round a bend and instead made a wider circle that took her off the track and through some bushes. The others heard Anna scream in terror, or possibly in exhilaration. They dismounted, followed Anna through the bushes, and found themselves on a hillside that gently sloped away beside a grove of chestnut trees. Anna was nowhere to be seen. The boys ran to the river calling her name. The river's edge was shallow and sandy. There were no bicycle tracks. The boys ran up and down the riverbank. One of the boys took off his clothes and waded into the shallows which flowed swiftly eastwards. He waded out fifty metres before the water reached his waist. He looked up and down the river, which was empty of traffic. There was not a boat to be seen and no evidence of a child. William ran up and down the meadow calling for Anna. Lizzie went into the trees and found the bike which had a buckled front wheel and then found Anna sitting with a little boy. The boy had bandaged Anna's knees with her socks and was now twisting the stems of wildflowers to make a floral crown for her hair. Anna looked up, saw Lizzie, and told her she thought this was a good place to have a picnic. Lizzie almost fainted with relief.

After lunch they walked along the riverbank. Anna claimed that her knees were not in the least bit sore because Camillo had picked special leaves to put on her cuts. William turned to take a backward glance towards Anna and Camillo. Anna wore her floral crown and the boy held her hand. William struggled to contain his emotions and choked. He took deep breaths. Lizzie asked why he was upset but William couldn't speak. Lizzie took his hand. William tried to distract himself and concentrated on the young lads who were describing how the mighty river flowed all the way across Italy from the Alps to the Adriatic fertilising the Lombardy plain which provided the finest corn, wheat and rice for polenta, pasta and risotto. William looked into the river and tried to ignore the feelings aroused by Anna's hand in Camillo's, and Lizzie's hand in his. The river's empty silence was very different from the Rhine that flows through Basel, and the Danube that flows through Vienna, both major thoroughfares for freight. There was no traffic on the Po.

They collected the broken bicycle from the forest and took their leave of the little Camillo. The boy shook hands politely with everyone. Anna whispered something to the Camillo and then the children kissed.

They had an early dinner and left the hotel for their box at the opera. Lizzie told them that the Lammermuirs were to the south of Edinburgh and that Lucia was an unfortunate woman who was prevented from marrying the man she loved and forced into marrying someone else. When the man she loved dies she goes mad.

William was amazed at the size of the theatre – a shoe box that seated three hundred but less on this occasion because there was no orchestra pit and half of the stalls had been removed to accommodate the orchestra. The performance did not begin at 8.30pm as advertised and there appeared to be no urgency. All the seats were taken but the hall was still filling up. When the conductor took his place at the podium there were as many people standing in the hall as there were seated. The three young lads who taught them how to ride bikes were among those standing in a crush at the back. William, Lizzie, and Anna pulled their seats to the very front of their box to allow another dozen to squeeze in and stand behind them. Many in the audience had brought their scores so that they could read as well as listen to Maestro Donizetti's music.

The orchestra was poor. During the overture the brass cracked their notes and a clarinet player ostentatiously changed his reed every time he leapt an octave. The intonation in the strings, especially the double basses, suggested that the players were deaf and that their performance might be appreciated by an audience similarly hard of hearing. And yet this audience listened attentively and those reading scores contributed the rustle of turning pages to the orchestration.

When the curtain opened, the performance of the singers was no better. Then Lucia made her entrance. The singer from Milan, Amalia Constanza, who had been hired by the commune to perform the role, was sensational. Her descent into madness was performed with total conviction. She could act as well as sing. Her technical virtuosity in the very highest reaches of the soprano's range was breathtaking. William had never witnessed so closely such a mesmerising performance and he and Lizzie and Anna joined in enthusiastically with the applause. The audience cheered, called out 'Brava!' and whistled. William wished he could put two fingers in his mouth and whistle. The three young lads who taught them to ride bikes were among the most enthusiastic whistlers. There was no need for a claque here. The audience had come to applaud and cheer. Mahler would have hated it. William decided to ask the bicycle teachers to show him how to whistle and when he got back to Vienna he would treat the audience in the Hofoper to his new skill. The performance was greeted with such enthusiasm that scenes had to be repeated, which required a singer to rise from the dead and die again. It was well after midnight when the curtain fell for the last time. After half an hour of curtain calls and bouquets the house lights went up and the musicians left the auditorium. The audience stayed. And then from behind the curtain a hand, clumsily searching, looked for the gap. William wondered how the gap in the curtains was so difficult to find, but then eventually a gloved hand reached through to pull back the curtain far enough for Amalia Constanza to emerge. The audience who had been waiting for this moment roared their appreciation, tossing flowers onto the stage. The soprano held her hands to her heart, tried to curtsey, then held her brow to let everyone know she was about to faint. Someone rushed from the wings and caught her just as she collapsed. From the opposite wing someone else emerged with a glass of water on a velvet cushion. She took a sip and miraculously recovered. The audience rushed to the front of the stage, tripping over the conductor's podium and knocking over the orchestra's music stands to present Amalia Constanza with more flowers. William thought it was sensational. Lizzie thought it wasn't exactly Walter Scott.

Dear Mother,

We lost Anna but then we found her sitting with a young spirit of the forest. You must come across spirits all the time but I have never seen anything as beautiful as this little spirit who comforted Anna, bandaged her wounded knees and put flowers in her hair. We shared our picnic with him and he looked after her, ensuring her plate was never empty, and then when we went for a walk he held her hand. Eight years old! Why can't I do this? I don't believe it's something you have to learn. Those two children didn't learn it, did they? Maybe children have it and then lose it when they grow up. Perhaps adults have forgotten innocence and behave towards each other clumsily because the children in us have fled. When I saw them walking hand in hand, Anna with bandaged knees, flowers in her hair and an attentive ear to the little boy's story, I was overwhelmed with their beauty and my own emptiness.

His name is Camillo Tarocci. He wants to learn to read and write but his father will not allow it. The local priest has arranged a place for him at the seminary but the child told the priest he didn't have a vocation. The priest has told him to go to the seminary to learn how to read and write, and not bother about whether he had a vocation or not. The boy's too frightened to tell his father. Anna has fallen in love with the little boy and so have I.

Your son, William

Next morning Anna didn't appear for breakfast. She wasn't in the room. Lizzie hadn't seen her since just before dawn when Anna had got up to go to the toilet. William ran downstairs to the three bikes, one with a buckled wheel, one good bike, and the third was missing. William set off as if he had been riding a bike all his life. He discovered Anna and Camillo in the same spot where Lizzie had found them the day before. They weren't surprised to see William. Anna told William that Camillo had run away from home and was going to join them on their tour of Italy.

Meanwhile, back at the hotel Lizzie had asked the hotel manager to call the police. The policeman appeared within minutes, out-of-breath and ill-tempered. He cut short Lizzie's description of Anna and demanded to know if there was another child involved. The policeman wagged his finger at Lizzie and said, 'Find one and you'll find the other!' When Anna and William returned to the hotel with Camillo, the little boy shrank at the sight of the policeman, who was his father. He tried to run away but his father caught up with him and pushed him over. The boy scrambled to his feet and his father pushed him over again, and again, and again, and so Camillo went tumbling home a step ahead of his violent father.

Anna fled to her room. Lizzie followed her, sat beside her, and stroked her hair as she lay face down on the pillow, sobbing. The hotel manager told William that it would be better for Anna if they moved on to Florence where there were so many beautiful things to see.

Anna had no intention of leaving without Camillo. She insisted that William and Lizzie fetch him. Then she said she would fetch him herself. Then she broke down and cried out, 'I'm sick of adults. They quarrel and shout at each other! Who can I play with? I have no one to talk to except for adults. It's rubbish. Ever since my sister died!' Anna's descent into the wilderness was as vertiginous as Lucia di Lammermoor's. Anna smashed a plate and ran to her room. William fetched one of the piccolos he had brought with him and sat outside Anna's room playing a slow air. Lizzie came upstairs when she heard the music, saw what William was doing and retreated. William moved from melancholy airs to haunting melodies, and then to pretty tunes. He played dances and then he played faster dances and Anna emerged from her room.

'What's that?

William explained that it was a magic flute and that no troubled heart could resist its call. He had two of them. The other was for her and he would give it to her that night when they got to Florence.

William prepared two envelopes of cash and asked for the bill. As he had expected, it was full of discounts and amounted to a sum considerably less than he had sealed in the envelope which he took from his pocket. The hotel manager acknowledged that William, presenting her with a sealed envelope, had ignored her bill, put his envelope in her drawer and thanked him. William then gave her the second envelope on which he had written – 'Per i tre biciclisti. Grazie. Il vostro amico, Guilliamo.' She took the envelope and told William that he was 'un grand'uomo.' She recommended a hotel in Florence run by a nephew of her sister-in-law and offered to ring and arrange their accommodation. William made room in the car for two large picnic baskets and a gift that the manager had wrapped for her sister-in-law's nephew. They set off for Florence.

That night in Florence William went to Lizzie and Anna's room. He waited until Lizzie had finished Anna's bedtime story, then presented Anna with a piccolo wrapped in a silk handkerchief. She would have her first lesson in the morning but for now he suggested she sleep with it under her pillow and fill the magic flute full of beautiful dreams.

An hour later and unable to get to sleep because of the lump under her pillow, Anna asked Lizzie if she believed what William had said about filling the flute with dreams. Lizzie said she didn't. Anna took it out from under her pillow, laid it on the bedside table, and went to sleep.

After breakfast William and Anna played scales on their piccolos, accompanying the Sunday morning church bells that rang out over Florence. Lizzie sat at the window with a view across the Arno and wondered at the differences between Sunday in Edinburgh and Sunday in Florence Whereas the streets of Edinburgh are empty the streets of Florence are packed with tourists seeking the Renaissance and Florentines seeking out each other. The cafés and bars were full of families – the middle generations helping to feed the elderly with one hand and their small children with the other hand. Lizzie remembered that the Italian cafes in Edinburgh were open on Sundays and that although everyone agreed Irish Catholics were good for nothing, Edinburgh's Presbyterian culture warmly welcomed Italian Catholics who ran ice cream cafés where Scottish Protestants could buy cigarettes on a Sunday.

William was so pleased with Anna's first piccolo lesson he was convinced she must have filled her tiny flute with the most delightful dreams and recommended she put it under her pillow again. Then the three of them, dressed in their Sunday best, went out to join the throng.

Michelangelo's 'Davide' was a huge disappointment. Anna could not believe the size of it. She thought Davide's large hands were grotesque. 'Is this supposed to be the same David that slew Goliath? I wonder how big the giant was?' Anna was more interested in the blocks of marble from which figures were emerging -– half-formed creatures, struggling to emerge from stone.

The queue for the Uffizi was impossible but they found a café where they ordered coffees and torte di riso. The little rice cakes were delightful. William in his halting Italian attempted to pay a compliment and told the waiter that they had eaten rice cakes in Vienna that were similar but with lemon, whereupon the waiter returned with the manager, who attempted to take the rice cakes away. William held on to the plate, protesting that the cakes were delicious. The manager did not appear to be reassured. 'Lemons! Who do you think we are, sir? Neapolitans? Our rice cakes never have lemon!'

Disappointed with Davide and shaken by the altercation in the café they decided to return to the hotel for a siesta. Two youngsters in the square outside the hotel were quarrelling. One pushed the other. There was a clumsy brawl and the flash of a blade. William gathered up Lizzie and Anna and shepherded them into the hotel.

As she got Anna ready for bed Lizzie told her that the fighting boys had probably made up their quarrel.

William sat in the car and waited for Mahler. Mahler told William that the police would probably want to interview anyone who witnessed the murder in the square and that it would be better for Lizzie and Anna if they all got out of Florence first thing in the morning. I suggest you drive to Lucca. It's not far. You ought to be able to stay out of trouble there and Lucca has a delightful small opera house.'

William asked Mahler not to go just yet.

Mahler asked William what he wanted.

'To make everything better,' answered William.

'Everything's fine.'

'No, it's not.'

'Yes, it is. You come to Italy chasing a dream and you discover a real world that you don't like. What's the problem with that? From where I'm sitting, William, a glimpse of the real world is worth a whole night of sweet dreams. Don't ask her to put the piccolo under her pillow. How's she supposed to get to sleep? It's hard for a child to see how people cope with their differences on the streets of Florence without having to deal with nonsense about magic flutes. By the way, I thought your piccolo lesson this morning was wonderful. Well done.' Mahler kissed him, ruffled his hair, and, without opening the door, got out of the car.

Lizzie opened the car door got in. 'Who were you taking to?'

'Mahler.'

'Do you often talk to him?'

'Yes.'

'Will you talk to me?'

'Yes.'

'I mustn't stay long. She's fast asleep. I don't want her to wake up and find me gone.'

'Are you real?'

'Of course I'm real. Why do you ask?'

'Because if you're not real we can stay here for as long as we like, and it won't matter. But if you are real then we can go back to the hotel and talk there.'

William asked for a bottle of grappa and two glasses and they went back to Lizzie's room where Anna, fast asleep, was snoring gently.

'What were you talking to Mahler about?'

'Oh, this and that. What to do in the morning.'

'And what did he say?'

'Leave Florence and move on.'

'Did you speak to Mahler when we were in Busseto?'

'I can't remember.'

'And in Venice?'

'I don't remember.'

'You can talk to me too,' she said.

'But you're real.'

'So is Anna. So is Italy. What happened in the square outside the hotel is real. The blood was real. You share things with your invisible friends that you need to share with us. You are so good at so many things, William. You are a delightful man. But even when we are in the same room with you I feel that you are not really there with us.'

'There's something the matter with me.'

'There's nothing the matter with you, William.'

'Yes, there is. I can't love.'

'That's not true.'

'It is. I was in love once and I will never love again.'

'Did she love you?'

'*He* loved me. I left him to follow Mahler and I broke his heart.'

Before retiring William asked the receptionist to book them a hotel in Lucca and a box at the Teatro del Giglio.

'Which hotel would you prefer, sir?'

'Isn't there someone in your family that runs a hotel in Lucca?'

'Of course there is.'

'Then we would like to stay in that one.'

'Would you like to attend a performance of *Madame Butterfly*?'

'That would be perfect. Thank you.'

The drive to Lucca should have been brief but the road was busy with horse-drawn carts packed with all manner of bric-a-brac, all of them on their way to Lucca. William brought a gift of an Easter egg for the hotel in Lucca from the hotel in Florence, even though it was a month until Easter and when they checked into their hotel they found their hotel rooms furnished with large Easter eggs. After Anna's music lesson William told her that she no longer needed to sleep with it under her pillow.

The three of them slept well past the sunrise. They had not been disturbed by the night's work outside their windows which had transformed Lucca into a vast flea market. There was no cobble within the walls of Lucca that did not support a market stall. From Saturday morning until Sunday evening you could buy whatever you wanted. Lizzie bought a red dress. William bought a top hat. Anna bought a tiger which was long dead and expertly stuffed. An adjacent stallholder offered to sell William a wheelbarrow to carry the tiger but William thought he could manage with the tiger on his head. Lizzie wore his top hat and Anna, who had nothing to carry, bought herself an ice cream.

Somebody with a camera tried to take a picture of the three of them but William, snarling at the photographer, put his head down and let the tiger lunge at him. The photographer pretended to be afraid.

Madame Butterfly in Lucca was every bit as good as *Lucia di Lammermoor* in Roncole. At first William did not recognise the soprano underneath the make-up she wore to suggest oriental features but from her first note William knew he was listening once more to Amalia di Constanza, the soprano from Milan who had been hired by the local opera company to perform *Butterfly*. William was thrilled by her performance and was moved when the entire audience joined in the *Humming Chorus*. William was developing a taste for small town opera. He loved the fluffed notes, the wayward intonation, and he especially loved the audience. It was so much more fun than the opera in Vienna.

After a full twenty minutes of curtain calls and bouquets it was well after midnight when the curtain fell for the last time and the house lights went up. The musicians left the orchestra pit but the audience stayed. Someone behind the curtain clumsily searched for the gap. William knew what was coming as Amalia di Constanza emerged. The audience who had been waiting for this moment stood and roared their thanks, tossing flowers onto the stage. The soprano held her hands to her heart, tried to curtsey, then held her brow to let everyone know she was about to faint. Someone rushed from the wings and held her just as she collapsed. From the opposite wing someone else emerged with a glass of water on a velvet cushion. She took a sip and miraculously recovered – a carefully rehearsed and perfectly choreographed repeat of her sensational curtain call in Roncole. The audience rushed the stage to kiss her hands and present her with flowers.

When they got back to the hotel they found the manager trying to comfort a chambermaid. He explained that the staff, recommended by the church and employed in the hotel as an act of charity, were nice girls but sometimes slow and occasionally prone to hysteria. The chambermaid had gone to the twin room to turn on the heating when she said she saw a wild animal. The manager told William she would be fine after a night's sleep and asked him to remember her in his prayers.

Saturday, March 2nd

Dear Mother,

We went to a performance of Madame Butterfly this evening in the small opera house in Lucca. There is something special about these small houses. In Vienna the audience has high expectations of the performance and no expectations of itself. They bring nothing to the performance. Here the audience's presence transforms the evening from a private experience into a communal one. I wonder if this is a religious response – as if the opera house is a church, the priests, the altar boys and the choir are the performers, and the audience is a congregation.

Anna bought a stuffed tiger at the market and although it had been dead for forty years it attacked one of the chambermaids when she came into the room to turn on the heating. The manager has asked me to pray for the poor woman.

I have told Lizzie that I was once in love with a man. I don't know what she thinks about that.

Anna is learning piccolo. When she has learned a few tunes she will need an accompanist. I am going to search the stalls tomorrow to find a snare drum. Will you help me to find one?

Thank you.
Guillaume

When William went to their room in the morning he found Lizzie and Anna and the chambermaid all kneeling beside the tiger which was lying on its side and having its tummy tickled.

After breakfast William, Lizzie and Anna strolled around the market stalls. Lizzie and Anna looked at everything while William looked only for a snare drum. After a while Lizzie asked William what he was looking for. William told her she'd see it when he found it. Lizzie told him how much more fun it would be if the three of them could share the quest. William told her he was looking for a snare drum.

'One like that?' asked Lizzie pointing to a snare drum that William had not seen.

Sunday, March 3rd

Dear Mother,

I have had another row with Lizzie. The more she complains about me the worse I get. She said the drum had nothing to do with you, that you never helped me to find it, and that she found it, not you. I am a useless friend to Lizzie just I was a useless son to you. Guillaume

They left Lucca and drove to the Hotel Sacre Cuore which sits on a hilltop outside Perugia overlooking a wide valley. It is a former convent and a rather grim-looking rectangular three-storeyed block of green-shuttered rooms facing east through all points of the compass from north to south. On a clear day you can count the arches on the basilica in Assisi which nestles on its hillside twenty kilometres away on the other side of the valley. The ambience of the hotel's former monastic life pervades every room and corridor. The walls are covered with Sacred Hearts and Madonnas. The guests come in small groups, often accompanied by a priest. They sing grace before meals and on Sundays they sing mass in the chapel which sits behind the hotel. The vines were already responding to the longer hours of sunshine and thrusting out green shoots.

In the chapel an artist was working on top of a scaffolding tower, cleaning and refurbishing a stained-glass window. Under the scaffolding piles of dust glowed with tiny bits of coloured glass. Anna would creep into the chapel and crawl under the scaffolding and sort through the dust and glass, choosing fragments and colours to take back to her room. She took down a small framed portrait of Pius X from her bedroom wall and, using this as a base, constructed a colourful yellow cockerel with blue and green tail feathers and a red comb. When she was happy with it she used plasticene to hold the tiny fragments together, and having removed Pius X and replaced him with her glass cockerel, she hung the frame in the window. When the early morning sun woke the roosters in the chicken coop behind the hotel kitchen, the rooster in Anna's window sparkled in response.

Every morning William and Anna played a reveille on piccolo and drum to greet the new day. They marched around the hotel waking up the last of the sleepy-heads and then into the breakfast room where they received the applause of their fellow guests.

The hotel grounds were extensive. Lawns gave way to parkland, then to cultivated land with vines and olives, and then finally to wilderness. After a week exploring their hilltop idyll William, Lizzie and Anna had still not found a boundary fence. Anna and Lizzie did, however, come upon a tent. There was a small gas stove with a kettle which was still warm. Pieces of glass arranged in the shape of a bird in flight sparkled on the artist's table. It had a yellow beak and a striking blue eye. Anna and Lizzie were taken aback, first by the secret world they had discovered, then by the artist's dog, and then by the artist himself who was carrying a rifle and a dead rabbit. He greeted the girls with quiet reserve, took out a penknife and, kneeling on the ground, expertly skinned the rabbit.

The following day after she had checked that the artist was working at the top of his scaffolding Anna stole away by herself to his encampment with her glass rooster and put it on the little table outside his tent. The artist's dog came out of the tent to greet her and, despite Anna's attempts to get the dog to stay, it followed her all the way back to the hotel. She went into the chapel and was about to tell the artist that his dog had followed her but the dog settled down comfortably underneath the scaffolding, so she said nothing and slipped away.

Over the next few days whenever Lizzie and Anna went for a walk they always ended up by the tent where Lizzie would leave a carefully wrapped sandwich or piece of cake and the dog invariably followed them back to the hotel and settled itself beneath the scaffolding. On the few occasions when they met the artist they discovered his name was Francesco and his dog was called Clara.

One day when Lizzie and Anna were making their way back to the hotel with Clara at their heels, the dog dived into the undergrowth. There was a terrible high-pitched squeal and Clara emerged with a rabbit in her mouth which she dropped at Lizzie's feet. Lizzie was horrified. Anna picked up the dead rabbit by its ears, took it back to Francesco's camp and left it outside the tent. Anna and Lizzie returned to the hotel alone. Clara stayed by the tent guarding the rabbit.

Lizzie got into a routine of collecting items from the breakfast buffet, wrapping them into a picnic and delivering them to the artist. Lizzie asked Anna to go with her because she didn't like to go on her own. They imagined that William was in his room. He was, in fact, at the top of the scaffolding with Francesco.

And then one day the tent was gone. Lizzie and Anna ran back to the chapel and discovered the scaffolding had also gone. William was there looking up at a stained-glass window which showed St Francis talking to the birds. An owl perched on a branch among the birds looked down towards St Francis and his brothers, one of whom looked like William.

Above the tree there were two angels which resembled Anna and Lizzie. The yellow rooster with the red comb and the blue tail feathers that Anna had made stood at St Francis's feet.

Monday March 25th

Dear Meddi,

We have stayed in Umbria since the beginning of March in a hotel which used to be a convent. It sits on top of a hill called Montebello which is well named because the view from the terrace is wide and beautiful. There was an artist camping in the hotel grounds and he worked on a stained-glass window in the hotel's chapel. Anna has been inspired to make things out of glass. Lizzie took food from the breakfast buffet every morning to leave at his tent and I have spent hours watching him work. I don't believe we have left the hotel grounds since we arrived here. While he was here none of us wanted to be anywhere else. Sometimes when I watched him work I felt so relaxed I fell asleep. His name is Francesco. He said that it didn't matter what I call the arrangement between Lizzie, Anna, and me when it was obvious that I was responsible for a wife and a child. He said he had no commitment and one day would be gone. That day has come. Lizzie is sad that he has gone. I may not be the only homosexual man she has fallen in love with. We are going to drive to Rome tomorrow leaving behind our portraits in the chapel window. The artist has given two angels the faces of Lizzie and Anna. I am a Franciscan brother. I suspect we will be looking at a lot of stained-glass over the next few days. William

They arrived in Rome after dark on Tuesday, March 26th and found their hotel in the Piazza della Rotunda. It was not until they opened the shutters in the morning that they discovered their hotel stood opposite the Pantheon. They ate breakfast at a table in the Piazza. Their order of three cornetti filled with custard, two coffees and a hot chocolate was brought to their table with glasses of iced water, crisps, nuts and biscuits. They set out on foot to explore Rome. They walked and walked and by the time they arrived at the Fontana di Trevi their feet hurt. Anna was taking off her socks and shoes to dip her sore feet in the water when she saw people throwing money into the fountain. Anna looked down and saw the floor of the fountain was covered in coins. She started to pick them up. She had nowhere to put them and so she gave them to a woman who was holding out her hands.

William hissed at her sharply, 'Come out right away!'
Anna refused.
William raised his voice. 'ANNA!'

The gathering crowd told him to leave the child alone. Someone gave Anna a bag and she waded back in to collect more money. Then there was a shrill whistle followed by two large policemen. When Anna refused to come out they waded in, picked her up and carried her to their police van. William and Lizzie ran after the policemen.

'We are her parents!!'

The policemen arrested William and Lizzie.

In court the policemen, now wearing dry uniforms, told the magistrate that they had caught the child stealing coins from the Fontana di Trevi and that her mother and father were accomplices.

The magistrate asked the policemen for their names. When the policemen identified themselves the magistrate told them that if either of them brought such nonsense into his court ever again he would personally see to it that they were fired.

'Yes, sir!'
'Now, get out.'
'Yes, sir.'

Then the magistrate asked Anna, 'Are you on holiday?'
'Yes.'
'Are you having a nice time?'
'Well, I suppose today could have been a better.'
'Did you take your shoes off because your feet were sore?'
'Yes.'
'And when you dipped your feet in the water you discovered that the fountain was full of coins?'
'Yes.'
'And what did you do?'
'I picked some of them up.'
'Brava! Would you like to go back to get more coins?'
'Yes.'
'Can I come too?'
'Of course you can.'
'I'm stuck here until five o'clock but I can meet you at the Fontana at 5.30.'

The magistrate told William and Lizzie, 'You have a wonderful daughter. I imagine you tried to stop her wading into the fountain and she refused. Ah! Children these days! It must be so difficult being a parent. She would like to go back to the Fontana to collect more coins and has asked me to accompany her. I would not accept her gracious invitation without your approval. May I? Wonderful! Let's all meet to at the Fontana at 5.30.'

The crowd at the Fontana cheered when the magistrate, a balding man who wore fisherman's waders and had a few strands of hair tied back in a ponytail, stepped into the fountain with the child, who had taken off her socks and shoes. They began collecting coins.

The crowd booed when a pair of municipal policemen turned up and waded towards the magistrate. When the magistrate identified himself the first policeman saluted and slipped. He tried to save himself by holding onto the second policeman and they both went over with a splash. The crowd cheered as the two wet policemen left the scene.

The magistrate thought it was time to leave when the people in the fountain collecting coins outnumbered those watching. As they got wetter the people playing in the fountain felt happier. When the carabinieri arrived the onlooking crowd were as wet as those in the fountain and they were all tossing coins at one other. By the time the carabiniere cleared the area there was more money in the fountain than there had been an hour before.

William and Lizzie took Anna back to the hotel to get dried and changed, and then met the magistrate at a restaurant in Piazza SS Apostoli where he had invited them for dinner. Most of the tables were taken up with groups of dining priests. The magistrate explained that, like grubs, who will only burrow into the best apples, so priests only ever eat in the best restaurants. After they had eaten the waiter brought three bottles of digestivo – a white one that tasted of liquorice, a green one that tasted of mint, and a brown one that tasted of chestnuts. The digestivos were replaced with an opened bottle of grappa and little cups of coffee. A priest who had been enjoying an alcoholic dinner at a nearby table got to his feet and made his way unsteadily to the door. He offered Anna a tipsy blessing and said he hoped she would grow up to marry a prince. She told him that she did not wish to marry a prince and that she intended to marry a priest. The manager held the door open for the priest who might otherwise have walked into it. The magistrate thanked Anna for the best fun he'd had all week and wished them a pleasant stay in Rome as he, also slightly tipsy, followed the priest into the darkness. When William inquired about the bill the waiter told him it was all settled. 'The magistrate is my brother.'

William suggested busking with piccolo and drum at the Colosseum, at the Forum, on the Spanish Steps and outside the Pantheon while Lizzie collected the money. Anna had a better idea and suggested William and Lizzie make a small investment in materials so that she could paint portraits in Piazza Navona. Within minutes of making her pitch a queue formed to have their portraits painted by the child. The other artists, who strictly controlled their numbers in the Piazza, didn't have the nerve to chase her away in front of her queue of admirers and for the rest of the week saw their takings slump as their potential customers waited patiently in line for Anna. At the end of the week one of the regular artists approached Anna to ask if she intended to return in the following weeks and was relieved to hear that she was leaving for Naples. She gave him her stool and easel to look after until she came back.

Naples, Monday April 1st

William parked the car outside the hotel and was immediately confronted by a small boy who offered to look after it. William gave him a coin. In the morning the little boy was joined by three friends and William handed over four coins. The number of little Neapolitans who presented themselves beside the car increased every day so that William carried a heavy pocket of change for his increasing band of little helpers. The shops selling religious artifacts were dressed in their most sombre tones of purple and black for Holy Week, but the streets were a colourful circus. William and Anna added piccolo and drum to the hustle and bustle of everyday Neapolitan street theatre. William, Lizzie, and Anna had never heard of Signor Pirandello but on half a dozen occasions they bumped into someone looking for him. They climbed Vesuvius and visited Pompeii.

Amalfi, Friday, April 5th

They arrived in Amalfi around 3pm on Good Friday. The town was closed and deserted. William had arranged to meet the local doctor who had agreed to rent them his house, an eleventh century villa that stood in grounds planted with seven thousand lemon trees. William parked the car at the school and the doctor came down from the villa with two donkeys to transport the baggage up to the house.

Over dinner the doctor told them how his parents had agreed to let a neighbour plant potatoes in rows between the lemon trees in return for half of the crop. This sharecropper had used the land for ten years without ever handing over a single potato. Then the sharecropper filed a claim to the land which he had cultivated for ten consecutive years. The court found in his favour. When William asked the doctor how he had retained his land after the court had found against his family, the doctor explained that his patients included honourable men who had settled the matter and the troublesome sharecropper had vanished from the neighbourhood.

The doctor invited William, Lizzie, and Anna to join him for the Easter Sunday meal and at 11 am on the Sunday morning the four of them left the villa on donkeys to climb the track to Ravello. The donkeys, surefooted, did not appear to suffer from vertigo, unlike William and Lizzie who clung to their animals with their eyes tight shut. Anna, with eyes wide open, thrilled to the huge panorama that opened beneath her. In the restaurant sixty people seated at six long tables stood to greet their doctor and his friends. On receiving toasts of welcome William, Lizzie Anna and William did their best to respond. After the fourth toast Anna stood on her chair and told the assembly that she had never seen such beautiful lemons. They were so big and so many that they must be the best lemon-growers in the world, and she lifted her glass of lemonade to congratulate them. A huge roar of approval was followed by a long round of applause.

There was no menu and courses were brought from the kitchen as they were ready –– anchovies and roasted peppers, squid and olives, a lasagna, roast lamb, green beans and salad, cheese, tiramisu, fruit, cake, coffee and glasses of limoncello. Anna developed a taste for the limoncello and had to be discouraged from making another speech. She had wanted to thank the honourable men who had restored their host's property but the doctor counselled silence.

The doctor recommended a day trip to the ruins at Paestum. On the way they stopped at Eboli for ice cream. The car was immediately surrounded by admirers who were surprised to discover that William intended to drive further south. It was such a beautiful car and the roads beyond Eboli were poor. They proceeded south and ignored the advice to stop at Eboli

The ruins at Paestum stood in meadows where cattle grazed. There were cows grazing outside the temples and cows asleep inside the temples. Sheep intermingled with the cattle and the two young lads looking after them played in the undergrowth. They were clearly very fond of each other as they held hands and kissed. Anna made several sketches before they drove back to Amalfi.

The doctor recommended a day out on Capri. 'If you're up for it,' he said, 'the best boat is the workers' ferry that leaves Sorrento at 6am. You'll get there easily if you leave here before five.' Lizzie roused the other two and got them out of the villa before dawn. The powerful aroma from Amalfi's bakers filled the early morning darkness with yeast. Anna and Lizzie took the boat to Capri while William waited in Sorrento to write his piece about Mahler's Ninth for the Vienna Philharmonic's press office.

Mahler sat beside him as William wrote on a blank page, 'Mahler's Ninth. A Symphony from Beyond the Grave.'

Mahler said, 'That's not true. I wrote the symphony while I was alive. Since my death I haven't had the time to write anything. How about, 'Mahler's Final Will and Testament'?'

'It doesn't sound as good as 'A Symphony from Beyond the Grave.' Editors prefer drama to truth.'

'I'd rather you didn't write anything about the symphony that isn't true. The symphony has nothing to do with death. Tell them the music is all about life.'

William started again.

'Mahler's Final Will and Testament.'

'Our special correspondent has had the good fortune to examine the score of Mahler's Ninth symphony and sends this report in advance of the premiere by the Vienna Philharmonic to be conducted by Bruno Walter on June 26th.

'Anyone who thinks Mahler's last symphony foreshadows the composer's untimely death is mistaken. Mahler's Ninth symphony is an explosion of creativity that erupts from every bar, launching brilliant firework displays to light up the darkness in a series of multi-coloured climaxes.

'The first movement opens with a hypnotic rhythm before introducing the falling second – a single downward step as a mother might rock her child to sleep. Then the dormant volcano erupts, throwing a dazzling display of fire into the sky. Listeners familiar with Mahler's music will now hold onto their seats in the knowledge there is much more of this to come. The gentle passages and the thrilling climaxes are all written within a harmonic structure that is full of surprises. The dissonance never grates but yearns for the resolution which the symphony will eventually find in its closing bars. Every question Mahler asks leads to another question and the listener's thirst for an answer will not be quenched until the very last page, which delivers an answer so profound it will not be revealed here but only in the concert hall on June 26th.

'The second movement is a Ländler reinvented in a series of variations that lift the dancers off their feet, sometimes exciting and at other times grotesque. Trombones perform a waltz of dancing elephants which cavort across the concert platform only to disappear as suddenly as they appeared. Mahler's listeners will be amazed to hear how the composer transforms the concert hall into a circus ring with dancing clowns, acrobats, jugglers, trapeze artists and tightrope walkers. Mahler himself is the mighty master of ceremonies who cracks his whip, sometimes laughing, sometimes mischievously mocking.

'The third movement is a startling display of counterpoint. This is music of the utmost sophistication, with so much happening and all of it at once. We have moved from the big top to the fairground. Strapped into our seats, we are taken by Mahler on hair-raising rides at dangerous speeds. The carousel, out of control, spins faster and faster. We hold on to our horses but the horses can't hold onto the carousel and fly off, carrying us with them.

'The fourth movement opens with the hymn, *Bleib bei mir Herr*, which sounds so familiar we will want to sing along. The harmonies are like those you might hear in church but sufficiently out of kilter to remind us that we are not in church, but in a concert hall. I will say no more about the development of this movement except to suggest, that when the symphony ends, we may have discovered another dimension to our humanity.'

'What do you think?'

'You have an interesting imagination, William. How did you know about the elephants?'

'When I read the score I saw elephants dancing.'

'When I wrote the music I saw them dancing too.'

'Really?'

'Yes, really.'

'Did I get anything else right?'

'No.'

William was crestfallen.

'I wouldn't have written about my symphony like that but then, I write music. I don't write *about* it, and I never read newspapers. I bow to your superior expertise and perhaps your volcano, circus, fairground, and hymn will help the box office to sell tickets. You did well to say nothing about the end of the symphony. Don't forget to tell Bruno

Walter I want four and a half minutes of silence before he puts down the baton – perhaps two or three seconds more.'

During the drive back to Amalfi Lizzie and Anna told William about their day on Capri. They had met a young Scotsman, Edward Mackenzie, who had shown them around the island. Lizzie was surprised to discover a compatriot, a Scot in every way except for his English accent. She was, however, embarrassed when Mr Mackenzie declared that the island had welcomed homosexuals since Roman times. Lizzie's hopes that Anna's command of English would not be sufficient to allow the child to understand were dashed when Anna told William that he should have come with them, that he'd missed a treat, that the island was full of people like him and she was sure he would have enjoyed himself there.

They left the Amalfi coast and drove back north by an inland route. William had thought Lizzie and Anna might have been interested in the monastery which sat on top of the mountain outside Cassino. It was more than a thousand years old. Anna and Lizzie were more taken with the ice cream café in Cassino. Lizzie liked the café interior which was identical to the ice cream café in Edinburgh where she often went on a Sunday. When the proprietor realised Lizzie came from Edinburgh he came out from behind his counter, wiped his hands on his apron, gave her a warm embrace and told her that his brother lived in Edinburgh, as did many young men from the Val di Comino. They had emigrated to the capital of Scotland, some of them from a little town high in the mountain called Picinsico. Anna and Lizzie wanted to go to Picinisco, Anna because it sounded romantic, Lizzie because she wanted to meet Italians with connections to Edinburgh. The ice cream man told them that the road went as far as Atina, and from there they could get a bit closer on donkeys. The last few kilometres were a difficult climb on foot up a steep track. The view back down to the valley below was breathtaking but it was unusual for anyone to attempt the journey before the month of May. He also told them that there was nowhere for them to stay in Picinisco.

The monastery offered generous hospitality to travellers who wished to spend time in prayer and meditation. William, Lizzie, and Anna asked if they could stay. Their retreat was unusual as the three of them left the monastery every day to go down to Cassino for ice cream. Anna spent most of her retreat working on her sketches of the ruins at Paestum. The monastic routine was so alien to Lizzie's Presbyterian ways that she felt she had landed on a different planet. The monastic peace was broken every morning at 2am when the monastery bell was immediately followed by several hundred pairs of feet crashing onto the floor above the guest quarters as monks leapt out of bed to begin their day of work and prayer.

After a week of monastery discipline William, Anna, and Lizzie spent an entirely different week in Spoleto where they did not get up for breakfast until 10am before beginning a day of holiday sightseeing. They drove to Norcia where they ate spaghetti with truffles, to Amatrice where they ate spaghetti with guanciale and tomatoes, to Montefalco where they drank Sagrantino, and up the steep hill to Todi for coffee and ice cream. Everywhere she went Lizzie found comfort in the age of the buildings. Spoleto's Romanesque cathedral had been a central landmark for more than eight hundred years and if you ignored the rumours of tectonic instability the landscape supported its ancient architecture with a reassuring and comforting endurance.

On their way north they stopped at Perugia where they were made welcome once more in the hotel on Montebello. They looked upon the stained-glass window in the chapel and Lizzie and William made separate pilgrimages to the spot where the artist had pitched his tent.

In Pisa they walked along Via Santa Maria towards the leaning tower. Anna saw it first – just the top of it looming over the rooftops on the right-hand side of the street as if it was about to fall onto the more vertical buildings. They ran into the Piazza de Duomo and there it was, leaning at an impossible angle just like it did on the tea-towels, postcards, ashtrays, and other knick-knacks on display in the tourist shops. Anna thought it looked so funny she couldn't stop giggling.

William, who had developed an appetite for Italian opera, reserved a box in Pisa for a performance of Bellini's *La Sonnambula*. The overture did not disappoint. It was committed, earnest, and played with intense concentration by players who would never be good enough to find a place in any conservatoire. William wanted to live in Italy to play in a band like this. When *La Sonnambula* made her entrance William immediately recognized the sleepwalker – the Milanese soprano, Amalia di Constanza. He knew that it would be well after midnight before the curtain fell for the last time. He knew that after the musicians had left the orchestra pit and the house lights had gone up the audience would remain until Amalia di Constanza emerged from behind the final curtain to accept her audience's love and devotion. Everyone else in the hall knew it, too. She didn't put a foot wrong and performed her final curtain call holding her hands to her heart, attempting a curtsey, wobbling, then holding her brow to let everyone know she was about to faint. Someone rushed from the wings and held her just as she collapsed. From the opposite wing someone else emerged with a glass of water on a velvet cushion. She took a sip and miraculously recovered. The audience rushed to the front to kiss her hands and present her with flowers.

On Wednesday May 1st all the shops were closed and remained closed until the following Monday as Italians celebrated Labour Day over a long weekend.

On Tuesday, May 7th. they drove north to Chiavari. In the warm spring sunshine they sat on the beach and watched holiday-makers playing in the surf. Anna wanted to go in the sea but neither she, nor William, nor Lizzie could swim. Anna insisted. William eventually agreed as long as they held hands and stayed in the shallows. As they stepped into the sea the gravelly sand dropped sharply beneath their feet and William was surprised, after only a few steps, to find the water up to his waist. Anna was thrilled. The first wave lifted them up. The second wave knocked them over. They swallowed salt water and tried to scramble ashore. Although each big wave took them towards the shore the sand beneath them dragged them back into the sea. William suggested that after the next wave they should try and crawl out of the water on all fours. The last wave picked them up and threw them back onto the sand. Anna was excited. William was exhausted.

They took the train to Romagnolo and explored the Cinque Terre walking from one town to another using the donkey trail on the ridge that connected the five towns. Lizzie, William, and Anna held on to each other and negotiated the narrow donkey trail by walking sideways. They insisted on holding on to Anna, not so much to protect her from the precipitous drop below the path as to deal with their own dizzying vertigo.

At the restaurant in Romagnolo they asked for 'Zuppa di Pesce'. The waiter apologised. The rough seas had kept the fishermen at home. He gave them lobster with spaghetti and hoped they would return tomorrow for the fish soup. But the rough seas on the following day kept the fisherman at home again and they ate pasta con vongole instead. When they returned on the third day the waiter saw them coming and from the door called out in triumph, 'Zuppa di Pesce!' When they had eaten their large bowls of fish soup they sipped small glasses of sciaccatrà, the local sweet red wine.

Genoa, May 12th

In Genoa, as a precaution, William did not carry all the lire himself but shared it with Lizzie and Anna, whose pockets might be safer than his own. This was not a precaution William had taken in Naples, where he was just as likely to be robbed, but William imagined the Neapolitan thief would be polite, whereas his Genoese counterpart might be less pleasant. Genoa, like Naples, was a busy port and put Lizzie in mind of Leith, where Edinburgh's better classes did not set foot.

They did have one striking encounter in Genoa, with a chef. They had ordered the turbot hoping for a dinner as good as the meal they had enjoyed in Venice. In the Genovese restaurant the chef emerged from the kitchen dressed in whites with a tall chef's hat, followed by a procession of uniformed sous-chefs and assistants. He approached the table, bowed, and apologised. There was no turbot. There was, however, an alternative which he hoped William would consider. He snapped his fingers and one of the sous-chefs presented William with a large fish on a platter. William had no idea what it was but showed his approval. The chef and his underlings, relieved, returned to the kitchen to cook it.

As they drove north the May warmth cooled and by the time they reached Bergamo it felt like winter again as fine snow powder from the mountains swirled above town. William thought they might stroll around the shops but Lizzie strode out, overtaking pedestrians as if she was late for an appointment. William and Anna ran after her. Lizzie was in a hurry to leave Bergamo and return to Vienna. She'd had enough of hotels, and sightseeing, and Italy.

CHAPTER 45

Mahler's 9th Symphony

Alma required an account of Anna's Grand Tour. She sat with a notebook and pen and listened to the list of places they had visited, the hotels, the restaurants, the walks, and the people they had met. William thought it best to say nothing about the magistrate and the coins in the Fontana di Trevi or the death of Gustav von Aschenbach in Venice. Alma listened to William and Lizzie with increasing irritation and made a note only of the operas Anna had attended – *Lucia di Lammermoor* in Roncole, *Madame Butterfly* in Lucca and *La Sonnambula* in Pisa.

'Tell me what my daughter has learned,' demanded Alma.

'She learned to ride a bike,' ventured Lizzie.

'Why?' demanded Alma.

William intervened, 'So that you and Anna could go out cycling together. Your late husband enjoyed cycling and when you went out on your bicycle you looked very graceful.'

Alma was taken aback by William's tone. She picked up Anna's sketch pad.

'What are these?'

'The ruins at Paestum. They're Greek,' answered William.

'And the sheep and the cows?'

'They're Greek too,' said Lizzie

William knew there was no room in this conversation for humour and told Alma that the ruins were not curated but stood among the grazing cattle as they had done for the last three thousand years.

'And who are those two?' asked Alma pointing to a sketch of two boys.

'The shepherd and the cowherd,' said William.

'And what are they doing?'

William looked at the drawing of the boys kissing each other and told Alma the boys were playing.

'And what else has my daughter learned?

'Her English is nearly fluent,' said Lizzie.

'So is her Italian, and she can play the piccolo,' added William.

'The piccolo? Whatever for?'

'She's a natural musician,' said William.

'She takes after her father,' added Lizzie.

'And her mother,' intervened William. 'She is a gifted child. Frau Müller has invited Anna to join her team at the Opera, who are designing and making the costumes for the new production of *Madame Butterfly*.'

'Fraulein Müller,' corrected Alma. 'Thank you, Miss Turner, that'll do for now. I would like to speak with Mr Hildebrand in private.' Lizzie stood up, thought of offering Alma an insolent curtsey, then thought better of it. Before she opened the door she turned and told Alma, 'Anna has no friends.'

'Neither do I,' responded Alma.

'And it's her birthday tomorrow,' said Lizzie as she left, closing the door more firmly than was necessary.

Alma gave William a thousand kronen and asked him to get something for Anna's birthday. 'You know her tastes.' Then she asked William to fetch the box from the sideboard. He brought it to her.

'Is this for Anna?' asked William

'No,' said Alma, 'it's for you.'

William had not been expecting anything. He was surprised and relieved. How strange and delightful that this prickly interview should end with a gift.

He opened the box. It contained a Luger pistol, a holster, and some ammunition.

'Do you know how to use it?' asked Alma.

William shook his head.

'Then learn.'

'Why?'

'Because I have enemies.'

William had been standing in his own room for a few minutes holding the box with the pistol in it. He wanted to put it down but didn't know where to put it. There was a knock on the door. Lizzie came in. 'I could kill that woman!' she hissed in a loud whisper. William gave her the box. She opened it, saw, the pistol, gasped, dropped it on the floor, took a couple of steps backwards, pressed herself against the wall and burst into tears. William approached her with his arms wide open. 'Don't touch me!' she screamed and pushed him away. He fell over and struck his head against the bedpost. When he recovered consciousness he found himself on the floor cradled in Lizzie's arms. He looked up at her face and asked, 'How did you know the sheep were Greek?'

'Thank God! You're alive,' she said, and kissed his head.

He winced and told her his head hurt.

She saw the bruise and the growing lump. 'You frightened me. What are you going to do with the gun?'

'I don't know what to do with it. It's not mine. It's Alma's.'

'What does she want you to do with it?'

'She wants me to be her bodyguard.'

'What does she want a bodyguard for?'

'She thinks someone wants to kill her.'

'That's ridiculous. Who would want to kill her?'

'Would you kiss my head again?'

She kissed his head. 'Why did you give it to me?'

'I didn't know what to do with it,' explained William.

'I said I could kill her and then you put a gun in my hands. I thought you really wanted me to kill her!'

William asked if she would kiss his head again.

'William, if you carry a gun someone will take it from you and shoot you.'

'Alma thinks Kokoschka's mother wants to kill her. She thinks she has seen her outside the house and imagines the woman is carrying a gun.'

'She's mad.'

'Kokoschka's mother?' asked William.

'No, Alma,' replied Lizzie

'Alma's not easy to love,' said William.

'Neither are you,' said Lizzie.

'What'll happen to us when Anna has grown up?'

'I'll go back to Edinburgh and you will find someone to love.'

'Why would anyone love me?' asked William.

'Because you're adorable.'

'You told Alma the sheep were Greek.'

'Alma never heard me. She didn't hear anything we said.'

'What will we do with the gun, Lizzie?'

'We?'

'What will I do with it, then?' asked William.

'Take it to a gunsmith and ask them to fix the safety catch so that it is jammed, then if someone takes it from you, they won't be able to shoot you with it.'

William fished the banknotes from his pocket and told Lizzie that Alma had given him a thousand kronen to buy something for Anna's birthday.

William and Lizzie went to the art shop and bought materials for Anna. Then they went to the gunsmith. William waited outside. Lizzie was only in the shop for five minutes.

'All done,' she said.

'That was quick.'

'The pistol Alma gave you was a brand new semi-automatic Lugar P08 and he couldn't bear to jam the safety-catch, so I sold it to him and he gave me the same pistol with a jammed safety catch he was about to repair. It's useless but it looks exactly like the other one.' She gave William the broken pistol and an envelope with a thousand kronen which the gunsmith had given her for the working pistol. The next day Alma gave her daughter paints, two stretched canvases, an easel and a palette, and William and Lizzie took Anna out to a smart restaurant where they spent the thousand kronen Lizzie had got from the sale of the pistol.

June 26th
The world premiere of Mahler's Ninth

William mounted the platform and replaced Bruno Walter's baton with Mahler's before returning to sit with Lizzie and Anna in the orchestra stalls. Alma and Kokoschka sat at the front of the circle with the other important people.

Alma wasn't looking forward to the performance. She had attended some rehearsals and didn't like it any better than her late husband's other symphonies. It sounded awkward and banal -– a betrayal of Mozart, Beethoven, Schubert, and Brahms. When it did occasionally show some Wagnerian promise it broke down into a cacophony of silly squeaks as if the music was laughing at itself. She had read with horror the newspaper article about volcanoes, fairgrounds, and circuses. She thought fairgrounds and circuses were Jewish and could not imagine what vulcanology had to do with musical composition. She was content to be fêted as the composer's widow but was far from content with the composition. Alma sat beside Kokoschka and sulked.

Kokoschka wasn't looking forward to the performance either. He was jealous of Mahler and didn't want to listen to Alma's late husband's music. He wanted to be alone with Alma and have her all to himself. His senses were suffocated by jealousy and although he sat in the same room as the huge orchestral forces that performed the symphony, he did not hear a note of the music.

Lizzie felt privileged to hear the first performance of Mahler's last work. Anna felt proud of her father. William listened on the edge of his seat with his mouth wide open. Disposed to hear eruptions, elephants dancing, and the thrill of the fairground, William did indeed hear all of that. He felt dizzy and to ease the vertigo which he found as terrifying as the donkey trail above the Cinque Terre he held on to the seat in front of him. He was able to settle himself only at the beginning of the last movement and allowed the calm of *Bleib bei mir, Herr* to soothe him. This last movement offered no more thrills, no more laughter, and no more mischief as the music flowed slowly towards its final stillness. William felt profoundly peaceful until Bruno Walter turned to the last page of the score. William had looked at that final page many times but had never heard the quotation from *Kindertotenlieder* until now. William sat bolt upright. Mahler must have been thinking about the death of his daughter as he approached the end of his symphony! He turned to look up at the balcony and through his own tears he saw Alma's. She too was taken aback. She had never paid close attention at any of the rehearsals and was not prepared for the reference which she immediately recognized, and as the passage struck home she too wept for the death of her child. Kokoschka, seeing Alma's tears, was overwhelmed with jealousy and anger. How dare she bring him to this grotesque ritual and make him listen to her dead husband's music while she sat there weeping? How dare she look backwards to Mahler instead of forwards to the future with him. Kokoschka and Alma had a furious row in the foyer. He stormed out of the building screaming, 'Let the dead bury their dead!'

William went onto the platform to retrieve the baton Walter had left on the podium. He looked at the last page of the score and there it was – the quotation from *Kindertotenlieder* carefully copied in his own hand. With Mahler's baton safely back in his pocket he took Lizzie and Anna home, then returned to the Konzertverein to fetch Alma from the reception before she drank too much.

June 27th

Alma wanted to go shopping. William was waiting in the car for her when Mahler got in and patted the pistol William carried in a holster under his jacket.

'Miss Turner negotiated a good deal with the gunsmith, don't you think?'

'It wasn't hers to sell,' said William.

'Whoever heard of an honest arms dealer?' asked Mahler. 'Were you pleased with my Ninth?'

'Of course I was. It was magnificent. I was surprised by the quotation on the last page.'

'But you carefully copied it. You must have noticed.'

'I didn't.'

'How long did Bruno Walter hold the silence at the end?'

'I can't remember. I was thinking about Maria and didn't hear the silence. Alma is pregnant. She's been visiting Gropius in Berlin. Alma doesn't know who the father is, but Kokoschka thinks it's his. He's delighted and wants to marry her. She wants an abortion.'

Mahler told William he didn't care who the father was and if William needed to discuss it he should talk to Meddi. 'If the old lady who runs the fruit shop disarms you,' said Mahler, 'she can't do any harm with a useless Luger semi-automatic P08. You will be safe, and so will Alma. Here she comes. Ciao for now, my brave bodyguard!'

Alma did not see Mahler getting out of the car as she got in. She patted William's jacket, felt the pistol in its holster by his shoulder, nodded her approval, and they drove to the greengrocer.

Alma and Meddi went for a few days holiday to Bregenz, a small town on the Bodensee on a narrow strip of Austrian territory between Germany and Switzerland where wealthy ladies travelled to deal with their unwanted pregnancies. Now that Alma was relieved of her burden she began to think it was time she and her daughter got to know one another better, so she arranged a mother-and-daughter trip to Berlin. Anna, who balked at the idea of spending time alone with her mother, agreed, but only if Meddi came too.

While they were away in Berlin William was tasked with taking Kokoschka to the new house in Semmering. Alma wanted Kokoschka to create a fresco on the wall above the fireplace. William drove and Kokoschka talked. He declared his love for Alma. He told William that Alma had the power to inspire genius, that she was a midwife to great art, and that when they were married he would become a genius greater even than Mahler. William did not feel obliged to feign an interest. Kokoschka left no gaps in his monologue and this suited William, who had no interest in joining the conversation. William was, however, fascinated to hear that Kokoschka could talk at such great length without apparently taking a breath. He wasn't listening to what Kokoschka was saying but rather listening for the moment when Kokoschka breathed. He never heard it. William's thoughts turned to

Johnny, who could play the trumpet without taking a breath because he had mastered the technique of circular breathing. Kokoschka appeared to be able to do this while talking. When Kokoschka was eventually exhausted he asked William to tell him what he knew about Alma's feelings for him. William told him that Alma didn't like Mahler's music. He could not have given Kokoschka a more valuable, more beautiful, more satisfying present. Kokoschka sat back in the passenger seat and with Alma's dislike of her dead husband's music he soothed his jealousy.

William left Kokoschka in the new house working on the fresco and drove back to Vienna.

On the drive back William told Mahler that the house in Semmering had yet to be connected to the electricity supply and that Kokoschka was having to work in the dark.

'But he can work during the hours of daylight?'

'It's almost as dark in the house during the day as it is during the night.'

'Why?'

'The way it's been constructed. The verandah which goes all the way around is sheltered by the overhanging pitched roof and all the rooms are in constant shadow.'

'Did Gropius design it?'

'No, it was Alma's idea. She read an article in a magazine that was illustrated with photographs of a house that belonged to an English writer who lived on Samoa. She cut it out, gave it to the builders, and told them to build her one like that. The house in Samoa wasn't dark because the verandah was only at the front. It was Alma's idea to have it all the way around. She also cut out a picture of the interior where there was a huge fireplace and asked the builders for an even bigger one in Semmering. Why would anyone want a fireplace in Samoa?'

'I don't know,' said Mahler. 'Maybe the English writer liked to write by the fireside.'

'I didn't know Alma was interested in English writers,' said William.

'She isn't. She's interested in the tension between Germany and England. Germany has commercial and strategic interests in Samoa where England stirred up a civil war between pro-German and anti-German natives. The article in the magazine described the English writer's attempt to keep the peace despite threats from his own government to deport him. The writer died a few years ago. The fighting between the natives goes on. Even though Samoa is on the other side of the world it causes tension here.'

'Why is Alma interested in diplomatic relations?'
'Because she's bored and hopes there will be a war.'
'But the British Queen and the German Kaiser are family.'
'That makes war more likely.'
'Why is Alma bored?'
'Too much sex.'
'That doesn't sound very boring.'
'Sex is more interesting to priests and other celibates like you, who have little experience of it. In Berlin, right now, Alma will be having sex with Gropius in the afternoon, with Meddi in the evening, and when she comes home she will have sex with Kokoschka in the morning, afternoon, and evening. So much sex with so many people becomes tiresome! Did you tell Kokoschka that Alma didn't like my music?'
'Yes.'
'He must have enjoyed that.'
'He wanted me to tell him which bits she disliked most so I told him, "the Jewish bits".'
'He must have enjoyed that, too.'
'He did. He thanked Christ he wasn't Jewish.'
'Better for him if he was.'
'Why?'
'Because she would rise to the challenge of cleansing him of his Judaism. She would cleanse all Europe from Judaism and provide Europe with a final solution to the Jewish problem if only she could marry them all. If you are not Jewish, Alma's not interested. She would like to humiliate Kokoschka, but he likes that so much she can't do it. She feels uncomfortable with his unusual tastes. Gropius isn't Jewish either, so that won't last long.'
'What about Meddi?'
'An oasis of calm.'
And Anna?'
'She doesn't miss a thing. It would be better for her if she could remain a child for longer, but she'll behave as if she's grown up long before she's ready for it – and long before you're ready for it.'
'Lizzie will deal with it.'
'If there's a war, Lizzie will go back to England.'
'She's Scottish,' said William.
'Whatever. When she goes you'll be on your own.'
'I never thought of that.'
'You just did.'

There was no family gathering on Christmas Eve and so they all avoided the previous year's difficulties. Anna celebrated Christmas in Vienna with William and Lizzie. Alma celebrated in Semmering with Kokoschka. The Molls went with their daughter Maria to visit Gretel in the asylum. Meddi went to visit her sisters in Oberkochen.

Anna made a large multi-coloured butterfly for Meddi. She carefully assembled her butterfly from the wings of real butterflies. Her construction avoided symmetry, the wings almost mirroring but not quite. William thought it was beautiful and said so. Lizzie thought it was cruel to destroy the lives of butterflies to create a work of art but didn't say so. Anna made a nativity for William and Meddi. Joseph and Mary looked like William and Lizzie. The ox bore a resemblance to her mother and the ass looked like Kokoschka. Lizzie gave Anna a book in English – 'Travels with a Donkey' by Mr. Stevenson. William gave Lizzie a map of Scotland and Anna a map of Italy.

The Schindlers, Mahlers and Molls gathered together in the spring, when Alma held a housewarming to celebrate her new home at Semmering. Everyone was required to be there. Servants served champagne to family, friends and invited local dignitaries. Alma's sister, Gretel, confined to an asylum where her health was deteriorating, was unable to attend.

A roaring fire blazed in Alma's enormous fireplace. Over the huge chimney-piece Kokoschka's fresco was covered by a large veil. Holding a corner of the veil Kokoschka stood in front of the fire and began to make a speech dedicating his painting to Alma, his muse. He would have said more but, worried that his trousers might catch fire, he stepped away from the fire taking the veil with him, prematurely revealing his fresco that showed the flames in the fireplace rising and spreading upwards and across the wall. Inside the flames the figures of two lovers entwined, Kokoschka and Alma, phoenixes locked in loving embrace.

Lizzie told William that she thought it strange that Kokoschka had painted himself and Alma in hell.

Anna whispered to William that she didn't think it was OK. He didn't know what she meant. Anna pointed to the letters 'OK' in the bottom right-hand corner.

Anna asked Kokoschka why he always painted Mama. 'Can't you paint anything else?' Kokoschka asked why he would paint anything else when he could paint someone as beautiful as her mother. Anna thought a good artist might want to reflect the wide and varied nature of the world. Kokoschka wondered if the child was mocking him and stepped away to refill his glass.

Alma asked Anna for her opinion and Anna told her mother that it was 'OK'.

Meddi asked Alma if Kokoschka's red pyjamas in the fresco were the pyjamas he had given to her. 'Yes,' said Alma, 'but I didn't like them so I gave them back.'

'You did well,' said Meddi.

Carl Moll thought it was a masterpiece. Alma didn't. To have Kokoschka running off with her up the wall in flames would be an unwelcome intrusion into the intimate moments she looked forward to sharing with other lovers in front of the fire. She decided to scrub Kokoschka out of her life and to whitewash the fresco. She went to Berlin to visit Gropius.

After his great success with *Madame Butterfly* Weingarter decided to produce more Italian opera and change the direction of the Hofoper's programming which since Mahler's time had leaned heavily on Wagner and German opera. He decided to present a double bill of *Cavalleria Rusticana* and *I Pagliacci*. The Hofoper's seamstresses were commissioned to provide a wardrobe of peasant costumes. Anna was looking forward to helping Meddi in the wardrobe, but Alma had other plans. She decided not to send her daughter to the Hofoper but instead to find Anna a 'proper' teacher. William drove Alma. Anna, and Lizzie to Semmering where they were to visit a neighbour whose two daughters had a private tutor. Alma proposed that her daughter should join her daughters for their lessons. Before they set off to visit the neighbour William asked Alma if she required him to be armed. Alma didn't think it would be necessary. William unbuckled the holster and laid aside the broken Luger P08.

Anna did not like the tutor, who spent the lessons reading stories in a monotonous drone. Anna was bored with his reading of the stories from the *Wunderhorn*. She didn't tell the tutor that her father's setting of the magical tale of *Das Klagende Lied* had excited and enthralled her. She did not profit from his English lessons because she spoke English better than him. During the music lessons the girls were given triangles and tambourines to accompany the tutor who sang nursery rhymes. Anna brought her piccolo and played variations of the melodies as the other two girls tried to keep time. To the dismay of her two fellow students, and the tutor, Anna wanted to learn mathematics.

She had heard that girls didn't do mathematics and had decided, therefore, that she would. They spent time every day learning times tables and doing sums. When William and Lizzie asked, 'What did you do in school today?' she entertained them with funny stories. In the evening she drew caricatures of the teacher which made him look like a Lutheran pastor wearing a black academic gown that was too big for him and a blue cap that matched his lapels. Anna's education had lasted for a month when Alma's neighbour suggested that Anna find a different tutor because Anna was 'so far ahead' of her own daughters that the current arrangement was 'inappropriate'.

Alma, who was now bored with living in the country, decided to sell the house and move back to Vienna where less than a year before she had been bored and decided to move to the country. She had been Mahler's widow now for more than two years and had had enough of that. She was determined to live in Vienna in her own right and rented a ten-roomed apartment on Elizabethstrasse where she could host social occasions, surrounding herself with very top people just as Gertrude Stein and Alice B Toklas did in Paris. She was tempted to revert to her maiden name, which might serve her just as well as her married name. Her father, Emile Schindler, had been a national treasure and a favourite of the Emperor. But having weighed up both names she decided Mahler was the more substantial and so it was Alma Mahler that returned to Vienna to be herself.

Alma sent William to Semmering to whitewash the fresco, oversee the sale of the house, and bring Alma's furniture back to Vienna.

On the way to Semmering William told Mahler he felt uneasy about scrubbing out Kokoschka's fresco.

'Don't you think the fresco adds to the value of the house?' asked William.

'No.'

'Why not?'

'If you want to buy a house that is dark all the year round but for the few minutes in the winter when the sun is low in the sky, you are unlikely to appreciate a fresco above the fireplace. And during these few minutes you are unlikely to be entertained by a portrait of the former owner and her lover climbing up the wall. Put your mind at rest, William. Scrub it out.'

'How will Kokoschka feel about that?'

'He'd better not find out.'

'Once I've scrubbed out the fresco, how do I sell the house?'

'Alma's lawyers will sell it. You need to be there to show their clients around. Have you got a torch?'

'No.'

'Then you may need to lead prospective buyers by the hand.'

'I'll get a torch.'

'Perhaps you could suggest to Alma's lawyers they advertise the sale in magazines for the partially sighted, or in the *Transylvanian Times*. It's an ideal home for people who keep nocturnal pets but would prefer to enjoy their company during the day, and for those who enjoy sex only at night the house offers new opportunities by extending the hours of darkness. Why are you driving so fast?'

'I want to get there before dark.'

'It's dark there all day, William, so please slow down. I see you have wallpapering tools on the back seat and several rolls of wallpaper. What for?'

'I'm going to paper over Kokoschka's fresco before I repaint the wall.'

'Why?'

'Because in two or three hundred years someone, curious to see what's behind the wallpaper, will peel it off and get a surprise. A genuine signed fresco by Kokoschka! It may not add to the value of the house today, but it will then.'

'That's very considerate of you.'

'Kokoschka might take the view that his fresco will add to the value of the house right now.'

'He will.'

'So when Alma sells the house he might ask her for a share of the sale.'

'He will.'

'So, there's going to be trouble.'

'Yes,' said Mahler.

Kokoschka was outraged to discover the house was up for sale. He confronted Alma in a storm of anger, shouting so loudly she couldn't make out what he was saying. He was angry about the abortion of his child and he was angry about the sale of his fresco, but he was prepared to forgive Alma everything if she married him. He was in a rage when he stormed out and slammed the door. He returned immediately and demanded compensation for the fresco which must have doubled the value of the house but he would settle for whatever she thought was fair, because he loved her. Alma laughed at him and he stormed out again slamming the door. He returned immediately. Alma was still laughing and he couldn't think of what to shout next, so he stormed out yet again, slamming the door for a third time.

Kokoschka was seen riding around Vienna in a carriage sitting beside a life-size doll which he had dressed to look like Alma. He painted the face and dressed the doll in clothes and a hat stolen from Alma's wardrobe. A hairdresser turned up at Kokoschka's with an appointment to do Alma's hair. He asked if Frau Mahler was at home. Kokoschka said, 'No, but her hair is in the drawing room,' and led the hairdresser to the seated manikin wearing a wig. At night he slept with the doll. Meanwhile Alma was in Berlin driving around town and sleeping with Gropius.

Alma's lawyers negotiated a price for the house in Semmering that was considerably more than it had cost to build. This had nothing to do with Kokoschka's fresco, which lay hidden behind thick wallpaper. It was down to the sharp practice of Alma's agents. They allowed the prospective purchasers to believe that Mahler had lived in the house before his untimely death. Mahler had indeed purchased the plot with a view to building a house where he would spend the rest of his life composing, but he had never set foot in it. It was built by Alma after her husband's death. The purchaser believed what he wanted to believe and was prepared to pay handsomely for a house previously inhabited by Mahler. It seemed Alma had contrived a considerable windfall. She sent a large sum of money to Kokoschka with a covering note to say that she had managed to sell the house for a good price and was happy to compensate him for the fresco. He realized that the cash was Alma's final farewell. His feelings of rejection were mollified by her generous financial settlement. He set up his easel in the garden in front of a funeral pyre, placed the manikin on top and painted a portrait of the doll burning in the flames.

The purchasers of the Semmering property withdrew from their contract when they discovered the house had been built a year after Mahler's death and sued Alma's lawyers for their sharp practice. When Alma discovered that the sale had fallen through and that she was still the owner of the house in Semmering she fired her lawyers and engaged a second firm of solicitors to sue the first firm for the money she had given to Kokoschka. Then she decided to keep the house and told William to take all the furniture he had brought to Vienna back to Semmering.

Christmas 1913

Anna spent hours with Lizzie making a model parrot with real feathers for Lizzie to give to William, and she spent hours with William dressing a doll for William to give to Lizzie. Anna discreetly kept her work with one a secret from the other. Meanwhile she made a set of nine Russian dolls for Lizzie and William and kept it a secret from both. On Christmas Eve William gave Lizzie the doll and a copy of L. Frank Baum's *The Wonderful Wizard of Oz*. The doll wore a sash identifying her as 'The Good Witch of the North.' Lizzie gave William Mr. Stevenson's *Treasure Island* and perched the parrot on his shoulder. William and Lizzie gave Anna Baedeker's 1913 *Guide to North Italy from Ravenna to Livorno* and promised to take her back to Italy for her birthday. Anna gave William and Lizzie a set of Russian dolls. The first doll was her father and the others opened to reveal her mother, Lizzie, William, Meddi, her grandparents, and her late sister, Maria. The last doll represented the little boy she had met in Roncole, Camillo Tarocci, wearing a clerical collar, the priest she intended to marry. Her plan was to make a new doll every Christmas, each to fit inside the last so that they become smaller and smaller until a magnifying glass was required to identify them.

CHAPTER 46

War

Two weeks after Anna's tenth birthday the Emperor's son was assassinated in Sarajevo. Austrian borders were closed, telephone lines and railway networks were commandeered by the military, who mobilised for war. Serbia was presented with an ultimatum. Germany mobilised to support her Austrian neighbour. Russia was treaty-bound to support Serbia, as were Britain and France. Italy was undecided about which side to join. Lizzie became an enemy alien in a hostile country. Alma suggested that William, Lizzie, and Anna should visit Trenkerhof in Altschluderbach, where they would be safer than in Vienna. She herself wanted to go to Berlin where Gropius had volunteered. When Alma told Kokoschka to volunteer he thought she must be joking. She convinced him that it would be harder for him as a conscript and that it was in his own interests to volunteer. So he did, and after she had waved goodbye to the reluctant volunteer in Vienna, Alma went to Berlin to wave a flag for her brave Gropius as he marched off to war.

Alma had told her daughter the war would be over by Christmas and that she would be safe in Toblach. When they arrived at Trenkerhof Anna reminded William and Lizzie that they had promised to take her to Italy. Anna was sent to her room while William and Lizzie consulted with Herr Trenker.

In the morning Herr Trenker had hitched the horse with no name to the wagon which was piled high with cheeses. William told Anna that Herr Trenker was going to the market at Belluno in Italy to sell his cheese and that Lizzie was going with him. Anna insisted on going too. William told Anna that she must stay in Toblach with him while Herr Trenker and Lizzie went to market. Anna flew into a rage and accused them of breaking promises and lying to her. She wanted to go to Italy with Lizzie. The child would not be calmed and half an hour later the four of them set off for Italy. Lizzie explained to Anna that they were not smuggling cheese. It was Lizzie herself who was being smuggled across the border. Now that William was no longer required to wait in Toblach with Anna, he was happy to be able to accompany Lizzie to Italy. Herr Trenker was also happy because the presence of the child would add an air of innocence to the wagon full of cheeses that concealed the presence of the young Scottish woman. The journey from Toblach to Belluno would take all day but at this time of the year they would be able to complete the ride in the long summer daylight.

It was a warm afternoon in the Southern Tyrol when Trenker stopped and ushered his three passengers under the tarpaulin and concealed them among the cheeses. He placed his passport in the horse's bridle above its right ear, pulled the tarpaulin back over his load and climbed on top of it where he lay in the sun and appeared to be asleep. The horse with no name continued along the road without a driver. The Austrian border guards were able to smell Herr Trenker's approach long before his wagon appeared. The horse stopped at the border. The border guard took the passport from the horse. 'Good afternoon, Herr Trenker. You have no need to declare your cheese. It declares itself.' He tossed the passport onto the sleeping wagon master who snored. The horse with no name snorted and trotted down the track to the Italian border.

'Stay where you are and don't move,' whispered Herr Trenker through the tarpaulin. 'I'm suffocating,' said William. 'That's not a problem, Herr Hildebrand, as long as you do it silently.' The horse with no name stopped at the Italian border where the Italian border guard helped himself to four cheeses. Removing the fourth he saw a pair of shoes. He pulled off the tarpaulin and found Anna, Lizzie, and William. 'Jesus, Mary and Joseph!' cried the astonished border guard. 'My name's Anna' retorted Anna, 'and they are William and Elizabeth!'

'How many more cheeses do you need?' asked Trenker.

'Another four?' suggested the border guard.

Trenker told him to take another eight. Four for today and four more for the day when they returned. He carried his heavy cheeses to the border hut, thinking only of the pleasure the twelve cheeses would bring to his mother, the priest, the nuns, his brothers and sisters, his cousins, his children, and his wife. He replaced the tarpaulin over the holy family and the horse with no name continued down the track to the market at Belluno.

Carrying only a small handbag with her overnight accessories and some cash, Lizzie took the train to Milan where she would change for Genoa and thence to Livorno to catch a ferry to Barcelona, then by train to Bilbao for a ferry to Southampton.

Herr Trenker sat in the back of his wagon with William and Anna. Using three large cheeses for seats they played cards as the horse with no name pulled the wagon back towards the border. When he saw the horse approaching the Italian border guard rushed into his hut and emerged with two bottles of wine in each hand. 'For you, from my father, who thanks you for the cheese. And these two are from our priest, Padre Polenta, who asks you to pray for peace.' Herr Trenker thanked the border guard and the horse with no name moved towards the Austrian border where the guard congratulated Herr Trenker on selling all his cheese. Herr Trenker introduced Herr Hildebrand, a citizen of Switzerland, and Fräuline Anna Mahler, a citizen of Austria. The guard looked at their documents and stiffened when he read in Anna's passport that she was the daughter of Gustav Mahler. He clicked his heels and bowed. Herr Trenker told the guard he would be happy to let him have the cheeses they were sitting on. The guard replied that he was, unfortunately, unable to accept gifts but complimented Herr Trenker on the cheese which his friend, the Italian border guard, had shared with him.

'What will you and your friend do if Italy and Austria go to war with each other?'

'The Italians will fight as our allies against the British,' replied the Austrian guard with certainty. 'I will be conscripted, although I would prefer to volunteer.'

'Why don't you volunteer?'

'Because I am not in a position to provide my own uniform and arms.'

'With your permission I would like to support the Austrian war effort.' Herr Trenker gave the border guard an envelope. 'If you do not buy the very finest cloth there will be enough left for you to arm yourself with a good rifle.' Herr Trenker asked God to protect the guard and asked the guard to protect Austria.

On the long drive home Herr Trenker asked William whether he thought it better to receive gifts in good faith like the Italian or in bad faith like the Austrian. William thought that was unfair on the Austrian who had accepted Trenker's generous offer of a uniform and rifle in support of the war effort.

'His family are poor,' said Trenker. 'He will find far better things to do with the cash than to dress and arm himself. If we need to pass this way again it would be well to have someone on the border who may be inclined to help us.'

Alma was thrilled by the outbreak of war. It was just what she needed to overcome her boredom. Before Gropius left to join his regiment of Hussars he and Alma promised to marry during his first leave.

Alma returned to Vienna and her salon in Elizabethstrasse. One morning a week Alma joined Meddi and the wardrobe team at the Hofoper, altering clothes for amputees. They turned out one-armed shirts and one one-legged trousers, and sometimes shirts with no arms.

Italy came into the war on the side of the British and the French, and Vienna lost its Italian teachers, artists, and restaurants. Anna's hopes of living in Italy until the war was over were dashed. Austria and Italy fought each other to a standstill in the Tyrol. In Toblach Herr Trenker's barns filled up with Austrian and Italian deserters and wounded. Weingartner had to rethink his plans for the Hofoper, where it was no longer possible to perform Italian opera. Dispatches from the front were greeted with outbursts of rejoicing. Rare reports of German setbacks were received with outbursts of anti-Semitism. Alma married Gropius. After the wedding-night he returned to his regiment and she returned to her salon where she met the young writer, Franz Werfel, younger even than Gropius and not so dull. Werfel worked in the propaganda office making up stories about brave soldiers. Although Alma was pregnant with her husband's child, she started an affair with Werfel.

Gropius got himself moved from a position where he had sustained minor wounds to a safer post in charge of a unit of dog handlers. Anna wrote to Gropius addressing him as 'Dear Stepfather', enquiring about his new job training dogs, which she thought must be very interesting. Alma wrote to him without any greeting to tell him how distressed she was to have fallen so far. Once the wife of the foremost musical artist of his generation she felt humiliated by her new husband's role as a dog handler. She told him to wash his hands before he wrote to her. Their daughter, Manon, was born on October 5[th.] 1916. Whenever Gropius was on leave, he visited his daughter. Alma was always relieved when he returned to his regiment.

William's duties included supervising the staff at Alma's salon in Elizabethstrasse and driving to Semmering four times a year to prepare the house for Alma's arrival. When Werfel was on leave from the propaganda office he accompanied Alma to her country house. When Alma was accompanied by Gropius, Franz Werfel remained in Vienna writing propaganda. On June 15th 1918 Alma took her daughter on a shopping spree to celebrate Anna's 14th birthday.

Anna applied her birthday make up with subtlety and finesse and wobbled on her birthday high heels through the door from childhood into a world of flirtation and sex. After Anna had gone to her room Alma opened a bottle of Benedictine. She asked William how old Anna was. William told Alma that her daughter was now fourteen. Alma had thought that Anna looked older and told William that Franz Werfel had his eye on her. William assured her that he would keep an eye on Werfel and that Anna would come to no harm. Alma thought that Anna and Werfel would make a fine couple. William couldn't believe what he was hearing and repeated, 'She's fourteen.'

'Werfel's twenty-eight,' replied Alma, 'and I'm thirty-nine. He's fourteen years older than her and I'm eleven years older than him. The difference between our differences is only three years, which hardly counts for anything.' William, lost in the fog of Alma's arithmetic, tried to grasp what he was hearing and could only repeat, 'She's fourteen.'

'So you keep saying. Next year she will be fifteen and then she will be sixteen. She is no longer a child.'

William was afraid to say any more lest he found himself trapped in a hideous joke.

Alma gave William a large envelope and asked him to open it. Gropius had sent her architectural drawings for the alterations to the verandah of her property in Semmering which would allow some daylight into the house.

'Does it smell of dogs?'

William sniffed the drawings. 'No.'

Alma put on a pair of gloves and William handed the drawings to her.

'Some wives get love letters from their warrior husbands. I get architectural drawings from a dog handler.'

Alma sniffed the papers and threw them back at William.

'Ugh! Dogs!!'

William suggested he might take the papers to Semmering and engage local builders to deal with the verandah.

'Do whatever you like. I need to wash my hands.'

William couldn't sleep. He thought of turning on the light but imagined he could talk to Mahler just as well in the darkness and he whispered, 'Are you there?'

'Yes, of course.'

'What would you do?'

'If I was alive she could not have married Gropius. Now that she is married to Gropius she is being unfaithful to him, not me, so I have nothing to say.'

'What about Anna?' asked William.

'Anna will do what she wants, with or without your approval. If you want to help her it would be better to let her explore her sexuality without your disapproval. If you lose her trust you will not be able to look after her and help her avoid pregnancy.'

'I'm out of my depth.'

'Your heart's in the right place. That'll have to do.'

'Alma said that Anna and Werfel would make a handsome couple.'

'That says more about Alma's state of mind that it says about Werfel. Anna will have nothing to do with him. Speak to Anna. She'll put your mind at rest. When you go to Semmering with the drawings, take Anna with you. She'll talk to you. She might have quite a lot to say for herself.'

On the way to Semmering Anna told William that she couldn't see what her Mama found attractive in Werfel. 'He's small and fat and smokes, his clothes are covered in ash, his teeth are brown, and his breath stinks. Can you imagine what it must be like to be touched by his nicotine-stained fingers? And as for being kissed by his smelly lips… Yuk!'

Before William met the builders, Anna made some alterations to the drawings. She added French windows to her room, which opened onto a balcony supported by a spiral staircase which led down to the garden. She told William that she intended to sit on the balcony and listen to the serenades of potential lovers before she invited the chosen one to climb the steps. William thought it was an excellent idea. He wanted to have a balcony and a spiral staircase outside his own room.

On the way back to Vienna Anna told William about Maria.

'Your sister?' asked William.

'No, Mama's little sister. Auntie Mary.'

'She doesn't like it when you call her that,' William reminded her.

'But I like teasing her. She's had a lot of boys. They'll do anything in return for sex. She makes them pay for it. They're nice boys. They used to bring her flowers and chocolates, but she'd rather have cash. That's very sensible, don't you think?'

William told Anna he thought she would be better off with the flowers and chocolates.

Anna told William that Maria was going to lend her one of her boyfriends.

'You might get pregnant.'

'Then you'll be an uncle.'

'I think you should speak to Meddi.'

'But Meddi sleeps with women.'

'That's not such a bad idea. You don't get pregnant, and Meddi tells me it's more fun.'

Anna giggled, laid her head on William's shoulder, and fell asleep.

William asked Meddi if he should get Anna a wider bed.

'Only if she asks for one. Otherwise it's none of your business.'

William told Meddi that he didn't know what to do.

'You don't have to do anything. You're doing fine. You're her friend. If she brings someone home just be friendly and hospitable.'

'I wish Lizzie was here. Lizzie would know what to do.'

'No, she wouldn't. She would frown, disapprove, be jealous, and Anna would flee. It's far better for Anna to feel welcome in her own home.'

'What about Alma? She will be angry. If something bad happens, it'll be my fault.'

'Don't you ever get tired of beating yourself up? A fourteen-year-old girl speaks in confidence to her thirty-five-year-old male friend about her sexual desires, and you wonder what's the matter with you! So do I! If you looked hard enough you could find gloom in a sunrise. Anna talks to you because she knows you'll listen. As long as she feels welcome at home she won't look for sex in shop doorways. Disapprove, and you'll chase her into the street. Of course you worry about her. But you're more worried about Alma, aren't you? Alma scares you. Alma's impulsive and reckless and enjoys the luxury of being crazy so you can't allow yourself any luxuries. You need to be there for Anna. Alma trusts you and so does her daughter. When Anna brings someone home you don't need to think about getting a bigger bed for her. Just make a bigger pot of coffee in the morning.'

The Austrian army in the Tyrol had planned for mountain warfare and were unprepared for what actually happened. The Italian soldiers retreated in disorder from Caporetto after a German gas attack. The fleeing Italian soldiers left the Veneto wide open to an Austrian advance. An army that had prepared for war in the mountains did not expect to leave the high ground and occupy the northern plains of Italy. At the beginning of November 1918 when the European war had decisively moved against the central powers, the Italians regrouped and won a far from glorious victory at Vittorio Veneto against the over-extended Austrians. The end of the war brought an end to the Austro-Hungarian Empire.

Herr Trenker did not survive the war. He was shot by an Austrian firing squad along with the Austrian and Italian deserters hiding in his barns, Some of these men were too badly wounded to stand before a firing squad and were shot in the barns where they lay. The Austrian soldiers took all the cheese, the horse with no name, and the wagon. Agnes, the cook, who concealed herself during the massacre, eventually emerged from her hiding place. She baked bread to give to the corpses lying in the barns and in the yard. She was eventually overcome by the stench of decomposing flesh and walked towards the lake shouting obscenities at the mountains and was never seen again. The victorious Italian army occupied the empty property. The map of Europe was re-drawn. Toblach, now in Italy, was renamed Dobbiaco.

CHAPTER 47

Another Grand Tour of Italy

Springtime 1919, and William fulfilled his promise to return to Italy with Anna. He asked Meddi to come with them. He wrote to Herr Trenker but got no reply. They had to cross the Italian border before reaching Altschluderbach, which was now in Italy. The Italian border guard examined their papers. William reminded him they had last met four years ago when Herr Trenker had given him some cheese. 'Of course I remember you. Please convey my best wishes to Herr Trenker. I hope that he had not been inconvenienced by the Italian border being moved into Austria.' Addressing Anna he said, 'Goodness! How you have grown since we last met!' and, mistaking Meddi for Lizzie, he said, 'And you, Fraulein Müller have not changed at all since we last had the pleasure of meeting.'

When William, Anna and Meddi visited Trenkerhof they discovered an Italian family living there who had never heard of Herr Trenker. The house still smelt of cheese. They spent the night in the hotel near the station. No one talked about the war.

They drove down from the mountains and entered Bologna in the late afternoon, found a hotel, then strolled into the centre of town. William knew that Bologna was famous for popes and sausages. He was interested in the sausages. He gazed through the windows of restaurants at the tables set for the evening meal. He stopped at one ristorante after another to take in the handwritten menus posted on the glass. He was intrigued that none of them offered spaghetti Bolognese. He had eaten spaghetti Bolognese in New York, Vienna, and Berlin but he couldn't find spaghetti Bolognese in Bologna. When William stopped to read the restaurant menus Meddi and Anna didn't wait for him and he spent much of the evening stroll running to catch up with them. The porticos which covered the walkways where Italians made their evening passaggiata were built wide enough and high enough to accommodate two horsemen passing each other. William, with eyes only for menus and restaurants, rushed past startled Italians, dressed in their best and strolling slowly. He did not notice the arches as he darted through the portici, and if there had been any horsemen William would not have seen them either. At the town centre they gazed up at the two leaning towers, Asinelli and Garisenda. Anna suggested that medieval Italian architects must have competed to see who could build the tower that leaned at the most precarious angle. There were many leaning towers in Venice but the twin towers in Bologna would have won the prize, seeing off the leaning tower of Pisa by several degrees.

William took them to a restaurant where they ate spaghetti with truffles, sausages with polenta, a green salad and a macedonia of fresh fruit. Next morning while Meddi and Anna were climbing Asinelli William went to a bar, where he met Mahler.

William told Mahler that Alma had given birth to a boy. 'Gropius thinks it is his child, but it's Werfel's. Alma wants a divorce but Gropius does not agree. Alma won't allow Gropius custody of their daughter, Manon. She adores the child and calls her an 'angel'. Manon is not Jewish, like Anna, and her new Jewish baby by Werfel.'

Mahler told William that Gropius would lose his appetite for a fight when he discovered his wife had produced a bastard. 'You and Meddi have done well to get Anna away from Austria so she doesn't have to witness Alma and Gropius tearing each other apart.'

William told Mahler that Gropius was more concerned about who had been fooling around with his drawings for the alterations to the house in Semmering than about who had been fooling around with his wife. The adultery that outraged him was the addition of a spiral staircase leading to the upstairs window of Anna's room.

William, Meddi and Anna arrived at Montebello in the late afternoon. The sun that rises above Assisi was setting behind Perugia. The hotel staff who warmly welcomed William and Lizzie stiffened upon meeting William and Meddi.

William and Anna took Meddi to the chapel to see the stained-glass window of St Francis talking to the birds. The two angels flew above the tree while Francis and his brothers stood below. The foliage on the tree seemed to have grown since William last looked and he couldn't find the owl. When Anna pointed to it William was taken aback.

'The owl looks just like the artist.'

'Of course it does,' said Anna. 'Didn't you know that?'

That night Meddi sat on the end of William's bed as he told her about Francesco, the stained-glass artist. Apprenticed to his father, Francesco had become a skilled stained-glass craftsman despite his father's insistence that he'd never be any good at it. Francesco never had a girlfriend. His mother had arranged a marriage for him to avoid a scandal. The couple muddled along together for four years before the wife became pregnant by a friend. Francesco's parents were delighted that their awkward son was at last presenting them with a grandchild. Francesco doted on the child and was a loving father until his wife went to the bishop to ask for an annulment of their marriage, which had never been consummated on account of her husband's perversity. Estranged from his wife, and his daughter, and his parents, Francesco took to the road with his dog and his tools and worked on stained-glass windows.

'Were you in love with him?'

'Yes,' said William.

'Was he in love with you?'

'Yes,' said William, 'but having lost his own daughter he would do nothing to come between me and Anna.'

'But Anna is not your daughter.'

'Not biologically, and not legally, but Francesco said that love has nothing to do with law or biology.'

'Were you and Francesco lovers?'

'I don't think so.'

'You don't know?'

'When he sketched me he would stroke my face and then draw what he felt rather than what he saw. He brought me to life first with his touch and then with his pencil. He stroked my eyebrows, my forehead, my nose, my lips, my ears, and he stroked my face for hours. Then he sketched it in minutes.'

'Show me.'

William slowly stroked Meddi's right eyebrow, moving his finger gently from left to right, measuring the sweep of its curve and letting his finger count every hair. Then he did the same for Meddi's left eyebrow. Then he touched her left ear on the outermost edge where he could count the dips and ridges in the cartilage, and only when he had committed the outer edge to memory did William move to the softer inner cartilage where Meddi could hear as well as feel his touch. They sat together in silence as William mapped Meddi's ears. The he began to explore Meddi's mouth. With his eyes closed William worked slowly, tracing his finger from the sensitive skin of her lower lip and exploring the changes in sensitivity between her lower lip and her throat. Every time William's finger returned from her chin to her lower lip Meddi's mouth opened slightly and William fixed the memory with his inner eye.

There was a loud rap at the door. A chambermaid came in with another set of towels. She stiffly walked around the bed and left them on the windowsill before leaving the room with her nose in the air.

William said, 'Christianity gave Eros poison to drink. He didn't die of it but degenerated to vice.'

'Did Francesco say that?' asked Meddi.

'No, Mahler did.'

'I don't believe Christianity has poisoned either of us,' said Meddi. 'What happened after he touched your face?'

'I fell asleep.'

Meddi stood up to go. 'The owl in the window,' she said, 'isn't looking at St Francis. It's looking at you.'

Before William fell asleep Mahler reminded him that although they might look like a family, he had returned to this hotel with a different woman, and that offended Italian sensibilities. In addition, the new woman was German and Mahler reminded him the war wounds were fresh. He suggested that when they went to Spoleto, to avoid raised eyebrows, they would be more comfortable if he didn't go back to the same hotel.

In Spoleto the painter and sculptor, Giovanni D'Agostino, worked in his studio from dawn until dusk. At 10am he went out for coffee and saw William, Lizzie and Anna sitting at a table. Giovanni drank his coffee at the bar and before going back to work asked if he might join the young family for a moment. He discovered that this unusual family comprised a Swiss, a German and an Austrian. He welcomed them to Spoleto and said he would be honoured if they would visit his studio and gallery which was just around the corner.

Meddi thought he wanted to sell them something.

Anna thought she would like to watch him work.

William thought he had beautiful blue eyes.

Giovanni D'Agostino wanted to make a portrait of Anna.

Giovanni didn't go back to work but sat in his studio and waited for them. They arrived and he gestured Anna to sit. He began the portrait. William and Meddi were taken aback by his presumption. Anna was delighted. Meddi decided she would wait with Anna and sat down. There was nowhere for William to sit so he stood behind the artist and watched him make the first few strokes. Giovanni asked him not to stand there. Meddi told William to leave and come back at one o'clock with panini and water. When William returned with the sandwiches no one seemed to have moved. Meddi took the sandwiches and suggested they all meet again back at the hotel. William asked when. Meddi didn't know. It was getting near dusk when Giovanni looked at his day's work, shook his head, painted over it and asked Anna to come back in the morning. Meddi asked Giovanni how long the portrait would take. Giovanni said, 'A few days.'

The following day Meddi asked William to go with Anna to Giovanni's studio while she explored Spoleto. Giovanni sent William out to get coffee. When William returned Anna had unfastened her blouse to reveal her left breast. Giovanni worked in silence and after three hours William said it was time for lunch. Giovanni pointed to the bag with the four panini which he had brought the day before. William ate one of them. Then he felt thirsty. Anna told William to go and get himself a drink and that she would see him later back at the hotel.

Meddi found Spoleto's *Museo del Tessile e di Costume* and decided not to spend any more time worrying about William and Anna. She couldn't decide which one of them was the chaperone but, on balance, she thought Anna was probably more able to look after herself than William. If fifteen-year-old Anna had an intimate experience with Giovanni D'Agostino it would be no more than her mother had experienced with Gustav Klimt. Instead of dwelling on William and Anna she immersed herself in five centuries of Italian textiles.

When Anna got back to the hotel she told William that Giovanni would be spending the evening in Bar Centrale. At dinner time William confessed he wasn't hungry. Meddi suggested he went to Bar Centrale.

'Can I?' asked William.

'Oh, for God's sake, William, I'm not your mother.'

William got up and left.

Anna told Meddi that when Giovanni looked at his day's work, he shook his head, painted it out, and asked her to come back in the morning. She told Meddi that Giovanni enjoyed sex but only with partners who let him pay for it. 'How do you think William will handle that?'

'I can't imagine,' said Meddi.

'Neither can I,' said Anna.

The following morning William didn't come down for breakfast. Meddi went to his room and discovered he wasn't there. Meddi and Alma arrived at the studio where they found Giovanni sitting at the canvas waiting for Anna. Meddi asked if he knew where William was. Giovanni pointed to the mezzanine at the top of a stepladder and said,

'Fast asleep and hungover. Come back in two hours with some coffee and we'll wake him then.'

Anna lowered the blouse from her left shoulder to resume yesterday's pose.

Two hours later Meddi returned with a tray of coffee.

'Don't move,' Giovanni called to Anna and he got up to re-adjust Anna's pose. Meddi climbed the stepladder with some difficulty, holding a cup of coffee in one hand and clinging to the rungs with the other. William was snoring and groaning. Meddi left the coffee beside him and climbed back down.

'Don't talk to each other,' ordered Giovanni.

Meddi blew Anna a kiss and left the studio to spend another day at the *Museo del Tessile e del Costume*.

She was happy among the textiles.

Anna and Giovanni were happy in the studio.

William was snoring.

William spent the rest of the week with Giovanni.

Meddi spent the rest of the week studying textiles in the museum.

Giovanni spent the rest of the week making the portrait and then painting over it at the end of every day.

Anna decided she would give Giovanni no more time to make her portrait than the six days it had taken God to create the world. At the end of the sixth day, when Giovanni was about to paint over his day's work, Anna took the brush from him, Meddi took the portrait and left the studio with Anna, leaving William to settle with the artist.

Anna's portrait showed only her head and shoulders in black and white. The portrait did not extend to her loosened blouse and left breast. Brush strokes of different shades of black applied to the canvas in layer after layer revealed her robust expression; brushstrokes of white streaking across and enlivening her forehead and cheeks revealed her fragility; the immaculate white that surrounded her wide-open dark eyes revealed her curiosity, and the line of her bared left shoulder merged with the panelled wooden wall behind to reveal her solidity.

'More than OK,' judged Meddi.

'Much better than OK,' agreed Anna.

'If this was a wanted poster you would immediately be arrested,' said William.

On the sabbath, before they left Spoleto, they went to visit Giovanni. They found him in his studio where he had been working all night on Anna's head in clay. Anna looked at the representation of herself. Face-on, the head narrowed to her nose with nothing beyond her eyes on either edge. Side-on, the head was elongated so that her profile resembled a fish. The resemblance to Anna was nevertheless striking and as you walked around it, the head appeared to move. When William walked around the sculpture, he found the apparent movement vertiginous and he reached out to the panelled wall to keep his balance. Anna promised one day to return and knew that she would. William wanted to say the same but knew that he never would. Giovanni presented him with a tiny sculpture standing on a block of wood. Only two inches high, it was a full-length sculpture of himself. They bade each other farewell.

April 30th, 1920

William sat at the wheel smiling as they drove north to Milan. He knew that Giovanni D'Agostino was a genius. Giovanni asked William for exactly the amount for the portrait that he had paid William for their sex together. The value of the portrait equal to the cost of their love was therefore, in William's eyes, priceless.

Their hotel rooms in Milan on the top floor at the corner of Via Giuseppe Mazzini and Piazza del Duomo offered them a fine view of the cathedral. They looked forward to celebrating May Day with the Milanese workers and anticipated the bands, banners, and holidays that would extend over the long Labour Day weekend. The hotel manager assured them they would be perfectly safe in the hotel. William thought it a strange welcome and put it down to a northern Italian reserve. They went out for dinner but returned to the hotel without eating when scuffles broke out in the street between gangs of angry Milanese fighting for control of the streets that led to the Piazza del Duomo. Back in the hotel they were unscathed but frightened. The manager scolded them for going out. They were ushered into a back room where a priest was leading prayers before a statue of the Madonna. They prayed for the safety of the hotel and its staff and placed their souls in the care of the Mother of God. They prayed for peace but, if there must be violence, they asked the Virgin Mary to ensure the communists got a good thrashing.

The manager told them not to leave the hotel, to close the shutters, and on no account to step out on to their balcony. The priest would be available all day to hear confessions and if they were unable to open the doors in the morning he would celebrate Mass in the hotel before breakfast.

William had seen no sign of social unrest anywhere else in Italy. In Bologna he had eyes only for restaurant menus, in Montebello for stained glass, and in Spoleto for Giovanni D'Agostino. He wondered if the present difficulty was peculiar to Milan. He had heard Alma and Franz Werfel arguing about politics and thought that was a problem peculiar to their relationship. Alma often accused Werfel of coffee house tittle tattle when he spoke about workers' rights. William now witnessed the subject of Alma's and Werfel's disagreements on the streets of Milan.

There was no sleep that night. They heard the crash of broken glass from shop windows as looters emptied jewellery stores and fashion houses. William went out onto the balcony and saw police on horseback scattering rioters. Barricades were built, torn down, and rebuilt. By morning socialists were in control of all the streets leading into the Piazza. Brass bands and drummers preceded marchers into the square. The music put William in mind of the first movement of Mahler's Third. Anna came to William's room and joined him on the balcony when she heard a marching band of piccolos and drums leading a procession of red-shirted Garibaldini triumphantly saluting as they marched down the street named after Mazzini. More red-shirted marchers followed, carrying a statue of the Madonna and bearing a huge banner which declared, *Il Partito Communista non e Ateo*. William thought this Madonna must be a different Madonna from the one in the hotel who had been asked to help give the communists a sound thrashing. Meddi came into William's room. She urged them to come away from the balcony but then she too was drawn to the colourful spectacle in the street below. William, Anna and Meddi could see over the buildings into the Piazza in front of the Cathedral. They heard the crowd cheering and singing but could not make out the speakers. The Square was full and the street below quiet when William saw soldiers jogging in formation towards the Piazza. More soldiers approached the Piazza from the other streets leading to the square. The tens of thousands in the Square did not realize they were trapped. The soldiers fired in the air. There was panic. William, Meddi and Anna retreated from the balcony and closed the shutters. Screams, sirens, and gunfire came from the street immediately below their window. They fled from the room to the landing where other guests on their knees fingered their rosaries.

Some demonstrators were trampled to death, others were suffocated in the crush, and some were shot. The story widely circulated in the newspapers described how the soldiers drafted into the Square to protect the House of God had been attacked by enemies of the Church and the State. The papers described the injuries suffered by 'our brave boys' who risked their lives to protect democracy and the right to peaceful protest. It was understood that there had been casualties among the demonstrators but the number of those dead or injured was not known.

CHAPTER 48

Anna Mahler. Franz Werfel.

William, Meddi, Anna, and her new friend, Rupert Koller, went out for dinner to celebrate Anna's sixteenth birthday. Anna was wearing a Celtic brooch which was identical to the 'badge of friendship' that Lizzie had given to William at Christmas eight years before and which he had carefully kept in its box. He asked Anna where she had got hers. She told him it was a birthday present from Lizzie. William was unpleasantly surprised to discover that Lizzie had been in contact with Anna. He had never been in touch with Lizzie. He was jealous of Anna and angry with Lizzie. He tried to show an interest in Anna's new friend but could think only about Lizzie. He tried not to stare but could not take his eyes away from Anna's brooch.

Anna hardly spent any time in Austria and lived with her boyfriend in Eberfeld in the Rhur where Rupert had been appointed chief conductor at the Municipal Opera House. William hardly saw Alma either. She was travelling with Franz Werfel. William lived by himself and looked after the empty houses in Vienna and Semmering. Meddi prodded William out of his melancholy, ordered coffee and discreetly asked the waiter to bring the birthday cake with the lighted candles. Anna and Rupert declined coffee and got up to leave. William followed Anna to the door and said, 'I need to talk to you, Anna.'

'I know what I'm doing, William. I'm sixteen.'

'Not about you. About Lizzie.'

'I'll see you tomorrow,' said Anna, and they left.

A waiter brought the birthday cake with sixteen lighted candles. William and Meddi sat in front of the abandoned cake.

'Do you think he loves her?' asked Meddi.

'I don't know,' answered William.

'I don't think he does,' said Meddi, 'and I don't think she loves him. What age are you?'

'Forty,' said William.

'I'm thirty-six,' said Meddi.

They blew the candles out together.

The other diners in the restaurant applauded and sang *Happy Birthday*.

Tuesday, June 17th

Anna came to Elizabethstrasse to collect her things to take to Eberfeld where she was planning to move in with Rupert. William wanted to know if Lizzie ever asked after him.

'No.'
'How is she?'
'Fine.'
'Tell me about her.'
'She's got a husband and two children. Guido is five and Elena is three.'
'Guido?' asked William.
'Her husband is Italian. His name is Tomaso Mancini. He has an ice cream café in Edinburgh and Lizzie is the manager.'
'How do you know all this?'
'She writes.'
'And she never asks after me?'
'She's a married woman, William.'
'But we were friends.'
'Maybe it's different for her.'
'Is she happy?'
'She enjoys the work, she loves her husband, and her children are healthy.'
'Do you think she'll ever come back to Vienna?'
'Whatever for?'
'I'd like to see her again.'
'Then you'll have to go to Edinburgh.'
'Have you got her address?'
'102, Pitt Street, Edinburgh 3. You'd better write it down before you forget it,' said Anna.
'I've just taken some bread out of the oven,' said William.
'It smells really good,' said Anna.
'Can I make you and Rupert some sandwiches for your journey.?'
'No, thanks. Rupert looks after whatever we need. Why don't you give the sandwiches to the wardrobe department at the opera? The staff will enjoy them for lunch.'

William gave her a picture postcard of a camel standing in front of a pyramid. It was addressed to Anna. On the back her mother had written, 'Weather fine. Wish you were here. Mama.'

December 24th 1920
Breitenstein
Semmering

Dear Mother,

I'm on my own this Christmas. Lizzie is married and living in Edinburgh. Anna is married and living in Elberfeld. Meddi is living with a musician from the orchestra and they are spending Christmas together in Vienna. I don't know where Alma and Werfel are. Alma's younger daughter, Manon, has been sent away to boarding school and I never see her. She was always happy to trust me with Mahler's daughter but has never asked me to look after Gropius's daughter. I look after Alma's country house.

I asked Alma for a new car and she bought a Benz saloon. This new car has a fixed roof and a heater. Driving is like sitting at home in front of the fire. It's very smart, with a running board and two spare tyres, one on either side. Alma has become wealthy. She manages Franz Werfel's affairs. Alma would never have dared to interfere in Mahler's affairs but with Werfel it's different. Alma is his literary agent. His books and lecture tours are very popular. She goes everywhere with him and she handles all the money.

In Vienna I manage her salon and look after her guests. In Semmering I look after the house and I repair the neighbours' cars. There are several cars parked outside that need repairing and, if the weather allows, I'll work on them over Christmas. There is a big future in automobiles.

Are you in touch with Mahler? After you died Mahler suggested I write to you. I don't know where to send the letters so I keep them and one day I will bring them to your grave in Basel.

I love you.
Guillaume

December 24th 1920
Breitenstein
Semmering

Dear Johnny,

I often think of you and I imagine that I see you in New York walking in the street carrying your trumpet. Sometimes I see you in Columbus

Circle, sometimes in Central Park. I always see you walking by yourself. Are you alone? I have been by myself ever since I left Vienna to go to New York with Mahler. When I arrived in New York I met someone in Central Park. He played the trumpet too. I ran away from him because he frightened me. The receptionist in the hotel frightened me too. I didn't want to get involved with anybody else. I have had two delightful adventures in Italy. I met a man in Perugia who works with stained glass. We spent a few days together. I will never forget him. I spent another few days with an artist in Spoleto. I have even slept with a woman who works at the opera in Vienna and she has also slept with Alma. If you and I ever meet perhaps we can share our adventures?

I can still hear you play. No other trumpeter sounds like you. Do you remember the first reading of Mahler's Fifth? Your solo trumpet opened the symphony. During the adagietto we sat on a freshly painted step and got paint on our trousers. You should see my trousers now. They're covered in oil and grease. I look after Alma's car. I am a much better mechanic than I ever was a musician. The neighbours bring me their cars to fix. There is a big future in automobiles.

Alma and her new husband, Franz Werfel, travel a lot but they never ask me to go with them. I will never come to America again but in my mind I can hear you play in Carnegie Hall. You would know I was in the audience and we would meet after the concert. You would forgive me and we'd go somewhere for hot dogs. Do you ever go to Chinatown? There's a restaurant there run by a German who is a terrible pianist. He murders Beethoven while you eat. The food is terrible, too. There's another restaurant in the same street which is always full of Chinese people. The food is great and there is an opium den upstairs. I wonder if we will ever see each other again.

Willie

Werfel was preparing a novel about an imaginary meeting between Verdi and Wagner in Venice. Werfel preferred Verdi to Wagner. Alma, who was his first reader and literary agent, adored Wagner and dismissed Verdi. Alma and Werfel spent several weeks together in Venice. Werfel was scouting locations for his book. She was looking at properties. She was especially interested in properties close to Wagner's former residence, Ca' Vendramin, on the Grand Canal, where she would be able to breathe the same air as the composer. She planned to purchase her Venetian property with Werfel's future royalties. She had given the copyright to a wealthy young publisher in Vienna, Paul von Zsolnay, in return for a huge advance. While Werfel visited Venetian restaurants, hotels, churches and galleries gathering material for his book, a gondolier working for a real estate agent showed Alma potential properties. At night Alma and Werfel quarrelled about music. Whenever Werfel spoke on behalf of Verdi Alma responded scornfully, 'Oom Pa-Pah! Oom Pa-Pah!' When they went to bed Werfel liked to imagine that Alma was an amputee. She did her best to satisfy his need and limped to bed with a crutch.

William drove Werfel from Vienna to Semmering in the new car. Alma had told Werfel to go to her country residence and not to come back to Vienna until he had finished his novel. Werfel understood that their relationship hinged on the quality of his writing and that Alma would settle for nothing less than genius. As William drove, he remembered the journey to Semmering with Kokoschka. Whereas Kokoschka had talked and talked, Werfel smoked and smoked. The disadvantage of taking a chain smoker on a long journey in a saloon car soon became obvious, as the air inside turned blue. William opened the window and the cold January air blasted in. It was a choice between freezing or choking. William enjoyed some relief when Werfel saw someone at the side of the road hobbling on crutches, insisted on sitting in the back of the saloon where he masturbated, and did not light up a cigarette until he had finished.

While Werfel was writing his novel William worked in the garden, provided Werfel's meals and repaired the neighbours' automobiles. Once a month he drove back to Vienna to fetch Alma and bring her to Semmering to inspect Werfel's writing.

Wednesday, May 18th 1921

Vienna no longer had an empire or an emperor but a full-scale production at the opera house was still known as a 'royal' opera or a 'royal' ballet and the Hofoper presented one or the other on every night of the year except for December 25th, the anniversary of Christ's birth, when the opera house was closed, and May 18th, the anniversary of Mahler's death when instead of an opera or ballet the musicians took to the stage and performed a Mahler symphony in memory of their late director. Alma accepted her invitation to the Mahler anniversary concert but had no intention of going. William had packed the luggage into the saloon and Alma was ready to be driven to Semmering, where

Werfel would read the latest pages from his Verdi novel. William wanted to go to the concert. He disconnected the exhaust pipe from the engine. When Alma was settled in the back of the car and ready to set off for Semmering William started the engine and there was a loud explosion. William tried again to start the car, creating a series of explosions. The police arrived, following reports of gunfire in the street. Alma went back to her apartment and William spent the afternoon underneath the car pretending to fix the problem but, in fact, enjoying a siesta. At around 6pm he reconnected the exhaust, cleaned himself up, had something to eat and went to the Hofoper for the concert. William sat at the front of the circle with Mahler's baton in his pocket. The Hofoper orchestra pit was empty as the musicians sat on the stage. The director of the opera, Richard Strauss, walked to the podium, shook hands with the leader, and raised his baton to begin Mahler's Fifth Symphony. Strauss looked to the trumpet section. The lead trumpet put his instrument to his lips – an unusual instrument with the upper tubing at a raised angle which sent the opening four notes of the symphony outwards and upwards into the Hofoper auditorium. William felt a sharp attack of vertigo followed by acute nausea. Unsteady and pale, he stood up. To avoid being sick over the patrons who were standing up to allow him to leave he vomited over the circle rail and onto the stalls below. He ran down the stairs and fled from the opera house and into the street. He ran to the Burgarten and leaned against a tree. He looked at the undigested food soiling his clothes and imagined the mess he had left behind him in the Hofoper. He took off his jacket, threw it away and rinsed his face in the pond. He crossed the Ringstrasse and let himself into the apartment in Elizabethstrasse. He washed and changed, found Alma and insisted that they both leave Vienna immediately. Alma protested that it was late. He told her that he'd fixed the car. It was ready now. They would cover the ninety kilometres before midnight, and they must leave now because tomorrow would be too late. Alma, puzzled by his insistence, followed him down the stairs and into the car. She sat in the back and told William he should do something about the unpleasant smell of stale cigarettes. He sat at the wheel and said nothing. She asked him why they could not wait until the morning. He lied to her about a communist demonstration and the police preparing for trouble.

Wednesday, May 25th

Von Zsolnay offered to pay Werfel handsomely for an account of his travels. Alma and Werfel set off for Egypt and Palestine. Alma wanted William to stay in Elizabethstrasse while they were away so that he could look after Anna who had recently separated from her husband, but William couldn't stay in the same city as Johnny and he told Alma that he urgently needed to return to Semmering.

'Whatever for?'

'To replace the soffits.'

Alma didn't know what he was talking about. William didn't know what he was talking about either, but nevertheless insisted that they must be replaced. William thought Anna was old enough to look after herself. She had only been married for six months, wasn't yet used to it, and would likely return to her husband after cooling off. Once he had dealt with the soffits William thought he might redecorate Werfel's study – anything to keep him in Semmering and away from Vienna and Johnny. He carried Alma's and Werfel's baggage upstairs and into their apartment and then drove straight back to Semmering.

Vienna, Sunday June 5th

Dear William,

I often go to Elizabethstrasse where Anna is living. She has asked me to visit her while her mother and Werfel are in Palestine. She will soon be seventeen and is looking forward to her birthday. She is well and looks back on her marriage as an interesting failure. She is impatient with the view that she was too young to be married. She may have been too young to love but she is certainly old enough to know that she was not loved. Her husband was in love with Mahler and proved his love by marrying his daughter. She has done well not to waste any more time with him. He is happy with his orchestra in Eberfeldt and she is happy with her freedom in Vienna. Anna doesn't need looking after but I visit Elizabethstrasse anyway because I hoped one day to see you. Anna told me that you are rarely in Vienna these days and that you spend your time in Semmering. I would like to come and visit but I need to write to you first.

I met your friend, Johnny, when we were both working in New York. He was known as 'Johnny Silence' because no one ever heard him speak. He communicated only with his trumpet. He had a studio in the Met where he started warming up at 7am for a 10am rehearsal with the Philharmonic in Carnegie Hall. I started going into work early because I liked hearing his exercises floating around the empty building. I noticed that he played his scales and arpeggios upwards only – he never played the answering descent. I thought the intonation of these ascending exercises sounded like questions and that he was waiting for an answer. One morning I prepared a coffee and cornetto and followed the sound of his trumpet. The door was open. I went in and left the breakfast. He stopped playing and said 'Danke.' I felt privileged. I thought I must be the only person in New York who knew he spoke German. I took him breakfast every morning and after a few weeks he graduated from 'Danke' to 'Danke Schön'. I often went to Carnegie Hall after work so that I could hear him play in the orchestra. I wondered what he did on evenings when there were no concerts and I asked him if he would like to come with me to the picture house. Dante's Inferno had just opened at Gane's Manhattan Theatre. I suggested we meet in the foyer of Carnegie Hall. After the film he insisted, silently, on walking me home and at my door he bade me 'Gute nacht.' I do not need to describe to you the development of our friendship. Johnny and I became intimate. You know us both well enough to understand how it goes. When I was given the opportunity to come to Vienna and work at the Hofoper Johnny broke down. He told me that you had left Vienna to go with the Mahlers to New York and now, when I told him I had an offer of work in Vienna, thanks to Frau Mahler, he found himself staring at the reflection of that first heartbreak. Johnny and I did what you and Johnny never did. We talked and made a decision together. We decided that I would take the job at the Hofoper and he would join me in Vienna as soon as an opportunity opened for him. When Richard Strauss took over the directorship at the Hofoper he immediately sent to New York for 'Mahler's trumpeter.' Johnny has been living with me since he returned to Vienna.

I know you will have difficulty reading this. I have not written to cause you pain. I am writing because we are friends and I will not give up on friendship. I believe that one day you and Johnny will also be friends.

With love,
Meddi

William was kneading dough when the doorbell rang. He was taken aback to find Meddi on the doorstep. He asked her if she was on her own.

'No.'

William froze. 'Meddi, I can't...'

'I've brought Anna with me. It's her birthday. I've brought a birthday cake, too.'

The taxi drove off. Anna, wearing a bonnet with a huge brim, waved at William and blew him a kiss.

William stood silently in the doorway until Meddi told him to go and greet Anna and carry her baggage indoors.

'Uncle William, it's my birthday and I want you to cook a birthday meal for us to celebrate!' She gave William a big kiss and her hat fell off. William picked it up.

Anna said, 'I'll take the hat. You take the bags.'

When Meddi saw the state of the house she suggested that William and Anna go shopping for food while she tidied up.

When they returned, Meddi had cleaned up the mess in the dining room and kitchen, picked flowers from the garden and put them in a vase on the table, collected all the loaves of bread she had found in the bathroom and stacked them like a woodpile against the exterior wall beneath the eaves.

'I've heard that your skills as a motor mechanic are in demand,' said Meddi.

William told her that he could make cars explode by disconnecting the exhaust and that he had spent all week making bread.

'I found the bread in the bathroom.'

William told her there were more loaves in the toilet.

'Why do you keep it all?'

'It seems a shame to waste it,' said William.

'If you filled the eaves with loaves right up to the roof we would be living in a gingerbread house! declared Anna. 'The birds would like that.'

'There's no ginger,' said William. 'So the birds will have to make do with a plain bread house without ginger.'

'Uncle William, you are so funny. Why are you not smiling?'

William massaged his face, trying to force a smile into shape and offered Anna different versions of a grimace.

'You're a bit of a miracle worker when it comes to loaves,' observed Anna. 'Can you do the same with fish?' She started to unpack the shopping. 'Here are two bottles of water that have already been turned into wine.'

William said he was tired and went to his room.

Meddi and Anna prepared the meal.

Anna and Meddi persuaded William to come and eat with them. After dinner Meddi brought the cake to the table and sang *Happy Birthday* for Anna. William sulked and blew all the candles out.

'I'm sure you two have got a lot to catch up on,' said Anna, cutting herself a slice of cake and taking it upstairs to bed.

William poured out two glasses of wine. He lifted his towards Meddi and they chinked their glasses. William said, 'I can turn wine into piss!' and he knocked back his glass in one gulp.

'I don't think you're well, William.'

'What do you care?'

'We care a great deal. Why do you think we came here?'

'I thought you only went with women.'

'Things change. You were part of the change.'

'So, it's all my fault?' barked William. He pushed the vase between them and hid behind the flowers.

Meddi moved the vase back so she could see William. 'I'm not going to be a stranger, William.'

'I didn't realise you slept with men.'

'You have a poor memory.'

'I thought that was special.'

'It was.'

'So, I wasn't the first...'

'You weren't. Who I sleep with now or in the future is none of your business.'

'I don't understand you,' snapped William, 'and you don't understand me'. He dragged the flowers back between them.

Meddi pushed the flowers away again and said, 'I'm not going to let you hide.'

William said nothing and pushed the flowers back between them. Meddi picked up the vase and removed the flowers from the table.

William put his hands over his face and peered at her through his fingers. Meddi took William's hands away from his face and held them in hers.

'When I slept with you, William, you thought about Johnny. When Johnny sleeps with me he doesn't think about you. He cares about me.'

William tried to take back his hands but Meddi held on tight.

She raised her voice. 'William! You're still thinking about Johnny! But these are my hands! Johnny is not here. I am!'

William tried again to take back his hands and Meddi felt his strength ebb.

'I won't let go,' she said.

Hand in hand they looked searchingly into each other's eyes.

'You've got a soul, William, and it's in pain. I'm not letting go until you give me some of your pain.'

'Does Johnny know you're here?'

'Yes. He knows that I care about you. It was one of the reasons he was drawn to me. She held on tightly and said, 'You brought us together.'

Silence.

Meddi told William that she and Johnny had gone to the Chinese restaurant where the chef prepared enormous beef spareribs for the German customers while the proprietor sat at the piano and murdered Beethoven. She told William that another time they went to the busy Chinese restaurant where they had to wait in a queue for a seat, and after eating they went to the opium den upstairs where she and Johnny smoked and fell asleep. She told him they had gone Christmas shopping to Macy's, had walked in Central Park, and ridden the ferry to Staten Island and back.

'Did you go to English lessons together?'

Meddi laughed. 'Johnny hardly speaks at all, never mind English.'

William looked away from Meddi's eyes, turned his gaze to their hands, and asked her if she and Johnny had gone to Madame Palladino's.

'Where?'

'Don't you remember? Madame Palladino? The lady who is in touch with the dead. When you and I went there we held hands.'

Meddi looked down at their hands locked together.

'Don't you remember?'

Meddi laughed. 'That old fraud!'

'Do you remember what she said?'

'No.'

'Mama said I had to go, and that Papa has to go too!'

'I don't know what you mean.'

'She contacted the dead and that's what she said. It wasn't Madame Palladino that said it. It was a voice from the dead. It was Mahler's daughter, Maria. That's when Mahler discovered that his wife wished him and their daughter dead. The cello hanging on the wall broke and fell to the floor. Don't you remember? As it was breaking up the screeching cello quoted a phrase from Mahler's *Kindertotenlieder* – the same phrase that Mahler quoted at the end of his Ninth Symphony. Don't you remember?'

'No.'

'You don't believe me, do you?'

Silence.

'You think I'm mad.'

Silence

'I loved Mahler,' said William.

'I know.'

'I didn't love Johnny.'

'You and Johnny were children.'

'Children know how to love. When they grow up, they forget.'

'We avoid love to avoid pain,' said Meddi. 'When we feel strong enough to cope with the pain, then we can love again. You and Johnny loved like children. You both suffered. Now we're grown up we must deal with our pain.'

William and Meddi looked up from their locked hands to Anna who was standing beside them. She cut herself another slice of cake and said 'Why don't you two stop holding hands and eat some cake?'

William and Meddi were not hungry for cake and found a way of double locking their hands by interlocking their fingers.

'You were a good father to Anna. Mahler would have been pleased.'

'Yes, he was pleased,' said William, 'but he didn't like it when Anna was in the motor car and I drove too fast.

Meddi nodded uncertainly. 'And you're a good mechanic. But look at your clothes! I'll make you some working clothes. You need to wear slops. I'll make you some with dungaree cloth and I'll bring them to you next time. They'll look good. They'll look even better when they're covered in oil. And I'll make you white aprons for when you need to bake bread. You'll be the best dressed mechanic and the best dressed baker in Semmering.'

'Do you make clothes for Johnny?'

'Yes. He's the best dressed trumpet player Vienna.'

'Mahler never cared how he dressed.'

'And then he met you. You cared. Johnny told me about the time you both sat on a step that had been freshly painted and got white stripes on your concert blacks.'

276

'That was the read-through for Mahler's Fifth. The opera performed it on Mahler's anniversary. I wanted to go but Alma doesn't like the symphony, she doesn't like anniversaries and anyway she needed me to drive her here so I missed it,' lied William. 'When are you coming back with the slops and the apron?'

'Soon,' replied Meddi.

'Don't bring Johnny. I'm not ready yet.'

'Neither is he,' said Meddi. 'Promise me one thing.'

'What?'

'You won't bake any more bread until I come back.'

'And what about all the bread you put outside?'

'Tomorrow we'll bury it in the garden and next spring you can grow vegetables.'

Werfel completed his Verdi book while William cooked for him wearing one of his new white aprons, looked after his neighbours' automobiles wearing his new blue slops and tended his garden wearing a beautifully tailored peasant's smock.

When the book was delivered to the publisher and the royalties were credited to Alma's account, Werfel and Anna set off once more on their travels. William became a permanent fixture in Semmering and only returned to Vienna to fetch or deposit Alma.

Werfel also became a permanent fixture in Semmering where he worked in his study writing the novels and plays which made Alma wealthy. She knew the difference between Werfel's literature and her late husband's towering genius. She also understood the difference between Werfel's royalties and her late husband's and relished the increased comfort in her standard of living. As Werfel became more successful he became more dependent on her and she wearied of him. She stayed in Vienna handling Werfel's business and receiving guests in her salon while he stayed in Semmering where William looked after him. Whenever Anna and her new man, the young composer, Ernst Kreneck, came to Semmering William looked after them too.

Alma's success in selling Werfel's work had given her a taste of the money that can be made from publishing, and she tasked herself with preparing Mahler's letters and her own diaries for publication. She also thought she could make money from the fragments of Mahler's last symphony and tasked Anna's new boyfriend, Kreneck, with transforming the sketches into a performable score. The young composer was horrified, but Alma insisted. Ten symphonies would be worth more than nine. She intended to earn good royalties from her own songs by publishing them at the same time as the new Mahler symphony.

Alma's diaries gave a one-sided account of her troubled marriage with Mahler and slandered many people that were still alive. Paul von Zsolnay's lawyers advised Alma that the diaries could not be published without changes. Alma refused to make any changes and locked her diaries away. Bruno Walter and the Vienna Philharmonic refused to perform the score that Kreneck made from Mahler's notebooks. Alma got the Opera House to do it instead. She published Mahler's letters and a facsimile of the original manuscript of the Tenth including Mahler's outpourings of love and grief scribbled in the margins, and an edition of her own songs, all of it to coincide with the premiere of Mahler's new symphony - all of it scandalous and successful.

The premier of the Tenth consisted of two movements – the long Adagio which Mahler had almost completed and the sketch for 'Purgatorio', which Kreneck had worked on. In one extraordinary moment during the Adagio the whole orchestra played the material Mahler had assembled for the entire movement in one huge chord of ear-splitting dissonance which abruptly ended leaving a solo trumpet all by itself screaming in a painfully high register for a suffocatingly, unconscionable, unplayable time. When the orchestra's trumpeters looked at the score they shook their heads. No one wanted to have a go. They stepped back from it and sent to the opera house for Johnny. William wasn't there to hear Mahler's Tenth. He stayed in his garden in Semmering.

When Alma visited Semmering William kept out of her way and worked in the garden or under a car. Only when Alma returned to Vienna did William venture back indoors, where he found Anna and Kreneck locked together in unhappiness. Anna was unhappy because she was dependent on her mother. Kreneck was unhappy because he was in love with Mahler, not his daughter. Werfel was unhappy because every time he asked Alma to marry him, she refused. She was anti-Semitic and increasingly drawn to the rise of fascism in Italy, and she continually argued with Werfel, who did not share her enthusiasm for fascism. She could be his muse, but not his wife. When Alma visited Venice she not only breathed the same air as her idol, Wagner, she also inhaled the strength of the new Italian government which was bringing to an end the social unrest which she blamed on the Jews. She believed that the German-speaking peoples required a strong leader of their own.

Sometimes William was required to drive Werfel around Germany on book-signing and lecture tours. On these occasions he left Anna and Kreneck strict instructions about watering the garden and feeding the chickens. William consulted the weather forecast every morning and called home every evening to check that his garden was in order.

CHAPTER 49

Meddi and Johnny Stanko

In Vienna Meddi and Johnny built a small soundproof studio at the bottom of the garden where Johnny practised. Johnny could play on any piece of metal tubing and produce beautiful sounds, not only on the trumpet but also on the barrels of the pistols and rifles which he kept in the studio. Johnny carefully maintained his trumpets, oiling valves and keeping the joints airtight, and he lavished the same care on the firearms which he took apart, oiled, and reassembled. Johnny had dozens of trumpet cases but only two trumpets. There was the trumpet his father had given him which he brought to the conservatoire when he arrived in Vienna as an eighteen-year-old student, and the trumpet he had designed and built for himself with a standard length of tubing but with the upper part of the horn raised from the horizontal at an angle of forty degrees. His hand-built horn suited his personality, allowing him to play introspectively towards the floor but nevertheless throwing his sound outwards and upwards into the auditorium. This trumpet required a larger case. The other cases contained small arms, rifles, and ammunition.

Johnny had joined the Republikanischer Schutzbund, a social democratic party and the largest party in Austria, denied power by a coalition of smaller right-wing parties which represented the interests of the Catholic church, the bosses and the countryside. Right-wing groups exercised power not only in parliament but also through their paramilitary forces on the street, where they clashed with the Schutzbund paramilitaries. Johnny was a Schutzbund quartermaster, procuring and maintaining arms for his party's military wing.

Once a week on a Thursday evening the Vienna Schutzbund Brass Ensemble would send a van round to Johnny's and take the new instruments in their cases to the band practice. While the band played very loudly at the front of the building, the trumpet cases were opened at the back of the building where the arms were assembled for military training.

All the brass players at the Hofoper had followed Johnny into the Schutzbund and on Thursday evenings, while some of the musicians were performing Johnny's arrangements of music from the operettas of Franz Lehar, others took their turn on the rifle range.

Early in the New Year of 1924 Anna and Kreneck left Semmering. They got married on January 15th and struck out on their own. Anna needed to get away from her mother while Kreneck finally expressed his love for Mahler's music by marrying the composer's daughter. Setting off on the same road as she had travelled with Rupert Koller, it did not take Anna and Kreneck long to arrive at the same destination.

William was kneading dough when the doorbell rang. He was surprised to find Meddi on the doorstep. He asked her if she was on her own.

'No.'

William froze. 'Meddi, I can't. I'm not ready yet.'

'I've brought Anna with me. It's her birthday. I've brought a birthday cake too.'

Anna, wearing a bonnet with a huge brim, waved at William and blew him a kiss.

William stood silently in the doorway until Meddi told him to go and greet Anna and carry her baggage indoors.

'Uncle William, it's my birthday and I want you to cook a birthday meal for us to celebrate!' She gave William a big kiss and her hat fell off. William picked it up.

Anna said, 'I'll take the hat. You take the bags.'

William dug potatoes, pulled up leeks and onions, picked spinach, cut some asparagus, collected rosemary, marjoram, thyme and half a dozen eggs. He killed and plucked a chicken and singed the stubble, just as cook in Trenkerhof had showed him all these years ago, filling the kitchen with the acrid smell of burning. William sliced the chicken in half and made stock with the lower part of the carcass and the wings. He roasted the upper half with the potatoes and onions to serve with spinach and asparagus, and he made a chicken stock with the lower part of the carcass for a potato and leek soup. They finished their celebration meal with Anna's birthday cake and William's first strawberries. Meddi lit twenty-four candles. They sang *Happy Birthday* and drank schnapps. Meddi told Anna that this was the last time she would have birthday candles as it was impolite to put twenty-five candles on a girl's birthday cake. Anna took this last opportunity to blow them all out. William asked her what she had wished for.

She said, 'I wish to go to Spoleto and become apprenticed to Giovanni D'Agostino, and I would like William to give me driving lessons and lend me the car.'

'Not tonight, Anna.'

Anna pretended to sulk, wished them both good night and said, 'I'm sure you two have got a lot to catch up on.'

William told Meddi he thought Anna looked happy for someone whose second marriage had collapsed.

'Perhaps it gets easier,' suggested Meddi. 'The next one will be even easier.'

'Surely she won't get married again,' said William. 'It doesn't suit her.'

'There's no limit to the number of times you can marry. Maybe she'll marry again when she finds someone who's never heard of her father.'

'And what about you?' asked William. 'Are you thinking of marrying?'

'Good heavens, no! Whatever are you thinking of?'

'You and Johnny.'

'We may not always be together.'

'But you're happy, Meddi, aren't you?'

'Yes.'

'And Johnny?

'He's happy. He enjoys his work. He's changing some of the orchestra's old-fashioned ideas and recommended the working practices he learned in America. He is the orchestra's representative on the Hofoper board and has organised the musicians into a union. He has convinced the administrators that the union is in their interests too.'

'What would Mahler think about that?'

'I'll ask him. I mean, I don't know. What do you think?'

Meddi told him that working conditions that are negotiated and agreed didn't change from one director to the next, so the quality of work at the Hofoper would be consistent whoever directed.

William wondered what the emperor would have thought about that.

'Austrians don't have an Emperor, William, and musicians are no longer employed on the same terms as Imperial soldiers. It'll be the same for the off-stage employees. I'm organising the wardrobe team into a union.'

'Alma won't be impressed,' suggested William.

'I don't intend to argue with her,' said Meddi.

'It would make a change. She quarrels with Werfel all the time. He's like you. He's for the workers. She never quarrelled with Mahler about politics. She wouldn't dare.'

Does she quarrel with you?' asked William.

'I admire her,' said Meddi. She's an unusual woman. She's powerful.'

'Is she for women?'

'She's for herself.'

'Are you for women?'

'I'm for workers. What about you, William?'

'I don't know.'

'You don't know your right from your left, do you?' Meddi took William's hands. 'But your heart's in the right place. How's your garden?'

'Fine. Whenever Alma comes she eats everything I grow and takes a lot of it back to Vienna with her. She's especially fond of asparagus. There's none left.'

'Why are you so annoyed with her?'

'She's selfish.'

'She looks after you, William. She's given you a home, a car, and a garden.'

'And Johnny's got you,' sulked William.

They looked up and found Anna standing beside them. 'I haven't got anybody, thank God, but I am going to have another slice of cake.' As she left Anna said, 'Why don't you two stop holding hands and eat some cake?'

William showed Meddi his garden. It was late in the evening but the midsummer twilight revealed a parade ground of vegetables standing at attention in the moonlight. Meddi asked William to stop being jealous of Johnny. There was so much he could do that Johnny would never be able to do. William told her that he could never do what Johnny did. 'Alma wanted me to be her bodyguard,' he said, 'and gave me a pistol to carry whenever we went out together. Lizzie took it to a gunsmith and swapped it for one that wouldn't shoot.' Meddi, afraid she might have let slip something about Johnny's role in the armoury of the Schutzbund, asked William what had brought the pistol to mind.

'Just something else I was no good at, like playing the viola.'

They wished each other a good night and Meddi said, 'Better to stick with what we're good at, William. Will you show me your garden again in the morning?'

They kissed each other good night.

Anna went to Spoleto where she worked with Giovanni D'Agostino. She made frames, stretched canvases, mixed paints, discussed his work, and sat for him. When Giovanni went out at night she used the studio to make work of her own.

With the publication of *St Paul Among the Jews* and his plays *Schweiger* and *Juarez and Maximilian* Werfel became the most famous writer in the German speaking world. Alma refused to marry him.

Meddi organised the union of the wardrobe staff at the Hofoper and affiliated her members with the newly unionised lighting and stage-hand workers.

The Viennese police kept a file on the Schutzbund and regularly invited members of the party in for questioning. Several Schutzbund members had been charged with plotting to overthrow the state. Those charged were always Jewish, which reinforced the impression that Jews were a threat to Austrian democracy. The conduct of the police was always very civilised. They sent an invitation to the person they wished to interview. The interview often resulted in a Jew losing his or her employment. At the end of every season the Hofoper and Philharmonic orchestras would fire some of the older musicians and replace them with younger players. Older musicians who were Jewish were always first to be replaced. Jews were often denounced to the police by their neighbours. When Johnny Stanko was invited to attend an interview at the police station his interrogator searched through Johnny's papers and saw that Johnny was not Jewish. The policeman told Johnny that, although there were many in Austria who disagreed with the policies of Schutzbund, it was his duty to maintain law and order so that all parties that disagreed could do so freely and in peace. He informed Johnny that he himself disagreed with the Schutzbund but that it was his duty to support Johnny's freedom to express his views peacefully, and he did so gladly. Johnny had not spoken during the interview but listened respectfully to his interrogator's commitment to democracy. The policeman gave Johnny his papers back and said, 'It would be a good idea if you married the lady you're living with.'

A policeman visited the Hofoper to speak with Meddi. She confirmed that she came from Oberkochen in Germany, that she had worked for twelve years in America and had returned to lead the costume department at Hofoper, where she organised the union. The policeman knew that union organisers were generally Jewish and male and he was curious to know why a woman like her, who was not Jewish, was drawn to this activity. Meddi explained that the union shared with the management the responsibility to look after the health, safety, and security of its employees and this helped the Hofoper to maintain its high standards. The policeman agreed that the Hofoper's standards were indeed of the highest quality and congratulated her on the work of the wardrobe team. He was pleased to have made her acquaintance, would continue to take an interest in her work, and wished to give her a word of advice. 'You are living with Herr Stanko – it would be a good idea, Fräuline, if you married him.'

In the mountains of Semmering in the tiny hamlet of Breitenstein, William cleared some wilderness on Alma's property to create an orchard. The fruit from the pear trees was his gift to a future generation. He looked forward to harvesting the apples, plums, and lemons within his own lifetime. As his trees put down their roots, so did William. He was working in the orchard on a sunny afternoon when he was interrupted by a policeman who invited him to attend an interview at the police station in Steinhaus the following morning. A car would pick him up at 8am.

The police car arrived punctually. William didn't tell Alma where he was going. She was fast asleep. She would probably still be asleep when he returned.

He was invited to sit while the police chief read his file. 'You were born in Basel, and you studied the viola at the Vienna Conservatoire where you met the director of the Opera, Herr Gustav Mahler. You entered his service and travelled with him to America. After his death you worked for his widow and you currently reside in her property in Breitenstein, where one of your duties is to maintain Frau Mahler's Benz Saloon.' William agreed that this was correct. The policeman invited William to follow him and took him to the garage where police vehicles were parked. 'We have a vacancy for a skilled mechanic who will maintain our automobiles. As you can see the vehicles are specialised.' William looked at armoured vehicles, vans designed to carry prisoners and saloon cars that looked straightforward until the policeman explained the engines had been enhanced for greater speed.

'We very much hope that you will accept the position and start work with us at your soonest convenience.'

'Can I think about it?'

'Of course, Guillaume. You are a Swiss national. You worked for the Jew, Mahler, and you live in Austria. You now have an opportunity to show your loyalty. May I call you Wilhelm? Let me have your answer tomorrow morning at 8am. Would you like to drive yourself home in one of these?' Holding the driver's door open the police chief said, 'I believe it's capable of a hundred kilometres an hour.'

William spent the day exploring the engine to discover the source of the enormous surge of power he had experienced while driving it. He cleaned himself up and prepared dinner.

William never joined Alma and Werfel for meals. Their quarrelling spoiled his appetite. He was happier eating on his own in the kitchen. Alma and William were surprised when William came to their table and asked if he could join them. He told them about the police proposal and that they expected him to accept. He described something of the interrogator's menace. Out of respect for the Jew, Werfel, William did not mention the policeman's reference to the Jew, Mahler. He told Alma he had to give them an answer at eight o'clock in the morning. Alma asked William to bring her coffee at 6.30am and said, 'We'll go together.'

The police chief bowed deeply. 'Frau Mahler! An exceptional honour.' He placed a cushion on her seat and the three of them sat down. Alma fixed the police chief with a powerful stare and started. 'Regarding your generous offer, Herr Hildebrand has returned this morning to give you a positive response. He is flattered by your attention and is honoured to be able to place his considerable skills at your service. I hope I do not embarrass Herr Hildebrand by referring to his extraordinary facility in the field of mechanical engineering, especially his diagnosis and treatment of motor vehicles which are as dear to him as the sick and elderly are to their doctor. Wilhelm will achieve in two days more than you would expect from a good mechanic in a week. He will begin his two days with you at 6am and finish by 3pm, when he must return to his studio, where' – staring at the crucifix the police chief was wearing – 'he is working on the manuscripts of Austria's greatest symphonist, Anton Bruckner. Wilhelm is responsible for preparing these manuscripts for the forthcoming complete edition of Bruckner's symphonies, which I am sure you will agree is a task of the utmost national and religious importance.' Alma stood up and, offering her hand to the police chief, said, 'Wilhelm will report to you tomorrow morning at 6am. God bless you.' The police chief clicked his heels and bowed deeply.

On the drive back to Breitenstein William told Alma that he didn't think he was that good.

'Well, you are,' she said.

And he asked Alma if she really thought that Bruckner was that good.

'He is,' she said.

William spent the rest of the day subjecting the engine of the police car to further study. When two policemen returned in Alma's Benz in order to collect their own car, Alma refused to let them have it. She assured them there must be a mistake as Herr Hildebrand needed the police vehicle to commute to the police station twice a week. Alma asked William to drive the policemen back to the police station in her car and in this way Alma took possession of both cars.

After dinner William sat in his new police car idling with the lever that put the engine into 'overdrive.' Mahler, sitting in the passenger seat, asked William how fast it would go. William thought it might do a hundred kilometres an hour, but that he had only got it up to seventy. Mahler told him that there were no roads in the mountains where it was safe to drive at that speed and advised William not to make any adjustments to Alma's car. William tried to explain that he didn't want to drive at a hundred but only wanted to satisfy himself that he understood the engineering that made such speeds possible. William asked Mahler what he thought of Bruckner's symphonies. Mahler thought they were best played where they were composed, on a church organ. He told William that he had a nose for orchestral music that was composed at a keyboard. 'It always sounds like a keyboard work which has been orchestrated. It is a different sound world from music composed for an orchestra.'

'I thought you liked Bruckner.'

'I do. As a man he's first-rate and as a composer of organ music, arranged for a large orchestra, he is also first-rate. But we were discussing the power of this vehicle's engine. You will be tempted to hurtle along the road as if you had been fired from a cannon.

William asked Mahler if he was ever tempted to ask the huge orchestras at his disposal to play *tutti* and *fortissimo*.

Mahler told him he was never tempted.

William reminded Mahler about the end of his Eighth when the huge orchestra was joined by an extra ten brass players.

Mahler conceded he had done so on that occasion but reminded William that art is not life. 'The sunrise in a work of art will not burn your eyes. Stare at the sunrise tomorrow morning and you'll blind yourself. Drive at a hundred kilometres an hour and you will kill yourself. How's Anna?'

'She keeps getting married and then coming back to her mother,' said William.

'That's because she doesn't need a husband.'

'What does she need?'

'Her mother.'

William told Mahler that Alma and Werfel fought all night.

'What about?'

'Getting married.'

'Will they marry?'

'Yes, but Werfel has to convert to Christianity first. He's going to receive instruction from a Catholic priest.'

'But Alma's a Protestant,' said Mahler.

'Werfel's decided to be a Catholic so they can keep on fighting.'

Mahler asked William if Anna was marrying anyone at the moment.

William told Mahler that Anna didn't have anyone in mind but that her mother was working on it. 'Alma told the police chief that I was working on the Bruckner manuscripts.'

'Not everything Alma says is true, William.'

'She told the police chief that Bruckner was Austria's greatest symphonist.'

'Like I said, William, not everything Alma says is true.'

The police chief asked William to drive him to Vienna on a mission of national importance. On the way to Vienna he told William all about the incompetence of the Viennese police. 'The capital of Austria,' he said, 'is teeming with communists and Jews and the local police behave as if they are powerless to do anything about it. They deploy neither intelligence nor force. We'll show them how it's done. Our intelligence informs us where the paramilitary wing of Schutzbund meets. We are on a reconnaissance mission. It will not be dangerous. There's nothing for you to worry about. We're only going to examine the territory and take photographs. When we get back to Semmering I'll make detailed drawings, front door, back door, fire escape, windows, then this time next week I will return with the force and eradicate the scum. Lethal force is the monopoly of the state, and on behalf of Austria we will deploy our force to destroy treasonable private militia.'

As William and the police chief were driving into Vienna the Schutzbund Brass Ensemble were rehearsing Johnny Stanko's arrangement of the waltz from *The Merry Widow*. At the back of the rehearsal room two Viennese policemen from the local constabulary listened respectfully. When the band stopped the policemen approached the platform and, after a few words with the conductor, they left. Johnny approached the podium and the conductor told him that it was probably nothing. The policemen were only looking for a place where their police band could rehearse. Johnny thought it was time for the Schutzbund brass band to look for another rehearsal room.

William and the Semmering police chief arrived as the two local policemen emerged from the hall. The Semmering police chief got out of the car, approached the local policemen, introduced himself and they exchanged salutes. The police chief discovered that the two local policemen were looking for a venue for their brass band to rehearse, that this hall was just what they were looking for, that the band rehearsing in the hall were excellent and they recommended the Semmering police chief to go in and listen. The police chief walked around the exterior taking photographs and then returned to the car and told William he was going inside.

When the police chief entered the hall the conductor stopped the rehearsal and asked the police chief if there was anything he could do for him. The police chief apologised for interrupting the rehearsal. He referred to his colleagues who had just left and hoped the band would not mind if he took some photographs. He complemented the conductor on the excellence of the band.

When he got back in the car the police chief smiled with satisfaction. He asked William to take him to an address where he wanted to spend a few hours with a lady known as Gradisca. She wasn't cheap but the police chief claimed her services on expenses. William went to visit Meddi at the Hofoper. As they drank hot chocolate and ate cake he told her how he and the Semmering Police Chief had spent the day. Then he returned to Gradisca's to wait for his boss.

The next morning in Semmering William worked in his orchard tending his baby fruit trees while in Vienna Johnny Stanko went to the landlord of the rehearsal rooms and informed him that they would no longer require the hall. He apologised for giving the landlord such short notice. There was, however, another band who needed the rehearsal space and who were able to move in immediately and to the satisfaction of all parties the local police band took over the tenancy from the Schutzbund Brass Ensemble.

The following week just after the local police band started their rehearsal, seven armoured vehicles from Semmering arrived outside the hall and fifty heavily-armed police surrounded the building. In the ensuing gun battle between the two police forces twenty-three policemen were killed, ten from the Semmering force and thirteen from the local Vienna force. Many others were injured.

Back in Semmering the police chief was given a loaded pistol and locked in his office. He sat at his desk, reluctant to add his own death to the twenty-three who had already died. After three days, not having heard a shot, his colleagues unlocked his office and entered. He was instructed to do his duty and not to bring the force into further disrepute. The police chief asked to see William.

William stood before the chief wearing the slops that Meddi had made for him covered in oil. The police chief asked him if he believed in God.

William said, 'No.'

'Do you believe in Heaven and Hell?'

'No.'

'Do you believe in damnation?'

'No'

'Then help me.'

He took William's hand and put it on the pistol. 'When I put the pistol in my mouth, pull the trigger.'

After a few seconds the police chief took the pistol out of his mouth and pleaded with William, 'Pull the fucking trigger!!' With both hands the police chief jammed the pistol back into his mouth. The explosion was deafening, the smell was acrid. When William opened his eyes he saw the wall was covered in blood and brains. The police chief was lying on the floor, still holding the pistol in his mouth as if he was eating it. The top of his head was missing. William felt something cold and moist against his skin slipping down towards his stomach. He undid his buttons and from beneath his shirt fished out one of the chief's eyes.

William was given a change of clothes and a large glass of brandy. Policemen stood in line and each man shook William's hand and thanked him as he was led to a car to be driven home.

Alma asked him how he had got on at work.

William told her that he had killed the chief of police.

Alma earned a fortune as Werfel's literary agent and Paul von Zsolnay also earned a fortune as Werfel's publisher. Alma now identified Paul von Zsolnay as the person to supply her with grandchildren and arranged a marriage between her daughter and Werfel's publisher.

Anna married Paul von Zsolnay and they went on honeymoon to Egypt.

Werfel converted to Christianity and married Alma.

Before Alma and Werfel left for a honeymoon to Palestine, Werfel visited the synagogue where, in a simple ceremony, he was welcomed back into Judaism.

William went back to his garden.

Paul von Zsolnay hoped that his marriage to Anna Mahler would help him move towards the mainstream of Austria's business and cultural life and away from the Judaism of his birth. He advised Alma to invest Werfel's royalties in property and recommended a mansion in Hohe Warte which would propel his new in-laws and himself into their proper place at the very top of Vienna's elite. The salon that Alma hosted in her new palace included not only the most important people in Vienna's business and cultural circles but also the Austrian chancellor and his ministers.

Meddi had taken little interest in Alma's affairs, giving herself entirely to union affairs at the Opera and supporting Johnny in his role of quartermaster to the military wing of the Schutzbund. But now that senior members of the Austrian government had become Alma's regular guests, Meddi too became a regular visitor so that she could keep her ears open around senior government officials.

Meddi helped Alma receive her guests and Alma looked on admiringly as Meddi flirted with the Chancellor and his ministers. She walked in the garden arm-in-arm with elder statesman and listened carefully to the problems they faced trying to run the country. She became particularly close to the Minister for Foreign Affairs, the Defence Minister, the Minister for Internal Security and the Chief Justice. She would often go home with one of them in their ministerial cars and allow them a quick kiss and cuddle in the back seat before seeing them off and telling the driver to take her back to Hohe Warte from where she would walk home to tell Johnny everything she had discovered. As a result of Meddi's spying, the Schutzbund's military wing had access to better intelligence than Austria's security services.

The Schutzbund brass band now rehearsed in a church hall near the cemetery at Grinzing on the outskirts of Vienna. Johnny thought the cemetery would be the ideal place to conceal the armoury. Johnny waited for opportunities to bury weapons in broad daylight when no one was looking rather than to conceal them furtively at night when it was more likely to attract attention.

A good opportunity arrived when Alma's daughter, Manon, died of pneumonia after contracting polio while on holiday with her mother in Venice. Her funeral in Grinzing cemetery on April 24th 1934 was a grand affair. There were so many cars with so many mourners that the cemetery soon became a traffic jam and chauffeurs unable to drive their limousines close to the funeral had to drop off very important passengers and leave them to walk to the graveside.

Meddi was at Manon's funeral, where she held the arm of the weeping Chief Justice. Johnny attended another funeral taking place at the same time. He was one of six pall-bearers carrying a heavy coffin to a far corner of the cemetery. The priest with brush and pail and full regalia prayed over the coffin as the military wing of the Schutzbund lowered a hundred rifles and a dozen grenades into the ground. Twenty-three years earlier this same priest, carrying the same brush and pail, sprinkled holy water over the coffin of Maria, Alma's first daughter, on the last steps of her journey to her father's grave. William had paid him the going rate – forty crowns. Now, Johnny paid him at the same rate but in the new currency, a hundred and fifty schillings, which, because of Austria's inflation, was equivalent to one and a half million crowns.

To Mrs. Elizabeth Mancini
102, Pitt Street
Edinburgh 3

From William Hildebrand
c/o Mahler
Breitenstein
Semmering
Austria

Dear Mrs Mancini,

I hope you will not be cross with me for writing to you. Anna gave me your address but she says it is very poor behaviour for an unmarried man to write to a married woman. Please forgive my bad manners.

It is twenty years since we said goodbye when you took the train to Livorno. So much has happened over the years that I don't know where to start.

Anna came to visit with Meddi last week. She has a daughter by her third husband, Paul von Zsolnay. She is also pregnant by a man with whom she has been having an affair. We celebrated her thirtieth birthday together before Meddi took Anna to the sanitorium in Bregenz where Alma goes for her abortions. Alma is furious with her Jewish daughter for making such a mess of her third marriage, especially as Anna's ex-husband is Franz Werfel's publisher. After living with Alma for so long it all seems quite normal to me.

I look after Franz Werfel and in my spare time I cultivate a garden and an orchard. Alma used to live in Vienna but at the moment she lives here with Werfel. She's always on the move. First she moved from a large apartment in Elizabethstrasse to a mansion in Hohe Warte which she bought with Werfel's royalties, and where she entertained the Chancellor and his ministers and all manner of very important people. She flirted with them all. She even flirted with a Catholic priest who instructed her in his faith. He baptised her and they started having an affair. Werfel knows all about it and doesn't mind because it keeps her out of his way. When Alma's daughter with Gropius died, she sold the mansion in Vienna and the Casa Mahler in Venice, two properties filled with memories of Manon. Now Alma lives with us. She quarrels with her husband every day. Werfel supports the Spanish Republicans while Alma is for Franco. Werfel is relieved when she goes back to Vienna to see her priest.

Anna told me about your husband, Mr Mancini, and your children, Guido and Elena, and she told me you are managing one of your husband's ice cream parlours. I imagine it looks just like the cafe we visited in Cassino. Do you remember that day? We bought huge ice creams and you and Anna wanted to climb the hill to Picinisco but there was no road and the snow had not yet melted.

There is so much more I would like to say and perhaps I will write again. I hope you will forgive my intrusion. I wanted to spend a few minutes with you and to greet you as your friend, William.

'Do you think I should send it?'
'Why not?' answered Mahler.
'Isn't it "poor behaviour", like Anna said?'
'No, I don't think so. You have given her some news and you have congratulated her on her family life.'
'I didn't tell her that I killed the police chief.'
'I'm glad you didn't.'
'Meddi told me I must never speak about that to anyone.'

'She's right'

'Meddi told me she wouldn't be in touch with me for a while and that I mustn't try to contact her.'

'She's probably working on something at the Opera which needs to be kept secret.'

'She could tell me.'

'But she won't, because she knows you are not discreet. But you can say whatever you like to me – you know it will go no further,' said Mahler.

'One of his eyes ended up inside my shirt. I can still feel it slithering down my chest. It was firm and wet and sticky, and when I fished it out it was huge! I didn't know eyes were so big.'

'What did you do with it?'

'I gave it to one of the policemen.'

'What did he say?'

'He congratulated me for doing what their cowardly chief failed to do.'

'You aren't sure that you pulled the trigger. You were both holding the gun when it went off.'

'The police chief believed that if he pulled the trigger he would be damned forever to the circle of Hell reserved for suicides, but that he could escape this fate if he asked someone else to do it. To avoid going to Hell with the suicides he asked me to take my chance in Hell with the murderers. Does that make any sense?'

'None,' said Mahler

'What kind of God would permit divine justice to serve such self-interested manipulation? '

'A stupid God.'

'Will this stupid God send me to Hell with the murderers?'

'There is no hell.'

'Are you sure?'

'Yes,' said Mahler.

'Does Alma believe in God?

'I think that's very likely,' said Mahler. 'She's having an affair with a priest.'

'That's an unusual path to God.'

'She's an unusual woman,' said Mahler.

'If you commit adultery with a priest, then confess your sin to that same priest, and God goes along with that and forgives you, then he must be mad.'

'But you don't believe in God,' Mahler reminded William.

'But Alma and her priest do,' said William

'The God they believe in created human nature and knows that *post coitum omnes animal triste est*. God also understands Latin and, in their moment of sadness, the gift of absolution is an act of kindness.'

'If I were to go to confession, do you think the priest would like to have sex with me?' asked William.

'Perhaps if he finds your confession arousing. But it's better to have sex first, then go to confession afterwards. That way allows you to work with divine justice rather than against it.'

'Is sex ever straightforward?' asked William.

'Yes,' said Mahler. 'Compared to her odd couplings with Kokoschka and Werfel, Alma's relationship with her priest is very straightforward.'

'Is my letter to Lizzie straightforward?'

'Your account of Anna's marriages, pregnancies and abortions is not very sympathetic. Anna will have expressed herself differently in her own letters, but I don't think Lizzie will be offended by your tone. She knows you well. She will be interested in your news. Don't expect a reply.'

After the death of Manon, Alma lived in Semmering with Werfel. William spent most of his time in the garden. It was a relief for both Werfel and William when she came out of mourning and left Semmering to go travelling. She tried to establish a better relationship with Anna and took her on holiday to Berlin. This was an exhilarating trip for Alma who was thrilled by the swastikas that flew all over the city, but it was a perilous adventure for Anna who was half Jewish. Alma derived her income from the music of one Jew and the literature of another, and prudently closed her German bank accounts and deposited her fortune in Switzerland. She no longer had an address in Vienna but took an apartment in the Hotel Ambassador where she received her priest.

When Alma was with her priest in Vienna Franz Werfel worked in peace and quiet and at table enjoyed the produce of William's garden without having to digest Alma's Nazi sympathies. Werfel ate alone and then after dinner he read his day's work to William. The new book was about the persecution and genocide of the Armenian people in Turkey. Werfel was aware that this would be read as a warning to Jews in Europe and that his book would be banned in Germany, where he had been expelled for the Prussian Academy of Arts. As long as Austria remained strong and able to protect its citizens, he was safe. He was the most important writer in Austria and had been awarded the Austrian Cross of Merit for Art and Scholarship. The security of Werfel and all the Jews in Austria depended on the survival of the state. Werfel was a keen supporter of the Chancellor, Dollfuss, whose regime was underpinned by the Catholic Church. William wondered how Werfel could support one Catholic dictator, Chancellor Dollfuss, and oppose another, General Franco. When Dollfuss was assassinated by Austrian Nazis he was replaced by Kurt von Schuschnigg who banned the Nazi party and imprisoned its leaders. Werfel wrote speeches for the new Chancellor and received him as a guest in Semmering.

William enjoyed his garden as much in the winter months as he did in the warmer seasons. It was the season for preparing and planning. He planted vines with a view to making his own wine. Werfel bought him a greenhouse where he could start his seedlings early and asked him to get rid of the chickens. Werfel found the supply of fresh eggs agreeable but was not prepared to put up with the noise. For Chancellor's Schuschnigg's proposed visit in February William prepared a banquet.

The meal was ready. Werfel was waiting impatiently. William answered the door, not to the Chancellor, but to the postman who delivered a telegram. William found it on the dining table after Werfel had retired to his study.

'Regret unable to come for dinner. Advise you leave Austria immediately. Schuschnigg.'

CHAPTER 50

Flight from Europe

Austria woke up the following morning to the news that Schuschnigg had preserved Austria's integrity by agreeing to the German Chancellor's demands and had released the imprisoned Nazis and appointed a senior Nazi as Minister of the Interior. By midday Alma arrived in Semmering. Two hours later Meddi arrived. She told William that Anna was with her. William went out to help Anna with her luggage and found her standing beside Johnny. Anna walked past William into the house. Johnny asked William if they could talk in William's car. When they were in the car Johnny said, 'Take me to the station.' They drove in silence. At the station Johnny got out of the car, leaving a briefcase on the passenger seat. He took a wallet from his inside pocket and gave it to William. 'Here are Meddi's papers. You should have stayed in America, both of you.' He opened the briefcase. It was full of US dollars. 'I never sold my trumpet. I robbed a bank.' He closed the briefcase, said, 'Vorbei', got out of the car, and walked into the station.

When William returned to the house Meddi anxiously looked for Johnny. William gave her the wallet with her documents and told her he had taken Johnny to the station. Meddi ran out of the house calling out his name.

William took the brief case to his room. When Meddi came back to the house. She would allow no one to comfort her. William said nothing about the money. He knew he was to use it to pay for Meddi's safety.

Anna wanted to go to London. Alma did not. London was cold. The food was terrible. There were no German newspapers. She couldn't speak English. She wanted to go to Paris.

'But you can't speak French,' said Werfel.

'But you can,' she said, looking at William.

The following morning Alma, Werfel, Meddi and William left Austria by train with Anna, who accompanied them as far as Paris. She proceeded to London by herself.

They stayed in Paris while Hitler annexed Austria and occupied the Low Countries. When the French police began to round up German speakers as enemy aliens they moved to Vichy and when the Wehrmacht invaded France they moved to Marseilles. When the Vichy regime agreed to deport German refugees they needed to get out of France and that was not possible without exit visas. Hotels in Marseilles were reluctant to take in Germans emigrants who were regarded, to Alma's horror, as communists and Jews. The luxurious Hôtel Louvre et Paix was, however, able to accommodate them, in return for a substantial quantity of William's dollars. Alma, afraid of being identified as a communist or a Jew, would not leave her room. Werfel, on the verge of a nervous breakdown, stayed in bed. William gazed out of his window at the yachts taking the early morning breeze on the silver crested waves of the Mediterranean that stretched from the beach beneath his window, where the children played, all the way to the horizon and beyond to the coast of North Africa. As he was gazing out to sea, Meddi knocked at the door and asked William to take her out.

'Where do you want to go?'

'To buy clothes.'

'Meddi! Alma has twenty-two suitcases full of clothes!'

'Everything we wear tells the whole world that we're German. We need clothes to make us look invisible. Come. I need you to do the talking.'

A few hours later, walking hand in hand back to the hotel and wearing their new clothes, they smiled and nodded to everyone who greeted them with a friendly 'Bonjour.'

They stopped on the promenade, looked out to sea, and William asked Meddi if she recognized the man, sixty paces or so to their right, who was also gazing out to sea.

'I think he's following us.'

'But he's ahead of us,' said Meddi.

'He knows where we're going. He walked behind us on the way to the shops. He's walking in front of us now because he knows we're going back to the hotel. I don't think he minds us noticing him.'

They continued to the hotel with their shadow walking ahead.

They sat in the hotel bar with two glasses of white wine when their shadow approached and asked in formal German whether he might join them. William answered in formal German that he didn't speak German. The shadow asked again in good French if he might join them and William replied in perfect French that he didn't speak French either. Meddi looked away and tried not to laugh. The shadow then asked in his native Brooklyn whether it might be easier if they cut the crap and spoke English.

He introduced himself. 'Varian Fry. Emergency Rescue Committee. My job is to shift high profile refugees outta here. If I can get Mrs Mahler and Mr Werfel back to the States it would look good for my organisation and we'd get more funding to rescue more of you people.'

Meddi and William were speechless.

'You're not Gestapo?' asked Meddi.

'Hell, no! 'Scuse my language, lady. Do either of you know how I can get in touch with Mr Chagall? Painter. First name, Marc. Paints cows. No? OK. Let's just deal with Mahler and Werfel for now. I've got contacts in the Portuguese consulate. They'll give you the papers you need to get into Spain. We need to go to the consulate as soon as you can get Mahler and Werfel ready.'

After Fry had gone William asked Meddi if she thought Mr Fry knew that Portugal and Spain were different.

'Of course he does,' said Meddi. 'Not all Americans are as stupid as they sound.'

Next morning they set off in a taxi for the Portuguese Consulate. Alma, Werfel and Meddi travelled in silence. Alma was counselled to say she was Austrian but not draw attention to herself by declaring, as Fry had often overheard, that she was neither a Jew nor a communist. William paid for the taxi in dollars.

The Portuguese Consulate was surrounded by gendarmes who waved Fry and his party away. Fry sent them back to the hotel in the taxi.

Rumours of what happened at the Portuguese Consulate got back to the hotel before the taxi. The Consul, in a fit of insanity, had thrown all his paperwork out of the window and shot himself. When Fry returned to the hotel he confirmed the story although he himself didn't believe it. He had spoken to the Consul the previous evening and he had been relaxed and even jovial.

Werfel had gone straight to bed and tried to calm himself with a pack of cigarettes, but the hotel's French cigarettes were too rough and burned his throat. Fry's American cigarettes were too smooth and tasted of nothing. Werfel felt ready to die. Alma nursed him. Meddi wrote to Johnny – a letter she could never post because it would lead the police directly to him. William, Meddi and Varian Fry sat in the hotel bar and discussed what to do next.

Fry asked William if he had enough dollars to pay the taxi driver to take them to Bordeaux where they could get papers and possibly a berth on a ship to the States.

'I have a contact in Bordeaux who can furnish you with exit visas and new passports.'

'We have passports.'

'If we do it this way you will have new identities. Not cheap. Have you got enough dollars to handle it?'

William nodded.

'We should leave right away. Bring only what you can carry. No time to delay. The odds lengthen by the day, my friend.'

They left for Bordeaux the following morning. William travelled with his briefcase full of dollars, Alma with her Bruckner and Mahler manuscripts. Meddi and Werfel carried a trunk each, full of clothes for Alma. Fry carried a pistol and some ammunition. The taxi driver wanted the fare in advance. William gave him half.

As they neared Avignon the road was full of traffic coming the other way, with news that the Germans had just taken the town. The driver turned south to Arles and stayed well to the south below the German lines and only turned north to Bordeaux when he reached the coast. They arrived in the early hours of the morning during a bombing raid. Fry directed the driver to the forger who was expecting them. As they got out of the car two soldiers carrying automatic weapons dragged a man out of the house, pushed him against the wall and gunned him down with machine gun fire. The taxi driver immediately reversed, turned, and drove away in a scream of tyres leaving his passengers standing beside the bloody remains of the forger. Werfel collapsed.

There was a moment of complete silence – no cars, no footsteps, no birds – and then life resumed. People came out of their houses. Two neighbours took away the body and an elderly lady brought Werfel a chair and a glass of water. Once Werfel was back on his feet they found a bar.

William gave the barman some dollars and asked him to give his friends a hot meal. Fry wanted to know where he was going. William said he was going to get a car. Fry pointed to William's case, patted his shoulder holster, told him he needed a buddy, and insisted on going with him.

Later that afternoon William drove back to the café in a new Citroën Traction Avant. Fry got out of the car, gathered up Meddi, Alma and Werfel and they set off on the long drive back to Marseilles. Werfel, slumped in the back of the car, didn't care where they were going. Alma did care and looked forward to being reunited with her clothes. Meddi was afraid for Johnny. She was afraid that he would not survive and that he would die alone. Her impotence left her shaking. Alma fished out a bottle of Benedictine from the lining of her coat, gave it to Meddi and asked William to turn up the heating. Meddi took a swig and let the alcohol course through her veins. She thought how much easier it would be for Alma to abandon her husband, go back to Vienna and join the Nazis rather than try and escape with him. She herself wanted to go back to Vienna to be with Johnny and join the resistance. Instead, she had to go wherever William was taking her. William had often spoken to her about his weakness and his feelings of emptiness and she had often tried to soothe his trouble by assuring him his heart was in the right place. Now, in their crisis, it was William's hands and feet, on the steering wheel and on the throttle, that were in the right place. Fry with the map on his knee sat up front with William and directed him south towards Toulouse. William loved the car. It was a new car. It was his car. He marvelled at the engineering of the front wheel drive. He felt empowered, and whenever the road allowed he let the car have full throttle, transferring the power he felt within himself to the driving wheels which were up front beside and beneath him. The suspension was a miracle. No one looked to hold on as he cornered. He felt as if he was driving a magic carpet. No one told him to slow down. William was in control and flying.

Night had fallen and they were an hour short of Toulouse when in the rear-view mirror William saw a fire in the sky. The fire appeared to be following them. The noise of the fire in the sky got louder - a furious, metallic, high-pitched mechanical grinding and screaming. As the fire passed overhead the noise was deafening and everyone instinctively ducked. A huge blaze appeared in front of the windscreen and William braked. The fire hit the road a hundred metres in front of them with an enormous explosion. The light, heat, the smell of aviation fuel and the acrid black smoke of burning rubber overwhelmed the car. William thrust the car into reverse. Alma prayed for a miracle. Fry saw the sign to Lourdes and barked, 'Go right!' William spun the wheel and pushed the car through the gears, driving at top speed away from the wreckage of the burning aircraft that blocked the road to Toulouse.

They arrived in Lourdes in the early hours of the morning and Alma, Werfel and Fry slept late in the Hotel Vatican. William examined his car and sank into a deep melancholy. The paintwork was blistered and burned. The satisfying smell of new leather upholstery now smelt of burnt toast.

They stayed in Lourdes for three weeks. Werfel, whose nerves were shattered, had no problem playing the role of a sick man on pilgrimage. He was ill and didn't want to leave his bed, but Alma and Meddi encouraged him to get into a three-wheeled bath chair so they could wheel him to the grotto where they could better conceal themselves among the crowds. They walked in a slow procession with thousands of others who recited over and over, *Je vous salue, Marie, pleine de grâce; le Seigneur est avec vous. Vous êtes bénie entre toutes le femmes, et Jésus, le fruit de vos entrailles, est beni. Sainte Marie, Mère de Dieu, priez pour nous pauvres pêcheurs, maintenant et à l'heure de notre mort, ainsi soit-il.* By the time they had heard the prayer a thousand times Alma and Meddi knew it off by heart. Werfel lay in the bath chair wearing a straw hat against the mid-summer southern French sunshine and took no interest in the proceedings until he opened his eyes and discovered that Lourdes was full of pilgrims hobbling on crutches. Alma sensed something within her husband waking up and asked him if he was all right. He said he was feeling much better.

Fry explored all the little booths around town which displayed working models with hundreds of moving parts. An exhibit of a village with a priest who rang a church bell, a cable car which went to the top of the hill, a water wheel and a fairground, all of which could be set in motion in return for a few coins. Another booth displayed a model railway on a mountainside with a passenger train that climbed to the top in a spiral that took it in and out of tunnels and then spiralled back down again before pulling into the station at the foot of the hill. Fry's favourite was a working model of *Snow White and the Seven Dwarves*. He loved the film, and here they were marching off to work singing, 'Hi Ho! Hi Ho!' He revisited this booth again and again trying to remember the seven names but could only ever remember six of them, and never the same six.

William drove his car to a body shop in Tarbes where, after counting out a roll of US dollars, the boss thought he might be able to restore William's Traction Avant. It would take around two weeks.

Alma did not realize the full extent of her husband's miraculous recovery until he asked her to join him in bed and insisted on sex.

Werfel wanted to go to the grotto every morning where the sight of so many crutches perked him up. In the afternoon he joined the procession that followed the blessed sacrament and sang 'Ave Maria' over and over, and then in the evening he marched in torchlight procession singing 'Ave Maria' all over again. At night Alma, exhausted from a day of walking, praying and singing, had to deal with Werfel's new-found sexual energy.

William and Werfel made daily trips to the baths on the far side of the grotto where the sick could immerse themselves in the holy water that sprang from the ground where the Virgin Mary had appeared to Bernadette. They undressed and were held in the arms of strong young male volunteers who plunged them into the holy water. Pilgrims dressed without drying. There was no need for a towel. The holy water miraculously evaporated in the midsummer sunshine. Werfel stood at the grotto with William and before the statue of the Virgin Mary he asked William to witness his solemn oath. Werfel swore that if he got out of this alive he would write a book about Mary's apparition to Bernadette.

The body shop did a miraculous job on the Traction Avant. The paintwork and glass were restored to their original condition and, to thank William for his very generous payment, the body shop fitted the car with four new white-walled tyres.

They left Lourdes and kept close to the Pyrenees until they reached Perpignan, where they stopped to eat. Varian Fry met his colleague from the Emergency Rescue Team, Richard Ball, who was on his way to the border town of Cerbère with Lion and Marta Feuchtwanger. Having been stripped of their German citizenship, the Feuchtwangers could not get an exit visa and the only way out for them was to climb over the Pyrenees at night, avoiding the French border controls.

Varian Fry continued eastward to Marseilles with his party where they returned to the Hotel Louvre et Paix and Alma was reunited with her luggage.

Fry was pleased to discover more celebrities. Heinrich and Nellie Mann had arrived in Marseilles. The Manns had heard rumours that Mahler and Werfel had succeeded in getting out of France through Bordeaux and were planning to do the same when they stumbled into each other in the hotel foyer. Fry's delight at finding two more famous clients was not reciprocated by the Manns who were disappointed to see that the Mahler-Werfel escape attempt from Bordeaux had failed.

Alma gazed out to sea searching the horizon for the ship that would come to rescue them.

Meddi searched the horizon for news about Johnny.

William searched under the bonnet of his car to discover how Citroen engineers had transmitted the power of the engine to the front wheels.

Werfel searched the Marseilles bookshops for anything he could find about Bernadette Soubirous and the apparition she saw at Lourdes. He spent his evenings discussing literature with Heinrich Mann. Alma spent her evenings avoiding Nellie Mann whom she considered to be vulgar.

Fry and Ball spent their evenings planning to get Mahler and Werfel to undertake the same journey as the Feuchtwangers who had successfully got out of France over the Pyrenees. Getting into Spain presented no difficulty. The problem was getting out of France without exit visas. The climb over the Pyrenees had to be undertaken without alerting French border guards. Ball had employed a shepherd to guide Lion and Marta Feuchtwanger over the hills while he took their luggage on the train from Cerbère and met up with the Feuchtwangers in Figueres. It hadn't cost the earth – a few dollars for the shepherd and 400 American cigarettes for the customs check.

Alma declared that the Pyrenees were not very high – nothing like the Austrian mountains where she and Mahler climbed every morning before he settled down to a day's composing and if Marta Feuchtwanger could do it so could she. And if Lion Feuchtwanger could do it so could Werfel. Fry would take their luggage by train to Figueres where they could all meet again in Spain.

The following morning Fry and Ball met them at Marseilles railway station. Alma had brought twelve suitcases. They all got off at Cerbère except Fry, who stayed on the train with the luggage. Ball left them all in a restaurant while he went off to meet his shepherd. They made for the foothills under cover of darkness. It was a warm night and the refugees felt encouraged when the moon rose. Their guide would have preferred a much darker night. They followed a single file track in silence. Heinrich Mann couldn't keep up. Nellie Mann nagged her husband to hurry up and complained to the guide, demanding that he slow down. Alma loudly told Nellie to 'be quiet!' The guide stopped every five minutes to allow the Manns to catch up, urging them all to be quiet. In the distance hunting dogs called out to each other across the moonlit hills. After three hours the mossy ground gave way to stones and gravel. The guide stopped to let them rest and gave them some chocolate. He told William that everyone must stay close and keep hard to the right. There was a sheer drop on their left. He took seven lengths of rope from his knapsack, one each so they could hold on to each other. He explained that they could not be tied together because if one of them fell they would all fall. There would be another rest and another piece of chocolate in an hour. It was 3am and the moon had set when they reached the summit. They rested for ten minutes. Their clothes were torn, their knees bruised, their hands and feet bleeding.

Heinrich Mann refused to go any further. The guide would not wait for him and set off. William, Alma, Werfel and Meddi limped after the guide. Nellie waited with her husband.

Descending was harder work than climbing. They abandoned the ropes that kept them close to each other, slipped on the scree and slid down on their backsides in a rattle of gravel and stones, overtaking their guide who moved down the slopes sure-footed as a mountain goat. At a spot where the descent fell away steeply down a gravel slope the guide sat, pulled Alma on top of him, kicked himself forward and slid down the slope on his backside holding Alma in his arms. When the dust settled Alma found she was now able to put her feet down on a grassy hillside. The others, who didn't get a lift from the guide, had to pick their way gingerly over the gravel and down the slope from the upper world of rocks and high places into a grassy world of moss and wildflowers.

By 7am they reached a road where a horse and cart was waiting for them. Guide and driver greeted each other in silence and then the guide turned and set off up the hill and back to France. The driver started for Figueres. William looked up the hill but saw no sign of Heinrich and Nellie Mann.

Fry was waiting for them at the railway station. He gave William the train tickets from Figueres to Barcelona, the address of a hotel in Barcelona, the train tickets from Barcelona to Madrid, and from there to Lisbon, and he gave them the papers for their passage from Lisbon to New York. He told William the guide had returned to collect Heinrich and Nellie Mann who would join them in Barcelona.

Before the train left Figueres William gave Fry the keys to the Traction Avant and told him to keep the briefcase which 'contained some funding to get others out of France.' Varian Fry was astonished at the vast sum of money he had been carrying for William and didn't know how to thank him.

'Don't thank me,' said William. 'Thank Johnny.'

End of Part 2

PART THREE

1940-1965

William and Leonard Bernstein

CHAPTER 51

William Meets Leonard

After the first war the German language steadily disappeared from the city streets of New York, and during the second war it vanished. Alma felt like a foreigner in the city where she had once felt at home. Meddi spoke English well, William hesitantly, Alma and Werfel not at all.

William and Meddi, looking like a couple on their second honeymoon, sat on the ferry to Staten Island, ate in Chinatown, and walked hand-in-hand through Central Park. They talked about Anna as if she was their own daughter who had only just left home. Anna, now living in London, had married for the fourth time. They talked about Johnny, the man they had both loved. Meddi asked William to describe to her again the journey with Johnny when William drove him from the house in Semmering to the station. William repeated it faithfully.

'He gave me your papers. He told me that both of us should have stayed in America. He gave me the suitcase full of dollar bills and told me not to worry about the money – he hadn't sold his trumpet. He told me that he'd robbed a bank and then he got out of the car, said "Vorbei" and walked into the station.'

Meddi asked him to tell her again and every time William repeated the story word for word and every time Meddi searched between the words for the meaning. William only ever told her what Johnny said. She knew there must be more to the story.

'Why did he say, "Vorbei?" Why did he tell you not to worry and that he hadn't sold his trumpet? He would never have sold his trumpet.'

William didn't fill the gaps because they were not for Meddi. They were for himself. He never told Meddi that he had sold his own viola and given Johnny half the cash. He never told her that Johnny had said "Vorbei" – "It's over" – just before he got on the train at Vienna's Westbahnhof station to go to America with Mahler all these years ago, and that when Johnny gave him the money and Meddi's papers and walked into the station at Semmering to take the train back to Vienna his "Vorbei" referred to the painful wound Johnny had suffered at William's hands thirty years before.

William asked Meddi where she thought he got all that money.

'He told you. He robbed a bank.'

William was astonished. 'Surely you don't believe that!'

Meddi told him about Johnny's role as quartermaster for the military wing of the Schutzbund, and that the procurement of weapons was financed by bank robberies. She told him that she and Johnny had decided to escape together with the Mahlers and only now did she understand that Johnny had never intended to escape. She loved him for getting her safely out of Europe and hated herself for leaving without him. William knew that, if she had a choice, she would rather die with Johnny in Austria than be walking with him in Central Park. Johnny had chosen to stay in Austria, to live, and probably die, without her.

William went to Carnegie Hall to listen to the Philharmonic when Bruno Walter was conducting. He would visit Walter in the conductor's room and deliver a greeting from Alma. Bruno Walter always returned the compliment. William lied about the first and never delivered the second. Alma never sent any greetings to Bruno Walter because she felt that he threatened to usurp her place as the senior guardian of her late husband's legacy. She also lost patience with Franz Werfel who had compromised her role as Mahler's widow by marrying her. She was happier being Mahler's widow.

Alma decided to get out of New York and go west to Beverly Hills where Thomas and Heinrich Mann, Berthold Brecht, Schönberg, Korngold and other German emigrés now lived and worked, writing scripts and music for Hollywood. Meddi found work in costumes at Metro-Goldwyn-Mayer, Franz Werfel started work on his book about Bernadette and William persuaded Alma to buy him an Oldsmobile. When Werfel finally grew tired of Alma's anti-Semitism he rented a place where he could work in peace. He bought William a portable Remington. William learned to touch type and copied Werfel's handwritten manuscript of *The Song of Bernadette*.

The book was a publishing sensation, and with the sale of the film rights Alma was once more a very wealthy woman. She threw lavish parties for her German neighbours. When America joined the war against the Axis, Japanese immigrants were rounded up and interned. German and Italian immigrants loudly declared themselves to be anti-fascists and contributed enthusiastically to Hollywood's war propaganda machine but otherwise kept a low profile. Alma's profile was never low. The abundant food and drink at her parties was of the highest quality. Her guests accepted her hospitality but were nervous about her fascist sympathies. Werfel spent less and less time at home and more and more time on the road promoting his book. When Werfel's publishers needed him in New York, Alma and Werfel crossed the continent by train. They arrived in late December and stayed at the St Moritz Hotel where Alma kept a salon to receive her guests. That's where William first laid eyes on the most beautiful man he had ever seen. Leonard Bernstein was standing just a few feet across the room from William talking to the New York Philharmonic's guest conductor, Bruno Walter. William stood beside Bruno Walter and listened to Walter telling Leonard Bernstein that he looked forward to the day when an American orchestra would be led by an American conductor. Walter introduced William. 'Herr Hildebrand works for Frau Werfel.' Bernstein smiled, said 'Hi,' and immediately returned to the conversation with Walter about American conductors. He gave Walter a list of American composers, including himself, to be introduced to American audiences by American orchestras led by American conductors, including himself. William saw Bernstein coming to the end of his cigarette and went to fetch an ashtray. He held it out to Bernstein who stubbed out his cigarette and lit another. William stood with the ashtray while Walter described the tasks he had undertaken as assistant conductor to Mahler at the Opera in Vienna. Bernstein told Walter all about his own first symphony. There were six cigarette stubs in the ashtray when Bruno Walter excused himself and left to use the washroom. Bernstein scanned the room for another important person to talk to and sidled over to Bruno Zirato, general manager of the New York Philharmonic. William remembered him from Mahler's days at the Met when he had been Enrico Caruso's secretary.

When Bruno Walter came back from the washroom he approached William, who was standing by himself. 'Bernstein is a hugely gifted boy who leaves everything to the last minute. He lacks discipline. If he gets the job as assistant to Rodzinski at the Philharmonic he'll have to polish Rodzinski's shoes, darn his socks, load his revolver, clean his shirts and clean up scores. He'll have to learn every note of every programme and then sit at the back while Rodzinski conducts. Bernstein doesn't have that kind of patience. He will need help. I would vouch for him if I knew you were around.'

'Load his revolver?' queried William.

'Yes,' said Bruno Walter. 'Rodzinski exercises his right to bear arms twenty-four hours a day and always carries a loaded revolver onto the platform. He never conducts without it.'

In the early afternoon of December 31st William knocked on Bernstein's door. Bernstein answered and William introduced himself as a friend of Bruno Walter. Bernstein did not recognise him and asked what he wanted.

'I want to help you.'

'I'm busy,' replied Bernstein.

'I know,' said William. 'That's why I'm offering to help you.'

'How can you help me?' asked Bernstein.

'I used to work for Mahler,' replied William.

'Frau Mahler?' asked Bernstein.

'Herr Mahler,' replied William.

'Gustav Mahler?'

'Yes.'

'Sprichst du Deutsch?' asked Bernstein.

William replied, 'Ja.'

'How does Mahler's Third start?'

'Eight horns in unison,' answered William.

'And the Fourth?'

'Sleigh bells.'

'The Fifth?'

'Solo trumpet.'

'How does the Sixth end?'

'A single plucked bottom A on the basses,' replied William.

Bernstein let William come in.

William entered a room where the table, chairs and floor were covered in manuscript.

'My symphony.' said Bernstein. 'The deadline for the competition is midnight tonight. I'll wash. You dry.'

Bernstein sat on the floor correcting sheets and passed them up to William who sat at the table copying the music as quickly as Bernstein corrected it. Sometimes William rejected a sheet, returning it to Bernstein for further correction as if handing back a dirty plate. William only left his seat to empty Leonard Bernstein's ashtray. The two of them created a clean copy of the score before midnight.

'Let's celebrate,' cried out Lenny.

William's heart leapt.

Lenny filled two tumblers with malt whisky and downed his.

'Does Mahler's Sixth really finish with a plucked note on the basses?'

'Yes.'

'Wow!' said Lenny.

311

He gave William the manuscript of his First Symphony.

'The competition says it's got to be anonymous, so you deliver it.'

Lenny scribbled out the address for William who got up to leave without drinking his tumblerful of whisky. Lenny picked up William's whisky and followed him to the door. 'Happy New Year, pal.' Lenny kissed William on the lips. William felt Bernstein's tongue. Then Bernstein drank William's whisky.

William organised the packing and travel arrangements for Alma's journey back home on the 20th Century, the overnight train to Chicago, which connected with the Superchief to San Francisco, from where Alma and Werfel would ride south to Los Angeles. William booked their cases through to Los Angeles so there would be no handling of luggage in Chicago or San Francisco and he boarded the train with Alma and Werfel. Just before its 6pm departure William stepped down from the carriage onto the red-carpeted platform and whispered 'Vorbei' to himself as the train pulled out of Grand Central Station without him.

William assumed, correctly, that he would not be missed on the journey west and that he would be easily replaced in Hollywood by any number of good solid Germans of Aryan stock who would be happy to drive Alma's Oldsmobile and open the door to her guests. Werfel would have no problem finding a replacement to type up his manuscripts. William had a few dollars in his pocket to see him through the next two or three days but otherwise, like Leonard Bernstein, he was penniless.

He sat on a bench in Central Park and discussed the situation with Mahler, who began by thanking William for his loyal service to Alma. He agreed with William that there was now nothing more he could do for her. Mahler told William that Alma's marriage with Werfel had settled into a stable and mutual hostility which would sustain them until death. Sooner or later Werfel's sixty cigarettes a day or Alma's daily bottle of Benedictine would finish one of them off.

William confessed that he had gone to the station with Alma and Werfel unsure of his next step until the moment he stepped off the train.

'You've done it before, as you well know. Why did you whisper "Vorbei" as the train pulled out? That was a bit dramatic, don't you think?'

'I abandoned them, just as I abandoned Johnny.'

'You've got that back to front. You're the one who's alone in New York with no money. You've managed to get yourself abandoned. You have a real gift for it.'

'What do you think I should do?,' asked William.

'You know exactly what to do. You want a part in the Leonard Bernstein story, and when you get it you'll play it well. Bruno Walter has already given you the outline. Leonard Bernstein will become the assistant conductor at the Philharmonic. The boy is a genius. He sleeps with men on Mondays, Wednesdays, and Fridays, with women on Tuesdays, Thursdays, and Saturdays, and with both on Sundays. He has orgasms when he conducts. He has an erotic engagement with life, and his passion will literally turn on a whole new generation of listeners. He will conquer America, then he'll conquer the world, and he'll take my music with him. Once Bruno puts the boy's feet on the first step at the Philharmonic there will be no going back. But Walter is afraid the boy will go up like a rocket and come down like the stick, which is why he wants you to look after him. You are to be Apollo to Bernstein's Dionysius. Bruno Walter thinks you can control the explosion, answer the door, sober him up, make the coffee and get him to the gig on time. Bruno's got a high opinion of you, William. He thinks you know more about my music than he does. The New York Philharmonic archive will have the scores of all the music I conducted and they're marked up, either by you or by me. You attended all the rehearsals. You could show Mr Walter and Mr Bernstein how I conducted them. Next time Bruno's in town get my scores from the archive and go through them with Walter. Get young Bernstein to attend these meetings and Bruno's rehearsals. Before the fall, Bernstein will take up the position of assistant conductor and before the end of the year he'll conduct the orchestra. Walter is conducting all this week, so why don't you start right away? Don't wait to be asked. Just go right ahead and set the chairs, music stands and risers on the platform and reset everything during the interval as required, organise the piano tuner before the concert and clear the platform after the concert and re-set it for the next day's rehearsal. The Philharmonic need someone who doesn't have to be told what to do. Here's another thing. Bruno's got a girlfriend. She's half his age. Americans have less understanding of these affairs than we have. The girl is the youngest daughter of Alma's neighbour, Thomas Mann, and she is married to an English poet who is homosexual. They married so that she could get out of Germany safely and into America. Her husband is only interested in boys and the marriage is unconsummated. As you know, Bruno Walter is also married. His wife has been in hospital ever since their daughter was murdered. He's terrified of a scandal but cannot give up his young mistress. If you and

Bruno's mistress were to become friends, it would give Bruno some cover. You've done it before. You're very good at it.'

William discovered a room on the top floor of Carnegie Hall which was filled with broken chairs, risers and music stands. William repaired them all and returned them to the furniture store beneath the platform. Then he refurnished the room, turning it into a studio for himself. On January 13th he stood at the back of the hall and listened to a concert performed by the Duke Ellington Orchestra.

Rodzinski, the Philharmonic's chief conductor, took whole weeks away to tend the animals he kept in his upstate pig farm and Bruno Walter was his regular deputy. Walter would climb the stairs to William's 'office' on the top floor and work there with William on the programmes, studying Mahler's scores from the archive. Bruno Walter always invited the boy, Bernstein, to join them. The markings told half the story. William's eye-witness account of Mahler's rehearsals told the other half.

So Bruno Walter conducted Mozart symphonies, as Mahler did, with a chamber orchestra, giving half of the musicians the night off, and for Beethoven symphonies he brought in extra hands, as Mahler did, to perform with larger forces including the E-flat clarinet which Mahler had inserted into the score and to which the late Henry Krehbiel, music critic of the Tribune, had harshly objected. Older members of the audience listening to Bruno Walter's interpretations recognised that the music was as good as it was in Mahler's day.

William became a fixture at Carnegie Hall and whenever he passed the big burly Neapolitan general manager in the corridor, Bruno Zirato would greet him with a cheerful 'Buongiorno.'

William wrote a review of Herr Walter's performance of Beethoven's Seventh, describing Walter's performance as 'one of the happiest evenings of music- making New York had heard in many years,' and went on to say that the 'gaiety forever preserved in Beethoven's score shone a light in dark wartimes that pointed the world to a better place.' When he read the review and the by-line, 'Avi Bacharach,' Bruno Zirato marched into the offices of the New York Evening Post with a loaded gun looking for the reviewer – 'the bastard that wrote the article about Caruso wanking in the monkey house.' Bruno Zirato was disarmed by two policemen and marched from the newspaper office back to Carnegie Hall. They asked William if this man was, as he claimed, the general manager of the Philharmonic Orchestra. William confirmed that he was. The policemen let him go and asked William to 'calm the lunatic down.' William took Zirato back to the manager's office where he slumped in a chair and wept. 'They took my gun,' he sobbed.

When Bruno Walter returned to New York for another fortnight of guest conducting he brought Erica Mann with him and presented William with a portable phonograph. Together they listened to *The Alpine Symphony* which Strauss had recorded the previous year with the Bavarian Symphony. William and Walter marked up the score following the composer's own recording.

William sat in the conductor's box with Erica Mann, a beautiful and intelligent young woman who reminded William of Meddi when she was younger. She had her hair short, and wore a three-piece trouser suit, a gold watch chain and a rose in her lapel. She had left Germany after visiting Theresienstadt where she had spent the day inspecting the highly-skilled work produced in the camp workshops by smiling inmates. She had enjoyed an evening concert performance of *The Bartered Bride*. But when she returned, uninvited, the following week, she discovered the camp was entirely different from the model village she had been shown the previous week. All the previous week's inmates had disappeared. Her persistent efforts to find out what was going on in the camps were a thorn in the side of the Nazi regime and they revoked her German citizenship. She married W H Auden to get out of Germany and into the USA, where she was able to join her father in Hollywood. Although she described the Nazi regime as a gang of thieves and racists she did not believe the rumours that the inmates who disappeared from the camps had been murdered. She thought it more likely that they had been deported to the east, possibly to the Ukraine. She deplored the régime's racial laws, which oversaw the deportation of Jews and the Aryanisation of their property, but she did not imagine the régime planned to exterminate Europe's Jewish population. It was difficult to believe the stories of mass executions at Belsen and Buchenwald while at the same time listening to the excellence of Richard Strauss's 1941 Bavarian Symphony Orchestra recording of his *Alpine Symphony*.

Bruno Walter booked a room for Erica in his hotel and allowed William to use it while Erica was in town. They entered and left the hotel as a threesome. William and Erica appeared to be a couple and Bruno looked like William's father-in-law. Bruno Walter invariably slept late, and Erica and William often took breakfast together in the hotel's dining room. She enjoyed William's stories about Bruno in the Mahler years in Vienna. She told him that her relations with Bruno were not as they appeared. Bruno Walter was devastated by the death of his daughter, murdered by the man Walter had chosen to be her husband. She told him that Walter's wife had locked herself away, a catatonic recluse, and was possibly insane. 'I look after him,' Erica said. 'But the world only knows one story for two people who leave a hotel room together. That story does not describe Bruno and me.'

She told William about her father's dim view of Alma's overblown and tipsy Beverly Hills hospitality and Werfel's overblown, crowd-pleasing literature. Erica, using the breakfast table to mime Alma playing the piano, sang *Falling in Love Again* in a Marlene Dietrich baritone. As she went to the buffet to refill her coffee she could do a magnificent take on Alma's unsteady plodding across the room to refill her Benedictine glass. William told her that Alma had required him to act as her armed bodyguard when they went shopping. 'No!' gasped Erica wide-eyed, as the pair of them traded gossip.

One morning over breakfast, remembering Mahler's New York years, William told Erica about the Met's *Bartered Bride* – the Czech dancers, the costumes and the resounding success. She confessed she'd only ever heard one performance and that was when she had visited Theresienstadt. She had some photographs and went to her room to fetch them. She came back with the photo album, laughing that her 'old man' Bruno was still asleep. She gave William the album and drew her chair beside him to share the pictures. There were several photographs of the orchestra. The musicians were not wearing concert blacks but were dressed in casual civilian clothes. William's eye was drawn to the back row on the right of the picture where the leader of the trumpet section was playing an instrument whose horn was raised at an angle of forty degrees. William stared at the picture of Johnny. He did not want to return the photograph to Erica and she let him keep it.

William looked forward to the meetings he had with Bruno Walter in the top floor studio at the Carnegie, where they would prepare the score for the next Philharmonic concert. It wasn't only for the pleasure of telling Bruno Walter how Mahler conducted; it was also for the thrill of sitting in the same room as Leonard Bernstein. At one meeting Bruno Walter wanted to know how Bernstein would conduct a silent downbeat. The boy, ignoring the question, asked who would conduct if Bruno was suddenly indisposed. Bruno Walter returned to the subject of the silent downbeat and only when he was satisfied that the topic had been properly discussed did he refer to Bernstein's question regarding his own hypothetical indisposition. To Bernstein's disappointment

Walter said, 'If I'm indisposed and can't conduct then I'd call Rodzinsky and tell him to get his ass down here right away.' Walter asked Bernstein what he proposed to do if the American military called him up to serve his country. Bernstein said it would be 'an honour'. Bruno Walter acknowledged that was the correct answer but it was also the wrong answer and until he got himself declared unfit for military service, Walter assured him, that he would never secure the post of assistant conductor and would therefore never be given the opportunity to stand in for anyone. 'You sort out your draft, then we'll worry about my health. Until you've fixed that I will never be indisposed!' After the meeting William emptied the ashtrays and opened the window.

Later that day Walter called Rodzinsky and told him the boy was nearly ready and that when he was offered the job it wouldn't cost the orchestra very much in the way of a salary because the boy would probably do it for nothing.

William often sat at the back of the piano bar where Bernstein played jazz. William wondered what Mahler would say if he ever heard this music.

Mahler told William he thought it was harmonically tedious. He got bored listening to the right hand scampering up and down the scales while the left shifted from one augmented, diminished, or flattened harmony to the next in a sequence repeated to the point where he lost interest. He thought the left hand was eating too many cream cakes while the right ran around like a headless chicken. He thought the improvisation was 'a waste of a good tune' and enjoyed the moment when the improviser ran out of ideas and returned to the melody. What Mahler liked was the rhythm. He had danced with orchestras as he conducted Ländlers and waltzes and encouraged his musicians to move with the rhythm as they played. He had spent years on the podium finding ways to get his musicians to play 'off' the beat – to 'lose the one' – to get away from the endless tick-tock of time which made so much music sound like clockwork.

'What did you call the music?'

'Jazz,' said William.

'Jazz,' repeated Mahler with approval. I love the way it moves.'

Mahler confessed that when he listened to jazz he couldn't sit still.

'It don't mean a thing if it ain't got that swing,' said William.

'That's right,' agreed Mahler.

Bernstein was a protégé of the conductor Koussevitzky, who advised him to give up his interest in jazz. He was also a protégé of the composer

Aaron Copeland, who advised him to concentrate on conducting. Neither took much interest in his composing and both advised him to drop his interest in Broadway and concentrate on more serious business. But with American soldiers crossing the Pacific and the Atlantic to wage war against Japan and Germany it seemed likely that Bernstein's next step would not be taken in concert blacks but in military uniform. When he was called up for his interview the draft board was better prepared than Bernstein. They had read the references which described his importance to the development of American musical life. The medical board showed little interest in the evidence which Bernstein presented describing his chronic asthma and sent him back into civilian life where he was expected to create a rich cultural environment for American heroes to inhabit after the war. Bernstein told everyone that he was disappointed to be denied the opportunity of serving his country and enthusiastically resumed his career in American music.

He kept a camp bed in William's studio on the top floor of Carnegie Hall for the nights he never made it back to his own apartment. After a stiff coffee and a cigarette he got up and was ready to spend the morning looking through Mahler's scores from the Philharmonic archive. One day Bernstein asked William if Mahler was a composer who conducted or a conductor who composed. William told him that Mahler was a performer whose instrument was the orchestra and that he performed the music that he wanted to hear and that he composed what he wanted to perform. In his composing hut Mahler appeared to be solitary but was never lonely. His symphonies were conversations with the composers who came before him. Bernstein asked William if Mahler ever had conversations with composers who came after him.

'Shostakovich's scherzos are a conversation with Mahler's scherzos,' answered William.

'Anybody else?'

'You, when you're ready.'

On his 25th birthday, August 25th 1943, Leonard Bernstein received a call from Rodzinski offering him the job as assistant conductor of the New York Philharmonic, which meant that he now got paid for what he had already been doing all summer. Rodzinski was never indisposed and whenever he retired to his pig farm the guest conductor, Bruno Walter, was never indisposed either. The chain-smoking asthmatic young assistant conductor was probably less healthy than his two senior colleagues.

On November 11th and 12th Bernstein studied the scores with William and Bruno Walter for the November 13th Saturday afternoon concert of Schumann's *Manfred* Overture; *Theme, Variations and Finale* by Miklós Rózsa; Richard Strauss's *Don Quixote,* and the Prelude to Wagner's *Die Meistersinger*. The orchestra knew the pieces well, and Bernstein had conducted the *Prelude* recently with the Boston Pops. William and Bernstein attended Bruno Walter's morning rehearsal on the Thursday. William had copied out the scores for Bernstein, which included all of Bruno Walter's markings. He sat next to Bernstein during the rehearsal, highlighting some of the more dangerous moments, in particular the opening of the Schumann, which starts with a silent downbeat. After the rehearsal Bruno Walter invited William and Bernstein back to the hotel for lunch. Over their meal Bernstein talked about the concert that evening at the Town Hall which included his composition *I Hate Music*. He told Walter that his parents were coming from Boston to hear it. Bruno Walter asked if his parents were going to stay the night. Bernstein, suspecting nothing, said that they were. Bruno Walter said, 'Good. Are you ready then?' Bernstein said that he was, but that the evening was in the hands of the musicians. He proposed to enjoy the concert sitting in the audience beside his parents. Bruno Walter asked again, this time making it clear that he wanted to know if Bernstein was ready to conduct the New York Philharmonic.

'When?' snapped Bernstein eagerly.

'Tomorrow,' answered Bruno Walter.

Bernstein leapt up from the table. 'I gotta phone Pops! I gotta cancel the Town Hall. I need to rehearse the Philharmonic in the morning'. Bruno Walter told him sharply, 'Sit down! You'll do no such thing. You will not breathe a word until the Press Office have formally notified everyone who needs to know. You will go to your concert at the Town Hall tonight. You will say nothing to your parents. You will not have a rehearsal with the Philharmonic in the morning. The concert's at 3pm. It'll be broadcast coast-to-coast on network radio. I just need you to tell me that you're ready.'

Bernstein stared at Bruno Walter and his eyes welled up with tears, 'Too damn right I'm ready!'

'Good,' said Walter. 'Enjoy yourself at the Town hall tonight, then come to my room in the morning, where you'll find me indisposed. We'll go through the scores again. When you step out on that podium tomorrow afternoon in front of the orchestra you will know every note.'

As Bruno got up from the table he told Bernstein that he would make the conductor's box available to his family but reminded him not to say a word to anyone until the Press Office released the information in the morning.

After Bruno had left the table Bernstein asked William, 'Did you know about this?'

'Yes,' said William.

'Fuck you,' said Bernstein and planted a kiss on William's lips.

CHAPTER 52

Bernstein's Assistant

At 2.55pm on Saturday, November 13th 1943 William walked onto the platform at Carnegie Hall and placed Mahler's baton on the podium. At 3pm the manager of the New York Philharmonic Orchestra announced that Mr. Walter was indisposed. Everyone already knew that. No one in the hall knew that the indisposed Mr Walter, wearing dark glasses and a hat, was sitting behind Bernstein's family in the conductor's box. The atmosphere in the hall was tight with anticipation, and when the manager announced that the concert would be conducted by Mr Bernstein the audience broke into applause. The leader of the orchestra took his seat and received the customary gentle applause. In the wings Bernstein asked William to kick him up the backside. He turned, bent over, and spread his tails. William hesitated. 'Come on!' shouted Bernstein. 'Kick my ass.' William did as he was told and Bernstein marched onto the platform looking neither right nor left. The orchestra leapt to their feet and stood to attention. The audience greeted the kid with generous applause which continued after he had reached the podium. Bernstein turned to acknowledge the applause, ignored the shout of 'Go on, my boy!' from his dad in the conductor's box and lit the auditorium with a huge smile. He turned to face the orchestra and before the applause died gave the silent downbeat. The orchestra came in together on the up. At the end of the Schumann Bernstein thanked the orchestra, turned to the audience, shyly acknowledged their applause and left the podium. William was waiting in the wings with a lighted cigarette. Bernstein inhaled deeply before returning to the platform to conduct Rózsa's *Theme, Variations and Finale*. That also went well and the applause, broadcast live from coast to coast, rang around Carnegie Hall again as William waited in the wings with another lighted cigarette. Bernstein returned for the *Don Quixote*. When he brought Strauss's tone poem to a close the audience knew they were witnessing the birth of a star. Bernstein didn't turn to them immediately but first brought the principal cello to his feet and shook hands with him. Then he asked the principal viola to stand, left the podium and approached her. She offered him her hand. He took her in his arms and kissed her on the lips. The audience cheered. He acknowledged the applause without stepping back onto the podium but stood with his musicians on the platform and bowed deeply. William, waiting in the wings, admired the humility and the showmanship and wondered how long the humility would last. He lit another cigarette and when Bernstein left the platform William placed it on Bernstein's lower lip and read out a telegram from Koussevitzky – 'Listening now. Wonderful.'

The programme had been designed to fill the hour sponsored by the United States Rubber Company and the radio broadcast ended with the Strauss. The *Meistersinger Prelude* was not broadcast, which was just as well because Bernstein, now emotionally spent, contributed very little to a performance that went by him in a blur. He accompanied the orchestra waving his arms, dancing and tapping his feet on the podium as the musicians performed the piece they knew well. William waited in the wings with a chalice of 12-year-old Bowmore and another cigarette. Bernstein downed the whisky and inhaled the tobacco before returning to the platform. After the audience had called him back for the eighth time Bernstein had smoked another three cigarettes and finished more than half the bottle of whisky.

In the conductor's box Bruno Walter shook hands with Bernstein's family and congratulated them on their son's successful début. Mr and Mrs Bernstein didn't know who he was. Bruno Walter left Carnegie Hall with two notes for Bernstein. The first was about stamina; without it the second half of a concert would always be less than the first. The second was about tapping his feet. Nowhere in the score did the composer ask for percussion from the conductor. Bruno Walter felt confident that Bernstein would work on his stamina. He doubted he would ever succeed in getting Bernstein to keep his feet still.

Bernstein took a shower and William towelled the naked conductor dry. Bernstein asked him why he had put a baton on the podium. 'You know I don't use one,' he said.

'A lucky charm,' said William.

'Pour me another whisky.'

'Later' said William, lighting him another cigarette. 'Your Mum and Dad are waiting.'

The triumph of the young American who had taken over at the last minute from the indisposed Mr Walter made the front pages of the newspapers and on the inside pages the music critics endorsed the opinion of the Carnegie Hall audience. The New York Tribune's chief critic welcomed the new conductor, praised the New York Philharmonic for handing the baton to one so inexperienced but so promising, described the Prelude as 'lacklustre,' and looked forward to the day when Mr Bernstein would conduct Wagner with the same authority he had displayed with the Schumann, Rósza and Strauss. The Tribune editor spiked his senior music critic's review and published instead the review sent to him by Avi Bacharach which better matched the paper's front-page headline, 'Carnegie Hall Rocked by New Kid on the Block.' Bacharach wrote that the excitement generated by the young American conductor reminded the audience of the glorious concerts led by Gustav Mahler. Bacharach's praise was unreserved, especially for the maturity and bravery with which the young maestro had faced the music's dangerous and challenging difficulties, praise underpinned by the reviewer's detailed knowledge of the scores Mr Bernstein had conducted.

Bruno Zirato asked William to come to his office to discuss the November - December programme. He wanted to offer Mr Bernstein another concert, and the sooner the better. William pointed to Mahler's Sixth, which Rodzinski was due to conduct for the following Sunday's broadcast. Zirato shook his head. 'Bruno Walter won't be here to hold his hand.'

'I'm here,' said William.

The door burst open and the New York Tribune's chief music critic stormed in. 'Who the fuck is Avi Bacharach? I'm gonna kill him.'

'I dunno who he is,' said Zirato, 'but when you find out, come back and let me know, because I wanna kill him too. And next time knock on the door. Didn't your mother teach you no manners? Now clear off. I'm busy.'

'What's the matter with him?' asked William.

'Maurice writes good reviews and gets little presents from the orchestra. He's worried that I'm going to give his presents to this Bacharach guy instead. Where were we?'

'Mr Bernstein conducting the Mahler next Sunday.'

'Only if Bruno Walter stays in town.'

'What about that Mendelssohn?' asked Zirato, pointing to a Thursday evening in December. 'Mendelssohn's easy. Mahler's complicated.'

'See what Bruno Walter thinks,' suggested William.

'Is Walter easy or complicated?' asked Zirato.

'Easy,' replied William.

'Bernstein?'

'Complicated,' replied William.

The following morning William helped Erica Mann pack her bags for the train journey back west and joined her and Bruno for lunch. William asked Bruno what he thought of Mahler's Sixth.

'Dynamite,' answered Bruno Walter.

'And Bernstein?'

'Dynamite.'

'I think it would be a good idea to let Bernstein stand in for Rodzinski next Sunday.'

'Mahler's Sixth?' asked Walter

'Yes.'

'Why would Rodzinski let him do that?' asked Walter.

'Because Bernstein puts the New York Philharmonic on the front pages of the newspapers,' answered William.

'Rodzinski would rather be on the front pages himself,' said Walter.

'He knows that's not going to happen. Give the concert to Bernstein, the papers will run with it, and Rodzinski can take the credit for being a generous and wise star maker.'

'Rodzinski will want me to stay, but I've got three cowboy films in Hollywood this Saturday.'

'Tell Rodzinski that I'll look after Mr Bernstein.'

'It's never been performed in America before. Are you seriously suggesting the kid conducts the American premier of Mahler's Sixth?'

'Yes.'

'And what if he doesn't manage? Have you thought about the scale of the disaster?'

'Yes. It's the same the size as the triumph when he pulls it off. The radio listening figures will go through the roof. The United States Rubber Company will sponsor more radio time. Bernstein will put Mahler on the map and Rodzinski can spend an extra week on the farm with his pigs.'

'Is that all? asked Walter.

'No.'

'Walter waited. 'What else?'

'Mahler will put his fingerprints on Bernstein's soul.'

'So, you study the score with Bernstein and you supervise the rehearsals, but on the day of the concert he's the conductor. Will he do what you tell him to do?'

'Yes.'

'How can you be sure?'

'Because you do what I tell you to do.'

Walter sat with his eyes closed for a minute and then pushed his chair back from the table, stood up and said to William and Erica, 'Why don't you two say your fond farewells while I call Rodzinski?'

Erica told William that she had never heard anyone speak to Bruno Walter like that. William told her it was quite straightforward. 'I know what Mahler wants and Bruno Walter knows that I know.'

William took the photo of the Theresienstadt orchestra from his inside pocket to return it to Erica. 'It's all right,' she said. 'Keep it.'

Bruno Walter returned and announced it was all fixed. He told William that Zirato and Rodzinski had already discussed the idea and had quarrelled.

'Rodzinski gave me the casting vote,' said Walter. 'I'll need to race through Saturday's recording session in jig time to get home for the Mahler broadcast.'

'What films are you doing?' asked William.

'*Buffalo Bill, Tall in the Saddle* and *The Yellow Rose of Texas*.'

'Music good?' asked William.

'Sensational,' lied Walter. 'You know the correct order of movements for the Mahler?'

'Of course,' said William, truthfully.

William waited outside the offices of the New York Tribune and approached the senior music critic as he was leaving the building for his lunchtime drink. He called out 'Maurice.' Maurice turned and looked at the stranger.

William greeted him politely, 'Good afternoon, sir,' and offered the critic his hand. 'Let's go for a drink together.'

The critic snatched back his hand and snapped, 'You a faggot?'

'No, sir. I work for Mr Zirato at the New York Philharmonic.'

'Doing what, stranger?'

'I put out the chairs, sir,' answered William.

'I write about music, not furniture.'

'Mr Bacharach writes about music too and if the Tribune publishes any more of his stuff you may need to start learning about furniture.'

They walked into a bar. William bought two large whiskies.

'It has come to Mr Zirato's attention that you wish to kill Mr Bacharach. Mr Zirato wondered if silencing Mr Bacharach would be sufficient to meet your needs. Mr Zirato has honourable friends who will guarantee Mr Bacharach's silence at a small cost. Mr Zirato does not wish to be associated with this cost and requests that, in return for

Mr Bacharach's silence, you redirect the cash you receive from his office on publication of your reviews and deliver it to my office which is on the top floor. I will then personally complete the transaction that guarantees Mr Bacharach's silence. That silence will be maintained as long as this arrangement is strictly adhered to. Our contract is, of course, entirely dependent upon your own silence.'

William didn't wait for an answer, told Maurice it was a pleasure doing business with him, downed his whiskey, and left the bar. William walked back to Carnegie Hall with a smile. No one had ever called him 'a faggot' before.

On Tuesday, November 16th William waited in his studio for Bernstein. Lenny burst into the room. 'Hey, Bill,' he cried. 'You're right. It finishes with a low plucked A on the basses.' He threw the score of Mahler's Sixth onto the table.

'You're late,' said William.

'I've been up all night reading this.'

'It's a big job, Mr Bernstein, and I expect to start on time.'

They got down to work. Bernstein thought the violent opening sounded like the universe going to war. William told Bernstein that Mahler avoided programmes and that the violent opening was music that sounded like music, not warfare. William did however concede Alma's claim that the second theme was a portrait of herself.

'If Alma says the second theme is a portrait of herself, then I'm saying the first theme is the sound of Hitler's blitzkrieg.' Mr Bernstein got to his feet and marched on the spot, stamping his boots on the floor with his right had raised in a fascist salute. William reminded Bernstein that Mahler died in 1911 and knew nothing of the first war, never mind this one. Bernstein protested, 'Mahler was a prophet and saw what was coming.' William didn't want to argue and suggested Bernstein conduct the first bars again without moving his feet. This time Bernstein used the clenched fist of his right hand to smash the glass windows of Jewish shops on Kristallnacht, punching the air like a boxer training for the big fight. William rolled with the punches. The orchestra didn't know what was about to hit them and William guessed they were going to love it.

Bernstein was concerned about the preponderance of A major in the first movement that was supposed to be in A minor. 'Which is it?' he asked. 'Both,' William answered. 'Mahler composed in the crack between major and minor.'

They discussed the cowbells before the last restatement of the march. William told Bernstein that Mahler liked to walk in the mountains, where the sound of cowbells was ubiquitous. The sheep and goats on the grassy meadows near the summit inhabit a different world from the valley below. The cowbells are the last sound you might hear as you float upwards from the summit into the realm of the spirits.'

'I dig,' said Bernstein.

They moved on to the second movement, which in Bernstein's score was the *Andante* and in William's score the *Scherzo*. William had decided not to argue the order of the movements with Bernstein because there was only one way he was prepared to let Bernstein do it – *Scherzo*, then *Andante*. He told Bernstein, 'You're the conductor. You decide. But you need to know that Mahler couldn't conduct *Scherzo*, then *Andante*, because it was too hot for him to handle. Maybe it's too hot for you too, but the only way you'll get an orgasm is *Scherzo*, then *Andante*', and he replaced Bernstein's score with his own. There was no further discussion.

As Bernstein turned the pages William told him, 'The *Scherzo* opens with same violence as the first movement. The march is in three instead of four and the stressed beat shifts from bar to bar. The violent stamping gives way to a melody which suggests a nostalgic look at two children walking hand-in-hand before the brass interrupts, laughing scornfully at the simplicity of a melody which can't defend itself against their sneering.

'Your audience is now ready for the *Andante*'s achingly tuneful melodies. Oboe and horn turn in surprising ways over a strange but beautiful harmonic structure that no one has ever heard before. Flutes and piccolos run crystal-clear through the meadow, accompanied by solo violin washing away the violence of the opening movements. As you cross the brow of every hill your ear meets more and yet more pleasing sounds until you reach the last summit and look down on a vast ocean of sound spreading before your ears. Then, just when you thought you had achieved safety, dark clouds gather on the horizon and the ocean starts to boil. The listener's serenity is shattered and the final movement lays waste to the whole symphony. That's what Mahler couldn't do. He was unable to embrace the safety and security of his beautiful *Andante,* knowing that it was to be immediately followed by its destruction. The darkness in the final movement races across the symphony like the shadow of an eclipse, obliterating cowbells and mountain streams as it covers the soundscape in a nothingness nailed down by hammer blows. All attempts at the major fail. Minor prevails, and the symphony ends with that deathly plucked bottom A on the basses. Do you see what comes after?' asked William.

Bernstein turned the page and said, 'Nothing.'

'That's right,' said William. 'The symphony doesn't end until you're sure that everyone in the auditorium has heard nothing.'

William told Bernstein that he'd visited the carpentry workshop at the Met and commissioned a large wooden hammer and anvil for the tallest and strongest player in the percussion section to make the hammer blows.

'Rodzinsky is not convinced you can manage this and would rather conduct it himself. If you're late again Rodzinsky will take over from you. Make sure you're early for the first rehearsal. I've got to go now to find you some cowbells.'

Bruno Zirato ran into William in the foyer and asked him where he was going.

'To get cowbells for the concert.'

'Someone else can get the cowbells. I need you in my office.' He called to someone up a ladder, 'What are you doing?'

'Cleaning windows, sir.'

'Here's $100. Get me a set of cowbells.'

'Where can I get cowbells?'

'Go to a music shop. If they haven't got any, go to a fucking farm!'

Zirato bounded up the stairs to his office two at a time and told William he needed a press release. 'I don't want any of the crap the Press Office writes. I need good crap.' Zirato told him to sit at his desk and write a hundred and fifty words and that he'd come back for them in half an hour.

William sat at Zirato's typewriter, took a sheet of New York Philharmonic notepaper and was about to write when he noticed on Bruno Zirato's desk the wire from the United States Rubber Company asking for a meeting to discuss sponsorship of New York Philharmonic performances conducted by Bernstein.

Then William wrote.

The eagerly awaited American premiere of Gustav Mahler's Sixth Symphony, to be conducted by Mr Bernstein at Carnegie Hall and broadcast coast-to-coast on Saturday afternoon, is now sold out. In advance of the radio broadcast, suppliers of electrical goods have reported a run on wireless receivers. The shelves at Macy's are empty and the store is hoping new stock arrives before Saturday's broadcast.

Great music binds our communities and those with wireless receivers will be opening their doors to neighbours in a display of good old-fashioned American hospitality. Meanwhile the offices of the New York Philharmonic have been inundated with offers of sponsorship from business leaders wishing to be associated with the huge public interest in the orchestra's forthcoming programmes, a development which guarantees the future of excellent music both in Carnegie Hall and on the air.

Enc. Photographs.

1) The empty shelves at Macy's.

2) Leonard Bernstein

(150 words)

There was a knock at the door. The window cleaner entered Zirato's office with a set of cowbells and said, 'They need cleaning, but they sound OK.'

'Where did you get them?' asked William.

'My brother works at the children's farm in the Bronx. I gave him the $100. He wants them back after the concert.'

When Zirato came back to the office he wanted to know what the bad smell was. William shook the cowbells and said it was goatshit. Zirato read the press release and told William it was bullshit – but beautiful. He called down to the box office and told them Saturday's concert was sold out.

'I know it's not,' he barked, 'but it is now! How many tickets are left? Then make a list of the next five hundred customers, tell them there's a chance they might get a return, then get back to them and sell the tickets on Saturday morning.

Then Zirato called the press office. 'Get down to Macy's with a photographer, buy all the radios and get a photograph of the empty shelves. I don't know what you're supposed to do with them. You think of something! That's what you're paid for! Give them to orphanages, hospitals, old peoples' homes, prisons. OK! Not prisons! Anywhere that'll interest the newspapers and make us look good. And clear a desk for Mr Hildebrand. He's joining the Press Office. He'll be down right away.' He slammed down the phone and told William to write the programme for Saturday's concert and not to go home until he'd done it. William did not remind Zirato that his home was on the top floor.

At 2.55pm on Saturday November 20th William walked onto the platform at Carnegie Hall and put Mahler's baton on the podium. At 3pm he kicked the conductor's ass and Mr Bernstein walked onto the platform to conduct Mahler's Sixth Symphony.

Mahler approved of the performance but was disappointed that William had indulged Mr Bernstein's wild imagination. William told Mahler that Mr Bernstein's imagination was the fuel that drove the performance. Mahler reminded William that he never had Hitler in mind when he wrote the first movement. 'All I had in mind was music.' William told Mahler that whatever he had in mind was no concern of the listener, who would make of it what they would. When William said he thought that Bernstein's was the best performance he had heard, Mahler raised an eyebrow. Mahler knew that William had heard the symphony three times before, each time conducted by himself. William told Mahler that there were many ways to conduct the symphony well and only one way of doing it poorly.

'And what way is that?' asked Mahler.
'The way you did it,' replied William.
'You would never have spoken to me that way when I was alive.'
'That's right,' said William.
'So. what's changed? asked Mahler.
'I have,' said William.
'You have,' agreed Mahler. 'But I haven't. A good teacher will tell you where to look but not what to see. I don't want you telling audiences what to hear. That's the problem I had with that miserable critic whose name I forget.'
'I've forgotten it too,' answered William.
'Whatsisname wasn't able to listen to music until someone told him what to hear.'
'I didn't tell Bernstein about Hitler. It was his own idea. All I told him was to keep his feet still,' protested William.
'What about the programme notes you wrote for Mr Zirato which referred to Hitler's Blitzkrieg, Kristallnacht, Alma's theme, cowbells ushering you into the spiritual world, and, most embarrassingly, that I am a prophet? – notes you gave to the radio announcer, the audience and the press, notes that made it into the reviews. The most shameless plagiarist was the music critic of the New York Tribune. His review,' said Mahler, 'could have been written by Avi Bacharach.'

William apologised and asked Mahler if he was cross.

'No. I was pleased with the music. I hadn't heard the symphony with the *Andante* after the *Scherzo* since the dress rehearsal in Essen.'

'Alma was furious,' said William. 'She was listening on the radio and when she heard the order of the inner movements she sent Mr Zirato a telegram to let him know she would have nothing further to do with the orchestra or Mr Bernstein.'

'She'll change her mind when she gets the royalty cheque. It'll be the first of many,' said Mahler. 'Bernstein will make her a very merry widow.'

William asked Mahler what he thought of the hammer blows.

'I'm glad you never told him that I originally had seven in mind. Three were quite enough. The big wooden mallet was good, but I didn't expect Mr Bernstein to join in. I was surprised when he stamped his own right boot onto the podium with the first hammer blow, and again when he accompanied the second blow by slamming both fists down onto the score with such force that he lowered his desk by eighteen inches and had to put on spectacles in order to see it. But that pales in comparison with the third mighty crash when Mr Bernstein leapt up from the podium, arms outstretched, landing at exactly the moment the hammer hit the anvil.... and you claim that you told him to keep his feet still! That boy will never keep still. And why should he? The orchestra were electrified. The audience were electrified. Over a million of them. This is big, William. Look after him.'

Knock at the door. William looked down at a child who gave him an envelope addressed to 'Avi Bacharach'.

'Who gave you this?' asked William.

'He said you'd know.'

'And what's your name,' asked William.

'Richard' answered the child.

William gave Richard a quarter.

Inside the envelope William found a ten-dollar bill. He was surprised to discover that Maurice was so cheap.

William travelled on the train with Leonard Bernstein from New York to Boston to conduct Bernstein's *Jeremiah* symphony. The invitation from the Boston Symphony Orchestra was an honour. To have his own work included on the programme was an even greater honour, and Bernstein had agreed to Boston's proposal without telling his employers at the New York Philharmonic. Bernstein sat opposite William and worked on his music for the Jerome Robbins ballet, *Fancy Free*. Bernstein looked up from his work and said to William, 'You would be amazed at the sound these notes make!' He laid his papers aside and fell asleep. William remembered the train journey to Leiden when Mahler sitting opposite had looked up from the manuscript of his Eighth Symphony and said those very same words.

The train made an unscheduled stop at Providence. A porter ran along the platform calling out, 'Mr Bernstein!'

William opened the carriage window. 'Yes?'

The young lad asked, 'Are you Mr Bernstein?'

William said, 'Yes.'

'Telegram for you, sir,'

William read, 'Rodzinski indisposed. Return to New York immediately.'

The boy waited for an answer.

William wrote three words on a piece of Bernstein's manuscript paper – 'Find someone else' – folded the paper, handed it to the porter and gave him a dollar. The porter told William that he had heard him on the radio, that it was a privilege to meet him, and then ran off. The station master waved his flag, and the train resumed its journey to Boston as Bernstein slept.

While Bernstein was sleeping William looked at his *Fancy Free* manuscript. The ballet had something of Duke Ellington about it – the swing that Mahler liked.

Bernstein went to see Rodzinsky to tell him how well *Jeremiah* had gone in Boston. Rodzinski hit Bernstein as hard as he could and threw him out of his office. Bernstein, holding his face, staggered up to William's room. William and the young boy, Richard, were making a model aeroplane. William gave the boy a dollar and sent him out to get a piece of meat for Bernstein's black eye. Richard wanted to know what sort of meat to get.

'Anything,' answered William.

'Not pork,' snapped Bernstein.

Richard ran off.

'What's up with Rodzinski?' asked Bernstein as William looked into his eye.

'He's impotent,' answered William.

'Sure as hell doesn't feel like it.'

'He wants to fire you and he can't.'

'What did I do?'

'You made yourself indispensable.'

'What am I supposed to do about that?'

'Look at the Philharmonic programme, then schedule your *Fancy Free* rehearsals for evenings when there are no concerts.'

'And the *Fancy Free* performances?'

'What about them?' asked William.

'I'm going to conduct them.'

'I'll get Bruno Walter to cover Carnegie Hall while you conduct *Fancy Free* at the Met.'

'You can fix that?'

'Yes.'

'You're a genius' said Bernstein.

'I know,' said William.

Bernstein took William in his arms and planted a kiss on his lips.

Young Richard came in with the meat. 'You're a pair of kissing queers and I'm only a kid. I could get damaged. I oughta report you!'

During the *Fancy Free* rehearsals William timed entrances and exits with a stopwatch and converted the seconds into bars which Bernstein composed on the spot while young Richard brought plasters for injured dancers, water for thirsty singers, towels for sweating musicians, and cigarettes for Mr Bernstein and himself. William told the child that only the composer was allowed to smoke. The child didn't pay any attention to William but ran here and there with a cigarette in his mouth, fetching and carrying whatever was urgently needed.

Before the first performance of *Fancy Free* at the Met William put Mahler's baton on the podium and kicked Bernstein ass.

'Did you ever kick Mahler's ass when he worked here?' asked Bernstein.

'No.'

'Why not?'

'He never performed any of his own music here.'

Bernstein smiled with satisfaction, thanked William, and strutted to the podium at the Met to conduct his own music. William watched from the wings and wondered if there was anything Leonard Bernstein couldn't do. Bruno Walter and Erica Mann had crossed the continent from Hollywood to look after Philharmonic business in New York while *Fancy Free* ran for a fortnight at the Met. Erica Mann sat beside young Richard in the director's box and after every show Erica, William and young Richard went to a diner for hot dogs and soda pop. Richard asked William if Erica was his girlfriend. William said she was. Young Richard was impressed.

All performances of *Fancy Free* were sold out. The audiences loved it. So did the critics. Bernstein received a note of congratulations from Rodzinski, who invited him to conduct the ballet music for a Philharmonic performance in Carnegie Hall in a programme to include Bernstein's own Jeremiah symphony. Bernstein also received an invitation to guest conduct the Los Angeles Philharmonic.

Rodzinski left a fat brown envelope on William's table and asked if there was anything else William needed.

'A good piano,' answered William.

'Of course,' replied Rodzinski.

'What's all that money for?' asked Mahler.

'Providing solutions to all the problems Mr Bernstein creates.'

'What are you going to do with it?'

'School fees for young Richard,' replied William.

'And the piano?'

'Lessons,' replied William.

It took five men all morning to hoist the baby grand up five floors to William's studio and one man an hour and a half to tune it.

'Wow!' said young Richard. 'Is that for Mr Bernstein?'

'No,' said William. 'It's for you!'

An hour later.

'Wow! said Mr Bernstein. 'Is that for me?'

'No,' said William, 'It's for young Richard. You're giving him piano lessons.'

An hour later Bernstein and young Richard were sitting at the piano with William Collins' *Scales and Studies for Beginners*. Bernstein told Richard that every key was a different room and that he should try to find his way around without bumping into the furniture. He said that each room had its own map, drawn to scale, and that each scale had its own shape. C was straightforward like an open book and you could wear F sharp like a black boot. D was a vase with two handles and E had four legs like two birds perched on a branch.

Everyday Bernstein and young Richard spent an hour together at the piano. William sat in the corner and listened to the young boy taking his fingers for a run up and down the keys. William took his own itchy fingers to the music store on West 57th Street where he bought a viola.

Bernstein did not invite William to accompany him to Los Angeles. William had discussed the programmes, marked the scores, and spent several days showing Bernstein how Mahler conducted his Fifth Symphony. At the station William felt awkward as Bernstein and two of his pals, Adolph Green and Berry Comden, boarded the train for the journey west as if they were going on holiday together. William was jealous. The train pulled out, taking the happy trio west, and William and Richard walked back to the studio. Richard sat at the piano and mourned the absence of his piano teacher by exploring the minor keys. It was not the best time for William to enrol young Richard in All Hallows, the Christian Brothers School in the Bronx.

While Richard was experiencing his first day at school a telegram arrived from Los Angeles for William.

'Need help. Come immediately. Lenny.'

William wired back, 'Find someone else', then went to collect Richard from school.

'What did you do at school?'

'Nothing.'

'Nothing? You must have done something.'

'One of the teachers showed me how to clean my knob.'

'To clean what?'

'To clean my knob. You pull on your foreskin, pinch it tight shut, pee into it, then let go without getting piss all over yourself. It rinses your knob and keeps it clean. I tried it and it tickles.'

'Did the teacher touch you?'

'No.'

When they got back to Carnegie Hall William wired Bernstein.

'Ignore last. On our way. William.'

The Los Angeles Philharmonic had provided Bernstein with a large house, a piano, and a car. William was pleased with the kitchen and the car. Richard was pleased with the piano. He practiced in the morning while Bernstein slept. Afternoons Bernstein rehearsed with the Philharmonic. Evenings he worked with Comden and Green on the new musical, *On the Town*. William cooked, did the laundry, emptied the ashtrays, drove Bernstein to the rehearsals, sat at the back of the hall and took notes, put Mahler's baton on the podium and kicked Bernstein's ass before the concerts, waited in the wings with a lighted cigarette and a bottle of twelve-year-old Bowmore and purred with pleasure during the half hour Bernstein spent every day sitting at the piano with young Richard.

Bernstein was given two days rehearsals for each concert. William told him that Mahler would have refused to present his Fifth Symphony with less than three days of rehearsals and would ask for four to ensure that he got three. Bernstein asked to meet the orchestra manager and succeeded in getting three for the Mahler concert but at the cost of losing one elsewhere in the programme William didn't think that outcome was satisfactory until he discovered that Bernstein had sacrificed a rehearsal of Tchaikovsky's Sixth.

Mahler did not think that a great loss and told William that Tchaikovsky's Sixth would go just as well without any rehearsal at all. Mahler went further and told William it would probably go even better without a conductor.

At the rehearsals for Mahler's Fifth William's heart ached with memories of Johnny as it always did when the solo first trumpet opened the symphony. The musicians were good readers and Bernstein let the players concentrate on the dots. It was all going well until the *Adagietto*, the movement for strings that William first heard when he sat behind the percussion with Johnny on a freshly painted step in the Grosser Musikvereinsaal in Vienna. William was puzzled at Bernstein's funereal pace. He assumed Bernstein took it slowly to allow the sight-reading strings the space to read their way through the movement.

With an hour to go at the end of the second rehearsal Bernstein dismissed everyone except the strings to work with them on the Adagietto. Bernstein took it even slower. William suffered until he could stand it no more and approached the podium. When Bernstein found William standing beside him he woke as if from a dream. The two men stared at each other. William whispered in Bernstein's ear. When Bernstein left the platform with William it appeared to the musicians that their young conductor had just received an urgent message. Bernstein was furious with William for interrupting his rehearsal.

'It's a song,' protested William.

'Where's the fucking singer?' hissed Bernstein, in a rage.

'At that tempo,' said William, you just strangled her!'

'OK, smart ass! You do it.'

William went to the podium and told the orchestra that the conductor wished to sit at the back of the hall and hear the movement played at a different tempo. William took Mahler's baton from his inside pocket, counted three silent bars, then opened the movement. Once he had set the tempo William found he was able to hold it back in some places and move it on in others. He completed the movement in less than half the time Bernstein had taken. As the last note died the orchestra players tapped their feet in appreciation.

William left the podium and returned to Bernstein sitting at the back who glared at him and growled, 'I like it!' Back on the podium Bernstein said, 'Thank you, gentlemen,' and he turned and offered William some brief applause, which the orchestra seconded.

Later that evening, after dinner, while Bernstein, Comden, and Green wrote *On the Town*, William and young Richard washed up. William set his bread to rise, and as the bread took shape, so did the musical. In the morning the room was strewn with empty bottles and overflowing ashtrays. The musical team surfaced around midday to the smell of coffee and fresh bread. William took Bernstein his breakfast in bed.

'The *Adagietto*'s a love song for Alma, isn't it?' said Bernstein.

'Yes,' said William.

'Come here,' said Bernstein, and pulling William towards him planted a huge kiss on his lips.

After he had showered, shaved, and dressed, Bernstein sat at the piano with young Richard for half an hour. William loved them both.

Meddi came to visit. She brought William a copy of an article from the *Los Angeles Times* about a Red Cross visit to Theresienstadt illustrated with a photograph of the orchestra. She pointed to the trumpet player. William recognised the trumpet but not the player. William looked closely, and still more closely, until all he could see were the dots that formed the player's face. No matter how William joined the dots of newsprint they did not form the face of the man he knew. Meddi, desperate to see Johnny, saw only Johnny, and convinced herself he was in the Theresienstadt orchestra, alive and safe. William knew the trumpet player was not Johnny, that Johnny was not in Theresienstadt and that he was likely to be in great danger. William kept his thoughts to himself.

While Bernstein, Comden, and Green worked on their musical. William, Meddi, and Richard did the housework. Richard told Meddi that Mr Bernstein was giving him piano lessons. Meddi thought he was a lucky boy. Richard asked Meddi if she was William's girlfriend. She said she was. William flicked soapy water into Richard's face. Richard told Meddi that William had another girlfriend called Erica. William flicked more soapy water at Richard. Meddi told Richard that William had a lot of girlfriends and that he was a good friend to many people. She reached for a towel to dry the soapy water from Richard's face.

Meddi told William that Anna had got married in London to Anatole Fistoulari, a Ukranian conductor, and she asked if William had heard from Lizzie. He hadn't.

'Who are Anna and Lizzie?' asked Richard.

'Two more girlfriends,' replied William.

Young Richard was impressed.

William looked at Erica's photograph of the Theresienstadt orchestra which showed Johnny sitting with his instrument in the trumpet section and compared it with Meddi's later picture in the *Los Angeles Times* which showed the same trumpet but a different trumpeter. He spent a troubled night dwelling on the difference between the two photographs.

On the Town conquered Broadway and Leonard Bernstein stood at the pinnacle of New York's musical and classical worlds. William left the first night party when he was too tired to party anymore. Bernstein didn't leave until first light. Instead of going home, drunk and dishevelled, he climbed the stairs to William's studio at the top of Carnegie Hall and woke William.

Koussevitzky had told Bernstein he could have the directorship of the New York City Symphony for the next season when Stokowski took a sabbatical, and then he could have the directorship of the Boston Symphony Orchestra as soon as Koussevitzky felt ready to hand it over to him, but on condition that he gave up writing musicals. It was one or the other. It was time to choose. Koussevitzky told him that if he chose Broadway then there was nothing he could do for him. Koussevitzky wanted to know if Bernstein's ambition was to work with a symphony orchestra or a theatre pit band. Koussevitzky insisted on an immediate answer. Bernstein told Koussevitzky what he wanted to hear and spent the first night party drowning his decision in alcohol.

Bernstein asked William why he couldn't work in both the theatre and the concert hall. William didn't know.

'At the very moment I get the prize it's snatched away from me because...because of what? The size of the band? The address of the auditorium? *On the Town* isn't just a musical. It's far too musical to be a musical.'

'Time will be the judge of that,' said William. 'Great music will be performed in fifty years, and in fifty years after that.

'So why does he insist I quit?'

'Because on Broadway you're only as good as your last hit. If the next one flops, you're finished.'

'There isn't going to be a next one.'

'The New York City Symphony's not a bad idea,' said William. 'You stay in New York. You choose your musicians. You choose your programme. The audience is young. You'll give Rodzinski and the

Philharmonic a run for their money and when you get the Boston orchestra you'll make music all over the world. Nobody's telling you not to compose. You just need to stay away from Broadway ...and maybe not forever.'

Bernstein fell asleep on William's sofa. He woke up to a piano and viola duet of Beethoven's *Ecossaises*. When William and young Richard finished Bernstein said, 'I didn't know you could play the viola.'

'Neither did I,' said William.

At the end of the war America welcomed back its victorious soldiers and Mr Bernstein had the pick of the demobbed musicians. They carried their instruments up five floors to William's room to audition for the new season of New York City Symphony concerts. William answered the door to a trumpet player who gave Bernstein the music for Tchaikovsky's *Danse Napolitaine* from *Swan Lake*. Bernstein sat at the piano ready to accompany him as the musician played a few scales to warm up his instrument. There was no mistaking the trumpet. It was Johnny's. William froze. William joined the dots and recognised the musician from Meddi's newspaper picture of the Theresienstadt orchestra with this stranger holding Johnny's trumpet. Bernstein, impressed with the audition, asked to see the instrument whose horn was raised from the horizontal through forty degrees. The trumpeter explained that he had designed and built it himself. Bernstein told him to give his name and address to William.

That night William went to visit Shai Levy at the address in Lower Manhattan which the trumpet player had given. Mr Levy was pleased to see William and assumed, correctly, that Mr Bernstein wanted to offer him a position in the New York City Symphony Orchestra.

William asked Mr Levy what he had done in the war.

'Bit of this, bit of that. Intelligence, top secret,' said Mr Levy tapping his nose.

William took the photograph of the Theresienstadt Orchestra from his pocket, the earlier newspaper picture with Johnny holding the trumpet that Erica Mann had given him, showed it to Mr Levy and said, 'The Theresienstadt Orchestra with you on trumpet.' Mr Levy looked at the picture and paled. 'That's you, isn't it?' said William, inviting Mr Levy to lie. 'There's no mistaking that trumpet.'

'Yes, that's me,' agreed Mr Levy, looking at the picture of Johnny.

'Well, said William, 'it's good for you that you play so well. I understand that all the musicians in the orchestra survived. Those who couldn't find a place in the orchestra were less fortunate. But now the war is over, Mr Levy, let's look forward to the future. May I inform Mr Bernstein that you would be happy to accept a position in his orchestra? He wants you to consider leading the trumpets.'

'Of course,' said Levy. 'Delighted and honoured to accept. And your name is...?'

'Hildebrand. Bill Hildebrand.'

They shook hands.

'Bill, can I ask you a favour. Do you have a copy of the picture?'

'No. This is the only one. But you can have it if you want. Can you do me a favour? Play me a note on your trumpet.'

Mr Levy took the trumpet from its case and playfully asked William what note he would like.

William hesitated as if making a difficult decision and then asked for middle C.

Shai Levy put the trumpet to his lips and William heaved against the instrument with all his weight and pushed the trumpet into the back of Levy's throat, breaking Levy's front teeth and knocking him over. With Levy on the floor and blood pouring from his mouth, William pushed and pulled the trumpet in and out of Levy's throat, breaking all his teeth. Levy's face was covered in blood and broken teeth. William pulled the horn out of Levy's mouth, but the mouthpiece was lodged in his throat. Levy couldn't breathe and his eyes were bulging. William put his hand into Levy's mouth, got hold of the mouthpiece and pulled it out. He wiped the blood from the trumpet on Levy's bedsheets and replaced the trumpet in its case. He put the picture of Johnny in the case beside the trumpet.

'You won't be needing this anymore,' said William, putting on his hat. 'Get out of New York tonight, Mr Levy. If you are still here in the morning I'll arrange for you to meet Johnny Stanko's friends. They are not as gentle as me.'

That night Shai Levy boarded the Staten Island Ferry wearing a scarf around his broken mouth and his pockets full of stones, Half-way across he slipped over the side and disappeared beneath the waves.

William and young Richard were reading the Arnold Bax Viola Sonata when Bruno Zirato knocked on the studio door and introduced William to young Richard's father. Zirato told William to conclude the matter quietly. The angry man told William he had come to take his runaway boy back to Chicago. He dragged Richard out from under the piano and pushed him through the door. The boy tried to run ahead of the angry parent who caught up with him and pushed him down the stairs. Whenever the boy tried to get up, he was pushed over again and so they went down five flights of stairs with the boy's feet hardly touching the ground.

William spent the night grieving in his armchair. He slept fitfully, dozing in and out of nightmares.

A ferociously angry eight-year-old Anna Mahler visited him in his sleep. She and William were in a hotel in Italy near the River Po. She scolded William for his failure to protect young Camillo from his angry father. 'Children are not the property of their parents,' she told him. 'To care for us is an obligation. Good intentions are worthless. No one gives a damn whether your heart's in the right place if you are never there when you are needed.'

Shai Levy floated into his sleep and the words that swam out of his mouth were fish. The fish told William not to judge anyone who had survived the camps. Survivors suffered their own judgment. The fish showed William the long queue of camp survivors, all suicides, lined up behind him in an outer circle of hell. Shai Levy pointed to a darker, deeper place where souls who had no experience of the camps and yet passed judgement on the survivors drowned in their own self-righteousness.

Then young Richard's father burst into the room and William woke up. The man held a pistol and demanded to know where his son was.

'He's not here,' answered William.

Young Richard's father fired a shot into the ceiling. 'Tell me where he is, Mr Hildebrand, or I'll blow your brains out!' A bullet whistled past William's ear.

'I don't know,' stammered William weakly, covering his face with his hands.

There was a third shot. William felt no pain. He wondered if he might be dead. He reached to his forehead and searched for the bullet wound, looked through his fingers and saw Rodzinski holding a pistol at the end of his outstretched arm. Richard's father lay on the floor. Behind Rodzinski stood Bruno Zirato carrying a greetings card, a pen, and a pained expression on his face. 'I told you to conclude the matter quietly. Here, sign this.' It was a card from the New York Philharmonic Orchestra offering Alma Mahler their deepest sympathy on the death of her husband, Franz Werfel. Behind Zirato stood Mr Bernstein who had come to give young Richard his piano lesson. Zirato stepped backwards over the body and got Bernstein to sign the card as well.

When William returned to his top floor studio after a morning's work in the Philharmonic's Press Office he found young Richard at the piano with a lady wearing a suit who introduced herself as Miss Coates. 'Leonard is so busy what with this and that and…I don't know… sometimes he doesn't know whether he's coming or going,' fussed Miss Coates. 'Leonard and I have looked at all his commitments, and you, my talented young man,' she said, turning to her new pupil, 'are a priority. I taught Leonard everything he knows, and now I'm taking over your lessons. And what, may I ask, is your role?' she asked. William described himself as a good friend and left the room so teacher and pupil could resume his studies. As she was leaving Carnegie Hall Miss Coates found William in the Press Office and told him, 'The man who died here was not young Richard's father. Piotr Tomasek died in Poland in 1938 and Richard came to America with the man who died here last week, his uncle, Stefan Tomasek, a very nasty piece of work, and good riddance. You appear to be *in loco parentis*. He is a talented young musician. Please discourage him from visiting jazz clubs. It has been a pleasure meeting him …. and you,' she added. 'I will come on Mondays, Wednesdays, and Fridays at 10am sharp. You will join us for the Friday lesson with your viola. And please see to it that he cleans his teeth before his lessons.' She offered William a limp handshake.

Bernstein asked William to look after the stage management for the City Symphony concerts. William told Bernstein that he was paid to fulfil that role for the Philharmonic at Carnegie Hall and that he should find someone else. However, after re-setting the stage for the second half of the Philharmonic's Carnegie Hall concert William was able to run to the New York Symphony's concert at the City Arts Centre to wait in the wings for Mr Bernstein with a lighted cigarette and a bottle of twelve-year-old Bowmore.

William could not imagine Miss Coates lighting cigarettes or pouring whisky for Bernstein. William, who had never felt threatened by the men in Bernstein's life, nevertheless felt uncomfortable with the arrival of this formidable piano teacher. Then Felicia Montealegre arrived on the scene, a Chilean actress who had fallen in love with Leonard.

The Federal Government sent Bernstein to Czechoslovakia to represent America at the Prague Spring Festival in 1946. William Hildebrand and Leonard Bernstein flew into Prague in a US Army plane which refuelled in Iceland, Greenland, Ireland, and France. Bernstein had never been abroad. William hadn't been to Prague since the premier of Mahler's Sixth. At the end of Bernstein's first rehearsal the orchestra played the overture to *The Bartered Bride*, an orchestral roar of freedom to welcome the American conductor.

Afterwards in the bar William sat with the trumpet section and asked after Johnny Stanko. They were reluctant to talk about Johnny with a stranger. Someone thought he might have gone to America. William assured them that Johnny Stanko was not in America. If he was in America William would have known. William showed them the picture of Johnny in the Theresienstadt orchestra and the musicians fell silent.

'Some bastard turned up in New York with Johnny's trumpet. I want to know what happened to Johnny!' demanded William.

Lenny came to the table with four beers and kissed each trumpeter on the head. 'That's some sound you guys make. You not only blew down the walls of Jericho, you blew them so damn far away nobody's ever gonna find them! Drink up, boys.'

As William was leaving, one of the trumpeters followed him. He wanted to know where he could find the musician who had Johnny's trumpet. William didn't know where he was.

'If you ever find out, let me know.' The trumpet player wrote down his address, gave it to William and said, 'I need to kill that bastard. He broke Johnny's teeth.'

William said, 'I don't know where he is, but he'll never play again.'

'How come?'

'Because I broke his teeth.'

'So maybe he's gone to Florida and eats mush? Do you know where Johnny went after that bastard broke his teeth?'

The trumpeter waited, glaring at William in contemptuous silence, then said, 'Auschwitz! You should've killed the bastard.'

When they checked into London's Hyde Park Hotel Bernstein went straight to bed with a throat infection. The London Philharmonic Orchestra was poor. The programmes Bernstein had to conduct were boring. The hotel was terrible. The food was awful. The weather was worse. Bernstein couldn't buy a scarf to wrap around his sore throat because he didn't have the necessary ration cards. He was, however, given a dose of penicillin for his sore throat and it worked miracles.

William got in touch with Anna Mahler who was living in London with her sixteen-year-old daughter by Paul Zsolnay and her two-year-old daughter by Anatole Fistoulari. She left the older daughter in charge of the younger and went out for dinner with William to celebrate her forty-second birthday. The Italian restaurants in London, which had become 'Swiss Restaurants' during the war, were now recovering their former identities, but with the food shortages they could not serve what William and Anna hoped to find. They settled at a table and reminisced about the meals they had shared in Italy. Anna remembered the restaurant in Rome where she told the priest who recommended she marry a prince that she intended to marry a priest. She confessed she might have been better with a prince or a priest rather than the second-rate conductors she had married, and congratulated William for teaming up with the very best –first her father, and now the young American wunderkind. William asked if she would like to hear Bernstein conduct the London Philharmonic, but she declined. Ever since she married Fistoulari she had given up listening to music.

They kept their coats on in the cold restaurant and warmed their hands by the candle stuck into the empty flask of Chianti. She told William that the summer in London lasted three weeks and didn't start until the end of July. She had decided to take her two girls to America where they could eat proper food and keep warm.

Anna asked after Meddi. William told her she worked in Hollywood designing clothes for Marlene Dietrich, Greta Garbo, Bette Davis and Ava Gardner.

William wanted to know if Anna had heard from Lizzie. Anna told him that Mrs Mancini was a widow. When Italy declared war on Britain Lizzie's husband, Tomasso, had been interned with their son, Guido, in prison camps which held the entire British population of Italian men. Father and son had been separated when Mr Mancini and another two thousand enemy aliens were deported to Canada. Mr Mancini was lost when the ship was torpedoed by a German U-boat and went down in the Atlantic. There were very few survivors. Guido had spent the war digging latrines with the Pioneer Corps and was now back in Edinburgh helping his mother. Mrs Mancini and her daughter, Elena, had managed to keep the shop open with the support of their Scottish neighbours. She felt no bitterness towards the police who had arrested her husband. They had known her husband as 'Tam the Man' and had apologised profusely to him and Lizzie on the night of his arrest, assuring them both that there must have been some kind of mistake, that he'd be home in the morning, and that it was all Mussolini's fault. As the tragedy unfolded the local police station did what they could to help Mrs Mancini. Her bitterness, a very concentrated grade of sour, was reserved for the Edinburgh Italians who had never acknowledged her because Tomasso had married outside the Italian community. Mr and Mrs Mancini had never attended the picnics, dances, and religious ceremonies organised by the Italian community, she had never become a Catholic, her husband had never observed his faith and the Edinburgh Italian community ignored them both. Her son, Guido, now twenty-six, was running the business. The café was always full of policemen from the local station and Guido employed a young lad to run with their bets to the dog track at Powderhall Stadium. Guido and his father had only ever spoken Italian to each other and so he was now fluent in two languages and two cultures. He was ambitious and could see no way forward for a cafe when milk, butter, sugar, and eggs were rationed. There were plenty of fish in the sea and potatoes under the ground and Guido tried to talk his mother into doing fish and chips. Guido pushed his way into the post-war reconstruction of Italian life in the city. He wanted to drive a nice car and he wanted the other Edinburgh Italians to see him driving it. On Sunday mornings he attended Mass at Saint Mary's Cathedral and took his sister, Elena, with him. Young Italian girls noticed him, and young Italian boys noticed his sister.

'I'd like to go and visit Lizzie,' said William.

'Leave her alone,' said Anna. 'The memory of you has a big place in her heart. The presence of you has none. You will only disturb her'.

Bernstein wanted to talk to Benjamin Britten about *Peter Grimes,* which Koussevitzky had commissioned for Tanglewood, so William went to Glyndebourne with Bernstein where Britten was rehearsing *The Rape of Lucretia.*

Then they went to Leicester where Bernstein conducted the Philharmonic. Leicester was even more dreary than London. Back in London and insufferably lonely, Bernstein cruised Soho from one rejection to another. No one had heard of him. There were no parties. The orchestra couldn't play in tune. The only thing that Bernstein enjoyed in England was the *Times* crossword which William brought to him with his breakfast every morning. Before William opened the curtains to let in the day Bernstein got William to sing out a clue.

'One across. Composer of Harlem shuffle. Five letters.'

'Mahler,' answered Bernstein.

'Mahler never composed the Harlem Shuffle,' objected William.

'I know,' yawned Bernstein. 'This coffee smells awful.'

Bernstein couldn't wait to get back to the States but was invited to extend his stay for a week to conduct *Fancy Free* for Ballet Theatre's Independence Day Gala at the Royal Opera House on July 4th.

William took the train to Edinburgh.

There are special city panoramas that lift your heart. Perhaps the Manhattan skyline from an incoming transatlantic liner or the Rialto from a vaporetto steaming towards San Marco, but for William nothing matched Edinburgh's castle rearing up behind the Scott monument as you leave Waverley station. William looked up at the early afternoon sunshine and wondered at the city centre spread out before him in a deep green valley which rises to the tall tenements standing on a ridge to your left climbing to the castle on its massive rock, and on the right, the gardens and a bustling main street overlooked by the monument to Walter Scott.

William made his way down the hill to Pitt Street. He found Mancini's café closed and boarded up. William went into Clark's bar next door and bought himself a beer. He asked the barman about the café and discovered, despite the barman's almost impenetrable accent, that it had been boarded up ever since the window was smashed in the anti-Italian riots the day Mussolini declared war. Mrs Mancini had nevertheless kept her boarded-up café open until the family moved away six months ago. The barman didn't know where they'd gone.

William finished his drink and walked down the hill past a butcher's shop with a display of rabbits hanging in the window to a newsagent at the corner where he bought a paper. The newsagent told William that Mancini's shop had been let to a local businessman who intended to retail electrical goods. She told him that Mrs Mancini's son, Guido, had married one of the Toscani girls and was now managing Toscani's fish and chip shop in Grindlay Street. The family lived above the shop.

William found the chip shop which stood opposite the Usher Hall and the Royal Lyceum Theatre. William waited in the queue which ran from the counter, out the door and onto the pavement. Through the window he immediately recognised Guido and Elena. He saw Lizzie in their eyes and in the way they moved. Guido was dipping fish in batter and his sister was serving the customers. William looked around but couldn't see Lizzie. When Elena asked if she could help, William could barely speak. Staring into Elena's eyes, William saw only her mother and wanted to ask Elena about Lizzie but choked and asked for something to eat.

'Fish?' suggested Elena.

'Yes.'
'And chips?' suggested Elena.
'Yes.'
'Salt and sauce?'
'Yes.'

She shook the salt cellar over his fish supper and splashed it with a thin brown sauce that smelled of vinegar before wrapping it in a pink newspaper with last week's football results. He gave her half a crown and got sixpence change. He wanted to tell her that he had hidden with her mother under a tarpaulin among Herr Trenker's cheeses when they had successfully smuggled Lizzie out of Austria and into Italy at the outbreak of the first war, but he bit his lip and pointed to a large jar of pickled eggs. She climbed onto the first step of a stool and reached up for the jar. Now William could see her from head to foot. He gazed up at the grace and elegance of the girl who was the same age as her mother when William had waved his last goodbye. He gave her back the sixpence to pay for the egg. She gave him a threepenny bit change and looked towards the next customer. It was now or never. William unbuttoned his lip and in a voice that was far too loud asked after Mrs Mancini. 'She's very well, thank you,' said Elena and she whispered something to her brother. Guido approached William with a generous open smile and asked if he might tell his mother who was asking after her. William's jaw locked, and his mouth fixed open as if he was about to howl. Guido asked, 'Are you all right?' William exhaled, nodded, whispered "Vorbei", and left the shop. He walked a few paces towards Lothian Road when someone tapped him on the shoulder and gave him the fish supper and pickled egg he'd left on the counter.

Mr Bernstein worked for five weeks in Tanglewood with a cast of students on the premier of *Peter Grimes*. During those hectic weeks William visited Tanglewood as often as he could get away from Carnegie Hall. He drove the car, fetched and carried, emptied ash trays, provided food and, largely invisible, was ignored by everyone except Miss Coates, who treated him like a servant. At the first night party Benjamin Britten declared the premiere 'not bad for a bunch of students.' The young English composer got Mr Bernstein's younger brother to sit on his knee. Felicia Montealegre, now Mr Bernstein's fiancée, felt increasingly lonely as she moved from one guest to another without finding anyone to talk to. She eventually settled on William. They sat outside. She offered William a cigarette. William declined.

'My fiancé won't take one from me either. What's the matter with my cigarettes?'

'They're tipped,' answered William. 'He doesn't smoke tipped cigarettes.'

Felicia tore the tip off a cigarette and offered it to William.

'Thanks, but I don't smoke.'

She threw it away and lit a tipped cigarette for herself.

'Do you disapprove of me?'

'Smoking?' asked William.

'No. Getting married to Lenny.'

'No.'

'Then you're the first person I've met tonight. His piano teacher disapproves of me because there's only room for one woman in his life and that's her. His sister disapproves of me for the same reason. His mother and father disapprove of me because I'm not Jewish. All his boyfriends disapprove of me because I'm a girl. The only one of them that isn't in love with Lenny is the smug English pervert who fancies Lenny's little brother. I suppose you're in love with Lenny, too.'

'We're good friends,' answered William.

'That makes a change' she said, exhaling a lungful of smoke. 'I didn't understand that I would be sharing my fiancé with so many others.'

William took Felicia's hand and told her that Mr Bernstein certainly loved her, that he loved women, that he loved men too, and that Mr Bernstein would be no stranger to any other category of human sexuality. 'He loves everybody.'

'Is it possible to be married to someone like that?' she asked.

William told Felicia stories about the married couples he knew – Alma and Gustav Mahler, Richard and Pauline Strauss, Alma and Franz Werfel, and Anna Mahler, four times married and still counting.'

'Did you ever marry?' she asked.

'No.'

'Have you ever been in love?'

'Yes.'

'With other men?' asked Felicia.

'Yes.'

'Do you think it helps that I look like a boy?'

'You don't look like a boy.'

'Look at me! Tall! Short hair. No curves. I am a boy!'

'That's not why Mr Bernstein finds you attractive. He finds you attractive because you are a beautiful woman.'

Bernstein came into the garden. 'There you are! What are you doing out here?'

'I'm getting to know your friend, William. He's my favourite of all your friends.'

'I want you to meet the composer.'

'I'd rather stay here with William.'

'I need your help,' pleaded Mr Bernstein. 'He's got my baby brother on his knee and I need you to distract him while I get Burton out of there.' Mr Bernstein put his arm around Felicia and swept her out of her chair and back into the house. She turned to William and said, 'I'll be right back.'

William waited. When he heard four hands at two pianos playing Gershwin's *Rhapsody in Blue* he went inside and discovered Bernstein at one piano and Richard Tomasek at the other. Felicia was standing close to Bernstein who played all the notes that Gershwin wrote. Tomasek improvised, quoting Bach, Chopin, Liszt, and, much to everyone's amusement, Bernstein himself. Huge applause from everyone except Helen Coates. Then Richard launched into a Cole Porter medley and Bernstein croaked the words. Richard moved from one key to another but could not find one that suited Bernstein.

February 14th 1947

Valentine's Day, and the newspaper was full of small ads placed by men professing their love for women. A small headline caught William's eye.

Toothless corpse dredged from the Hudson.

Police are unable to identify the badly decomposed human remains found in shallow water. They are appealing for information. A police spokesman said 'One possible clue to the identity of the deceased male is the unusual condition of his teeth, all of which were broken. The deceased was wearing a leather jacket which was made in Poland. The zipped pockets were full of stones. The death is not being treated as suspicious.

CHAPTER 53

On Tour with Bernstein

Miss Coates summoned William to her office and informed him that he would be travelling to Palestine at the beginning of April with Mr. Bernstein, who had accepted a two-week engagement in Tel Aviv. Mr Bernstein's parents would accompany their son and William would be responsible for the safety, health, and welfare of the party. Thereafter, William would travel with Mr Bernstein to Vienna, Prague, Paris, Brussels, and The Hague.

William nodded in silent acknowledgement. This instruction would require him to resign his position at the New York Philharmonic, whose season did not finish until the end of April. He suggested that young Richard should join the party for the valuable experience such a trip would afford. She demurred, informing William that it was not a holiday but a politically sensitive, historically significant, and vital contribution to the building of the Jewish state, that Mr Bernstein's parents were pilgrims travelling to the Chosen Land to witness the birth of the nation, and that it was William's responsibility to ensure that their pilgrimage did not detract from their son's professional responsibilities. She told William that it was Mr Bernstein himself who required his attendance. William wondered if perhaps she had wanted to go herself and had been passed over. 'I will stay here,' she continued with an air of martyrdom, 'and take responsibility for Master Tomasek's piano studies.'

Bernstein asked William if Miss Coates had talked to him about Tel Aviv.

'Yes.'

'You're coming then?'

'Yes.'

'Great!'

William told Bernstein that he had told Bruno Zirato about his new job and handed in his notice.

'Good,' said Mr Bernstein, who had given no thought to William's position with the New York Philharmonic. Mr Bernstein recovered himself in time to suggest that William speak to Miss Coates about joining the payroll. William told Mr Bernstein that he would not speak to Miss Coates, and that he did not want to work for Miss Coates, but he was happy to work for Mr Bernstein.

They left New York on Wednesday April 9th and crossed the Atlantic on the SS America. On the first day into the voyage William told Mr Bernstein that he had arranged for his parents to travel as the captain's guests, with places at his table and a suite in his private quarters.

'My darling boy!' exclaimed Mr Bernstein as he hugged William close to him. 'However did you manage that?'

'You will be giving a concert on Sunday afternoon for the Sailors' Pension Fund. Mahler always gave a concert for the Sailors' Pension Fund.'

Bernstein's parents were thrilled with the new arrangements. Lenny took great pleasure in their delight, and all the credit for the arrangement.

In Tel Aviv William looked at the Mediterranean rolling onto the Palestinian shore and saw the same sea that washed the coast at Marseilles and Amalfi. When he walked along the boulevards that skirted the promenade he looked up at buildings that were European, although rather more modern than the French or Italian seaside architecture. A few steps back from the sea in the narrow lanes of the old town William found himself in the Levant, where market traders bought and sold fruit and vegetables, meat and fish, nuts, gold and silver, copper, tin, metalwork and jewellery, clothes and textiles, carpets and birds, flowers, shrubs, lemon trees, orange trees, olive trees, coffee, tea, tobacco, candles, incense and furniture, with more and yet more around every corner. The stalls were under canvas stretching across the narrow lanes from one rooftop to another and shadowed by the tenements on either side, so that every market street felt like the aisle of a tall, tented cathedral. In the morning William rose early while Bernstein slept late. He explored the souk, inhaling the exotic perfumes and admiring the flowing colourful clothing which did not identify the various brands of Judaism, Christianity and Islam among the buyers and sellers. The traders, all brown-skinned, dark-eyed, swarthy Semitic people worked together in the vast sprawling market. William wished he was dressed in a long flowing tunic with sandals on his feet and a knotted headscarf against the sun rather than the costume of the German, Polish, Czech, and Russian Jews who had arrived in Palestine over the last twenty years and lived in the modern white buildings along the seafront, a few metres away but a world apart from the Palestinians, Armenians, Egyptians, Turks, Greeks, Spaniards, and Lebanese who lived cheek by jowl in the old town, sat together in cafés, smoked, drank tea and traded to ports throughout the Mediterranean and into the Black Sea.

Around 11am Bernstein drank his coffee with a sweet and savoury breakfast of Turkish delight and olives, or halva and capers, baclava and anchovies, sugared almonds and humous, or bowls of deep-fried pasta dipped in honey with a soft goats' cheese. Bernstein, who would die for a cigarette, ate the breakfast that William brought him from the souk before he lit up his first of the day. He read the scores and in the afternoon rehearsed for the evening concerts which were performed in Tel Aviv's cinemas. The audiences loved their young, handsome, Jewish, American hero. The adulation for Lenny went far beyond anything he had experienced in America and after every concert the curtain calls went on and on and on well into the night. William waited in the wings with a lighted cigarette and a chalice of the twelve-year-old Bowmore, and although Lenny puffed between every call, William cut out the whisky after Lenny returned for his tenth bow – a cue for Lenny to call out to the orchestra, 'C'mon everybody, on your feet, 'cos this is everybody's show!'

Leonard Bernstein only once referred to the explosions. He told William it was remarkable how many of them coincided with his downbeat. At first William thought they must be fireworks but soon came to understand that there was a power struggle going on. The violence became more evident when Bernstein took the orchestra into the fertile hinterland to perform for the troops. The musicians played in the open air for soldiers who arrived in tanks and armoured vehicles, enjoying a day's furlough from the job of establishing the Jewish state. The orchestra, uniformed in concert blacks, played a repertoire of European music for the military, uniformed in desert khaki.

The Palestine Symphony Orchestra begged Leonard Bernstein to be their permanent conductor, but he had commitments in Europe before returning to America where the directorship of the Boston Symphony Orchestra would become vacant upon Koussevitzky's retirement.

On receiving intelligence that the Vienna Philharmonic Orchestra was an unregenerate Nazi organisation that mirrored the feelings of the Viennese, Bernstein cancelled his Austrian visit and went directly from Tel Aviv to Prague.

After the first Czech concert William joined the trumpet section in the bar. They ignored him. William interrupted their conversation to tell them that the guy who hurt Johnny was dead.

'You sure?' said the first trumpeter.

'Yes.'

'How do you know?'

'I killed him.'

'How did you kill him?'

'Drowned.'

'You drowned him?'

'Yes.'

'How did you feel when you drowned him?'

'Better.'

'I feel better too.' said the first trumpeter.

'So do I,' said the second trumpeter.

'So do I,' said the third.

'So do I,' said the fourth.

They banged their glasses on the table in applause and ordered William a beer.

In Paris William brought Mr Bernstein his breakfast in bed – coffee, croissants, and yesterday's London *Times*. Bernstein turned greedily to the crossword.

'Musical would be fine if shortened. Two letters. OK.'

'OK?' asked William.

'Yes,' said Bernstein. 'Oklahoma was too long. Now it's shortened, it's OK. This coffee's great!'

In Brussels Bernstein performed Aaron Copeland's Third Symphony. He shortened the final movement, cutting eight bars. Mr Copeland did not think it was OK.

In Amsterdam William showed Bernstein how Mahler got the Dutch orchestra to trip over itself at the beginning of his Fourth Symphony. The sleigh bells set the tempo which suddenly drops as the strings slowly climb three steps to the door of the symphony which they enter one after the other, stumbling over the threshold. Bernstein and the orchestra loved this mischief music-making so much they rehearsed these opening bars again and again for their own pleasure. William told Bernstein the difficulty Mahler faced in getting the leader of the orchestra to play the *scordatura* passages. Even if he agreed to play it badly in rehearsal, he always, to Mahler's frustration, played it well in performance. In Holland the orchestral leader had a sense of humour and readily agreed to Bernstein's request, to 'play it like you can't play it.' He did, and the entire string section applauded as their leader scraped and scratched his instrument like a novice. In the third movement Bernstein confidently led the orchestra from neo-classical Vienna to the outer reaches of the solar system and at the end of the fourth movement Lenny kissed the solo soprano long and hard and full on her lips.

Before leaving Holland William made a pilgrimage to Leiden in memory of Mahler's visit to Freud and bought himself a mature hard cheese spiced with caraway seeds.

Back in the USA Bernstein opened his new Symphony Orchestra season. The city insisted the orchestra support itself from ticket sales and, in return for limited funding, insisted on low ticket prices to attract a younger audience. Consequently, Bernstein could never afford sufficient rehearsal time and the quality of the playing suffered in comparison with its more illustrious Philharmonic neighbour. Despite the lack of funds Bernstein included Mahler's Second Symphony in the autumn programme

The New York Philharmonic programmed Mahler's Ninth, conducted by Bruno Walter, on the same night as the New York Symphony was scheduled to play Mahler's Second. Walter wanted to hear Bernstein conduct the Second and Bernstein wanted to hear Walter do the Ninth. Avi Bacharach wrote an article for the *Herald Tribune* arguing that New Yorkers must be permitted the opportunity to attend both concerts and that the orchestras should therefore perform on consecutive nights. The two managements agreed, and Bernstein suggested they toss for who went first. Walter, not inclined to gamble, yielded precedence to the young conductor, so the New York Symphony went first with Mahler's Second.

Before the concert William placed Mahler's baton on the podium although Bernstein had still never used it. Bernstein walked to the podium, acknowledged the orchestra and then turned to the audience and announced that there would be a short interval after the first movement. He opened the symphony without singers in the choir stalls and without soloists on the platform. After the first movement the audience sat in silence as Bernstein left the platform. The silence was broken by the obligatory snuffles and coughs. The musicians sat on stage and waited. When the musicians started to chat amongst themselves the audience did the same as the chorus filled the choir stalls and three of the four soloists took their places beside the conductor's podium. Bernstein returned and opened the second movement, a delightfully straightforward dance interrupted by three interludes that were diabolically far from straightforward. William had told Bernstein the first part is a waltz danced in a ballroom and the second part is the same but seen through the distorted glass. The third movement, a mischievous ballet where Christianity dances with Judaism, was followed by a song in which the singer tells an angel to get out of her way because 'We are from God and to God we will return'. The last movement started with the choir still seated and silent. An off-stage horn had the audience looking around. The last creatures on earth, two birds, played by piccolo and flute, circled in the air above the seated choir who whispered 'Auferstehn' so quietly there were corners in the hall where it was inaudible. One of the sopranos in the front row of choristers soared away from her colleagues and peeling away from them like an acrobatic pilot in an aerial display she made her way slowly through the orchestra walking, singing, and finishing her solo precisely as she reached her place beside the other three soloists. The choir remained seated until their final fortissimo 'Auferstehn', when a hundred singers sprang to their feet and fired a huge 'Auferstehn' into the hall to awaken the dead, commanding them to 'rise again'. The final drama occurred between the penultimate and last notes of the symphony when Bernstein leapt into the air and filled the auditorium with the sound of himself crashing down onto the podium before bringing in the last triumphant sound. The audience also leapt to its feet, loudly cheering, and gave the symphony a standing ovation. William was waiting in the wings for Bernstein with the usual glass of twelve-year-old Bowmore and a lighted cigarette. Bernstein returned to the wings thirteen times for thirteen draws on his cigarette and thirteen swigs of whisky before returning to the audience with an enthusiastic alcohol-fuelled 'C'mon everybody – on your feet, 'cos this is everybody's show.' Nearly everybody on the platform heard the mezzo soprano hiss, 'You could have fuckin' fooled me!'

In the green room Walter congratulated Bernstein on a superb performance and told him Mahler would have loved the staging, especially the interval between the first and second movements. He congratulated Bernstein on placing the solo soprano in the front seat of the women's choir and giving her a solo procession to the front of the platform as she sang. And as for the moment the choir leapt to their feet before that final 'Auferstehn!'? Walter had never seen anything like it but knew that Mahler, the director of the Opera, would have approved.

He did not comment on Lenny's 'leap.' Bernstein was very happy with Walter's comments on the staging of the symphony and did not acknowledge that William had choreographed the entire performance, except for the leap at the end.

William sat next to Mr Bernstein during the following evening's Philharmonic concert. Between each of the movements nobody coughed, no one cleared their throat, no one shuffled in their seat, and the silence generated by each movement was profound. Despite his own success on the previous evening with Mahler's Second, Bernstein was beginning to feel jealous of Walter's Ninth, which Mahler himself had never conducted. During the second movement Ländler Bernstein couldn't keep still and danced in his seat. Bernstein's dancing became more pronounced during the third movement *Rondo*. William laid his hand on Bernstein's knee and became Bernstein's dancing partner. Bernstein laid his own hand firmly over William's hand. At the beginning of the final movement the audience recognized the hymn *Abide with Me* but were taken aback by the adventurous harmonic structure that underpinned the familiar melody. Bernstein admired Irving Berlin's skill with scissors and paste when he recognised the string arrangement for the Bing Crosby recording of *A White Christmas*. Bruno Walter stood immobile with his baton raised during the last few bars of the symphony, leaving the musicians to find their own way to the close. No one was sure when the symphony ended as the last sounds wormed their timeless way into the consciousness of the audience where they would unravel eternally. As the audience listened to the silence Bruno Walter stood immobile and remained still for … no one knew how long. Time had stopped. After an eternity, a small shuffling sound, a throat clearing, and a cough, Carnegie Hall broke into a respectful, warm, and then lengthy applause. Walter returned three times, brought the orchestra to its feet, and then the musicians and conductor left the podium. When the applause finished the audience remained in the auditorium, heads bowed in contemplation. From that moment Bernstein formed the belief that whereas Mahler had written the first eight symphonies for himself, he had written this ninth symphony for him.

Bernstein congratulated Walter on the risks he had taken with the tempo, especially the mad career at the end of the *Rondo* when the symphony nearly spilled over, and the remarkable the long silence at the end. Bruno Walter told Bernstein that Mahler had asked for four and a half minutes of silence. William, who knew that Mahler had asked for no such thing and that he, William, had conceived the silence that follows the symphony all by himself, added, 'Maybe two or three seconds more than that.' Bernstein said, 'Someday someone will be brave enough to try it.'

Walter suggested Bernstein use a baton. Mahler always did. 'I like using my fingers,' said Bernstein.

Walter said, 'Your fingers don't point to very much except perhaps to the musician who is ready to make his entry. Your pointed finger reassures the audience that you are on the right page but annoys the musician who can read his part perfectly well. In any case, if he or she has fallen asleep, your pointed finger comes too late to wake them up. Mahler used the fingers of his left hand, his eyes, his eyebrows, his mouth, his head, shoulders, arms, hands, hips, knees, and baton, and never made a noise with his feet.'

The reviews compared Bernstein's Second unfavourably with Walter's Ninth. When William found Bernstein surrounded by the papers looking glum he told him these poor reviews were nothing compared to the stinkers Mahler got. Bernstein cheered up and tossed aside the papers as if he cared about the reviews even less than Mahler.

'Bruno told me Mahler would have loved it,' said Bernstein. 'That's good enough for me.'

'You're right,' said William, who had discussed the concert at length with Mahler. 'Mahler loved it all, except for the big leap at the end.'

'What leap?'

'You jumped up and crashed two steel-capped Cuban-heeled cowboy boots onto the podium in unison.'

Bernstein, who had no memory of the leap, didn't know what William was talking about.

The Palestine Symphony Orchestra kept calling Bernstein with invitations, but the security in the region had deteriorated. Last year's bombs were Jewish. This year there were Arab bombs and Bernstein didn't feel it was safe to return. Besides, Koussevitzky was due to retire and Bernstein had an eye on the Boston orchestra. Also, there were invitations to guest-conduct orchestras all over the world, even from Vienna and Berlin. However, the German and Austrian orchestras did not take to Bernstein's style and neither of the orchestras wanted to play Mahler's Second Symphony which Bernstein was owning as a signature piece. Bernstein understood that their coolness towards him reflected the Nazism that persisted in Vienna and Berlin. The bad reviews in the Austrian and German press pushed Bernstein to identify more closely with Mahler and he shrugged off their anti-Semitism as he imagined Mahler had done. William, however, noticed a difference. Whereas Mahler had conducted orchestras that contained large numbers of Jewish musicians, the orchestras in Austria and Germany in 1948 contained none. The Jewish musicians had all been murdered. There were, instead, musicians in the Berlin and Vienna orchestras who only four years previously would have marched Bernstein and his family into a gas chamber. There were no longer any synagogues in Vienna or Berlin.

In Vienna William walked the streets revisiting his youth. He stood outside Mahler's apartment in Auenbruggergasse. He looked up at the windows of the apartment he had shared with Johnny. He stopped at Freud's door and visited Alma's mother's apartment. He discovered that Carl Moll had killed himself when the Russians took Berlin. He drank coffee in the café where Suttner and the claquers had often met to pour scorn on Mahler.

Although Helen Coates had booked all the travel and accommodation, William called ahead to the Hotel Continental in Munich and, speaking French, booked a suite for himself. He told the receptionist which suite he required and was delighted to discover it was available. He asked the hotel to install a piano. William hired a car and drove Bernstein from Vienna to Munich. Bernstein sat in Mahler's seat as William told him stories about journeys he and Mahler had made together and how Mahler had always turned the heater up to imagine he was sitting at home in front of the fire. At the Hotel Continental William showed Bernstein to his suite and told him they were the same rooms Mahler had used when he came to Munich for the premier of his Eighth and he gave Bernstein a copy of the piano reduction. Bernstein took William in his arms and kissed him. Apart from the hours rehearsing and performing with the Munich orchestra Bernstein never left Mahler's suite, where he sat at the piano reading Mahler's Eighth. The receptionist who had given the hotel's best rooms to a Jew was fired.

They visited the Berlin camp for displaced persons run by the Americans. The camp orchestra consisted entirely of Jews. The musicians pleaded with Bernstein to accept the musical directorship of the Palestine orchestra and to take them to Israel with him.

Bernstein wanted William to drive him to Italy and so the pair of them cancelled Helen Coates's travel arrangements and Bernstein sat in the car in Mahler's seat in front of the hearth composing as they drove from Berlin to Milan. William walked the streets where he had once fled the pitched battles between communists and fascists.

Back in the USA Miss Coates, who was trying to keep control of the Bernstein finances, was outraged to discover the expenses William had run up in Europe – hiring a car, booking the Hotel Continental suite and now ordering the London *Times* to be delivered to Mr Bernstein in New York. William suggested she discuss the matter with Mr Bernstein. When she told Bernstein that he was spending more than he earned and that it had to stop, he fired her.

Koussevitzky announced his retirement. The Boston Board decided, to Bernstein's surprise, not to hire him. He immediately got in touch with the Palestine Orchestra and offered to conduct their autumn season. Before setting off for Palestine Bernstein re-hired Miss Coates to make all the arrangements for the travel and accommodation and instructed her to work on a deal with MGM, who wanted to film *On the Town* with Gene Kelly and Frank Sinatra.

Bernstein and William arrived in Haifa to find the Promised Land nervously surrounded by hostile Arab states. The British had lost control of their mandate and were trying to extricate themselves before they suffered any more casualties at the hands of the Irgun terrorists who had assassinated the UN mediator, made war on Arabs and defied the United Nations in defence of the settlements they had made on Arab land. The Palestine Symphony Orchestra changed its name to the Israeli Symphony Orchestra. Bernstein arranged for the German text of Mahler's Second Symphony to be translated into Hebrew and mounted a huge production which he performed for audiences in Tel Aviv and Jerusalem and gave al fresco performances in occupied territories for settlers and soldiers. 'Rise Again' called the choir to its Jewish audience. Bernstein's 'Rise Again' was not addressed to the dead but to the living, urging them to rise and take the land God had promised.

William, in his suit and leather shoes, did not feel safe visiting the Levantine traders in the souk for ingredients to prepare exotic breakfasts as he had done during their previous visit. Unlike Bernstein, William had no emotional connection with this land or its armed inhabitants.

William declined the arrangement to travel in the middle of the night without lights to the airport in a bullet-proof car and he cancelled the flight to Rome, making alternative arrangements to sail with Bernstein from Tel Aviv to Italy where Bernstein had been engaged to conduct the Santa Cecilia orchestra before flying home to the USA.

During the voyage Bernstein bathed naked under the Mediterranean sun and listened to William's hilarious account of Mahler's experience with the Santa Cecilia Orchestra. William told Bernstein that the Roman musicians who turned up for rehearsals were the poor readers, that the good readers only turned up for the concerts, that it was a small orchestra because many of the musicians were required to attend family weddings, christenings, first communions or funerals, and that the concert master was likely to be on holiday. Bernstein roared with laughter and didn't believe a word of it.

On a map the Mediterranean looks small, but from the top deck of the ship where Bernstein lay sunning himself, it appeared to be a vast ocean with no sight of land until they reached Italy's Adriatic Coast. William and Bernstein stepped ashore in Venice. They had an hour in Venice before taking the train to Rome from the new Santa Lucia railway station. William tried to persuade Bernstein to have lunch in a fish restaurant he knew near the Campo San Barnabo but Bernstein wanted to look at the opera house. As the guide showed them around La Fenice Bernstein told William that one day he would conduct an opera there.

'Which one?' asked William.

'I haven't composed it yet,' replied Bernstein.

CHAPTER 54

Johnny Stanko's Trumpet

Back in the USA William and Bernstein set off for MGM's Hollywood studios. Bernstein needed to edit *On the Town* to fit Gene Kelly's choreography.

William turned up at Meddi's with Johnny's trumpet in its case. She put the case on the table and opened it. Neither of them spoke as Meddi ran her fingers over the brass tubing. She fingered the valves. She put her ear to the trumpet as you would listen to the sound of the waves in a seashell. Then she folded her arms around the trumpet, held it to her breast and silently sobbed, rocking slowly backwards and forwards in her chair. The three of them – Meddi, William and the trumpet – sat together in silence for an hour or more until William moved his chair close to Meddi and took her in his arms. He held her, she held the trumpet, and with his free hand he gently stroked the brass tubing as she had done. William thought about threesomes – Father, Son and Holy Ghost; Jesus, Mary and Joseph; Heaven, Hell, and Purgatory; beginning, middle, and end, the triad whose middle note steps down from major to minor in its bitter sweetness. Meddi had no such thoughts and concentrated only on feeling the cold at the tips of her fingers as she caressed the metal of the instrument she cradled in her arms. It was nearly midnight when William realised Meddi had fallen asleep. He left her holding the trumpet and went out into the street to find a cab.

The next morning he called MGM and discovered that Meddi had not shown up at work. He took a cab to her door. He waited outside and listened to her trying to get a note out of a trumpet. Sometimes she found a note but then her lip gave way and the sound collapsed. William waited until it sounded like she might be taking a break. He knocked on the door. Meddi – wide awake, alert, and excited – opened the door and announced she was learning to play the trumpet. Her upper lip was bruised. William advised her to find a teacher before she hurt herself.

On the table there was a jewellery box. She opened it and showed William the tooth she had found in the mouthpiece. Meddi gazed at the last remains of Johnny, William looked at the last remains of Shai Levy, the man who had sent Johnny to his death.

'Johnny's dead,' she told him.

'Yes,' said William.

'Where did he die?'

'Auschwitz,' said William.

'How did you get the trumpet?'

'A friend of Johnny's from Theresienstadt brought it to me in New York,' lied William.'

Meddi got her photograph of the Theresienstadt orchestra and pointed to the musician she had long suspected was not Johnny.

'Him?'

'Yes,' said William.

'Please say thank you to him from me.'

On June 15th Bernstein went with William to Alma Mahler's Beverly Hills mansion to celebrate Anna's birthday. Bernstein, unhappy with the way MGM was developing *On the Town*, was in a bad mood. William admired the 1948 Oldsmobile Futuramic 98 convertible, finished in Nantucket Cream with red interior, which was parked in the drive. William told Bernstein that he needed a car and that he should have one like this. He opened the door to look inside.

'Please don't touch the car, sir!'

William and Bernstein turned to a man standing at the front door with a clipboard.

He looked them up and down. 'Names?'

William answered, 'Mr Bernstein and Mr Hildebrand.'

The butler made a display of looking at his list until he had located and ticked off both names.

'Which one of you is Mr Bernstein?' he asked.

Bernstein pointed at William and said, 'Him.'

The Beverly Hill Germans always turned up for Alma's feasts. Her hospitality was legendary and Germans like Thomas Mann, who didn't like Alma, nevertheless turned up to eat and drink. She had booked staff from the usual agency with the stipulation not to send her any negroes. She had asked for a quartet but there was a misunderstanding and the agency sent her a modern jazz quartet. Alma wanted to send them away, but Anna insisted they stay and play for her. It was her birthday and she would have what she wanted. The trumpet player was a negro.

A lady wearing bright red lipstick gave her coat to the trumpet player and approached William, greeting him loudly with, 'Lenny darling! I love your music. She farted, looked around, and said, 'I can smell dog. I'm allergic to dogs.'

The trumpet player gave the flatulent lady's coat to the butler.

Alma had already eaten a vast amount and, unable to eat any more, went to the bathroom to vomit before returning for second helpings – eating, as she said, 'the Roman way.'

Nellie Mann gave her empty glass to the trumpet player. Meddi took the glass from the trumpet player to give to the butler. Meddi asked the musician if he took on students. He told her that he didn't like it round here and that he was going back to New York. Meddi told him that she was working on a movie that was going to be shot on location in New York and asked if she might enquire about lessons when they were both back east. He agreed and gave her his card: 'Jon Gillespie. Weddings and Bar Mitzvahs.' Meddi would not have blamed Mr Gillespie, if he thought she was an eccentric old lady given the strange behaviour of some of Alma's other guests. She told Jon Gillespie about her special trumpet, how it was built and why it was built that way, describing its unusual specifications in a language that demonstrated some expertise. She asked him if he would like to see it, invited him to lunch and gave him her card: 'Mechtilde Müller. Metro-Goldwyn-Mayer'. He gave her another of his own cards, a different one from a different pocket. This one said: 'Jon Gillespie. Concert and Recording Artist'. They arranged to meet at MGM studios the following day.

Anna told William and Meddi that she was going to Italy. She had been in touch with Giovanni who wanted her to come and work in his studio.

'Giovanni?' asked William, not knowing who Anna was referring to.

'Giovanni in Spoleto! Giovanni D'Agostino. You can't have forgotten him. Or have you had so many lovers you no longer remember one from another?'

Anna continued, 'What I'd like for my birthday is for you two to get married and adopt my children so that I can go to Italy and work with Giovanni in his studio. What do you say?'

Meddi told Anna that they had often thought of getting married but up until now neither of them had found anyone who was willing to have them.

An anxious young man clutching a manuscript pleaded with the butler, who pointed to William. He came over to William and said, 'Lenny, I have written a symphony and I know you'll just love it.' Bernstein, standing behind William, was in conversation with Bruno Walter, Erica Mann, her father Thomas, and her husband, Wystan. Bernstein had only just realised that Wystan Hugh was 'W H' and that he was talking to the same Auden whose *Age of Anxiety* was the subject of his Second Symphony. Auden told Bernstein that he did not understand how poetry could be translated into music. To translate poetry into another language was almost impossible. To translate poetry into no language at all was ridiculous. William heard Auden say to Bernstein that he was not interested in his symphony. William took the words from Auden's mouth and rudely repeated them. 'I'm not interested in your symphony,' he said to the unwelcome composer and turned away from him to join the conversation going on behind him.

Erica Mann said, 'William, let's you and me swap. I'll look after Lenny. He knows how to treat a lady. You go to the Edinburgh Festival with Bruno and show him how to use a knife and fork. I went there with him two years ago. It's a cold, windy city and Bruno's idea of taking his girl out for dinner is to sit on a bench outside the concert hall in the wind and rain using your fingers to eat fish and chips wrapped in newspaper.' Walter told William he was welcome to come to Edinburgh with him if Lenny could spare him and that he would treat William to a fish supper from the shop opposite the concert hall. It was one of the finest pleasures of the Edinburgh Festival.

Bruno Walter talked about Edinburgh and its Festival, but William only wanted to hear about the fish and chip shop. Walter said it was a festival of peace. 'Soldiers have put down their weapons. Now it's time for musicians to pick up their instruments.' Bernstein wanted to know how Walter had managed to get the Vienna Philharmonic to Edinburgh.

'It's such a cheap gig, Bruno.'

'That's right, Lenny. So cheap no one wanted to go. But when the Vienna players agreed to it, everyone else fell in line.'

'How did you persuade them to go to Scotland for next to nothing?'

Walter tapped his nose. 'There's a big American pot that pays for de-Nazification. The managers of the fund thought it would be a good idea to send the Viennese Nazis to a festival city to play music composed by one Jew and conducted by another. It'll take more than a trip to Edinburgh to clean them up, but it was a start,' said Walter. 'Viennese musicianship runs deeper than their Nazism and I put the orchestra back in touch with the years when Mahler directed the Hofoper and Vienna stood at the very summit of music making. Not like it is now, the broken capital of a defeated country with an opera house in ruins.'

'How do you feel about conducting a band of Nazis?' asked Bernstein.

'I let go of the past and think of the future,' said Walter.

'They don't like me,' complained Bernstein.

'That's because you can't keep your feet still.'

Bernstein looked at his shoes.

Erica said they were going back to Edinburgh in August for a recital of songs by Schumann, Schubert and Brahms – 'Bruno at the piano and his star singer, Kathleen what's her name?'

'Kathleen von der Erde,' teased Walter.

'Yes, her,' continued Erica. 'He likes her so much he'd crawl over broken glass to stick matchsticks in her shit.'

'Very fucking poetic, darling!' said Auden.

The jazz quartet kicked off. They had no music and improvised freely. Bernstein and Meddi wandered over to the musicians. Bernstein stood by the piano itching to join in. She closed her eyes and listened to the trumpet.

Alma, glassy-eyed, worked the room, offering herself up to the homage of her guests and accepting their compliments on her wealth and fine taste in husbands. Anna accompanied Alma on her tour of the room. Whenever Anna referred to her mother as Alma Mahler-Gropius-Werfel Alma referred to her daughter as Anna Koller-Kreneck-Zsolnay-Fistoulari. Guests remarked how Anna took after her mother.

Heinrich Mann stood as far away from Thomas Mann as the room allowed and the brothers ignored each other.

William introduced himself to the butler, who clicked his heels and identified himself as August Hess. William discovered that Hess did everything that he himself used to do for Alma and perhaps more now that Werfel had died. William was especially interested in the Oldsmobile. Hess offered to take him for a ride. William suggested he pick up Mr Hildebrand and himself at the hotel in the morning and take them to the airport.

'August!' called Alma.

'Coming,' and Hess ran off to attend to her.

William found a bathroom. He heard Auden's voice behind the locked door.

'It was to get her out of Europe – a marriage of convenience which is very convenient for old Bruno. He doesn't fuck his wife; I don't fuck my wife. So, he fucks mine, and we all live happily ever after.'

William knew it could be a while before that bathroom was free and went in search of another one.

When the band took a break, Leonard Bernstein played Chopin's *Raindrops,* then Bruno Walter sat beside Bernstein and they played

Mozart's *Sonata for Four Hands* in D Major. The lady who was allergic to dogs spoke to the trumpeter who pointed to the butler. She approached the butler. 'The n****r says you've got my coat. She farted and said, 'I'm allergic to n****rs. I can't believe Alma hired one.'

As William was leaving, Hess, the butler, questioned William about his name, 'Bernstein's a Jewish name. Amber. The burning stone. But you're not Jewish.'

'No,' said William.

'Neither am I,' said Hess, and he told William that he had not fled from Germany like all the other Germans in Beverly Hills who were Jewish. He never had any quarrel with the Third Reich and had been touring America singing roles in his own opera company when the war broke out and his company went bust. That's when he became Alma's chauffeur. He did odd jobs during the day and in the evenings sang Wagner for Alma while she accompanied him on the piano.

'Alma bought me the car. Isn't she beautiful?'

William assumed Hess was referring to the car and said, 'Yes.'

As Hess kept calling him Mr Bernstein, William said nothing about his own relationship with Alma. Hess agreed to come to the hotel the next day and take him and Mr Hildebrand to the airport in the Oldsmobile.

Mr Bernstein wanted to know why William had arranged for a Nazi to drive them to the airport.

'Because he's got a beautiful car,' said William.

In the airport bar Bernstein lined up three large whiskies. He drank one each for Adolph Green and Betty Comden with whom he'd written the songs for *On the Town*. 'They used to be my friends, but they've written four new songs to replace the four they had written with me. Who needs enemies when you've got friends like that?' The third whisky was for Arthur Freed, the *On the Town* producer. 'He called my music "a bit Prokofiev".'

On the plane Bernstein started reading *Romeo and Juliet*. He told William he was going to do another musical with Jerome Robbins based on the play.

'It's a romance between a Catholic boy and a Jewish girl, doomed as their families fight a turf war on the streets of New York when Passover coincides with Easter. The bastards at MGM won't get their hands on it.'

'I hope your *Romeo and Juliet* won't be "too Prokofiev," said William. Bernstein told William to shut up, read two more pages, then fell asleep with his head on William's shoulder.

MGM shot *On the Town* on the streets of New York and there was pandemonium as crowds gathered every time Frank Sinatra stepped onto the pavement. Meddi visited Mr Gillespie who gave her trumpet lessons. She soon realized Mr Gillespie was more interested in the trumpet than in her. He asked if he could borrow it. She dithered. She didn't want Jon Gillespie to touch Johnny's trumpet and she wanted to hear him play it. Both. William took charge and carried the trumpet as he walked with her to the Village Vanguard.

Trumpeter and bassist stood on the bandstand and behind them, at the piano and with his back to the audience, Dick Tomasek. William stepped onto the bandstand and gave Gillespie Meddi's trumpet. William smiled at young Richard whose face was drawn and gaunt, his eyes unseeing. The smile he returned to William did not suggest any recognition. Gillespie breathed melody into the trumpet. Richard clothed it in harmony. Richard accompanied Gillespie's spontaneity with unusual harmonic sequences that swept the well-known melodies of the American songbook to far away and unknown territory. At the end of the gig Mr. Gillespie wiped down Johnny's trumpet, brought it over to Meddi and carefully put it back in its case. William wanted to speak to Richard, but the pianist had gone.

Bernstein wanted to come off the road and compose but his love of the platform, the musicians, and the audiences drove him from one orchestra and one concert hall to another. William, constantly on the road with Bernstein, rarely returned to his studio in Carnegie Hall where Richard slept all morning, played the piano all afternoon, stage managed the orchestra in the evenings and played in the clubs all night. Bruno Zirato gave Richard a wage and ten dollars every time the New York Post published one of Maurice's reviews. Richard spent it all on heroin.

CHAPTER 55

Edinburgh Festival 1950

William and Bernstein arrived at the Usher Hall in Edinburgh to perform two concerts with the French Radio Orchestra at the Fourth Edinburgh International Festival. Bernstein had a few hours rehearsal to prepare Brandenburg Five, Shostakovich's Fifth Symphony, and a Liszt Fantasia with Marcel Dupré at the Usher Hall's organ. The Festival's budget did not extend to having the organ tuned and the orchestra had to make small but difficult adjustments to be able to perform with it.

William went through several handkerchiefs mopping Bernstein's troubled brow. As always, he left Mahler's baton on the podium.

The following day William needed several more handkerchiefs as Bernstein prepared his second concert for Aug 23rd, where he would conduct the first Beethoven piano concerto from the piano. It can be done if the orchestra knows the concerto well enough to play with their eyes shut. Bernstein spent August 22nd. rehearsing French musicians, who needed eyes very wide open.

At the rehearsal break the hall manager asked the orchestra, 'Who wants fish and chips for half a crown?' He went across the road to Guido's with fifteen pounds and ten shillings and an order for sixty-two suppers. The hall manager told William that Guido fried thousands of fish suppers during the festival for the musicians and thousands more for the audiences. 'That's some fryin' eh? He's still in the shop cleaning up after midnight. The generous tip he gives me is one of the good things about my job. The downside is that every year someone in the audience croaks. See when they come in? Some of them can hardly walk. It's a miracle there's only two or three corpses a year. When you see these ancient geezers inching their way into the hall you'd think there'd be one every night. Could be tomorrow tonight. We usually get them out of the hall without disturbing the concert. It takes the ambulance only a few minutes to get down from the Infirmary. There's nae hurry to get back to the hospital because they're usually deid before we get them into the ambulance. A thousand fish suppers during the festival and that's just the Usher Hall. There's the Lyceum an a'. That shop's a wee gold mine, I'm tellin' ye. And now they've got the restaurant an' a'.'

William stood outside the Usher Hall and looked at the chip shop 'Pesce e Patate' and the restaurant next door called 'Pizza e Pasta.' The restaurant was busy. A sign on the door said it was closed for a private party. William glanced through the window, saw balloons, and heard the party singing, 'Compleanno a te, Compleanno a te, Compleanno Arnaldo, Compleanno a te.' Mother and father blew out the candles on a huge cake in front of the one-year-old in his high-chair. William passed by the window quickly and went into the chip shop next door. He looked at eight large portraits on the wall – photographs of Guido Mancini with Bruno Walter, Kathleen Ferrier, William Furtwängler, Sir Malcolm Sargent, Sir Adrian Boult, Rafael Kubelik, Carlo Zecchi and Vittorio Gui.

William stood outside the Usher Hall eating his fish supper when someone passing by said, 'Gie's a chip, pal!' William gave him the fish supper and went into the bar on the corner of Lothian Road. The barman offered him a pint of heavy or a pint of light. William, thinking he would be safer with the light, was surprised to be given a large glass of beer that was almost black.

The barman said the pub was quiet because there was no concert in the hall and there was a private party in the restaurant, otherwise it would have been busy. The restaurant customers took a ticket then waited there until there was a table for them. William told the barman he thought there was a birthday party in the restaurant.

'Yes. The wee boy's one. Guido's son and heir. The wean'll keep old Mrs Mancini busy. Puir wumman. Lost her man in the war.'

After replacing glasses on the shelf the barman returned to William and told him that Guido had opened the restaurant two years ago when the La Scala orchestra came. They played for a week and the Italian boys ate there every day. 'You couldn't get a seat. They queued up outside, then they queued up in here, and people have been queuing ever since.'

"Pizza e Pasta' e 'Pesce e Patate',' said William. 'I Quattro Piselli'

The barman didn't know what William meant. 'I Quattro Piselli' – it's Italian for 'The Four Peas',' said William.

Bernstein spent his rehearsal time preparing the orchestra and left no time to prepare himself. The concert didn't go well. The Edinburgh audience didn't think much of the flash American. They thought his performance as soloist and conductor was a circus act. After the concert

Mr Bernstein dined with the Festival Director, Mr Hunter, in 'Pizza e Pasta'. William did not go with them. He took the remains of the twelve-year-old Bowmore to the hotel and left it in Bernstein's room. He picked up the copy of the *Times* open at the crossword and looked at the first clue – 'Fragment of Messiah heard, part of a cycle.' Mr Bernstein had filled in 'Handlebar.' William couldn't see why.

CHAPTER 56

Hollywood and HUAC

Bernstein's mentor and spiritual father, Koussevitzky, died. It was Koussevitzky who had insisted Bernstein choose serious music or Broadway. Bernstein now felt free to do both. He wrote *Trouble in Tahiti*, a musical that was more than 'a bit Prokofiev'. He also wrote *Wonderful Town* which won a Tony Award for best Broadway musical, and a violin concerto for Isaac Stern. He composed *Candide* and *West Side Story*, became a television personality, and, after an on- and-off engagement to Felicia, he finally married her.

With so much new music William and Mr Bernstein would sit opposite one another correcting and copying until the wee small hours. 'I'll wash – you dry', said Bernstein, recalling the first time they had worked together when Bernstein corrected, and William copied, Bernstein's *Jeremiah* symphony.

William advised Bernstein that his royalties would be doubled if he followed Richard Strauss's example and retained the ownership of his own copyright. Bernstein thought 'Amber Music' would be a good name for the new publishing company. William thought the bi-syllabic 'Amber' left the name up in the air and suggested 'Amberson', the third syllable properly grounding it. Bernstein agreed and encouraged William to improve his relations with Helen Coates. 'Let her supervise the accounts and deal with the legal stuff, and you can promote the catalogue.' Bernstein left Helen and William to get on with it, and each other, while he went to South America on honeymoon.

Hollywood came looking for music. Sam Spiegel wanted Bernstein to write the music for his movie *On the Waterfront*. William knew that after his experience with *On the Town* Bernstein would not work in Hollywood again and that he wouldn't work anywhere with the director, Elia Kazan, who had named colleagues to the House Un-American Activities Committee. But when Spiegel sent a rough-cut Bernstein saw it was a great film, wrote the music, and went with William to Hollywood to record it.

In Hollywood William found Meddi anxious because she had been invited to attend a House Un-American Activities Committee hearing. She didn't want to go. William said he would go with her.

Thursday April 15th 1954

Meddi was questioned by Mr Richard Nixon

'Good morning, Mrs Müller.'

'Miss Müller', she corrected him.

'Forgive me, Miss Müller. May I call you Meddi?'

'Mechtilde.'

'Mechtilde – did I pronounce that right? - you are the senior mistress in the costume department at Metro-Goldwyn-Mayer where, in addition to your role of designing and making costumes, you organise the seamstress's union. You're her lawyer?'

'A friend,' said William.

'Thank you both for coming to see me. I am Mr Nixon. I won't keep you long. My colleagues and I have been looking at the activities of the Emergency Rescue Committee which enabled refugees like yourself to escape from Europe and settle in America. The First Lady took a special interest in this initiative and many of the refugees became American citizens on Mrs Roosevelt's personal recommendation – yourself, Mrs Mahler, the late Mr Werfel...' He thumbed through the files on the table in front of him and stopped at the file bearing William's photograph. He looked up at William. '...and your 'friend'. It may be necessary to ask the court to deliver a judgement on the legality of procedures involving the First Lady which gave refugees citizenship of the United States of America without proper judicial oversight, but in the short term we feel it would be more effective if we could simply establish that the new Americans who have recently joined us are de facto as well as *de jure* citizens. You are not Jewish, Mechtilde, so we ask ourselves, why are you a refugee? Is it because you are an anti-fascist, and if you are an anti-fascist, are you a communist? You were a member of the Austrian Schutzbund in Vienna – a socialist party with a paramilitary wing which was supplied by criminal activities.'

Nixon extracted a photograph from the file and showed Meddi the picture of the Theresienstadt orchestra. Meddi's hand immediately went to the locket she wore around her neck which contained the tooth she found in the mouthpiece of Johnny's trumpet.

'Do you know this man?' asked Mr Nixon, pointing to Shai Levy holding Johnny Stanko's trumpet.

'No,' she answered truthfully.

'We have six statements from your colleagues at Metro-Goldwyn-Mayer attesting to your involvement with the paramilitary wing of the

Schutzbund and your intimate involvement with one of its leaders. I'm not looking for any comment from you, Mechtilde, regarding these facts. I only wish to note that you are now sixty-eight years old and I advise that it would be in your own interest to retire.'

He turned to William's file. 'Mr Hildebrand, born in Basel, Switzerland, formerly resident in Vienna and employed by Mrs Mahler-Werfel, now resident in New York and employed by Mr Bernstein. And how is Mr Bernstein?'

'Very well, thank you, sir,' answered William.

'I wasn't expecting you, Mr Hildebrand. Thank you for coming all the way from New York to see me. When you were resident in Vienna, did you ever come across a musician employed by the Vienna Philharmonic Orchestra named Mr Stanko?'

William looked his interrogator straight in the eye, blushed and said firmly, 'No, sir!'

'Good. Please calm yourself, Mr Hildebrand. You have nothing to worry about. Would you describe Mr Bernstein as a good American patriot?'

'A what?'

'A patriot, Mr Hildebrand. Do you know what a patriot is?'

'Yes, sir.'

'Are you a patriot?'

'Yes, sir.'

'Well, then, is Mr Bernstein a patriot, like you?'

'Yes, sir.'

'That's good. You are a very young-looking seventy-two-year-old, Mr Hildebrand. You're not thinking of retiring, are you?'

'No, sir.'

'Good. It would be so much better for us all if you were to continue working for Mr Bernstein. We'd rather you stayed here than be returned to Vienna. If you feel your boss does anything that you consider to be unpatriotic, here's my number.' He gave William his card. 'If you mention to Mr Bernstein that you came to see me, he will not be happy, so we should keep this conversation between ourselves. On behalf of the House Un-American Activities Committee I would like to wish you both a very Happy Easter.'

To get away from the noise of the traffic Meddi took William into a diner where she ordered two Cokes. Meddi proposed a toast, 'To the land of the free.' They chinked bottles, and Meddi said, 'Prost!'

William asked Meddi if she thought he should throw away Mr Nixon's phone number. She thought that would be a political act which would be out of character for William.

William suggested he give it to her to dispose of. She thought that was a political act no different from his first proposal.

'What should I do, then?' pleaded William.

She suggested the course of action which best suited his character was to leave it in his pocket where he would forget about it and one day it would disappear all by itself and he wouldn't even notice it was gone.

'Am I really seventy-two?' asked William.

'Yes,' replied Meddi.

'How did that happen?'

'It happened because you were born four years before me.'

'I hadn't been counting,' confessed William. 'Seventy-two is quite old, isn't it? But Mr Nixon thought I was very young-looking.'

'And you trust him?'

'No,' replied William.

'But everything he said was true. The only lie I heard was the one you told when you said you didn't know Johnny.'

'It wasn't a very good lie, was it?'

'No, but he was pleased to hear it.'

'Do you think he believed me?'

'Of course not.'

'Did the Emergency Rescue Committee rescue communists as well as us?'

'Probably. But they don't rescue communists anymore. They only rescue Nazis now.'

'Does Mr Nixon think I'm a communist?'

'Mr Nixon knows that you haven't got a political thought in your head.'

William drank his Coke.

'...but your heart's in the right place,' added Meddi.

'Why did he wish us a Happy Easter?'

'He wanted us to know how much he enjoyed humiliating us.'

'Is it Easter then?'

'On Sunday,' she replied. 'Do you know what day of the week it is?'

William thought about it and confessed he didn't.

'But at least you know how old you are,' she reassured him.

William went back to the hotel. Bernstein was in a bad mood. The studio had insisted that Bernstein's involvement with the movie ended with the composition of the score. They had specifically asked Bernstein to stay away from the studio during the recording, which was now in the hands of a conductor answerable only to the studio. Bernstein wanted to go to the nearest bar and from there to the airport and never to set foot in Hollywood again.

Bernstein lined up whiskies and William made a call to the studio, discovered the name of the conductor, called his agent, said he was calling on behalf of Leonard Bernstein, and was put straight through to the twenty-five-year-old who had been hired to conduct the music and play the piano part. William suggested to the young conductor that it would be better for him to concentrate on directing the musicians and have Mr Bernstein play the piano part. 'If you run into any problems, Mr Bernstein would then be on hand to help you solve them. No need for any paperwork. Credit yourself as both conductor and pianist, and if anyone asks who the pianist is, he would like to be known as Lenny Amberson.'

William re-joined Mr Bernstein at the bar and told him the deal. Mr Bernstein ordered two more whiskies, shook hands with William, and then pulled him over and planted a huge kiss on William's lips.

The recording session went smoothly. Mr Amberson played the piano as if he'd written the part himself and Mr Bernstein congratulated the young conductor, Mr Previn, on his excellent interpretation of the music.

Meddi went back to work. Everything was the same as it had been the day before. The routines, the teamwork, the camaraderie – everything that Meddi had worked hard to put in place – was all still there. Nothing had changed. But for Meddi everything had changed. Meddi stuck it out until the end of the week. She hoped, like the phone number in William's pocket, that she could forget about the poison Mr Nixon had dropped into her ear until it evaporated all by itself and she wouldn't even notice it had gone. But every indiscreet word she had dropped over coffee, or in the ladies' room, which now filled Mr Nixon's files, haunted her. The smiles she shared with colleagues looked and felt like grimaces. She felt betrayed, quit her job at MGM, and went back east with William where she became a trustee of the Costume Institute in New York.

CHAPTER 57

'West Side Story'

William rarely invited the confidence of a mirror but now, shaving or dressing, he lingered to examine the seventy-two years written in his face.

William told Mahler that he had only just realized he was seventy-two.

'Is there something special about seventy-two?'

'No. It's just that birthdays come and go and I never noticed them. I haven't been counting and it seems that I have suddenly become old.'

'I'm still only fifty,' said Mahler.

'You always looked older than me,' said William. 'You still do, but orchestral musicians who used to look like grandfathers are now boys and girls. I'm feeling old and tired.'

'Bit late for a mid-life crisis,' said Mahler.

'Mr Nixon hoped that I wouldn't have to be returned to Vienna.'

'That was an empty threat. He wants you to keep working, and so do I.'

'Do you want me to keep an eye on Bernstein's patriotism?'

'No, but I would like you to help him with his difficulties.'

'His marriage?'

'No. His music. Mr Bernstein wants to compose, but to make a living he needs to conduct. He needs the money and the applause. He gets neither, composing. The only way to earn money from composing is to do what Richard Strauss did and write big operas and have them performed all over the world. *Candide* was a flop. *West Side Story* will flop too. He gets depressed and deals with his depression by going all over the world conducting. This leaves him no to time to compose.'

'He's never at home, and Felicia's unhappy,' interrupted William.

'Never mind her just now. Let's think about music. There is so much about Mr Bernstein that reminds me of myself. I conducted from October until April and composed in the summer. Bernstein should have his own orchestra and his own opera house, like I had. He has just finished an engagement in Israel, is about to begin a series of concerts in England and, as we speak, he's conducting Maria Callas in *La Sonnambula* at La Scala in Milan. Leonard Bernstein and Maria Callas should be doing *La Sonnambula* in New York. The Met is a better opera house, the orchestra's better, and it's on his doorstep. And look at Dimitri Mitropoulos. He's old!'

'He's younger than me,' interrupted William.

'Yes, but he looks older, he's not well, and he's coming to the end of his time with the New York Philharmonic. Why doesn't Mr Bernstein share the directorship of the orchestra with Mitropoulos, and when Dimitri steps down he can have the orchestra all to himself.'

'But he wants to be famous all over the world,' interrupted William.

'Of course he does! But you don't have to go all over the world to do that. Look at Frank Sinatra. He's famous all over the world and doesn't have to go anywhere because the records he sells all over the world are all recorded in America. Mr Bernstein needs to think about recording. And then there's television! He doesn't have to set foot outside New York. And in the summer he could retreat to somewhere quiet and peaceful to compose.'

'How do you think I could fix that?' asked William.

'Get Helen Coates to speak to him about money. She needs him to understand that he's broke and running further into debt. She can show him that, however handsome the La Scala fee, once his lavish expenses in Tel Aviv, Milan and London are paid he doesn't have enough left to pay for the apartment on Central Park, nor the cook, nor the nanny. Let Miss Coates spell it out. She's good at that sort of thing. He'll probably fire her, then hire her again a few days later.

Then you could have a word with Bruno Zirato at the New York Philharmonic. He knows you and likes you, respects you, and, although he looks a lot older, he's the same age as you. He needs Bernstein. The orchestra has a contract with Columbia Records and Bruno Zirato would rather have Bernstein's face on the cover of the records than Mr. Mitropoulos's. I have nothing against Mitropoulos. He's a fine conductor and has performed all my symphonies with the Philharmonic. The musicians are now familiar with my music, thanks to him. But when the orchestra records my music, I'd rather they were led by Mr Bernstein.'

'I could tell him how you conducted your work,' interrupted William.

'There's no need for that. Let him treat the score as a modest proposal and he'll come up with his own ideas. But you could try and get him to use the baton. I don't like the way he waggles his fingers. He's supposed to be conducting an orchestra not playing the piano. Now, regarding the record contract. I suggest you ask Bruno Zirato to approach Columbia Records and propose the orchestra record a complete cycle of my symphonies to be issued separately, and eventually in a complete edition, with his picture on the sleeve of each long-playing record and my picture on the front of the box set.'

'What about his marriage?' asked William.

'Fix the music problem and the wife problem will disappear.'

'I don't think so,' said William. 'Their marriage isn't a musical problem. It's cultural and sexual. When Bernstein's away his Jewish family invade Felicia's home and look after her children. When he's at home they come and look after him. Felicia wants her own family and not a walk-on part in his family. And she would rather have him to herself than share him with his boyfriends. It's easier for her to sleep alone when he's on the road. It's not so easy sleeping alone when he's in New York.'

'You know I'm no good at that sort of thing,' said Mahler. 'Talk to Meddi.'

Two o'clock in the afternoon. Meddi and William entered the Village Vanguard, William carrying the trumpet.

'It belonged to the man I loved,' said Meddi to John Gillespie. 'He was the first trumpeter in Vienna, first trumpeter in Prague and then first trumpeter in the camp orchestra in Theresienstadt, before he was murdered. I want you to breathe life into it.'

'You want me to play it for you?' he asked.

'I would like you to have it.'

'Ma'am, let me level with you. Your boyfriend played the finest trumpet I've ever seen. There's nobody got a finer trumpet than this. And there's nobody I know can afford to buy it, least of all me.'

'When the rest of us fled,' said Meddi, 'the man who built this trumpet stayed to resist Hitler. When the Gestapo picked him up, they thought he was just a trumpet player and they put him in Theresienstadt to play in the camp orchestra. They didn't realize he was a soldier and that this trumpet was his weapon. Do you have any use for a trumpet like that?'

Jon Gillespie took the trumpet from its case, pushed the mouthpiece into place and stepped onto the bandstand. He played Reveille, then played it an octave higher, then he danced between the two octaves filling the space with runs and flurries of notes, transforming a military call into a blizzard of scales, arpeggios and glissandos, skiing a precipitous slope then abruptly turning to ski back up the mountain, off piste, with no hesitancy and an eye only for the summit, which he reached with an ear-shattering top C and then, without taking a breath, with cheeks bulging and the horn pointing to the ceiling, he stepped up another semitone to a C# that ended with an explosion of tiny lightbulbs in the chandelier above the bandstand. The room filled with the echo of the C# and the tinkling of broken glass that fell around Mr Gillespie. The silence which followed was broken by the barman who appeared on the bandstand with a broom and shovel. 'Did you just play a top C, Dizzy?'

'C# baby. C#! Go to war with a trumpet like this,' said Mr Gillespie, 'and the walls of Jericho ain't got no chance.' He blew the spit out of the horn, removed the mouthpiece, and put the trumpet back in its case.

'Mr Gillespie, you've got your own battles to fight, and if you'll accept it, I want you to take it,' said Meddi.

'Take it to the conservatoire, ma'am, and get someone to tell you what it's worth before you think of giving it away.'

'It's worth far more than money, Mr Gillespie. Take it.'

William, Meddi, Mr Gillespie, and the barman leaning on his broom all looked at the trumpet. Then the barman said, 'Take the lady's trumpet.'

Mr Gillespie shut the case and said, 'I'm sorry about your boyfriend. There's nothing I can do about that. I'll take the trumpet if you'll accept $100 a month. And you gotta know, ma'am, neither of us is gonna live long enough to get close to what the trumpet's worth.'

Meddi and Gillespie shook hands.

William told Mr Gillespie that the last time they'd met he'd played the trumpet very quietly, with the music sculpted at the lower end of the trumpet's register.

'That was Dick Tomasek's trio,' said Mr Gillespie. 'Dick didn't play with screamers. No drummer neither. Just melody and harmony. That's where he explored the bruised melancholy in all these old songs. He played 'My Funny Valentine' like it was Chopin. He wanted to taste every note, so he never played fast, and he didn't like to disturb the harmony, so he never played loud. Slow and quiet. The kid was a genius.'

'How's he doing?' asked William.

'Died in Paris. The heroin in Paris was pure. He overdosed on pure heroin. The kid was a genius.'

Outside in the street William breathed deeply and quickly to try and quell his rising nausea. Meddi held on to him and he held onto the railing. The sharp intake of oxygen eased the contraction in his stomach and when he felt he had it under control he let go the railing and let

Meddi hold him. Meddi felt the numb lifelessness of the sobbing body she held in her arms. They did not speak. She knew there were no words to fill the emptiness a father feels at the loss of his son.

They walked from the Village Vanguard to St Vincent's Triangle and sat on a bench.

She said, 'You loved him.'

He turned away from her and said, 'Why don't you make something nice for Felicia to wear?'

They walked north to Bernstein's apartment on Central Park.

Two weeks later Felicia Montealegre skipped all the way to her audition dressed in the new suit Meddi had made, feeling like the successful actress she was.

William went to visit Bruno Zirato.

Bruno agreed with William that Leonard Bernstein was a shoo-in for the directorship of the New York Philharmonic Orchestra, if only...

'If only...?' asked William.

'If only he was here. It would be easier to hire God. God is everywhere. Lenny is everywhere, except New York. The board would never let me give him the job.'

'He needs to come off the road, settle down, conduct during the season and compose in the summer,' said William.

'So, I'm gonna kidnap him and lock him up?' asked Bruno. 'It's a free country, William. You're not allowed to do that in America. He becomes the artistic director of the New York Philharmonic Orchestra, and then what? The Israel Philharmonic call up and says, "Hey, Lenny, come to Tel Aviv." "Yes, Amos." Then the Vienna Phil. call up. "Yes, Gunther!" Then Amsterdam. "Yes, Ruud." Then Milan. "Hey, Lenny, Maria won't sing unless you conduct." "OK, Giuseppe, tell Maria I'll be right over." Have you ever heard Lenny say, "No!" Imagine if he'd been born a woman!'

'He has to settle down, have his own orchestra and to compose.' said William.

'There's no money composing.' said Bruno. 'Didn't Mahler tell you that? You don't compose for money. You compose for the audience of the future, not for royalties today. *Candide*? Great music. Flop! *Trouble in Tahiti*? Great music. Flop. *On the Waterfront*? Great music. Who won the Oscar for best score?'

'I can't remember,' said William.

'Neither can I,' said Bruno. 'But it wasn't Lenny. And when *West Side Story* flops he'll leave New York and maybe we won't see him ever again.'

'And if it's a hit they'll be queuing up all the way from Broadway to Carnegie Hall to hear Mr Bernstein conduct.'

'If only...'

'If only, what?'

'If only I could tear up his passport.'

'You might not have to,' said William. 'It needs to be renewed. Nobody joined more left-wing organisations than Lenny. He never said no to anyone. His name is on so many lists. Lenny was promiscuous. He went to hear Shostakovich address the Cultural and Scientific Congress for World Peace where Shostakovich declared western music to be decadent and bourgeois and denounced Stravinsky as the lackey of American warmongers.'

'Nobody, least of all Shostakovich, believes any of that nonsense,' said Bruno.

'But the FBI believe all sorts of nonsense,' said William. 'Why don't you tell them that Bernstein spent several hours with the Soviet delegation in the Waldorf Astoria where he discussed politics with Shostakovich. The FBI knows nothing about music. All they know is that Shostakovich is a 'red' – an elite 'red'.'

William took Mr Nixon's telephone number from his jacket pocket and gave it to Bruno.

'I thought Lenny was your friend,' said Bruno.

'He is my friend.'

'And you want me to turn him in.'

'Tough love,' said William.

'If you're so tough, why don't you turn him in yourself?'

'I'm not as tough as you,' said William.

'You're a very bad man,' said Bruno.

'During the delay in his passport renewal, why don't you give him the Philharmonic directorship and when he needs his passport back, say, for example, to take the orchestra on tour to the Soviet Union and show the Russians the superiority of Western culture, then you could find him a good lawyer. There's something else you can do for me. The studio at the top – it's a big bright space. Ideal for an artist's studio. I'd like to invite Anna Mahler to come to New York. She paints. So does Felicia. I think it would be nice for Bernstein to have his wife and

Mahler's daughter upstairs working together while he's in the hall rehearsing the orchestra.'

'If only…' said Bruno.

'If only, what?' asked William.

'If only it was available. It's young Richard's room,' said Bruno.

'Richard died of a heroin overdose in Paris,' said William.

Anna Mahler accepted William's invitation to celebrate her birthday in New York and made him promise not to put any candles on her birthday cake.

Leonard was working on *West Side Story* and never came home. Felicia had taken the children to visit her family in Chile. Anna, Meddi and William celebrated Anna's birthday. William prepared a wide skillet of paella which looked like a work of abstract expressionist art – chestnut mushrooms, sea-bleached squid, flamingo pink prawns and fiery sunset chorizo, all dripped onto a yellow canvas of saffron rice sprouting glossy shards of green pepper. Anna asked William to pay her compliments to Felicia's cook. William told Anna that the cook had gone to Chile with Felicia and that the paella was all his own work. William happily confessed that he spent very little time in the office these days and stayed at home in the kitchen, where Felicia's cook had shown him how to prepare food Spanish style. He liked the kitchen better than the office, where he thought Helen Coates was happy working on her own. She was a good administrator. He was a good cook.

Anna knew a different story. She'd heard that William made all the big decisions.

'Don't be silly,' chided William.

'That's what Bruno told me,' countered Anna.

'Bruno Walter?' asked William.

'No, Bruno Zirato. He called me up and offered me studio space in the loft at Carnegie Hall. That was music to my ears. Mama was driving me mad. I hate it when she introduces me to her Nazi friends as her 'Jewish daughter' A four-times-married, fifty-four- year-old woman should not be living with her mother.'

'Fifty-four!' exclaimed William, who had put fifty candles on Anna's cake.

'Bruno told me,' continued Anna, 'that you fixed Bernstein's appointment to lead New York Philharmonic, and that you'd fixed a record contract for him to record all of Dad's symphonies, and that you'd fixed it for me to have a studio in the loft at Carnegie Hall where

I could work. He told me that you convinced the board that Bernstein would not go gallivanting around the world anymore but stay in New York. And that Helen Coates's lawyers had drawn up a document as thick as a New York telephone directory but you tore it in half with your bare hands and wrote on a single sheet of paper how long and for how much, and Lenny and Bruno signed it. Oh, and he thought I might like to share the loft with Lenny's wife, who paints a bit. You fixed all of that... and this paella.'

Meddi added, 'And his heart's in the right place too.'

'And if I have to paint with Lenny's wife to earn my supper, I'll have seconds.' Anna took another helping of paella and poured the last of the wine into her glass.

William went into the kitchen to fetch another bottle from the fridge. He removed the fifty candles from Anna's cake, filled the little holes with rum, and smoothed icing over the pitted surface.

They sang *Happy Birthday,* ate the cake and drank the wine. Meddi told Anna that she was now on the board of the New York Costume Institute and that she hoped one day to go back to Italy to revisit the Textile Museum in Spoleto.

'Then you must come and visit me!' declared Anna. 'I go to Spoleto every year to work with Giovanni. He sculpts. I paint.'

'How is he?' asked William.

'He's even older than you, Uncle William.'

'Uncle William?' queried William.

'That's what me and Giovanni like to call you.'

William wanted to know if she still had the portrait that Giovanni painted.

She said that she had kept it on the bedroom wall where it had looked down on her four marriages. None of her husbands liked it. They said it didn't look like her, but she liked it because it looked like she felt. None of her husbands recognised the portrait because none of them knew her like Giovanni knew her. She had taken it back to Spoleto and given it to Giovanni. He was delighted. He said it was the only portrait he had ever finished. William and Meddi remembered Anna snatching the brush from Giovanni's hand and stealing away from his studio with the painting before he could paint over it and start again. Anna poured herself another glass of wine and explained why sculpting worked better for Giovanni than painting. 'Instead of a blank canvas he starts with a great lump of plaster. He still has the same problem about never being able to finish, and as he works the figure gets thinner and thinner until he has to stop before it disappears.'

Meddi gave Anna a copy of Hans Bethge's *Die Chinesische Flöte* and William gave her the Vienna Philharmonic's recording of *Das Lied von der Erde* conducted by Bruno Walter, with Kathleen Ferrier.

'Poor Bruno,' said Anna. 'He's not been himself since Kathleen died. She was his precious jewel. He only wanted to make music with her. Now he doesn't do much anymore. He's old and tired.'

'He's the same age as me,' said William.

'Then how come you look so young, Uncle William?' She kissed his head, kissed Meddi's cheek, wished them both good night and retired to her room.

William knocked on Anna's door. 'I wondered if you had heard from Lizzie.'

'Yes, she writes to me every year on my birthday.'

'So, you've just had a letter?'

'No. If she sent me a card this year, it'll be in Los Angeles.'

'I'll go and get it for you,' offered William.

'Why would you want to do a stupid thing like that?'

'So that you could tell me how she's doing.'

'She's doing fine. Her children have opened a restaurant in Edinburgh near the concert hall. Bruno Walter loves it. Says it's the only reason for going to Edinburgh. She's got two grandchildren. Arnaldo's seven and Maria's five. That's about it,' concluded Anna.

'Doesn't she ever ask after me?' pleaded William.

'No.'

'Do you write to her?'

'Yes'

'Do you tell her how I'm doing?'

'No.'

'That's hard to believe.'

'Only if you believe everything always has to be about you.'

'It was never just about me. For nearly six years it was about the three of us. We were together – you, me and Lizzie. You and Lizzie write to each other and you ask me to believe that neither of you ever mention me, not ever, not once. How do you think I feel about that?'

'Are you going to tell me?' asked Anna.

'Yes! It's incomprehensible and I want to understand it. How come you two write to each other and I get frozen out? What's the matter with me? What have I done to deserve that?'

'What is it about men? They do so much and understand so little. Lizzie knows what you did to get her out of Austria. Mama knows what you did to get her out of Europe. Bruno Walter knows what you've done for Lenny, so does Bruno Zirato, and now you've asked me to come here so that you can do something for Lenny's wife. On and on you go like the Francis of A-fuckin'-ssisi that looks like you in the stained-glass window in Perugia. The glass artist loved you. Everybody loves you and you're too stupid to see it. For Chrissakes, William, my Dad loved you!! For the last forty years Giovanni's been painting a portrait of you and him – both of you, the lion and a lamb lying together. He'll never finish it. He thinks of you with love and affection, like everybody else except the one person who fell hopelessly in love with you and who still is in love with you. She's a widow, a mother, and a grandmother. She keeps her family together and she keeps herself together and scourges her feelings for you. It's hard and it's harsh.'

'So, she does ask after me.'

'Yes.'

'Harshly?'

'You weren't easy. Sometimes you weren't there for her when she needed you. Mama wouldn't let me go to Dad's funeral, so I made her take me and she got fired. You weren't there. You just fucked off and left us to deal with it on our own.'

'Your father asked me to go to Maernigg to fetch Maria so that she could be buried beside him. It was his dying wish. I missed the funeral so I could fetch your sister to rest in peace beside your father.'

After a long silence Anna put her arms around William and whispered in his ear, 'I'm sorry.'

'Thank you for telling me about Mrs Mancini,' said William.

'You're supposed to know these things without being told,' said Anna

'I'm an idiot.'

'Yes, that's right. You are.'

Bernstein left the theatre and walked into the nearest bar where he set up five large whiskies. Bernstein didn't acknowledge William's presence but stared at each glass, identified them, then knocked them back. The first three whiskies were the three pieces of music that had been cut from *West Side Story* for being 'too operatic.' The fourth was for the choreographer who had made the cuts, 'Mr Smartass, Jerome Robbins', who insisted his name appear on the theatre poster in a box all by itself. The fifth was for Koussevitzky, Bernstein's mentor and teacher, who had told him not to go near Broadway if he wanted a career in serious music. Bernstein looked up to the heavens, apologised to his spiritual father, promised he'd never set foot in Broadway again, and swallowed the last whisky.

'Let's talk about the Charles Ives rehearsal,' suggested William, referring to the rehearsal at the Carnegie hall the previous day. 'Mahler would have enjoyed it.'

'The chaos?' asked Bernstein.

'No, the music. It's everything Mahler thought a symphony should be.'

'Chaos? asked Bernstein.

'Especially chaos,' answered William.

'There's the chaos Ives wrote, and there's the chaos the orchestra played,' said Bernstein. 'They're different.'

William ordered another two whiskies. 'Shall I tell you what Mahler would do?'

'I'm listening,' said Bernstein as he downed his sixth whisky.

'He'd use the baton that I leave on the podium for you.'

'I never use a baton.'

'The musicians are struggling to read the music. Every bar is a challenge. Sometimes they're following different time signatures. When some parts are speeding up others are slowing down. They need all the help they can get. They take turns to snatch glimpses of the conductor and all they get is mother goose teaching them how to fly.'

William downed his whisky and Bernstein ordered two more.

'I keep the baton in my pocket,' said William, and he tapped his jacket. 'I leave it on the podium for you and then I put it back in my pocket.'

'And I never use it.' said Bernstein.

William took it from his pocket and held it up between them. 'When Mahler was unable to continue his last rehearsal with the New York Philharmonic I took him back to the hotel. I kept his baton.'

William gave the baton to Bernstein. 'I think you should use it.'

Bernstein kissed William long and hard then turned to the bartender, but William thought they'd both had enough. He took Bernstein's hand, pulled him off the barstool and led him home.

'The box with Jerome's name in it,' said William, 'looks like a coffin.'

They staggered home hand in hand.

Sunday morning. Carnegie Hall and the orchestra revisited Charles Ives's *Holidays*. Bernstein used the baton. It didn't make any difference. The first movement, *George Washington's Birthday*, was chaotic, *Decoration Day* was more chaotic. Even more chaotic was the *Fourth of July* as Ives's *Holidays* careered to the final movement, *Thanksgiving*, when the symphony collapsed under the weight of its own complexity.

In the bar afterwards Bernstein told William that America had to be able to hear its own music. 'Charles Ives is one of our own, and if my orchestra doesn't play it, nobody will.' William suggested that a second conductor on the platform would help. Bernstein thought that was a crazy idea. William agreed it was crazy, but it was a solution to a problem presented by crazy music. Bernstein thought for a moment and then said he would never invite anyone else onto the platform to conduct with him. William offered to do it without being asked. The two of them went back to Bernstein's studio and marked up their scores.

At the next rehearsal William sat on the platform among the violas with his own score, his back to the podium, and a mirror in which he could see Bernstein standing behind him conducting with Mahler's baton. Bernstein led the strings and woodwind and William conducted the brass and percussion. The chaos that ensued had more to do with Ives's sophistication and humour than the unintended chaos the orchestra had created at the previous rehearsals.

The luxury of an assistant conductor during the rehearsals became a necessity for the performance. William had asked Bernstein if he could be credited 'Assistant Conductor' and have his name in a box in the concert programme Bernstein said, 'No', cuffed William's ears, and kissed him.

For the premier of *Holidays* Bruno Zirato placed a 'Good Luck' card beside the mirror on William's music stand. William took the platform with the orchestra, left Mahler's baton on the podium and sat with the violas. Bernstein took the platform on his own, turned to acknowledge the applause, and then raised Mahler's baton to lead the orchestra slowly through the sounds of a freezing February evening to a warm brightly lit barn where they celebrated Washington's birthday playing several dances simultaneously in an exhilarating helter-skelter ride of carefully controlled chaos constructed from fragments of tunes that everybody knew but nobody had ever heard played all at once. On it went on until *Thanksgiving,* which ended with the audience on its feet giving Bernstein and his orchestra a standing ovation. There was no mention in the concert programme of the Assistant Conductor.

CHAPTER 58

A Gay Bar in Tokyo

With the Soviet Union camped in Eastern Europe, the United States of America kept an eye on its own backyard. The White House proposed a goodwill diplomatic mission to South American capitals enhanced by the presence of the New York Philharmonic Orchestra conducted by Leonard Bernstein. Generous finances were put at the orchestra's disposal. Bruno Zirato organised the concerts and Helen Coates booked the flights and hotels. In order that Bernstein could travel abroad on behalf of the United States government the White House insisted that the FBI withdraw its objection to renewing Bernstein's passport. The FBI suggested that Bernstein hire a lawyer, one of their own, a well-known communist hunter who had cleared out Reds from under many beds. This lawyer, a consigliere to the Kennedy family, wasn't cheap. For five thousand dollars he helped Bernstein compose a letter declaring his love for the United States, his undying patriotism, and his regrets for the bad company he had kept in his youth and, before the ink was dry, Bernstein had his new passport.

The orchestral tour was a huge success. The New York Philharmonic criss-crossed the Andes, visiting eleven countries, opening each performance with the national anthem of their hosts before delivering concerts of mainly American music, some of it written by Bernstein himself. The performances were greeted with wild enthusiasm by South American audiences. William was on hand as Assistant Conductor and stage manager, and kept the Green Rooms well stocked with cigarettes and whisky. Meddi and Anna Mahler were Felicia's constant companions. Felicia wore outfits tailored for each of the countries she visited, incorporating elements of traditional costume in national colours designed by Meddi and cut with all the chic and glamour of New York *haute couture*. Anna Mahler kept a pictorial diary of the tour in sketches and water colours.

The United States Government's diplomatic mission was less successful. The diplomats would have been better advised to travel with the orchestra, but they decided to travel separately and moved around in limousines flanked by motorbike outriders. Crowds that had gathered to welcome the musicians demonstrated their hostility to the state officials, chanting insults and throwing fruit and eggs at the diplomats. Arrests were made and miscreants released within the hour so that they could get to the concerts in time.

By the time the orchestra got to Santiago the Vice President decided to book into the same hotel as Bernstein, where he hoped to escape the hostile vigils held nightly outside the diplomats' hotels. In the bar after the concert Mr Nixon sat with Mr and Mrs Bernstein, Meddi and William. The Vice President snapped his fingers and barked an order for a large scotch on the rocks. He looked at Meddi and William and asked where they had met before. Meddi said she thought it might have been in Los Angeles. Mr Nixon looked from her to William and then to Bernstein and wondered if it might have been during his stint at HUAC. His scotch on the rocks never arrived. 'They hate us,' said the Vice President. Meddi put her hand on William's arm and William kept his mouth shut.

The South American adventure was a cultural success. The White House was fulsome in its thanks to the musicians for bringing the hand of Uncle Sam's friendship into its backyard. Bruno Zirato was approached by the White House regarding a series of concerts in the Soviet Union. Bruno cannily quoted for the orchestra and when that was agreed he returned to the table to negotiate a separate deal for Mr Bernstein and his entourage.

This time the accompanying diplomatic mission to Russia consisted only of a small number of low-grade staffers keen to accept the opportunity to travel. Bernstein looked forward to conducting Shostakovich in Moscow and to presenting the music of Stravinsky to Russians. William travelled with a suitcase containing enough American cigarettes for the duration. He understood that there would be no difficulty obtaining alcohol in Russia but that it would be impossible to find copies of the London *Times* for Mr Bernstein's breakfast crossword.

Russian audiences loved the performances as much as the South American audiences had done. The Russian critics were less impressed. They found Bernstein's movement on the podium, his foot stamping and cries of anguish, a vulgar and offensive intrusion, and they were outraged when Bernstein addressed the audience to point out aspects of the music they were about to hear. The arrogance and gall of the American conductor which so insulted the critics nevertheless charmed audiences, who had never experienced anything quite so informal in a concert hall. Rather than forbid him to speak to the audience,

Bernstein's hosts asked if he would share his thoughts with them before going onto the podium and they successfully dissuaded him from airing his view that Shostakovich's Fifth Symphony anticipated Khrushchev's denunciation of Stalin.

The orchestra's minders were ever present. They accompanied Bernstein and William on a visit to the Moscow State Conservatory, where Bernstein addressed the students on the violence in Stravinsky's *Rite of Spring*. Then they attended a matinée at the Bolshoi. On the way from the Conservatory to the Bolshoi William listened to music spilling out of the open windows as students practised. The cacophony swirling above Moscow's streets sounded just like the music of Charles Ives.

Bernstein wanted to get in touch with Boris Pasternak. Following the publication of *Dr Zhivago* in Europe, Pasternak had been forbidden by the Soviet Union to accept his Nobel Prize. So Bernstein thought it best not to seek the help of his Russian minder and constant companion and instead asked William to discreetly ask one of the junior American diplomatic staff attached to the orchestra to contact someone at the Moscow State University who spoke English, to communicate Mr Bernstein's interest in Russian Literature, and to invite them for drinks with Mr Bernstein in the hotel bar. Bernstein was looking forward to a scene of cloak and dagger cold war intrigue when Professor Peshkov promptly arrived from the university carrying a folder of his unpublished poems. Bernstein's minder asked if he could read the poems. Peshkov gave the poems to Bernstein's minder and excused himself so that he might wash his hands. William followed him. Bernstein's minder got up to follow them both, but Bernstein took his hand and insisted he read Professor Peshkov's poems to him. Meanwhile, in the washroom William told Professor Peshkov that Mr Bernstein wished to contact Boris Pasternak. Peshkov went to the hotel reception and asked for a telephone directory, looked up Boris Pasternak's number, wrote it down on the hotel notepaper and gave it to William. Meanwhile, Bernstein, who didn't understand a word of Russian, declared himself to be very moved by Peshkov's poems and said he would present the poems to his father who was born in the Ukraine. Peshkov had a good command of English and an excellent taste in malt whisky. Over the course of two hours he drank a lot of whisky and, for the benefit of Bernstein's minder he extolled Maxim Gorky and denigrated Pasternak.

Bernstein was delighted that William had got Pasternak's number but disappointed to learn that it was listed in the telephone directory.

Bernstein picked up the telephone in his suite, announced to anyone who might be listening that he was calling Boris Pasternak, and dialled the number. He invited Mr Pasternak to attend his performance of Shostakovich's Fifth Symphony. Pasternak, in his halting and very formal English, told Bernstein that he was 'most honoured' and asked for two tickets to be left in his name. He requested Mr Bernstein's permission to meet him after the concert to thank him personally and invited him to his home for dinner 'on the evening of day after the concert'. Half an hour later Mr Pasternak called back to inform Mr Bernstein that he was unfortunately not able to attend the concert and was, with 'the deepest regret', withdrawing the invitation to dinner in his home. The following morning a young lad came to the hotel with a note for 'Mr Bernstein'. It was from Mr Pasternak asking Bernstein to ignore the second telephone conversation of the previous day, and to say how much he was looking forward to the concert and to welcoming Mr Bernstein to his home for dinner.

William went for a walk on his own. The minder ran after him and asked where he was going. William said he was going to the Conservatory. The minder, torn between following William and staying in the hotel with Bernstein, threw up his arms in exasperation. Five minutes later a car drew up alongside William. The driver offered him a lift. William said that he preferred to walk. The driver thought it was about to rain. William looked up at the cloudless Moscow blue September sky and bade the driver 'Good morning.' The driver got out of his car and told William that he would accompany him in case he got lost or was confronted by a pickpocket. William told his unwelcome companion that he had heard that Moscow, unlike American cities, was law-abiding and free from crime. 'Yes,' agreed his companion, 'except for pickpockets who prey on foreigners.' William pulled the pockets of his coat inside out to show that his pockets were empty. 'Elephant's ears' said William. At first his companion was puzzled and then he roared with laughter. 'Elephant's ears!' he called out over again. 'Elephant's ears! You Americans are wonderful! Such great humour. Elephant's ears! Unfortunately, we have very few elephants in Russia. Perhaps none.' William asked him if he had an umbrella in his car. He said he did. William suggested he go back to the car and fetch it just in case it rained. His new minder said that if he went back to the car to get the umbrella, he knew that William would turn a corner, hide in a doorway, and then he would get into big trouble with his boss. 'Anyway,' he said looking up at the cloudless sky, 'it isn't going to rain.'

When they reached the Conservatory William observed that it was named after Tchaikovsky. His companion expressed his admiration for the great Russian composer. William said that he admired an institution proud to be named after a homosexual. William's new minder said that William had got that all wrong. None of Russia's great artists were homosexuals. William should not be so naive as to believe American propaganda. He asked William if it was true that black people in America were arrested, beaten, and hanged from trees. William was unable say, 'You should not be so naive as to believe Soviet propaganda.' Instead, William asked if there were many black people in Russia. 'Very few. Probably none,' answered the minder. 'Just like elephants?' asked William. His minder roared with laughter and put his arm around William as they walked toward the Bolshoi Theatre along the street where the students practise at their open windows. William listened to the universal language of students rehearsing music, making sounds too simple and yet too complex for words. It was the sound of Vienna at the beginning of the century, of Prague immediately after the war, and listening to the students in Moscow William wondered how long a society could remain closed when music poured freely from open windows. His minder said if he was looking for a girl, he could take him to the right place. William thanked him but said he would now like to return to the hotel.

Back home, and on the eve of President Kennedy's inauguration Frank Sinatra organised a fund-raising gala for which Bernstein composed a fanfare. After the rehearsal William drove Bernstein back to the hotel where they were due to change into their glad rags and black ties. A blizzard had been blowing all day and the snow lay deep and crisp and even. William was driving with Bernstein in the front passenger seat. The actress, Bette Davis, and the leader of the orchestra, Felix Slatkin, sat in the back. They got stuck in the snow and never made it back to the hotel. William explained to a police patrol who they were and where they needed to be. The Bernstein limousine was abandoned and the passengers were returned to the venue in a police vehicle with chains on its tyres. Bernstein sat up front with the driver. Felix, William, and Bette Davis sat in the back, the actress sitting on William's lap. William held on to the door with his right hand but didn't know where to put his left hand without disturbing Bette Davis. He sat holding his left hand in the air above Bette Davis's knee. She unbuttoned her coat and whispered into William's ear, 'You can lay your hand on my right breast, sweetheart.'

Bernstein tried leaving the summer-time free to compose but was unable follow Mahler's example. When the Philharmonic season ended, Bernstein left New York and conducted orchestras all over the world. He didn't need the money. The Philharmonic salary was handsome. *West Side Story* ran and ran, and when the film opened the royalties continued to pour in. Bernstein needed more than money. He needed audiences and their applause. When he dwelt on the lack of composing time he had inflicted on himself, and the thin collection of his composed works, he sank into dark depressions and only climbed out of his melancholy by travelling and conducting. He set off for Japan, taking William with him.

Japanese appreciation of western classical music was stubbornly conservative. They only listened to the German classical and romantic tradition, preferably conducted by Herbert von Karajan. They weren't ready for Leonard Bernstein.

Bernstein visited the Tokyo Music College where he inspired and championed young Japanese composers and conductors. The youngsters responded to him with enthusiasm but the concert audiences found his performance at the podium and the repertoire he performed 'too American' for their taste. He knew that Karajan's Japanese concerts always ended with a standing ovation which starkly contrasted with his own reception. William observed Bernstein's prickly sensitivity every time Karajan's name cropped up. William thought he could help.

William pulled up a stool next to Bernstein in the hotel bar and ordered two whiskies. He told Bernstein all about Suttner and the claque at the Vienna Opera House and how Mahler tried to stop it. William told Bernstein that Mahler never understood how much a well-timed burst of applause could transform an evening and lift both the performance and the audience. Performers liked to receive applause. All the audience needed was a little encouragement. William was proud of his expertise. He told Bernstein that when he and his friend auditioned for the Vienna claque, they were set the task of stimulating applause for a baritone. Baritones rarely, if ever, stop the show and it was a difficult audition made even more difficult because the applause had to be stimulated as the soprano was about to launch into a famous aria.

'The baritone was good, and we did it. The baritone basked in the warmth of the auditorium's approval as the soprano waited. The audience congratulated itself on its sophisticated appreciation of a fine singer. The rest of the cast, in response to this discerning and deserving audience, performed excellently. The newspaper reviews were fabulous. We got the job and Mahler tried to get rid of us.'

William continued, 'Stimulating applause is a team effort. You can't do it on your own. There is nothing worse than the sound of one person in the audience clapping. A foolish interruption is always followed by the silence of disapproval. The first clap must be followed by a cascade of clapping. If a claquer fails to achieve it he cannot rectify his mistake. Before he can bring his hands together for a second time it's already too late. At the sound of the first clap the other claquers located around the auditorium must immediately bring their hands together to stimulate the whole auditorium.'

Bernstein had arranged to meet some of his music college students later that evening to crawl round Tokyo's gay bars and he invited William to join them. William had never been to a gay bar before. He went out with the forty-year-old conductor and his twenty-year-old students. The waiter who served their table declared himself delighted to look after three generations. The students understood what the waiter said but not the forty-year-old Bernstein who considered himself to be of the same generation as the youngsters and the eighty-year-old who had no idea how old he was.

William spent the night telling his young audience stories about Mahler. The students hung on the old man's every word and Bernstein, who had never heard any of the stories before, was enthralled as William described how Mahler had sent plain clothes police into the Opera House to discover and arrest the claquers, and how the emperor had asked Mahler to calm down after some of his imperial family, who had been enthusiastically enjoying the evening, ended up in the police cells. He told them how Mahler supported Schönberg when audiences reacted violently to his difficult music and that during one concert Mahler had got involved in a brawl with someone who hated the music, threw a punch, and hurt his hand and how, when he got back home, he and William pretended that he had caught his hand in the car door. He told them about the night Mahler had gone out for a Christmas drink with the New York Philharmonic musicians, got lost and walked in circles around New York before finding his way home. William stood up and showed them all how Mahler walked, stopping every few steps to touch the back of one leg with the toe of the other. Bernstein tried it and fell over. William ordered a round of beers and showed them how Mahler would scratch the label off the bottle as he drank his beer. 'OK, everybody, scratch off your labels in honour of Gustav Mahler!' ordered Bernstein. William picked up one of the bottles with the label scratched off and told them that one day Schönberg had turned up with bottles of beer that had the labels already scratched off and that Mahler called him a cheeky young puppy and threw him out. Then he told them about the time Mahler had lost the buttons on his flies just before the concert was due to start and how he had tried to close his flies with safety pins. He got Bernstein to stand up and demonstrated the pose in which the stage manager found them. Everyone in the bar watching William's performance broke into applause. William told them that Mahler had taken the stage with his trousers on back to front and that no one noticed until he had turned to the audience at the end of the performance and bowed to acknowledge their applause giving the orchestra behind him an exclusive view of his underwear. William told them about Enrico Caruso masturbating in the New York Zoo monkey house, and how Pauline Strauss accused her husband of using too much toilet paper, that Alma never wore anything under her gowns and that one day she had turned up in the director's box at the Met wearing a hat and stole of fur made from the front part of a white wolf, its forelegs hanging over her breasts and its ears standing alert on the top of her head, and that the auditorium had responded with a chorus of wolf whistles. By the end of the evening William had recruited a claque made up of not only Bernstein's music students but the entire clientele of the gay bar.

 They all arranged to meet the following night in the bar for a dress rehearsal. William, concerned that a standing ovation would be more difficult to achieve than ordinary seated applause, carefully considered the final piece of music. William told Bernstein that he thought it would be easier to stimulate a standing ovation after a contemplative piece of music, one that disappeared and ended in a silence, rather than music that finished with a big bang, and suggested Barber's *Adagio*. Bernstein kissed William good night and retired to his suite with his new Japanese boyfriend.

 At the concert William placed his Japanese claquers around the auditorium, some singly, some in pairs, most in the orchestra stalls towards the front, with several couples in the grand circle. Bernstein conducted the *Adagio* moving only the baton in his right hand. and as the music faded and disappeared into silence Bernstein, standing still, kept his right hand raised and motionless. The audience sat in respectful silence. The claquers counted thirty seconds before they shuffled in their seats and coughed. Others in the audience joined in the coughing. Then the claquers stimulated the applause which opened quietly then grew in strength, and just as William felt the applause had reached its maximum he stood up. Two pairs on the other side of the hall sprang to their feet and began to applaud with their hands above their heads. Five solo claquers joined them, rising to their feet one after the other, apparently independently but carefully following the pulse of the *Adagio* that could still be felt all around the auditorium. When several more, who were not claquers, got to their feet, all the other claquers leapt up and called out together, not a shout of 'Bravo' but the deep satisfied and affirmative 'Yes.' By the time Bernstein turned to acknowledge the applause the entire audience was on its feet. After another long celebratory night in the bar the claquers carried William back to the hotel on their shoulders. The following day the newspapers carried rave reviews.

CHAPTER 59

The Chichester Psalms and The Opening Concert of the Nineteenth Edinburgh Festival

Dark days were not unusual for Bernstein who moved in and out of depression throughout his life. The darkness, fuelled by his inability to make time for composing, was further charged by the shadow of death stalking his family and friends. Felicia went to Chile to sit at her dying mother's bedside. Two of Bernstein's intimate friends died in dramatic circumstances – Dimitri Mitropoulos collapsed at the podium in Milan conducting Mahler's Seventh and Mark Blitzstein was murdered outside a gay bar in Martinique. Then President Kennedy was assassinated.

When William went to Bernstein's room to collect the breakfast tray, the London *Times* crossword had only one clue solved – *Composer's waste disposal unit containing old fishing equipment*. Bernstein had filled in 'Borodin' and had done no more. It was unusual for Mr Bernstein to get out of bed until the crossword was complete. William found Bernstein washed, shaved, dressed and at work in his study surrounded by pages of manuscript. In the shadow of the deaths of his friends and the President, Bernstein was working on a setting of the Jewish prayer for the dead

'I'll wash, you dry,' said Bernstein, and William sat beside him, carefully copying Bernstein's rough sketches into a comprehensible score. Page after page of Bernstein's music shook its fist at God until Bernstein brought his *Kaddish Symphony* to a defiant conclusion.

William rescued from Helen Coates's in-tray a letter from Dr Walter Hussey, the Dean of Chichester Cathedral in England. It was a very polite and hesitant inquiry asking whether it might be appropriate to ask Mr Bernstein to compose something for the Cathedral choristers – perhaps a setting of psalms. William replied on behalf of Bernstein and wrote a very encouraging invitation to Dr Hussey to sketch out his proposal. Dr Hussey replied with an outline of the musical forces available, a modest fee, and the suggestion that, 'It would be nice if the psalms carried a hint of *West Side Story* about them.'

As soon as he'd finished his Kaddish Symphony Bernstein started work on the *Chichester Psalms*. Ms Coates was annoyed with William for dealing with Chichester behind her back and complained about having to draw up a contract worth so little money. She decided it was time to do something about a chauffeur with ideas above his pay grade. She collected the correspondence with the NYPD regarding fines for traffic violations and the bills for bodywork repairs which showed not only the huge cost of maintaining William as a driver but also the danger to Bernstein and the public at large. Bernstein was amused at the long list of fines, especially as he himself had been at the wheel on all the occasions his car had jumped red lights. William, who was responsible for most of the scrapes and bumps, had never jumped red lights and was adamant that he had never reversed into the police car.

'Was that me?' asked Bernstein.

'Yes,' replied William.

Bernstein thought the best way to keep the Amberson family happy was to maintain William as his chauffeur but not allow him to drive anymore. He had another job for him. He asked William to prepare a set of conducting notes for all of Mahler's music, including whatever William may have gleaned from Bruno Walter's performances of *Das Lied von der Erde* and Mahler's Ninth. William agreed but had no intention of providing Bernstein with any notes. He knew Mahler had complete confidence in Bernstein to make his own recordings. William would have loved to hear Bernstein's recordings but knew he was unlikely to live long enough. He was eighty-two, slept for three hours every afternoon, and didn't think he could keep going much longer.

William didn't drive the car, didn't wait in the wings at the concert's end with cigarettes and whisky for Bernstein between curtain calls, didn't supervise the stage setting of chairs and music stands for the orchestra. He did, however, place Mahler's baton on the podium before each concert and retrieved it at the end. He also produced a beautifully copied manuscript of the *Chichester Psalms*. He listened to every note he copied and couldn't wait to hear it. Having shaken his fist at God in the *Kaddish Symphony* Bernstein now offered the *Psalms* to repair their relationship.

So that Bernstein would not be distracted from his composing William took responsibility for Bernstein's personal correspondence. Once he had perfected Bernstein's signature in all its different forms – 'LB', 'Lenny', 'Lenhutt', 'Leonard' and 'Leonard Bernstein', he answered the requests for signed photographs. Bernstein's hand was careful and neat and well within William's grasp. After a few days studying Bernstein's handwriting William could reproduce it precisely and so was able to answer requests for Bernstein's autograph with a signature that was identical to Bernstein's own hand. William became Mr Bernstein's amanuensis. In the early hours of the morning, after Mr Bernstein had finished his whisky and taken his pills, William sat by the bed taking dictation until Bernstein fell asleep. Many of Lenny's intimate letters were written and signed by William.

Being a celebrity didn't leave Leonard Bernstein with much time for rehearsals and so the New York Philharmonic took on four assistant conductors. There was no shortage of applicants. William attended all the rehearsals conducted by these assistants and took notes so that he could brief Bernstein when he turned up minutes before he was due on the platform to conduct the performance. William briefed Bernstein as they walked together from the green room to the platform. Sometimes Bernstein had only one question for William, 'Will I have an orgasm?' Occasionally, and then more frequently, when Bernstein was too busy elsewhere, an assistant conductor was able to take his relationship with orchestra beyond the rehearsal and go all the way to the performance. Everybody could hear what was happening to the quality of the Philharmonic's playing – the musicians, the critics, and the audience. The charisma of their absentee musical director papered over the cracks.

The one weekly performance that Bernstein never missed was the Saturday morning children's concert. Parents booked months in advance to take their children to listen to Lenny introduce and perform Mozart, Beethoven, Mahler and Shostakovich. Bernstein conducted his musicians and spoke to his audience of children who hung on every word.

After the concert Lenny would sit on the edge of the platform receiving the children one at a time and signing their programmes. William watched the queue of children eagerly waiting to speak to him and thought about how well Bernstein would perform the role of Christmas Santa. For those who preferred not to wait, William gave out photographs that he himself had signed earlier, 'With best wishes, Sincerely, Lenny,' in Bernstein's best handwriting.

William overheard a little girl telling Bernstein that when she grew up she was going to be a conductor. The child gave Mr Bernstein her programme to sign and said her name was Marin. Bernstein wrote, 'To Marian, best wishes, Leonard Bernstein.' She looked at the autograph with dismay and said, 'Marin, not Marian, silly!' Bernstein scored out 'Marian' and wrote 'Marin'. William quickly found another programme and wrote, 'Dear Marin, when you finish High School, come and join my conductor's class at Tanglewood. I look forward to seeing you there. I really mean it. Sincerely, Leonard.' William picked up Mahler's baton from the podium, put it in his inside pocket and ran after Marin and her parents. He found them in the foyer looking with disappointment at the corrected autograph. William called her name, 'Marin!' and gave the newly-signed autograph to the little girl, who squealed with delight.

Mahler wanted to know why William planned to go to Edinburgh after Chichester.

'I'm going to the opening concert of the Festival. I thought I might write a report on the Scottish Festival Chorus for Bernstein in case he needs a choir in England.'

'Very good. Now tell me why you really want to go to Edinburgh,' said Mahler.

'Mrs Mancini will be there. I would like to sit in the same hall as her one last time.'

'Oh,' said Mahler, 'I thought you were going to tell me that you wanted to hear my Eighth Symphony.'

'No,' said William. 'I've already heard it. Lizzie and I sat together in Munich at the premiere.'

'Can we talk seriously for a minute?' asked Mahler. 'Why didn't you give the little girl my baton? You were going to give it to her, but then you didn't.'

'She wouldn't know it was yours. She would have thought it was Bernstein's.'

'Indeed, she would, and it would have been more valuable to her for that. Too late now. The words you wrote on the programme will be sufficient. Now that you haven't given little Marin the baton, I wonder what you are going to do with it.'

'I don't know,' said William.

'Well, as I understand it, you are not thinking of returning from Edinburgh, so I don't know what you're going to do with it either.'

'It's funny how you and I often don't know the same things,' said William. 'Did you know that before I go to Edinburgh I intend to go to Basel and put the letters that I wrote to my mother on her grave?'

'Yes,' said Mahler. 'And before you go to Edinburgh, I suggest you write to my daughter and let her know about your plan. Don't tell her you are auditioning the Scottish Festival Chorus for Bernstein because she won't believe you. Just tell Anna you're going to the concert. She is in touch with Lizzie and will let her know what you're up to. By the way, I think our lives – yours, and mine – have made a small difference for the better.'

'Did you really say that?' asked William

'It's what you hope, isn't it? I think you might be right.'

'Thank you,' said William. 'Do you think you and I will ever meet again?'

'No,' said Mahler.

From William Hildebrand
New York
July 1965

Dear Anna,

I hope you are well. I'm sorry I missed your birthday this year. I'm writing to let you know that I'm going to Edinburgh to hear the opening concert of the Festival, your father's Eighth. Please send my love to Giovanni.

Yours, William.

From Anna
Spoleto
July 1965

Dear Mum,

Thank you for your last letter. I have given Giovanni your good wishes. He is now reconciled to the diagnosis. The doctors have told him that, with the very best care, he should be able to work for another six months. This might sound rather grim, but it isn't. I have never seen him so happy. The cancer has given him a new lease of life and every minute is precious. He is thinking of his legacy and is planning a retrospective of his work to be exhibited here in Spoleto next summer. The exhibition is likely to be posthumous. He has been thinking about his funeral. He wants a twenty-four-cork champagne salute over his grave. What are supposed to do with all that champagne? Giovanni has made a will. He's leaving me the studio. I'm going to stay here, look after his estate, and do my own work. What a stroke of luck that you and William took me to Spoleto all these years ago.

Forgive me for such a short letter but I need to post this today so that you will know in good time that William is coming to Edinburgh. He wrote to tell me that he was going to the Festival to hear the opening concert, Dad's Eighth. I thought you should know. Hugs and kisses,

Anna

William bought The Times at the newsagent around the corner from the hotel in Chichester, took it to Mr and Mrs Bernstein's breakfast table and read out the first clue – *Prelude to main trombone part* (5 letters).

'Intro',' replied Mr Bernstein.

Felicia applauded.

The performance of *Chichester Psalms* in the cathedral was a joy. Afterwards in the sacristy William bade farewell to Bernstein and Felicia. She kissed him on both cheeks. Leonard kissed him on the mouth. William said, 'Leonard, you're immortal now.' Bernstein was taken aback. It was the first time in twenty-five years William had called him by his first name.

In Bernstein's best handwriting, William wrote to Miss Coates.

Dear Miss Coates,

I have asked Mr Hildebrand to visit Basel and Edinburgh on my behalf before he returns to New York. He has access to the Amberson bank account and will be travelling first class and staying in the very best accommodation at Amberson's expense. William's outgoings should be tax deductible in the normal way.

Yours sincerely, Leonard

William took the train from Liverpool Street Station in London to Harwich for the night ferry to Holland. On board the *Köningin Wilhelmina* William immediately found himself in Holland. The crew were Dutch. The beer was Dutch and served in small glasses of half lager and half froth. The food was Dutch. The smell of cheese with caraway seeds transported William over fifty years to the day he spent on his own in Leiden while Mahler went for a walk with Freud. Barely five minutes out of Harwich and William could see the harbour lights rising and falling. The boat lurched and tossed. Through the lounge windows William watched Harwich appear and disappear as the ferry dipped and crashed into the rising sea. William remembered his first crossing to America which was rough, but this was worse. He was surprised the North Sea presented a more challenging environment than the Atlantic Ocean. He lay down in the cabin and the tossing ship rocked him to sleep. In the morning he showered and dressed in clean clothes. He left yesterday's clothes in the cabin. He had no need to carry laundry with him. He was travelling light and would travel lighter by the day so that when he reached his journey's end in Edinburgh he would have nothing left to carry.

In the railway station at the Hoek William recognized the Cyrillic alphabet on the train bound for Moscow. The departure board announced trains to Amsterdam, Rotterdam, Groningen, Copenhagen, Hamburg and Berlin. William boarded his train for Cologne and found his first-class seat in the restaurant car. Holland was waking up as William ate his breakfast on the train that glided past rows of neat housing. William caught glimpses of people through uncurtained windows getting ready for work or school. As he crossed the border into Germany William, listening to the rhythm of the wheels, imagined he was riding the same line that he and Mahler had ridden on their way back from Leiden to Vienna. When he reached Cologne William visited the cathedral and explored the newly-excavated Roman remains. As he waited to board his train for Basel William was excited by the noise, smell, and size of huge steam engines arriving and departing. He hoped one of these monsters would pull his train and was disappointed when a sleek electric locomotive brought the Basel train to the platform where he was waiting. In the restaurant car William watched the boats on the Rhine. After lunch William asked for a glass of sweet wine and a biscuit, then he asked for grappa and coffee, then he asked for a cigar which the steward cut and lit for him, then he fell asleep. He woke up as the train pulled into Basel's Badischer Banhof. William preferred to wait until the train had crossed the Rhine where he would get off at the Schweizerische Banhof. He took a taxi to the hotel, checked in, then walked to Schneidergasse where he found the Hasenburg and ordered a dish of *Leberlet mit Rösti*.

He slept well and missed the thunderstorm. When he woke up it was still raining with no sign of letting up. The hotel called a taxi, gave him an umbrella, and he set off for the Friedhof Cemetery on Hegenheimerstrasse. He asked the taxi to wait for him. William didn't know how to find his mother's grave. Many of the graves were overgrown. Many of the gravestones were illegible. The torrential rain deepened his sense of impotence. William started to examine the gravestones one by one when a stranger approached him and asked who he was looking for. William answered, 'Madame Madeleine Hildebrand.'

'Ah! Madeleine et Félicité. Les femmes amoureuses', and he took William to the grave.

William had not thought where he might put the letters. He had not brought a trowel to dig a hole to bury them. This torrential rain would destroy the letters before his mother had a chance to read them. He left the letters in his raincoat pocket, rolled up the coat, tucked it inside the umbrella, closed the umbrella and left it behind the gravestone. He pulled up weeds, nettles, and brambles to cover it and returned to the taxi. The driver pointed out that he had forgotten his coat and umbrella. William said he no longer needed them.

August 21st 1965
The Great Northern Hotel, King's Cross

William left the clothes he no longer needed in the hotel room and declined the hotel breakfast. He preferred to eat on the train. He settled into his first-class seat in the restaurant car of the Flying Scotsman that left King's Cross for Edinburgh at 10am. Four large men settled into the table on the other side of the aisle and in loud voices these four music critics complained about having to spend the weekend in Edinburgh. 'But needs must,' sighed the one with the striped blazer. 'Can't let that little Scotsman chappie, whatsisname, have the only word.' 'Conrad Wilson,' mumbled the one nearest the window. 'Just a kid,' offered the third. 'Might be good when he grows up and moves to London. Waiter!'

William opened his copy of the *Times* and turned to the crossword. *In brief fine state of musical theatre* (8 letters.) Nothing came to mind as he listened to their conversation.

The waiter approached the noisy table with his open notepad.

'What's a full English breakfast?'

'Sausage, bacon, eggs, sautéed potatoes, mushrooms, baked beans, fried bread and fried tomatoes, sir,' answered the waiter.

'I'll have a full English without the tomatoes.'

'What's the difference between a Full English Breakfast and a Full Scottish Breakfast?'

'The Scottish breakfast is served with a slice of black pudding, sir.'

'Is that the only difference?'

'Yes, sir.'

'Then I'll have a full English breakfast with a slice of black pudding.'

'Yes, sir.'

'What's the vegetarian breakfast?'

'Eggs, potatoes, mushrooms, tomatoes, baked beans and fried bread, sir.'

'You mean it's a full English breakfast but without the meat?'

'Yes, sir. You may have as many eggs as you wish.'

'Then I'll have a full English breakfast with three eggs.'

'How many eggs can I have?' rejoined the first.

'As many as you wish, sir.'

'I'll have four and let me have his tomatoes.'

'And for you, sir?'

The fourth journalist asked for a black coffee and a large brandy.

The waiter turned to William and raised his eyebrows. William nodded in sympathy. The waiter turned the page on his notepad and William ordered a kipper and poached eggs because he didn't want what the four music critics were having.

The waiter returned with the coffee and brandy.

'Is the Scottish orchestra any good?'

'Anyone who's any good comes to London. The Scottish band employs what's left behind.'

'And their conductor?'

'Alexander Gibson?'

'One of the 'left behind.'

'And Mahler?'

'Don't get me started.'

'Minor Austrian. Banal. Lots of crash bang wallop. Not much else.'

'Why would you open a festival with something like that?'

'Because it's a festival, dearie! You take risks, go for broke, and when it's broke, we give them a pat on the back for having a go.'

'We're going to applaud, then.'

'Depends how bad it is.'

'Anyone heard Mahler's Eighth?'

The one at the window refilled his brandy glass from a hip flask and said, 'Two movements. The first, a setting of *Veni Creator Spiritus*. The second, a setting of the last scene of Goethe's *Faust*.'

'What's the connection?'

'First movement implores the Holy Spirit to come down and the second invites Faust to go up.'

'Up and down?'

'Other way round -– down and then up.'

'Better to finish going up, don't you think?'

'Do we know anything about Mahler?'
'Wife cheated on him.'
'Impotent.'
'Tyrant.'
'Musicians hated him.'
'Vienna was thrilled when he went to New York.'
'And New York was thrilled when he went back to Vienna.'
'He went to New York?'
'Yes'
'What did he do there?'
'Conducted the Met and the New York Philharmonic.'
'Conductors shouldn't compose. Is it going to be cold in Edinburgh?'
'Of course it is! We're going north, old chap.'

The waiter brought William his kipper and saw the dismay on William's face as he looked down at the bones. From his brief time in Holland he knew that 'kip' meant chicken and wasn't expecting the waiter to bring him a fish.

'May I, sir?'

The waiter took Williams fish knife, removed the head, tail and skin from the fish, eased the flesh from the bones and left William with the fillets.

William thanked him.

'Excuse me, waiter, but I think we placed our order first.'

'Just coming, sir.'

William checked into his suite in the Caledonian Hotel, which was five minutes' walk from the Usher Hall. He would have settled for something less luxurious but the suite, including a grand piano, had become available after a cancellation. The vast number of dollars involved in securing the accommodation was of no interest to William.

William walked slowly up to the Usher Hall, stopping every few yards to catch his breath. Outside the Usher Hall he looked up at the restaurant on the other side of Grindlay Street and was amused to see that it was called '*I Quattro Piselli.*' He went into the Shakespeare Bar. He recognised the barman, asked for a pint of light and they started chatting. William manoeuvred the conversation towards the restaurant.

'I see it's called *I Quattro Piselli.*'

The barman laughed. 'That was my idea. It used to be 'Pasta e Pizza e Pesce e Patate – four p's. 'Quattro piselli' is the Italian for four peas. Clever, eh?'

'And it's a family business?' asked William.

'There's the old lady and her son and daughter. Her son's no' well. Fast cars, drink and the gamblin.' He's in a bad way. He's no' long for this world. The auld woman and her daughter are runnin' the place on their own. The wee laddie's in the choir and the auld yin's fair lookin' forward to the concert.'

William finished his pint, declined the barman's offer of another, left the pub and started to walk up Castle Hill towards the Royal Mile, but he ran out of breath and couldn't make it all the way up. He turned and slowly walked back down to the hotel, took the lift to his suite, and lay down. With her grandson in the choir, William was certain Lizzie would be in the hall.

William called room service and ordered a hot dog and a beer. He sat at the piano and picked out *Frère Jacques* with his right hand. The sound William heard was the solo bass that opens the third movement of Mahler's First. As the orchestra joined in and began to dance, William stood up from the piano and started to dance with them, slowly at first and then accelerating wildly as the Klezmer band pushed the wedding guests through their paces. At the end of the dance William threw himself onto the bed gasping for breath.

The kilted steward bringing William his beer and hotdog found him on the bed.

'You all right, sir?'

'Wine,' slurred William breathing deeply.

'I've brought you the beer that you asked for, sir. You had me worried there for a minute. A sip of beer should put some colour back into your cheeks. If you need anything else, sir, just let me know.'

William tried to reach out for the hot dog, but his right arm wouldn't move. William decided to lie still. He only needed enough breath for another twenty-four hours.

August 22nd

William took the brooch Lizzie had given him from its tartan box. He had never worn it and wasn't sure where to put it. He pinned it to his lapel. William took the lift to reception, limped to the desk, and despite the numbness that slurred his speech he managed to settle his account and take a taxi to the Usher Hall. The steward who helped him to his seat in the fourth row of the Grand Circle asked if he was all right. 'Wine,' said William. The steward told his colleagues to keep an eye on him. William scanned the audience. He didn't recognise anyone. He touched Mahler's baton in his inside pocket and wished Alexander Gibson good luck.

The opening blast on the organ and the choir's call for the Holy Spirit pinned William to his seat. He held on tight and flew back fifty-five years to the world premiere in Munich. This orchestra, choir, and soloists performing their Scottish premiere were every bit as good.

Towards the end of the second movement the soprano performing *Mater Gloriosa* walked down the central aisle to the front of the Grand Circle. William felt like he was in heaven. 'Genius!' he said to himself. 'Mahler would love it.' The singer was about to summon Faust into Heaven from her position above the audience in the orchestra stalls. An elderly lady on the other side of the aisle, two rows in front of William and a bit to his left, looked up. William's gaze locked onto hers. Lizzie only needed to turn her head a fraction more to catch sight of him. She caught sight of the brooch, smiled, and turned away. William's heart soared. His happiness at her smile, and his sadness as she looked away, were unbounded. Mater Gloriosa sang *Komm,* and William slipped through the crack between major and minor into the dateless dark.

Acknowledgments

I never asked permission but would like to acknowledge my thanks to William Ritter for the use of his first name. William Ritter (1867-1955) was a writer and critic who, like William Hildebrand, was Swiss and gay. Like Hildebrand he went to a Mahler concert only to jeer but found himself seduced by the composer's soundworld and fell in love with it. He spent the rest of his life defending Mahler from his critics and championing the music. When he died in 1955, aged 88, having lived an even longer life that William Hildebrand, he would have been aware of Leonard Bernstein. I hope he died happily knowing the music was in good hands.

I have never spoken to William Ritter but I suspect he would not recognise much of himself in William Hildebrand. I have however often spoken with Mahler. We talk to each other when I'm driving (he thinks I drive too fast) and when I'm listening to jazz (he loves Gil Evans, Carla Bley and Mike Gibbs). If talking to yourself is a first sign of madness then I have probably strayed past a point of no return by including some of these conversations in this book.

Thanks also to Henry Louis de la Grange for his magisterial four volumes of Mahler biography which is indispensable for anyone interested in the life of Mahler. I did have the privilege of (really) speaking with him when I was preparing 'Song & Dance Man' in 2003. I'm also grateful to Humphrey Burton for his biography of Leonard Bernstein and his many films about the conductor including the performance of Mahler's Second in Ely Cathedral in 1974 with the Edinburgh Festival Chorus. Our choirmaster, Arthur Oldham didn't think as much of Lenny as I do and told the choir a wicked story about our mezzo-soprano soloist Dame Janet Baker. After Lenny had taken 13 curtain calls he turned to the orchestra, choir and soloists and said, 'C'mon everybody! On your feet, 'cos this is everybody's show!' Arthur claimed he heard Janet Baker hiss, 'You could've 'f***ing fooled me!'

Thanks to the number 18 tram driver in Vienna who let me off at Grinzing and pointed out the cemetery where I could find Mahler's grave, the tour guide who showed me round Vienna Opera House, and the owners of the hotel in Steinbach where I sat in Mahler's composing hut and made a start on this work. What a joy to visit these places and match them up with the myths that surround them. For example, there is a story about Mahler insisting the maid carry his breakfast tray from the house in Mairnigg to the composing hut beside the Worthersee by alternative route in case his genius was disturbed by an accidental early morning encounter. When I climbed from the house to the composing hut it was clear the maid would have to go a different way, not because she was required to avoid Mahler, but because it would have been impossible to carry a breakfast tray up the steep slope where Mahler walked.

Thanks to all the hotels and restaurants in Italy for their hospitality over the years. I have described many of them in 'The Baton'. Thanks to Arnold and Anna Maran who took me to Casa Mahler in Spoleto, the studio where Anna Mahler lived and worked and which now houses many of her sculptures, to Jim Meloy who looked after me in New York when I was working on a completely different project, and to Beverly Sutehall for the baton I used in the original stage production.

To the young lad who came up to me in the Shakespeare Bar outside the Usher Hall after Mahler's Sixth and said, 'What brilliant tunes!' Nothing about the classical form, the tonal voyage or the order of the inner movements. Just the thrill of it all. Thankyou. It was the same for me!

Lastly thanks to Paul Ashton and Christa Jostock for reading the manuscript and trying to steer me away from banalities and towards good taste. I'm sorry they didn't succeed but I bear in mind a review of Mahler's Third where the critic, conceding the symphony did indeed contain 'vulgarity and kitsch,' proclaimed, 'yes - but what a voice!!' I cannot claim such a voice for my book but I can for the Edinburgh Festival Chorus with whom I once sang and to whom this book is dedicated. What a voice!

Printed in Great Britain
by Amazon